PENGUIN BOOKS

HIDING IN PLAIN SIGHT

Nuruddin Farah is the author of eleven previous novels, which have been translated into more than twenty languages and won numerous awards, including the Neustadt International Prize for Literature. Born in Baidoa, Somalia, he lives in Cape Town, South Africa, and Annandale-on-Hudson, New York, where he is a Distinguished Professor of Literature at Bard College.

——————

Praise for *Hiding in Plain Sight*

"This novel—Farah's twelfth—takes us deep into the domestic life of a sophisticated African family, with great emotional effect. . . . Each of the kids . . . becomes starkly real in their intelligence, ingenuity, anger, and grief. Even their outrageous mother (and her selfish choices) seems credible. . . . This family, our families, Africa and Europe and America, have never seemed closer in the way we live now—and this engaging novel, from its explosive beginning to its complex yet uplifting last scenes, shows us why." —Alan Cheuse, NPR

"Absorbing and provocative . . . [Farah] writes evocatively about everything from Nairobi traffic to Kenyan game reserves to, importantly, how Somalis are seen not just through the eyes of others, but through their own." —*USA Today* (4 stars)

"The rewards of reading . . . lie in Farah's sensitive exploration of grief and his depiction of a family's love for one another. . . . [He] is particularly adept at evoking the way in which the sight of a familiar face or place can trigger painful memories and how comfort can come to us from unexpected sources." —*The New York Times Book Review*

"Rattles the cage of conventional thinking about family, gender, and sexuality as they apply to the African context. At once conscientious and demanding, nuanced and aggressive, it is a novel that is sure to be featured in the year-end awards lists." —*Pittsburgh Post-Gazette*

"If [*The Kite Runner*] was up your alley, make sure to give this a go. Farah's twelfth novel spans countries, demographics, and histories, and is a pseudo-thriller that is boldly political and far-reaching." —Martha Stewart.com, Winter Book Club Pick

W9-BSY-637

HIDING IN PLAIN SIGHT

Nuruddin Farah

PENGUIN BOOKS

PENGUIN BOOKS

An imprint of Penguin Random House LLC
375 Hudson Street
New York, New York 10014
penguin.com

First published in the United States of America by Riverhead Books,
an imprint of Penguin Random House LLC, 2014
Published in Penguin Books 2015

THE LIBRARY OF CONGRESS HAS CATALOGED THE HARDCOVER EDITION AS FOLLOWS:
Farah, Nuruddin, date.
Hiding in plain sight / Nuruddin Farah.
p.   cm.
ISBN 978-1-594-63336-2 (hc.)
ISBN 978-1-594-63410-9 (pbk.)
1. Women photographers—Fiction.   2. Divorced women—Fiction.   3. Nieces—Fiction.
Nephews—Fiction. Kenya—Social conditions—Fiction.   6. Domestic fiction.   I. Title.
PR9396.9.F3H53   2014   2014028657
823'.914—dc23

Printed in the United States of America
1 3 5 7 9 10 8 6 4 2

Book design by Michelle McMillian

For Nicole Aragi
with much affection

HIDING IN PLAIN SIGHT

PROLOGUE

On his desk in the office, Aar has three photographs, one of each of his two teenage children and a third, the photo of a very beautiful woman, which occupies center stage. Unless he tells them who the woman is, nearly everyone assumes she is his wife, the mother of his children. But if they ask and he tells them that she is his sister, their faces turn sad, as if they are sorry that she is not his woman.

In a dream just before dawn, Aar keeps trying to corral a dozen ground squirrels into his apartment. Time and again, he fails miserably. In spite of this, he doesn't give up, and eventually he rounds up quite a few of them. But just as he attempts to shut the door on the last of the lot, he discerns in the hallway the presence of a familiar figure: Valerie, whom he thinks of as his former wife, although they have never actually divorced. But what on earth is she doing here? And why are the ground squirrels gathering around her, looking eagerly up at her as if she might offer them treats?

Indeed, Valerie is wearing an apron with huge pockets, from which she begins extracting seeds, nuts, dead insects, and other tidbits that she feeds to the rodents. Enraged, he utters a few choice expletives under his breath. Then he resumes his efforts to rally those nearest him, but he feels he hasn't a chance in hell to lure away the ones that are happily feeding around her. He doubts if he will succeed in doing what he has set out to do.

Aar hasn't set eyes on Valerie since she disappeared from his life and that of their children's a decade ago. Why would she make this sudden reappearance here in Mogadiscio, where he is living for only a short while—or, rather, in his dream there? And come to think of it, what have ground squirrels to do with her, or with either of them, for that matter? He watches in bemusement as some of the creatures, having eaten their fill, pirouette for the others, who applaud as squirrels do, rising on their hind legs and touching their palms together. Why is Valerie back in his life at just the point when he no longer misses her?

Aar's heart expands with great sorrow, yet he won't admit defeat. He triples his endeavor to pen in as many squirrels as he can, singling out the sated ones, who surrender more easily to his will. But when no more snacks are forthcoming, they look confused, and some manage to give him the slip while others come and go, entering the room at his behest and departing again at Valerie's insistence. In the ensuing chaos, with neither Valerie nor Aar willing to back down, frenzy sets in, and the poor things begin pushing and shoving one another, looking helpless and lost.

Just then, Aar feels the quiet presence of someone else on the periphery of his vision. A woman, elegantly dressed all in black, is placing a tripod within shooting distance and mounting a compact digital camera on it. Busy attending to the squirrels, Valerie does not take notice of her, but Aar recognizes Bella and wonders how come his sister did not bother to e-mail or phone to alert him to her arrival. How bizarre, and how unlike her! They had last met in Istanbul, when he was on his way to his current posting in Somalia. She had flown in from Brazil and they had spent nearly a week together. But here she is, in her birth city, where she hasn't set foot since 1991, when the two of them fled the fighting in Mogadiscio with their mother, first to Nairobi and then to Rome.

Silent, he watches Bella as she approaches and adjusts the position of her camera, her shadow lengthening, her face widening in a knowing grin as her eyes encounter Aar's. He is relaxed, no longer worried. Bella, more than anyone, gives him comfort. And Bella, more than anyone, discomfits Valerie, because if there is anything Valerie hates, it is having her picture taken when she hasn't prepared for it.

And lo and behold: The minute Valerie's eyes fix on Bella's camera and its attendant paraphernalia, she begins to make ponderous, ungainly movements. Hardly has another moment passed before she beats the undignified retreat of a vanquished rival, slinking away without so much as a word of self-justification or apology.

And Aar herds all the squirrels in.

Unsettled, his confidence shaken, Aar waits for his breathing to even out. He rubs his eyes until they are sore. For a moment, he has no idea whether it is night and he is still dreaming, or whether it is daytime and he is coming out of a deep reverie. He looks at the ceiling and studies the walls. Then his eyes focus on his feet, and he notices the jagged edges of his badly trimmed toenails. He looks at them as if for instructions as to what to do, as if they might tell him the answers to his many questions.

Aar has been in Mogadiscio for three months, seconded to the UN office in Somalia as logistics officer, charged with the task of facilitating moving the UN's Somalia staff back to Mogadiscio for the first time since Somalia collapsed into civil anarchy. In the interim, UN personnel assigned to Somalia have been operating out of Nairobi, flying up in the morning and returning before nightfall once or twice a month. Not surprisingly, it's been impossible to achieve viable results this way, and yet the staff is resistant to leaving Nairobi, where they and their families feel safe. Even Aar, Somali by birth, is happy to have his children boarding in a school in one of the Nairobi suburbs, and these days he too feels more secure in Nairobi than he does in Mogadiscio.

Yet his home here is a spacious studio apartment with a view of the sea and much of the international airport. At first, Aar lived in a sublet, but when his continued presence became necessary, he rented this apartment in a well-guarded, recently built complex, twenty apartments in all, each with two access points, one serving as a fire exit with steps leading down to a basement shelter in the event of a terrorist attack, the other facing a parking lot. Three-quarters of the occupants of the complex are foreign, and the remainder of them are of Somali descent, albeit with alien passports. A number of the studios accommodate multiple part-time residents who take turns living here. It makes sense to share because the cost of living in a secure place like this comes to an exorbitant two hundred U.S. dollars daily, including breakfast, buffet lunch, and a simple evening meal delivered to one's room. Residents of the larger apartments pay considerably more. And lately the UN and some of the embassies based in neighboring Kenya have taken to paying heavy retainers so they can have rooms, suites, or apartments of their choice available on short lets, sometimes for only half a day, where they can conduct a meeting and leave and not risk an overnight stay.

Hounded by the memory of his dream, Aar feels disconsolately hot one moment, and in the next, despondently cold, as if a life-threatening chill coursed through his blood. His life unfurls before him like a straw mat curling at the edges. But when he tries to smooth it out, his hands shake, and he hears a thunderclap in his head. Aar is a man a little past his midpoint in life and therefore unable to decide in which direction to move. He knows this is what the dream was about.

He makes an attempt to push his worry aside, walling off the nightmare and sidestepping his disorienting sense of dread. But what emerges instead is a memory from the evening before, when one of the UN drivers passed him a sealed envelope as he got out of the car. He'd thought nothing of it at the time, simply accepting it and stuffing it into the back pocket of his jeans. Undoubtedly it contained a request for a loan or a salary advance, he imagined, this being something of a daily occurrence with the workers. Often they ask Aar, as the only Somali of high rank here, to intercede with the Indian moneyman to facilitate these transactions.

But now he is full of anxiety to know the contents of the envelope. He gets out of bed, totteringly eager to satisfy his troubled curiosity. He finds his jeans on the floor where they have fallen and his shaking hand retrieves the envelope, which he tears open with his forefinger. And before he has given it much thought, he is staring at a single word, and a misspelled one at that: DETH!

He doesn't know what to make of the lone word. Did its author mean to write DEBT and misspell it? Or is Aar meant to read it as DEATH with a missing A? Aar is no fool. He is fully aware that among the UN's Somali staff there are Shabaab recruits, hordes of them, who will carry out a threat to kill on behalf of the terrorist organization. They go for soft targets, aiming for a publicity stunt. And nothing works better than killing foreigners—never mind their nationality, so long as they are of the infidel variety—in the name of Islam. On many an occasion, they've killed fellow Muslims, but do they care? The UN is a particular magnet for terrorist groups because of the huge international coverage any damage inflicted generates. Aar remembers when, back in 2003, al-Qaeda operatives used a bomb-laden cement truck to target the Canal Hotel in Baghdad where UN Special Representative Sérgio Vieira de Mello was staying, trapping him in the rubble for hours before he lost his life, as did twenty-one members of his staff.

He drops the envelope to the floor and, with his knees knocking, manages to pick up his mobile phone and ring Bella. He needs to speak to someone, not necessarily to discuss the letter and its brief but disturbing contents, but just to touch base, to share a moment of amity, evidence that he is still alive. But Bella does not answer.

Aar knows that further action will have to wait until tomorrow. He wonders if the driver who gave him the envelope will be back on duty then. He may already have reported to one of the terrorist cells to share his reconnoitering with Shabaab intelligence, who would most probably assign him to other duties elsewhere now that this part of the mission has been carried out.

Of course, Aar has expected threats from Shabaab to come his way since the day he arrived in Mogadiscio. And in a way, it annoys him that the menacing missive has come just when he is a couple of days from departing for R&R and a celebration of his son's birthday in Nairobi. If he manages to leave, he knows he won't be returning to Mogadiscio soon, maybe ever.

And now that he is deciding what his next step is to be, he feels a surge of further fear. His hands all of a sudden become conscious of each other and the uses to which he can put them. He secures the door and the windows, and he sets the alarm in hope that it will bring help if somebody breaks in. At eight in the morning, he is not sure if he is safer staying at home, where the alarm is now on, or going to work, where there is comfort in knowing that he is not alone. Then the trilling of his mobile phone startles him.

It's Keith Neville, the UN's local chief of security, an Englishman, who wants to call on him. Aar doesn't bother to ask why, and Keith Neville doesn't volunteer an explanation. Does he know about the letter from the driver? As soon as Aar rings off, he is seized by an urge to phone his children, Dahaba and Salif. He dials their numbers, feeling that it is essential for him to hear their voices, and they his. But, like Bella, they do not answer; and so he leaves them messages, in which he informs them that he is coming home to Nairobi a day earlier than previously arranged. He encounters the same worrying silence when he calls the home of the principal of their school and his wife, two generous souls who have been playing host to Dahaba and Salif in Nairobi. Again he leaves messages, telling Mr. and Mrs. Kariuki of his plan to arrive on the morrow.

In his desperate need to reach someone close to him, Aar rings Gunilla Johansson. Mercifully, she answers and, hearing the worry in his voice, wonders aloud if everything in Mogadiscio is well.

Gunilla is a colleague of Aar's back in Nairobi, and the two of them have recently become secret lovers, seeing a lot of each other when Aar is home and his children aren't around. The children have met Gunilla twice, the first time when they camped out together in the Rift Valley and the next on the one time she came to dinner. Undemanding, generous to a fault, Gunilla is the sort who understands Aar's predicament as the father of two teenagers who are difficult to please, immodestly possessive, and given to asking if there is something going on between him and any woman he greets. Still, he is unsure why he's kept the true intimacy of his relationship with her a secret, not only from the children but also from Bella, whom he's often told about his other women. He ascribes this to his general wariness about making a serious commitment after what happened with Valerie.

And yet it was she, not Mahdi or Fatima, his closest Somali friends in Nairobi, whom he took into his confidence on his last visit home, requesting that she store his essential documents, including the notarized photocopies of his passport, his most recent will, and the details of his bank accounts and other assets, in her safe box. She agreed and also insisted that he provide her with Bella's coordinates, just in case, along with those of Valerie and her lover. Bella's details he could readily provide, but as for Valerie, the best he could do was to give his former mother-in-law's e-mail and phone number.

Not only did he do all this, but he also gave her power of attorney over all his assets before he left for Somalia. He did not tell this to either the children or Bella. Perhaps this was because Aar leads a compartmentalized existence, and no one person, not even his sister, has access to the sum of his secrets.

Now Gunilla is asking why he sounds so feverish, on edge. He tells her that his days have been hectic lately and that he's been returning home exhausted. But he doesn't tell her about the letter. Nor does he tell her that he's been so restless that one day last week he woke up to find his feet on his pillow and his head where his feet ought to have been.

She says, "I am glad you're coming to Nairobi. It will be great to see you and for you to see the children."

They chat about this and that, and then he rings off to wait for the chief of security with the serenity of a man awaiting a pizza delivery.

The calmness doesn't last long, however. Keith Neville calls back to advise Aar not to open the door to anyone until he gets another call from Keith, which he should not answer, and then a text message from someone called RatRoute. Aar waits, his heart beating loudly in his ears, especially after the missed call from Keith. He draws gulps of nervous air into his lungs.

When Keith finally arrives, he is accompanied by a man who, like him, is wearing a sky-blue UN uniform and helmet, though the companion has larger feet, which Aar can make out through the peephole. The men carry themselves with a professionalism that sets them apart from the local ragtag soldiery. Aar deliberately keeps them waiting at the door until, growing restless, the other man draws close to Keith to say something. This affords Aar a glimpse of the man's face.

It's Cadde, Keith's deputy, who once served as a bodyguard to a radical religionist who is now a high-ranking Shabaab figure. Not that Cadde will ever admit to having been close to his former boss, now a wanted terrorist. Cadde is advisedly moderate in his ways, never openly condemning the young Somali women who work in the office and move about with their heads uncovered. He is soft-spoken and unusually polite. But Aar won't be humbugged, no sir.

Keith Neville, on the other hand, is a former bodybuilder gone to fat. When Aar opens the door at last, Keith is the first to enter, with the bearing of a great actor asked to do an uninspiring cameo in a bad movie. Face dotted with liver spots, eyes bulging and as red as beetroot, maybe from illicitly acquired beer and liquor, the Englishman has told Aar that he doesn't want to be in Somalia. A former marine and subsequently a mercenary with Ian Smith's Rhodesian army, lately of Blackwater and their ilk, who have employed him in Iraq and Afghanistan and Pakistan, he has done all the dirty work that a dirty man can get away with.

Now he says, "May I look around?"

"Go ahead. Please," says Aar.

The two men move in opposite directions. Keith enters the bedroom and then presumably the bathroom, and Cadde heads for the kitchen and, finding the door to the balcony locked, asks if Aar has a key and can open it for him. Aar is wise to the fact that many a security breach has resulted from an unlocked balcony. In Nairobi, where he has resided for a number of years, balconies often provide access points to burglars. Aar elects to lie, saying that he has no idea where the key is and that he has never opened the balcony door for fear that he might forget to lock it.

Back in the living room, Keith's wandering gaze falls on the photographs of Bella in various poses, and he stands there, staring at them. It is as if the man suddenly has no memory of the business that has brought him here. Still, Aar refrains from asking why they have come, his self-restraint greater than even his sense of unease. He has no wish to confront his demons now. But when Keith and Cadde join him in the kitchen, at last Aar asks, "Why are you here?"

Keith looks at Aar and then at Cadde and, smiling solicitously, explains, "My office has received intelligence from an unidentified source suggesting that you've been singled out as a terrorist target. And because of this, we've been asked to call round and talk to you."

Aar has no way of knowing whether the two of them are fishing for information or know more than they are letting on. He looks at Cadde for a long minute before he responds. "Does your unidentified source say why I've been singled out and in what way?"

Cadde turns away, avoiding Aar's glance, and Aar is struck with a sudden nausea; in fact, he is so panic-stricken that he thinks his knees may give way, forcing him to collapse to the floor. And because he can't bear the thought of that happening in the presence of these men, he makes his way to the chair closest to him and sits down. There is no point in engaging these men in further talk. He trains his eyes on Cadde, in hope of divining something from the man's body language, but when he fails to do so, he turns to Keith: "Can you say who your unidentified source is or how you know that I've been singled out?"

Keith exchanges a furtive glance with Cadde and then answers that he is not at liberty to share any information. That is the moment when Aar indicates that he wants them to leave. And they do.

Aar telephones his children again, and again each of their phones rings on and on until at last he gets their voice mail. He leaves them each a second message, his worry gaining in intensity. He paces back and forth as though he were in a cage, which in a sense he is, in this barricaded hotel in his native city, with armed guards roaming inside and outside, and stationed at all entrances.

Until a few hours ago, Aar felt safe here, especially being so close to the airport. All he has to do is pack his one suitcase and leave. And although he hates giving the impression that the mere suggestion of danger in the shape of a threatening letter is enough to make him flee, he is inclined to do just that. After all, he has the children to think of, having been a single parent to them since Valerie vanished.

When he thinks of Valerie, he thinks of their relationship as being like a rug: beautiful when first purchased but gone threadbare over time and then utterly disintegrating. He seldom mentions her in the presence of the children anymore, as he does not know what to tell them, how to explain that their mother evidently valued the love she shared with Padmini over the love she had for them.

The last time he heard from her was when Dahaba, at ten, had her first period. Valerie wrote to him from Pondicherry, where she and Padmini were running a hotel and restaurant, to tell him what to do. As if she could give this sort of advice from such a distance! Or had any right to after failing to remember so many of the children's birthdays with so much as a phone call, let alone a card or a present! When he responded angrily, she wrote back, "As a Muslim man, what do you know about raising a daughter? Your people chop it all off, don't they, and maybe feed it to a waiting cat?" From then on, Aar cut off all communication with her and relayed information only through the children's English grandmother, with whom he has remained on good terms and who gives him the latest about her daughter in return.

The years that have passed have dulled the edges of his rancor, and recently he has begun to pity Valerie, sensing that she may be regretting the choices she made. The children have lost interest in what their mother is up to. In fact, one of the things he would like to talk to them about is who will take care of them in the event of his death. Given the choice, he would like Bella to have them. Not that he would stand in the way of Valerie making a new bond with her children. After all, she carried them both in her womb for nine months, breast-fed them, cared for them, loved them—until she left. But it won't be easy for Valerie to win them over again, especially if Padmini is still in the picture.

That night, Aar books a flight to Nairobi for the following day. In the morning, he calls in sick—a terrible diarrhea, he says. He learns from his secretary, a Kenyan Somali who has little or no understanding of Mogadiscio's clan-infested politics, that Cadde has not returned to work since he and Keith visited Aar at his apartment, nor has Aar's driver. He tells her he's going to organize a taxi so he can quickly pick up a few documents he needs to work at home.

He leaves his suitcase in the taxi and slips into the office. It isn't files he is after, but a few photos—and not any of Bella's, surprisingly enough. The photos he feels compelled to have are the ones he himself took during that camping trip in the Rift Valley with Gunilla and his children. He is just on his way back out the door with them when Shabaab strikes.

1.

"Like beads unstrung," Bella says to Marcella.

"What a terrible thing death is!" says Marcella to Bella.

They hug for a long time, the elderly Italian woman holding the younger woman, each wailing louder than the other—their lamentation a survivor's threnody expressive of so huge a loss.

The doors of their respective apartments are open. They sob bitterly in the corridor, neither of them battling to hold back their keening. Some of the neighbors come out of their apartments and stand gawking at the women and exchanging questioning glances.

It is Bella's ill luck that she was one of the last to hear of Aar's death. When he was killed, she was finishing up a photo assignment in Bahia for the German magazine *GEO*. She had just cleared customs at Fiumicino when she came upon the headline in the Italian daily *La Republica*. According to witnesses, a suicide bomber blew up a car at the main entrance to the UN compound, then four heavily armed gunmen entered the building and a gun battle lasting more than an hour ensued. In all, twenty people lost their lives, fifteen of them Somalis and five foreigners, Aar among them.

Bella had barely finished the first paragraph when her legs buckled and she collapsed at the feet of a man offering her taxi service. When she came to, a throng of people had crowded around her and a fierce debate had ensued as to what to do with her. The taxi driver, an elderly Sicilian with a broad face sporting at least a week of stubble and a sweet smile showing only a few front teeth, bent down and helped her to sit up. "Signorina, take notice," he said. "You are in Rome, whose proud citizens frown on public weeping." He offered her a pile of paper napkins. "Here, dry your tears."

The taxi driver, a gentleman of rare breeding and charm, led her to his car and they sat together until she came to her senses. Then he drove her home, left his car parked illegally in the street, helped her up the stairway with her luggage, cameras and all, and refused to accept the fare.

On the drive, Bella used her phone to glean further details from the Internet. The attack was remarkable for its ruthlessness, which had attracted intense international attention. The body parts of the dead were found strewn about the outbuildings, so charred and mangled as to be unidentifiable. Aar's head was found far from where the rest of his body fell, although that was according to some of the unreliable Somali websites, which are given to exaggeration and releasing unverified information. Those body parts that were identifiably Somali were buried in a mass grave, and those of a recognizably paler shade were collected and put in containers to be catalogued later before being passed on to their next of kin.

Now, at the sight of her beloved friend and neighbor, who has been listening for her return, Bella is again undone. Marcella holds her until her sobbing ceases, then they retreat into Bella's apartment, still clinging tightly to each other.

Marcella makes her sit. "I'll make you tea with sugar, the way Somalis like it," Marcella says. Bella stares back at her, as if she doesn't understand the language or can't comprehend why anyone would have sugar in her tea. "Please," she says. Too weak to sit up straight and too jet-lagged to keep her eyes open, too exhausted to sleep and much too disoriented to take in all that has happened, Bella is at the point of losing control over her bodily movements.

Marcella sits down opposite her. The old woman has known Bella literally from birth. She remembers the day in 1981 when Hurdo came to have her second child at Mogadiscio's Digfer Hospital. It was a Muslim holiday and the hospital was short-staffed; Marcella, as head of obstetrics, was putting in a long shift, and it fell to her to perform the delivery. My lucky day, Hurdo always said. Hurdo and her husband, Digaaleh, were colleagues of Marcella's husband on the law faculty, and the two couples knew each other well. Hurdo was a much-adored professor of international law, having gained her higher degree from Bologna in the days when a large number of Somalis pursued their professional training in Italy.

There was an additional layer to the intimacy of Marcella's connection with Bella, in that she was among the few who knew of Hurdo's affair with Giorgio Fiori, a Dante scholar on the faculty of letters, and she suspected that Bella was Giorgio's child even before it was confirmed. So she had a certain proprietary feeling about Bella from the beginning, which was rekindled years later, when Marcella and her husband—who had died recently of lymphoma, poor soul—took on the role of surrogate parents to Bella in Rome, helping her to find her apartment opposite their own and watching after it when photography assignments took her far and wide.

Lately, Marcella has been losing more and more of her recall, fading like a cloth losing the brightness of its original dye. Now she is reaching for the memory of the last time she saw Aar, but it is earlier memories that surface. Aar was twelve years old when Bella was born. From the beginning, he had an older brother's protectiveness and affection for her, buying her toys with his own pocket money and helping with her studies (she was bad at mathematics and science). He'd encouraged her interest in photography; in fact, he bought her first camera and sat for her as she began to master her art. One of Marcella's great joys was to host brother and sister together, delighting in the way they comforted each other, holding hands and hugging at every opportunity. They had a deeper affection for each other than could exist between even the most intimate husband and wife, Marcella thinks. But still she can't retrieve the memory of Aar's last visit.

"When was Aar here last?" she asks.

But the question leads Bella to a dim hall lined with fogged mirrors, where she searches frenziedly for answers and, finding none, weeps some more. Marcella can't think of anything to say that might help, and so she says only, "Let me make the tea."

"Actually, I would prefer coffee," says Bella.

"Black or with milk?"

"A latte if possible."

Marcella knows how to work Bella's espresso machine and goes about feeding the grinder with coffee beans, apologizing for the hideous noise. She regrets that since her husband's death she hasn't been looking after the young woman's apartment as before. In the old days, she would often do the tidying herself or hire a Filipino woman to do it, services that Bella would insist on reimbursing with money and favors in return. Now Marcella notices the dishes in the sink; the books lying open, abandoned like orphans; the drawn curtains; the windows unopened for days on end so that the whole apartment emits a musty odor. This is not clean living, she thinks. In an effort to alleviate the dark mood, she parts the curtains to let in the daylight and opens the windows. She sets the coffee to brewing while she begins to clear away the clutter then interrupts herself to froth the milk and pour the *latte* into a large mug, worried that Bella might spill it in her state of discomposure.

"Here," she says, handing it to Bella. "This will do you good."

Bella receives the mug with both hands and murmurs her thanks. But she doesn't take a sip, not yet; it is too hot. And when she does, she continues to look dazed, her eyes unfocused, her hands trembling as she lifts the mug to her lips and lowers it again, untasted.

Marcella has noticed that the red button of the message machine is blinking. She knows that one of the messages is her own condolence, left earlier in the day, when she was still at work and Bella had not yet returned. But there may be more. She debates whether she should bring the messages to Bella's attention. After all, one or more may be from Aar, or from his colleagues. But Bella is staring ahead of her, looking at nothing, and Marcella decides not to mention it.

Bella looks up into Marcella's eyes, finding comfort in their warmth and familiarity. Then, as if remembering something, she tries to stand but nearly loses her balance before she steadies herself with her hands and sits back down, narrowly missing spilling her latte, which she still has not tasted.

"What do you need done? I'll do it. What?"

Apologetically, Bella says, "Could you please help bring in my camera cases? In my state, I left them outside, in the corridor."

"Gladly, and you stay put."

Marcella fetches the bags and asks if she should put them in the spare bedroom, which Bella rightly calls Aar's room, as it is always ready to receive him—the bed made, clean towels in a neat stack, his pile of reading material (much of it novels bought at airports) at bedside, a spare pair of pajamas and hotel slippers, all of it arranged neatly as he liked things kept. Bella has never allowed anyone else to stay there. So Marcella's question initially strikes her as almost insensitive, but after a moment of thought, she says, "Yes, in the guest room, please."

Marcella knows all about homage to the dead. She has only recently finished going through her late husband's things, getting rid of all but a handful that she left where he last placed them, cautioning the cleaning lady not to shift them. It is the prerogative of survivors to honor their dead and salute them the best way they can, she thinks.

When Marcella has finished moving the camera cases, Bella says, "Come and sit with me, please." Marcella obliges, settling at the bottom end of the couch where Bella has indicated she should. Soon enough, though, an uneasy silence descends, and with it, a gnawing feeling of despair. Marcella scans the far wall of the living room, which is lined with Bella's photographs, some of which have made her into one of the fashion industry's most sought-after photographers. Even so, Marcella's favorites are the family portraits, of Aar alone and with Valerie and his children at different ages. Bella has the true artist's knack for showing the ugliness inside those she detests, Marcella thinks, as can be discerned in the photographs she took of Valerie.

In an effort to ease the tension and hardness in Bella, Marcella takes the young woman's feet in her hands and gently massages them until she feels a kind of calmness taking hold both in her own as well as Bella's body. Then she blurts out, "Where is Aar's corpse?"

When Bella does not answer, Marcella persists. "Any idea when and where he will be interred?"

Marcella has always had this tendency to say the unspeakable in public, to ask the unanswerable in private. And before Bella can think what to say, the old woman says, "Will you have time to get there before his burial? I wouldn't go to that dreadful country if I were you—

but I can understand if you choose to do so. But I suppose, knowing them, they will not wait for your arrival."

Marcella's questions remind Bella how little even educated Europeans know about Islam, let alone about Somalis and their culture. "He'll have been buried before dark the same day he died," she says.

"Already buried—but where, when? Before dark?" Mercifully, Marcella stops herself before she blunders in deeper, and she stares at Bella in confusion. It is obvious that Marcella is upset with herself for asking inappropriate questions at such an inopportune time, but Bella waits to be certain Marcella is done before she says, "Aar was buried the same day he died."

"What a way to go!" This time not even Bella's expression of palpable distress is enough to keep Marcella from continuing in this vein. "What a way to end the noble life of a man who served everyone with honor, untainted integrity, and purpose."

At last, Bella, wincing, takes her first sip of the latte.

"Has anyone been in touch with you officially?"

Bella looks at the blinking answering machine, and Marcella goes to it and presses the button to play back the messages. A woman speaking in perfect English with a Nordic-sounding voice has made several attempts to leave a message. In the most recent, she scarcely gets past Bella's name before she bursts into tears and hangs up; the second time, she says, "Gunilla here," and then, "There's been terrible, terrible news from Mogadiscio—" She breaks off, then attempts to continue, stuttering, stopping, and weeping copiously before she again hangs up. On the third try, she says her piece, as if she were reading from a script: "Aar lost his life in a terrorist suicide bombing. The Somali authorities have ordered that his corpse and the others will all be interred in a mass grave in Mogadiscio."

Bella utters an Irish curse, wishing the killers hell and worse in the spirit of all the saints of every faith anywhere. This message is followed by several earlier messages from Aar, who sounded desperate to speak with his sister. At the sound of them, Bella breaks down again. Marcella shushes her, tapping her cheeks and then holding her face in her gentle hands until the weeping ends. And for the first time, Marcella allows herself to wonder to whom the responsibility of informing Aar's children and Valerie will fall.

Aloud she says, "Would you like me to call the children or had you rather do it yourself?"

Of course, Bella insists on being the one to tell her nephew and niece about their father's death. As for Valerie, Bella will start by calling her mother, who will know how to locate her if anyone can.

Bella remembers that the Hausa way of informing a relation living far away about the loss of a parent, a sibling, or another intimate is to send an emissary to deliver the news in person. The emissary dispatched on such a delicate mission does not share the sad news, however, until they are in close proximity to a place where a wide community of friends and relatives are on hand to provide support. A pity, Bella thinks, that whoever it was who called and left the news of Aar's death on the answering machine—or whoever turned it into international headline news—did not take a leaf from the Hausa book of etiquette.

Actually, Bella is not certain from whom she learned about this custom. Perhaps it was Marcella, come to think of it. As a former senior obstetrician at a Vatican-run hospital in one of Rome's poor neighborhoods, she had become deeply familiar with corpses and what becomes of them, depending on the faith of the dead and their relatives. She and Bella had often discussed the Irish and their wakes, the Yoruba and their drawn-out rituals, the Muslims, the Jews, the Zoroastrians, the Hindus, and the Catholics, each in their own way confronting the moment of death with a rationale that is unique to their culture and belief systems. But Bella suspects that it was not Marcella but her Malian lover who told her of the Hausa's sensitive handling of news of bereavement. And as much as she wishes she could spare Dahaba and Salif the pain of receiving the news in the same boorish way it came to her, she is aware that this is impossible in the age of the Internet and round-the-clock news channels that jabber on and on, forever upsetting one.

But before she can telephone her nephew and niece, she needs to stop Marcella from yammering away. She asks the old lady to go to her own apartment and call the airlines to buy Bella a business-class ticket to Nairobi on the next flight available. "Use my credit card," she says, offering it.

"Business class at short notice?"

"What's wrong with that?"

"It will be prohibitively expensive."

Bella says, "This is a once-in-a-lifetime purchase. Or at least I hope so."

With Marcella gone at last, Bella picks up the telephone to dial her nephew. It has barely begun to ring when her weeping and wailing starts anew. This is no good, she thinks, as the phone rings and rings. She hangs up without waiting for voice mail to kick in. To fortify her resolve, she pours herself a strong drink, which she downs in a single gulp. Thus hardened, she calls Wendy, Valerie's mother. The two women are fond of each other. What is more, Wendy got on very well with Aar and looked upon him with great approval, not only because she saw how devoted a father he was, but also because he gave her as much access to her grandchildren as she wished. For their part, Dahaba and Salif loved their grandmother and looked forward to spending a month a year with her in Leicester when the schools in Kenya closed for the summer.

As soon as she has recognized Bella's voice, Wendy lets out a long whimper and then stammers weepily, "I've been in a state since hearing of it. You know, I loved Aar more than I've cared for my own daughter."

"Where is she?" asks Bella. "Any idea?"

"She is currently in Uganda, with that woman."

Bella knows that there is no love lost between Wendy and Padmini, whom she blames for Valerie's decision to walk out on her marriage. But when Wendy offers to call and break the news of Aar's death to her daughter, Bella is all too glad to accept the offer.

They talk some more, and when Wendy speaks of being overwhelmed by the barbarity of the killings, Bella silently remembers something Hurdo once said after their country collapsed into anarchy and they fled Mogadiscio: "Death in Somalia seldom bothers to announce its arrival. In fact, death calls with the arrogance of a guest confident of receiving a warm welcome at any time, no questions asked."

The church bells in Trastevere chime, as if in tribute to Aar. Bella pictures death riding a tide of undulant waves of unheralded emotion—and she weeps again, unable to stop shaking, the hour as dark as a cave.

"And what do they say down in Somalia?" Wendy is asking.

Bella, despite herself, recounts some of the gorier details from one of the Somali websites, which reported without giving any evidence that one of the terrorists who entered the UN building after the suicide bombing held a knife to Aar's throat and then stood by, waiting and watching, until his blood drained like a goat being made halal.

"Shame on the lot of them," Wendy curses.

Bella knows that these terrorists aren't true Muslims. Yes, she is a secularist, no more than culturally Muslim. But with a mother born and raised a Muslim and a father born in Italy to Catholic parents and brought up a Christian, she believed she had the undisputed authority to choose her faith. In her youth, growing up in a Muslim country, she embraced her mother's faith. But she no longer thinks of herself as a true Muslim.

Wendy is saying, "Death is a given, isn't it?"

"We have no idea of the time of our dying."

"Nor of the manner of our dying."

Bella says, "It is only that Aar's death adds terror to the idea of death, the idea of dying, because he was unprepared for death and did not deserve to die in that infernal manner."

"He was a good man," Wendy affirms.

And they say their good-byes.

Unable to reach her niece and nephew on their mobile phones, Bella rings the home of their hosts, the principal of the school and his wife. Surely the attack has been headline news in Kenya as well. Finally, Catherine Kariuki, the wife of the principal, answers the phone. Bella asks if the children have heard the news. Catherine confirms that they have and that they are taking it very badly indeed.

"How do you mean?" asks Bella.

Catherine says that they seem to be traumatized and uncertain how to act. One minute they're a little weepy, the next minute one or the other of them says, "This was bound to happen, given where Dad was," and the other one commiserates.

"I would like to talk to them, please."

Catherine goes to call the children to the phone but soon comes back to say that not only won't they open the door to Dahaba's bedroom, where they've sequestered themselves, they also won't even acknowledge her knocking or her calls to them.

So Bella simply tells Catherine that she will be on a flight to Nairobi on the morrow, and the two of them burst into tears and weep and weep and weep until one or the other of them drops the line, and the next thing Bella knows, she is holding a dead phone in her hand and listening to approaching footsteps. Looking up, she realizes that Marcella has come back with the boarding pass for the plane ticket she has booked.

Bella puts the boarding pass in the external pouch of her shoulder bag and immediately sets about packing. She decides to take along with her a couple of camera cases in addition to the ones she has brought back from Bahia—who knows how long she'll need to stay in Nairobi; perhaps she'll even set up a studio there. She asks Marcella to bring up a couple more from the basement of the building, where Bella stores them. Bella packs her flash leads, hot-shoe-equipped units, and several other essential items. Often, Bella entrusts this job to a young half-Eritrean woman who serves as her assistant, but there isn't time for that. So, as Bella does not like surprises, she packs for all eventualities, such as whether the sun will bless her with its presence or fail to show, like a hurt lover. Bella knows of an Italian photographer who lost much of his work—a month's worth—because he hadn't prepared for the sudden dust storm that swept in after a gorgeous day in Omdurman, Sudan.

Marcella, bless her soul, keeps bringing sandwiches and drinks and asking questions. She expresses surprise at how much equipment and clothing Bella is packing. "Are you staying away for a long time?" she asks.

"What would you have me do instead?" Bella asks.

"Fetch the kids here."

"And then what?"

"Let them go to school here or in England with their grandmother, who would be more than willing to have them stay with her," Marcella says.

"Things seem a lot more complicated than that," Bella says, "what with a dead father and a delinquent mother who may turn up in hopes of having a say in what happens to them. Not to mention that there is the children's opinion to consider. Maybe they are happy where they are."

"So are you relocating back to Africa for good?" Marcella asks. "Is that what you are intending to do, *carissima*?"

"Aar's death changes all plans," Bella replies.

"Including where you'll live?"

"Everything," Bella affirms.

"And the apartment, what will you do about it?"

"Aar's death has changed everything," Bella says again.

"But you are so young and unfulfilled!" Marcella cries, once again unable to keep from speaking her mind.

Disturbed, Bella sits on the edge of the bed, where the camera cases are still open, and puts her head in her hands. She knows there is no simple way she can explain to Marcella or anyone else what it feels like to lose Aar. And now that death has deprived her of him, how she feels she is answering a call to serve, almost a religious calling. As a young woman, she saw herself as his appendage, breathing the very oxygen he breathed. She has never married, never committed herself loyally and fully to another person, man or woman, always and forever waiting for the summons, duty-bound, steadfast in her dedication to her beloved brother, like a hound to its master. She has never forgotten the assistance and love he provided to her when she was a young girl growing up. Now it is her turn to give him and his children all the devotion they require, setting aside her own needs and desires.

"Forgive me for being selfish," Marcella says.

Bella asks, "What are you talking about?"

"I was hoping you would be here when I go."

"Go where? Where will you go?"

"I meant when I die," Marcella says.

Bella is at a loss for words. After a pause, she says, "At the moment, Dahaba and Salif are my priority. You will always be there in my mind and my heart; and of course, I will rush to return if there is urgent need."

The truth is, Bella hasn't thought further than the next blind corner in a life marked by labyrinthine turns, as full of surprises as the paths that lead into and out of a casbah. The idea of travel, insofar as Bella is concerned, is bound up with the loading of cameras—the genesis of renewal via self-expression in everlasting images. But she feels in no condition to share all her inner tumult of worries and half-formed plans with Marcella.

"To me, you are the daughter I never had," says Marcella.

"You've told me that several times."

"I had a soft spot for Aar too."

"I've always been aware of that."

"I am bad at gaining control of my emotions."

"Don't give that a thought."

"And because Aar's death has shaken me to the marrow of my bones, I'm even more inept than usual."

Weeping once more, they hug.

Through her tears, Bella looks down at her bare feet. She must trim her toenails before she goes to catch her flight, she thinks, soak them in very hot salt water and trim the ugly lot, as hard as a young calf's hooves and just as dangerous, with their jagged edges. In Rio, where she visited her Brazilian lover, she hadn't the proper scissors with which to cut them, the airline having confiscated her last pair.

"What about Valerie?" Marcella asks.

"What about her?"

"Why can't she be with her children?"

How can Bella tell this bumbling, adorable fool that there is a right time and a wrong time and place to bring Valerie into the conversation. But Bella, though miffed, won't say boo to Marcella or speak ill of Valerie to her.

Marcella continues. "Remember, she is their mother and no one can prevent her from making a legal claim to the children as the only surviving parent."

Bella doesn't tell her the plan that is beginning to take shape in her head if such a thing threatens: fight all the way to the courts to stop it from happening. She instead speaks with long-winded caution, saying, "We haven't communicated, Valerie and I, for a very long time, and I have no idea what her plans will be when she hears of Aar's death."

"She is unbearably self-centered."

Bella wishes she had a quiet moment in which to plumb the depth of her grief alone, to give herself over to an instant of full-blown mourning before she gets a little rest and goes to catch her flight. Then she recalls how Marcella handled the loss of her husband of nearly sixty years: She slept. Bella has never known anyone who slept off her grief, but Marcella fell into a massive depression and slept and slept—not once leaving her bedroom for a whole month, during which time she remained utterly mute. At the end of what a mutual friend would later describe as Marcella's "mourning hibernation," the woman reemerged, and she seemed to think that the world around her was good again. And if you mentioned her husband's name, Marcella would speak of him as though he were out for a brief walk and would be back shortly.

Bella has no such luxury; she doesn't have a whole month in which to mourn. She has a nephew and niece to look after.

2.

With the aircraft doors closed and the plane ready to depart, Bella half listens to the flight attendant giving instructions she must have heard a million times over the years as she crossed oceans, changed continents, exchanged one time zone for another. It starts to dawn on her now that her body time is nowhere near the one her wristwatch is telling her, nor will it match the time it will be when the plane lands in Nairobi tomorrow. She is in her own time zone, much more jet-lagged than she has ever been, her brain little better equipped for thinking than a cabbage in the process of becoming sauerkraut.

Of course, Aar's death has been traumatizing, but it also comes on top of months of nearly nonstop travel. She has been putting together a book meant to document the outward migration of Somalis in pictures and words—nearly three million people in the space of a decade making a move from one of the least developed countries in the world to some of the most advanced. To that end, she has been traveling from Rome to several European countries where Somali refugee populations abound, and then to North America, including the cities of Toronto, Ottawa, Minneapolis, Columbus, and San Diego. From there, she was

off to Australia and New Zealand, after which she took the Brazil trip
for work and to visit with her lover there.

A life of quality *merde* mixed with quite a bit of weltschmerz.

Although she and Aar were not refugees, they were among the penultimate wave to leave Somalia, the last before the hemorrhage of a million and a half persons of all ages, classes, and educational backgrounds
who quit the country and then the continent, and ended up anywhere
that would take them. Two decades after the start of this stampede,
some clarity is emerging as to which of these expatriate communities is
thriving and which have stayed at the lowest rung of development. It
has been Bella's intention to document the successes and the failures
alike. Initially, she wanted to go to Somalia, maybe even visit Aar in
Mogadiscio. But now Bella thinks she may shelve the entire project or
at least postpone it until Dahaba and Salif are both out of school, their
lives settled and their futures on an even keel. A pity, because Bella had
been funding the project herself from her meager earnings, against the
advice of several friends, who suggested that she seek funding from one
of the European foundations or even from the UN's International La-
bour Organization.

As the plane levels at thirty thousand feet and the flight attendants
come around to offer drinks and snacks, Bella reminds herself that
Marcella forgot to give back her credit card. She discovered this while
waiting in the passenger lounge at the airport, but she realized it was
too late to do anything about it. Lucky she has plenty of cash from the
unused pile she returned with from Brazil and a couple of other credit
cards she always carries with her when she travels, in the event of an
emergency.

Instead of worrying needlessly about her credit card, Bella used
her time in the lounge to check her messages. Which is how she discovered a strange text informing her that Valerie and Padmini, her Asian-

British partner, have spent a night in a lockup in Kampala, Uganda, having been accused of engaging in illicit sex. The sender signed off only as "G," which Bella suspected stood for Gunilla Johansson, the colleague of her brother's in Nairobi who left her the message telling her of his death.

Following her hunch, she tried Gunilla's number and reached her. At the sound of her voice and the mention of Aar's name, the tears were back, this time with Gunilla's accompaniment. The two of them were so hopelessly emotional that Bella forgot to ask about Valerie and the mysterious text, and Gunilla did not manage to give her any information worth remembering. Then just before she boarded the flight, Bella telephoned Mahdi and Fatima, who were among Aar's closest friends in Nairobi and whose children were Dahaba and Salif's schoolmates. When Mahdi offers to meet her flight, Bella thanks him but declines, worried that she may be in an even worse state when she lands.

The business-class flight attendant gives Bella an elaborate menu printed in several languages; Bella takes it with both hands but doesn't bother to open or look at it. The idea of ordering food so soon after Aar's death appalls her. She declines the offer of the meal and closes her eyes, out of a combination of fatigue and the effort to fight the primal urge building up within her to take revenge against those who murdered her brother. When she opens her eyes, she says to the stewardess, her voice faltering, "Actually, I wouldn't mind having a coffee with some Baileys." The stewardess hesitates, looking embarrassed, as if deciding whether or not to tell Bella to wait until after the meals have been served. Then she disappears into the galley and returns with the creamy Irish stuff, as if she were serving at a Dublin wake.

Meanwhile, Bella engages her neighbor, a young Alemannic-speaking woman sporting an ostentatious coiffure, which must have cost her quite a bit, dyed in the colors of exotic birds and arranged in terraces. Her dress, by contrast, is scanty, her tank top bursting at the seams under the pressure of a well-developed chest. The shirt bears a slogan across the front promoting love in all forms, in German and English. Bella hopes that the woman is not on her way to Somalia or any other Muslim land, where she would surely be stoned on sight.

"Where are you headed?" Bella asks the woman.

"Nairobi," the woman replies.

"As a tourist?"

"I am going to marry my lover, who lives there."

Bella is tempted to know the gender of the young woman's betrothed—she can't help thinking of Valerie evidently languishing in Uganda—but then Kenya, next door, is the capital of gay culture in East Africa, an altogether different proposition. At any rate, she knows this is not her business and so choreographs the conversation in another direction.

"And this," Bella ventures, indicating the elaborate coiffure, "this is for the occasion?" She thinks of all the sacred texts—of Islam, of Judaism, of Sikhism—in which the growing or covering of hair plays an important part, welcoming this distraction from thinking about Aar's death.

"More or less."

"And where are you getting married?"

"In a church in the center of Nairobi."

She will go this far and no further. But when the plane hits a pocket of turbulence and the young woman, looking frightened, opens and closes her mouth without issuing a word, Bella leans forward and says, "It is all right. I am here, we are here." And then, surprising herself, she takes the woman's hand in hers, and they settle effortlessly into a place of mutual comfort, each deriving solace from the contact. Bella drops into a well of exhaustion, thinking ahead to her reunion with Dahaba and Salif, and imagining the hard times ahead for which she must prepare. But by the time the flight attendant comes to collect her cup, she is dead to the world, still holding the hand of the scantily dressed, heavy-chested woman with the fantastic hair with the tenderness of a lover. It isn't until her seatmate reclaims her hand, with the aim of going to the bathroom, that Bella wakes with a start. For a sleepy moment, she doesn't remember where she is and what on earth she is doing, and then she stays awake for the next few hours, wary and worried.

As much as she dislikes Valerie, Bella can't help wondering about the circumstances of her alleged arrest. You can't be cautious enough in a country that legally forbids same-sex lovemaking; you are bound to lay yourself open to blackmail and arrest if you engage in "inappropriate behavior," which has recently become synonymous with illegal behavior in a growing roster of places. In Dubai, a British heterosexual couple smooching in the lobby of their five-star hotel had been jailed for a year, for example.

In Bella's mind, freedoms are a package, so the freedoms denied daily to millions of citizens in Africa or the Middle East are bound up with the lack of democracy in these parts of the world. The choices individuals make in their private lives are just as important as the choices they make at the ballot box. Public displays of affection, whether between a man and a woman or two men or two women, are but expressions of democratic behavior. No one, not even the president of a country, should have the power and the authority to define love—including whom to love. So while Bella hasn't a kind word to say about Valerie, she is nonetheless sad to learn that she has been a victim of such repression. True, she and Padmini—particularly Padmini, being Uganda-born—should have known better than to visit a country where they might easily fall afoul of the law. The cynic in Bella wonders if unconsciously Valerie was trying to steal Aar's thunder by any means possible. He has been dead less than a week, after all.

And then she thinks, enough of Valerie, at least until she learns more about her situation from Gunilla. It is time she thought about other topics of greater personal relevance. Her niece and nephew are far more important than a foolish woman who gets herself locked up in a Ugandan jail.

At last she lowers her seat into a narrow bed and, turning and tossing in the confined space, wills herself to sleep.

She wakes when the service trolley rolls over the blanket that has been half covering her feet. She opens her eyes and stares at the flight attendant, waiting for the woman to apologize.

But the stewardess only says, "Breakfast?"

"How much more time until we land?" asks Bella.

"Two hours and a bit."

Bella orders water, juice, and coffee. When she gets back from the bathroom, she notices that the woman across the aisle is filling in the form for immigration into Kenya. She presses the call button above her seat and asks for a form for herself.

Bella has always found Kenya's entry form to be ill designed and clumsy. It never gives the traveler the needed space to write the answers. In addition, Kenya has lately been a problem country for Somalis, who are harassed from the moment they present their papers to the immigration officials and are asked relentlessly embarrassing questions. She fills in the form with trepidation, holding her pencil in midair as she frets over the best answers to give for "reason for visit" and "length of stay." She can't afford to be in a nervous state when she presents her documents and is questioned about them. She hopes that her

Italian passport, which boasts multiple entries into and exits out of numerous countries, will help allay anyone's worries that she may overstay her welcome in Kenya. Even so, her best option is to state that she is a photographer in the country as a tourist. Then the officer is bound to say, "Welcome, madam," and stamp her in.

The pilot announces, "Ladies and gentlemen, we have begun our descent," and all of a sudden the sky, which has been clear, turns leaden and gray, and clouds envelop the plane like curtains being drawn. It begins to rain heavily, each drop, which are as big as one of Bella's tears, splattering against the windows. What feels like a tropical storm is raging around them, as though the very heavens were angry. Outside the windows, lightning flashes as the plane careens down through the storm. The darkness becomes more intense and there is a loud banging, as if the wings were coming off the plane, and Bella can see nothing except the occasional flash of lightning and the endless gray clouds until suddenly the plane veers left, as if avoiding an oncoming object, then descends again with a lurch, and suddenly the clouds part and the ground is visible below them, very close.

The pilot lands safely despite the weather and taxis to a stop far from the terminal. He counsels calm, urging the passengers to remain seated, but he allows them to use their mobile phones as they wait for assistance.

There is nothing like sharing a near-death experience to bring people closer, even briefly. And later, when they've all gone their separate ways, they'll tell the same stories about it—the story of how the woman with the varicolored hair went berserk, or how another passenger threw off her seatbelt and bounced up and down like a dervish, madly reciting all the while what Bella took to be a Hindu prayer, or how a third was scared so witless that his eyes grew to the size of golf balls, the pupils dilated, and his Adam's apple went up and down as if he might be choking on his tongue. Amid the adrenalized frenzy, Bella kept calm, even managing to lend a hand to her fellow passengers. Somehow she was certain that this time death would spare her so that she could go care for her nephew and niece.

Now that they are safely on the ground, a general feeling of euphoria sets in, and soon the air is abuzz with the chatter of mobile-phone conversations. Bella can hear some of the passengers repeating the more vivid details of what occurred, and a couple of them are already embellishing the account in preparation for the moment when they will appear on the news.

After a very long wait, airport emergency services show up, and the cabin doors are finally opened. There is terrific chaos when the doors open and the passengers who are closest to the exit collide with the men and women who have been sent to deliver assistance to those in need. With several people shouting for attention at the same time, the mayhem seems likely to sabotage every good effort to provide help until the pilot enters the fray, once more advising restraint. He requests that all passengers not injured in the bumpy descent please sit and remain seated until those who need help receive it. A passenger in business class, accustomed to what he refers to as "the priority for which I paid," insists that he be the first to exit. It takes the shaming of several fellow passengers and the venomous reprimand of one of the male flight attendants to get him to settle down, but once he does, the mood of the other passengers takes a positive turn. With calmness prevailing, they collaborate in filing out of the aircraft and into the waiting buses in an orderly manner.

Bella, waiting her turn to disembark, negotiates her shoulder bag, heavy with her computer, with a big hard camera case made of shiny metal in her right hand, and a smaller matching case in her left. She is remembering previous, more pleasant visits to these parts, visits that she always looked forward to. Aar used to take her and his children to out-of-town restaurants such as the one in Naivasha, her favorite, which boasted gorgeous vistas, the blueness of the lake complementing a clear sky that extended in every direction. This visit, weighed down by death, will be very different.

Just as she is about to clamber on board the bus to the terminal, hauling her cases, a man approaches her too close for comfort. A tall, thin European, with chiseled features and a tan, is eyeing her as if debating whether to speak to her or not. His brazen stare puts her off and she doesn't bother to answer him when he says, "Will you have a drink with me if I were to ask you out? I'll show you a fabulous time, the best you've ever had in the company of a man."

For the first time, Bella wishes that she had allowed her sorrow to express itself, which might have discouraged such advances. Now she tries to cut him down with a look of bitter distaste that makes it obvious she wants nothing to do with him. She gets on the bus, retreating into the rear, where she stands next to the woman with the many-hued hair. The man gets on board as well, but he keeps his distance, contenting himself with glancing in her direction every now and then.

Immigration is a breeze. In fact, she has never seen a friendlier group of immigration officers. Chatty and apologetic for the difficult landing, they are quick to say "Welcome!" to every passenger who approaches. Nor does anyone bother to ask for the supposedly mandatory yellow fever certificate—this in an airport known for holding travelers for hours and extorting bribes from them.

And even though it takes a much longer time than usual for the luggage to be delivered to the cranky carousel, nobody complains. When Bella finally collects her other cases, she realizes that there is no need for her to rush; no one is meeting her. And so she heads toward the exit, dreading only mildly that the man who approached her earlier might make a further nuisance of himself, in which case she has decided to deal with him firmly and, if need be, crudely.

Bella pushes the loaded baggage trolley forward, feeling hot inside her black cotton shift. She walks slowly, her gait unsteady, her cheeks now wet with tears again, her sight blurred. She finds a bench to rest her exhausted bones on, sitting until the waves of nausea start to abate. She feels uncomfortable being so infirm in so public a place, but the familiarity of her surroundings relaxes her a little, even if there is no Aar to meet her or no taxi driver holding up a placard with her name. She lets herself sit and weep, not bothering to wipe away the tears. She asks herself why death, and why now? And why did death deprive her of her adored brother? Why has misfortune chosen to descend on her and her nephew and niece at a time when they are so ill prepared for loss?

A tall man standing nearby, a Masai from the looks of him, approaches. "Madam!" he says repeatedly, until she looks up. Once he has her full attention, he says, "Taxi," as if this were her name. Gradually other men join them, and one of them takes her by the arm, another grabs hold of her bags, a third insists that she ride in his taxi because he will give her a bargain price. She looks from one to the other, clearly miffed. She focuses her hard stare on the man who is trying to dispossess her of her computer bag and who already has in the grip of his right hand one of the camera cases. She restrains herself from speaking, but her expression and body language indicate clearly that she wants him to give back her bags.

Then the man who approached first, the Masai—she takes in his torn ears and his sharpened teeth—tries to put the others to shame, accusing them of being a disgrace to their profession and their nation.

Bella gives her face a quick wipe, as if the word "disgrace" is equally addressed to her. The mood changes, and nearly all of the taxi drivers step back, some of them moving on immediately and others mumbling their dissent and straggling away slowly, unhappy at being shut out. Bella beckons the Masai.

"Hotel 680, please."

"Yes, madam. Please follow me!"

He pushes the unwieldy trolley with her pile of heavy cases in the direction of the exit, and Bella hurries to keep pace with him to the open-air parking lot. When he opens the back door of the taxi, she indicates that she wants to sit in the front.

Nairobi traffic is atrocious, disorderly, and murderously slow. It's as if this city has a violent strain running in its veins. It's an in-between place, with many different tendencies pulling its residents in diverse directions, and it seems fitting to Bella that it started as a railway depot at the turn of the last century. In slapdash fashion, it has grown into a "self-help city," as an urban anthropologist has put it, in which the Africans must make do while European tourists are drawn by the promise of adventure and safari.

The taxi is Japanese-made and rickety, as if it could easily be pulled apart. It's hot too, but Bella dares not roll down the window, even a little, on account of the black fumes and white smoke emitted by the malfunctioning trucks ahead of them, which pollute the air as well with venomous bellowing. Bella sits with her computer bag between her knees, pondering the world outside. She is not sure of the name of the poet, but there is a line that she has always appreciated for its balance and alliteration: "It is beautiful, it is mournful, it is monotonous." To this she adds another line of her own composition: "There is glory in grief."

With the traffic at a standstill, the driver starts a conversation. "Madam, to what name do you answer? My own name is David."

Uncomfortable at giving the name by which she is known, Bella says, "Some of my friends call me Barni."

"What does Barni mean in your language?" he says.

"Something to do with a baby born with a birthmark."

"You were born bearing a birthmark?"

She improvises. "I was named after an ancestor."

"What is your country of origin?"

Bella doesn't fancy giving her life history to this stranger either, so she turns on the radio, which jabbers away in a language she does not comprehend.

David asks, "Do you understand this language?"

Several young men circulate among the cars with things to sell: fruit, combs, cell phone chargers, and shoelaces. People buy from them as they sit in traffic. Bella rolls down the window and prices several items just to engage these young men and women in conversation and avoid a further exchange with David.

"Barni, eh? That is a beautiful name," David says.

In truth, she is rich in names. Her mother called her Isabella, but only when she was upset with her, lengthening the vowels and rolling her tongue over its syllables. Bella is the name by which she is known outside her immediate circle. Barni is her middle name, which affords those who are most intimate with her the chance to address her as BB.

The question is not what is in a name, but rather how many of them she can answer to. She thinks it is a useful thing to have an array of names, each presenting her with different possibilities. Well aware that people she encounters rarely forget meeting her, even if they did so fleetingly. Yet she sometimes delights in denying having met someone and, if challenged, asks if they remember her name—whereupon she insists that she is called by a different name. Outside the Horn of Africa, she prefers the use of her Somali name; inside the Somali-speaking region, she is Bella.

A blind man with a boy for a guide pushes his way toward the car. He is as determined to get her attention as the street hawkers, it seems. He recites a Muslim prayer, wishing her safe passage, and touches her elbow when she isn't looking. She shrinks from the physical contact and rolls the window up again. Just then the traffic moves.

Presently, she spots a web in the corner of the floorboards, close to where her foot is resting, a web woven and then forsaken, and then she sees another, this one active, in which a bigger spider has recently trapped a tiny insect, which is now trying to wiggle its way out alive. Bella bends down and frees the insect, which shakes its whole body and then tenses, like a gymnast readying to somersault and hit the ground with his feet wide, balanced and firm. The spider goes in determined pursuit, and both vanish through a gaping hole in the floor of the car.

With nothing better to do, Bella returns her attention to the driver. She volunteers that she has missed Africa, missed the smell of night fires, the mellifluously tonal languages, and the calls of neighbors across a village courtyard after a day's hard work has left them too exhausted to bother with the formality of coming out of their homes.

The driver asks, "So you were born in Africa?"

"Born and brought up a Somali," she says.

"Both your parents are Somali, are they?"

Again Bella seizes up, and as the traffic moves a little faster, she revisits the most salient fact about her life, which is that for most of her early years she believed Digaaleh, nicknamed "Arab" on account of his very light skin, to be her biological father and Aar her full brother. She was seven when she first made the acquaintance of Giorgio Fiori in 1988. Fiori was then on a return visit to Mogadiscio in the capacity of leader of an Italian government delegation charged with determining if Italy should continue funding university education in Somalia and for how long.

Bella, as it happened, would meet her father again less than a year and a half later, when she and her mother and Aar fled the anarchy surrounding the collapse of Somalia to the coastal city of Mombasa, Kenya, where they were declared stateless and were made to stay in a refugee camp. Fiori came in person to take them out of the refugee camp and fly them to Nairobi, where he presented them with Italian visas so they could go with him to Rome. It was a couple of months later that Digaaleh, who had remained behind in Mogadiscio, had surgery on his prostate. Half a year later, he would be dead.

Bella remained in Rome with Fiori, who supplied her with the obligatory papers allowing her to remain in Italy and pursue her studies. When she was older, she moved into an adjacent one-bedroom apartment that he paid for so they could be in constant touch, sharing evening meals often and spending a great deal of time together. Still, she led her private life discreetly, never speaking of her Neapolitan lover, a cameraman working in the studios of Cinecittà, the film studios established by Benito Mussolini on the outskirts of Rome in 1937. No one could be more aware of the importance of Cinecittà than Bella, as she had been brought up on Italian cinema, popular during her days in Mogadiscio. Her Neapolitan lover showed her the precise location where *Ben-Hur* was shot, and they gave her a private tour of Teatro 5, where Federico Fellini made his most famous films.

Aar and Hurdo eventually relocated to Toronto, where they were first granted refugee status and later Canadian citizenship. Within a couple of years, Hurdo learned she had ovarian cancer. Aar cared for her even as he pursued his graduate studies in human migration. After Hurdo died, Aar joined the International Organization for Migration, an intergovernmental organization headquartered in Geneva.

It takes the taxi a little more than three hours to get to Bella's hotel. By the time she arrives, she is too exhausted to evaluate just how terribly the place has aged since her last stay, but she can see that the walls need more than a lick of paint and the chairs are sunken with use. She asks for the room she occupied a decade ago when she was on assignment here and met her Kenyan lover, HandsomeBoy Ngulu, who is no longer in the modeling business and now works for an NGO specializing in the eradication of illiteracy in Africa. But she still remembers him as an exemplary subject, patient, willing to do as many takes as she wanted, always smiling, forever prepared to make her happy.

What a disaster it was, their first lovemaking! But things began to improve with each night they spent together, and Bella still thinks of him as her *bell'uomo*. Now that Bella is in Nairobi, however, she thinks that she must seek out HandsomeBoy Ngulu to apprise him of her new situation and suggest that they cease being lovers; life now is just too complicated.

3.

In her hotel room, Bella takes a shower. Drying herself, she stands on the tips of her toes, craning her neck as though to see something beyond the scope of the mirror. She is a dark-eyed beauty with a prominent nose, heavier in the chest than she likes because of the attention it draws from men, even though she is overjoyed that she boasts the slimmest of waists for a woman her age and an African's high buttocks. Drop-dead gorgeous, she also strikes most people as charming, well read, and intelligent.

Which of her names goes with which of her attributes? She is a woman whose disposition is rarely at variance with other people's assumptions. She only reaches for the unattainable when it comes to photography, where her ambitions soar. And yet, not only as a woman but also as a Somali woman, she has had to defy harsh social conditioning to establish herself as a person equal in all respects to a man.

She puts on a robe and starts to unpack, but she makes very little headway, distracted as she is by several loose photographs of Aar that fall onto the table and floor. He is in different situations and in the company of different people, including his children, the photos having been taken when they met in Istanbul during what would turn out to be his final holiday. She looks at one of the photographs and remembers that somewhere she read that the French philosopher Roland Barthes thought that an interest in photography points to a preoccupation with death because it attests to the past existence of an object, person, or image in a never-ending present, but not necessarily to its continued existence.

Now, as Bella holds Aar's photograph before her, her mind wanders from where she stands to engage with a distant past, where she interrogates the meaning and quality of a life that Aar had been an essential constituent in. In the photograph, Aar stands before the Hagia Sophia Museum, the sun in his eyes, facing Bella as she takes his picture, the thought of death the furthest thing from their minds. But now, looking at the photograph and studying it with death-inspired intensity, Bella senses that the two of them were in a sense preparing for death. Otherwise, why take a photograph in front of a museum representing a distant era that is no longer part of anyone's present? That is to say, this photo, taken barely a year ago, now serves as a witness. And she listens to herself saying, as though to another, "Here we were, my brother and I, in Istanbul, marking our existence with this photograph, which now attests to his death." A question: Can one accept the existence of anything unless one can represent it in some form or image?

Of the many apocryphal tales about Bella, this is the one Hurdo repeated most often: Unlike other babies, she was not born with the residue of birth smeared all over her. Nor did she announce her arrival with the usual primeval cry. Instead, she emerged from the womb with a shock of long jet-black hair and an even-tempered, almost professional expression that put Marcella in mind of a competitive swimmer emerging from a pool after a hard workout.

Digaaleh suspected from the beginning that he was not the father. Indeed, very quickly the rumors circulating gained so much momentum that he couldn't ignore them. This did not improve his marriage, but to everyone's surprise, he continued to put on a good show despite his obvious loss of face. He neither spoke ill of Hurdo in public nor accused her in private. He treated Aar and Bella equally as his offspring, and behaved civilly to Giorgio Fiori. Only Fiori's wife, who had remained in Bologna with their son, found his fling unpardonable. As if to prove that all cats are not gray in the dark, she filed for divorce within a year of his return to Italy.

Hurdo, for her part, believing that a child's happiness is built on a parent's small gestures, devoted herself to the newborn, and in return, Bella gave her reasons for joy and a hopeful perspective on not only her daughter's future but also her own. Aar, now twelve, had longed for a sister, and he too reveled in Bella's presence. He was highly protective of her, even reprimanding his parents if Bella fussed in her crib and neither of them went to comfort her. When she was awake, he could be found sitting beside her, cooing sweet nothings to her. Once, when Bella took ill, Aar refused to go to school and nothing would make him leave her bedside, where he kept feeling her pulse, taking her temperature, or touching her forehead. When asked how his absence should be explained to his headmaster, he said to write that he was too sick to attend school; he couldn't be well if Bella wasn't.

When he had done anything to upset his mother, Aar learned that extra attentiveness to his sister would soften Hurdo toward him. They were a threesome, Hurdo, Aar, and Bella, flourishing together, never allowing anyone to come between them. For the first three years of

Bella's life, they lived just as they pleased, with no boundaries. And Bella appeared to benefit from their unusual closeness. She sat up at five months, had her first teeth at six, crawled at seven, and walked before her ninth month.

Yet Hurdo was aware that life couldn't go on like this forever, with the three of them continually in one another's hair, and she knew she would have to put a stop to some of Aar's boyish mischief. In self-admonishment, she repeated to herself the Somali proverb that a parent must refrain from showing her smiling teeth to her children lest her children start showing their naked bums. Gradually, she began to introduce some order into their lives.

Bella continued to thrive. The world is at my daughter's service and everyone in it is at her feet, Hurdo would say. Other children seemed to be infatuated with her. They threw tantrums when their parents arrived to fetch them home, crying their hearts out and insisting on staying longer and speaking of their wish to sleep in Bella's room. Yet the moment Aar came home from school, Bella lost interest in them. Sometimes she would shoo them away disdainfully so that she could follow Aar around, going where he went and sitting where he sat, endlessly telling him things. At five or six, she threatened to kill any girls she imagined as rivals for Aar's affection. In his absence, she often complained of feeling hunger. Asked what she craved, she would say that she longed for his return. Yet no amount of his indulgence seemed to satisfy her; Hurdo said he had the patience of a saint.

Hurdo spoke of her daughter's attachment as a form of infatuation, comparing it to an infatuation she remembered from her own childhood. "When I was three," Hurdo recounted to Marcella, "I felt drawn to a boy my age. My parents and the boy's parents were amused at first. Then came the time when my parents and the boy's parents quipped that the boy and I would marry."

Marcella said, "Still, to experience love as hunger is a brilliant way of dealing with a complicated emotion. How apt! Your daughter is very smart."

"Among Somalis," Hurdo explained, "love is looked upon as an affliction, a sickness for which there is no cure. We believe that love is unattainable because true desire is impossible."

Marcella thought that Bella's childhood crush on her brother might make her the kind of woman men fell for and women were wary of, even hated by them. And Hurdo too worried that the intensity of Bella's feelings for her brother were such that she might never allow herself to fall in love with anyone else.

But what was there to do? They would just have to see what would happen. And the bond between Bella and Aar stayed unbroken until Aar fell in love with a girl in Rome, and Bella went ballistic. Hurdo's every attempt to explain things only made matters worse. Always a bad eater, Bella became anorexic, in the terrifying grip of a hunger that to her was synonymous with pining.

Eventually, her despair abated, when, thanks to a photograph of her that appeared in a fancy Sunday supplement published in Rome, she became a celebrity and began to earn a lot of money as a teen model. Bella had the uncanny ability to make her eyes flame a metallic green, and what with her exceptional looks and captivating smile, several agencies vied to represent her. After consulting Hurdo, Fiori negotiated a very favorable agreement with her with one of the best-known of them. Hurdo was not surprised when Digaaleh rang them from Mogadiscio, raising his objections, disconsolately comparing Bella's work and the exploitation of her image to prostitution. Hurdo let him fume, seeing his reaction as that of a typical Somali father and knowing he could do nothing to stop Bella from pursuing her heart's pleasure, while earning good money to boot.

Digaaleh, however, insisted she had misunderstood his intentions. "Essentially, it depends whether one sees Bella as Somali and therefore Muslim—and Muslims don't go into modeling or exploit their image in exchange for cash—or Italian and therefore free to do as she pleases." But Hurdo cut him off, saying that Bella was indeed a free person, able to make her own choices in life, and that no one had the right to impose their cultural or religious dictates on her just because she hadn't yet attained the age of majority.

"I don't wish Giorgio to decide her fate," Digaaleh said.

"Well, if it comes to that, he will," Hurdo retorted, "because he is her father." Then she was hung up on him—and not long after, word came from Mogadiscio that he had died. And it wasn't until many years later, at Giorgio Fiori's funeral, that Bella heard about this heated exchange, from Marcella.

Bella has long been of the belief that there are no people on earth more narrow-minded or chauvinistic than Somalis, for whom appearances—the clothes one wears, the way one moves—matter enormously, especially when it comes to women. She recalls too that when she took up smoking and dressing in jeans, the Somalis she met in Rome, or Toronto whenever she visited, found both habits provocative and offensive in equal measure. (Looking at her fingers now, she can still see them in her memory as they were: stained brown with nicotine, as she held a fresh cigarette between them, lighting it with the butt of the previous one.)

It was Giorgio Fiori who sparked what would become Bella's true vocation, for it was in his house that she saw the first piece of art that ever took her fancy—the inspiration for making art herself. It was a carving from the Dogon in Mali—a simple figure with a cylindrical body, rods for arms, broken bits of colored glass for eyes, thrown together as if in haste—that she had glimpsed in silhouette at dusk in the house he rented during one of his intermittent teaching stints in Mogadiscio during her childhood. The natural light was fading and the electric lamps had not yet come on. The carving struck her as the most beautiful thing she had ever seen or held in her hand; she was very impressionable.

She did not know then that Fiori was her mother's secret lover, but as she held the piece, admiring its detail, she admired its owner by extension for choosing a work of such finesse. From that moment she began to adore him and to love her mother all the more for the adoration she sensed in her.

Fiori had other pieces too, which he would show her later. By then she knew that he was her father; speaking in Somali, he told her that he'd kept them hidden away from the prying eyes of the Somalis when he lived there, not knowing what impression the carvings might make on such an unlearned lot. As Muslims, perhaps they'd have accused him of engaging in idol worship. But none of the pieces, much as she admired them, inspired the same reaction as that first piece. She'd wanted to possess it, pure and simple. Of course she could have it, Giorgio said. Hurdo tried to persuade Bella to withdraw her demand, but Bella wouldn't back down. Hurdo explained that the piece was one of a series and Giorgio's favorite, and that it would upset the balance if the piece was separated from the rest. Nothing doing: Bella wanted that one and no other. In the end, she accepted a compromise: She could borrow the piece for a month and keep it in her room on her windowsill provided she took good care of it. Bella charged headlong into Giorgio, hugging him and blurting her thanks.

Each night, Bella went to sleep with the piece in her sight, and it was the first thing she looked at when she woke. It made her feel fulfilled, joyful, satisfied with life. She worked harder in school, earned better marks, and became more purposeful and organized. She volunteered to do the dishes when it was her turn without talking back to her mother. Giorgio couldn't make sense of his daughter's infatuation and predicted that it would be no more than a passing fad, like several others she'd gone through. But neither her devotion to the piece nor her interest in art nor her newfound sense of purpose and discipline wavered.

It was then that Aar bought her a Polaroid camera. She began to draw too, copying the sculpture in crayon from different angles. And then she began to photograph it with the Polaroid, shooting it again and again, as though possessed. One day, Aar walked in on her when she was at work, unwashed, sweaty, her room a mess. As she worked with unbreakable concentration, she looked like someone in another world. For the first time it occurred to him that with proper support she might become a serious photographer.

Next Aar bought her an inexpensive point-and-shoot, and she began to learn which camera to use to get the effects she was after. When the cost of developing the flood of photos she was taking became more than they could afford, Giorgio introduced her to an Italian colleague who trained her to develop her own negatives and helped her to set up her own darkroom in a closet, with Giorgio covering the outlay for materials as a gift for Bella's twelfth birthday.

With a view to becoming self-reliant, Bella began to photograph weddings and other occasions. At first she did so free of charge while she mastered the art of taking photos of unruly revelers in crowded circumstances. Next, she learned to take portraits outdoors because she had no studio. She noted that when people posed for portraits a differ- ent self came to the fore, a self behind the self they wished to present to others. And Bella discovered that the longer she held off before clicking the shutter, the more this hidden self emerged. She learned to wait for this hidden, this authentic self to emerge, surfacing after a display of nerves and fidgeting.

From childhood, Bella had wanted to free herself from her parents' constraints and blackmailing maneuvers, and she was determined to make her own way in the world, working hard and doing well in whatever profession she chose. At eighteen, Bella apprenticed herself to a photographer friend of her Neapolitan lover. With Fiori prepared to buy her the expensive cameras she required, she was able to set her mind on pursuing her vocation.

Yet even as she became successful, Bella remained dissatisfied with the companionship on offer. Always a picky eater, who at her heaviest weighed no more than forty-five kilos, she boasted of a waistline so thin that her first boyfriend, the Neapolitan cameraman, told her she looked like a waif who needing a little fattening. This put Bella in mind of a cow being pumped with supplements to make sure it fetched the highest price, and she showed the boyfriend the door—though not before he made a jibe about her incestuous relationship with her brother, whose name she had mentioned at every possible opportunity. She fired back, "And you are nowhere near as good, as lovable, as caring, or even as amusing as he. So be off with you!"

She continued to be romantically sought after, but no man seemed to suffice. Over time, she discovered, first to her disbelief and then to her amusement, that she was not jealous if a man she was with ogled other women or made passes at them in her presence, reasoning that neither the men nor the women they noticed mattered enough to justify her jealousy or disappointment. By the time Aar married Valerie, Bella had evolved her fantasy. She would have three lovers, she decided: one of them very, very handsome; another (with whom she would have at least one child) who was very, very intelligent; and for the third, she would choose a stud—a well-hung partner with whom she would enjoy sex. Little by little, the fantasy became reality.

HandsomeBoy was first. Bella met him on one of her first major freelance assignments, which involved shooting photographs of models and animals in Kenya for clothing businesses with Italian connections. HandsomeBoy had moved from his natal hamlet near the Tanzanian border to study sociology at the University of Nairobi. He worked part-time as a model to pay for his education. If asked, he and Bella wouldn't agree on which of them fell for the other first, each claiming to be the one to do so, such was their immediate attraction.

Her appreciation for sculpture persisted, and it was at a gallery show that she met Humboldt on a visit to her mother and brother in Toronto. A successful Brazilian sculptor of African descent, Humboldt was based in Rio and traveled the world as Bella did. He became her second lover, and the sex was great. In those days, nothing else mattered much, and neither of them had the desire to enter into a long-term relationship. Since then, they meet as their schedules permit, in hotels in various cities, for a week, for a day.

Five years into this second relationship, on a day when she was in New York, she attended a lecture by Cisse Drahme, a Malian philosopher of note. He was speaking on "The Wonders of Dogon Astronomy," and after the lecture, she was invited to join a group at a bar, which led to a dinner for two and then a meeting of the minds that has blossomed for more than ten years. And thus Bella fulfilled her fantasy of three lovers.

Within reason, any of them would drop what he is doing and go where she chooses to meet up with her. She has keys to their houses or apartments, and she can come and go as she pleases, while none of them even has her exact address. All they know is that she lives in Rome. The arrangement has served Bella very well. She has had to curb neither her love life nor her professional ambitions. But now?

A journalist for an Italian daily newspaper once asked Bella, "What makes you think that a nervous subject makes a more interesting photo than a calm one?" And Bella replied, "As a child, when I had to get a shot, I feared the jab of the needle, just as I hated the nurse saying not to think about the pain. I mean to wait until the person photographed no longer thinks of what I am doing. That way, I am in charge. And I like being in charge, in total control."

The journalist asked, "Do you believe that photography is a matter of power, with the photographer lording it over the subject? Is this what you are trying to say?"

That was indeed how Bella felt. "I like to think that my subjects are as powerless as a rabbit caught in the headlights of an oncoming car."

"Isn't that an unhealthy attitude to hold?"

"I am a woman," Bella explained, "and a Somali one at that."

"How do you mean?" the journalist asked.

Bella found it difficult to explain, but she tried. She talked about how the colonized Asians, Africans, North American Indians, and Australian aboriginals had been eroticized and trivialized by their colonizers. And just as American photographers produced naked portraits of Native Americans or Africans for the tourist trade, women photographed in the nude were put to similar service. Bella asked, "If that is not power that allows the mighty to lord over the weak, I don't know what is."

But lately, the journalist observed, Bella had been photographing children more and more, especially Somali children. Why was that?

Bella pointed out that she had never photographed anyone in the nude or eroticized any of her subjects. "Please note," she said, "that I make sure they look straight into the camera. I let them laugh and gesticulate naturally instead of shaping their bodies into objects of desire."

"When does photography become art?" the journalist asked.

The photographer achieved the status of artist by virtue of his lenses, his choice of paper, his mastery of printing and tone, Bella said. And she spoke of her favorite photographers, many of whom were also painters, and the works she regarded as their masterpieces, such as Stieglitz's *The Terminal* and the nude portraits he'd made of his wife, Georgia O'Keeffe. For a time, early on in her career, he'd been the only photographer she idolized. But the more Bella developed her own style, the wider the range of photographers she admired. Still, she remained partial to the photo, which reminded her of a painting. She had always believed that photography owes its existence to painting. "I would like my photographs to think of their favorite painters," she said.

The journalist pointed out that Somalis, whether male or female, are physically reserved. "They are undemonstrative. It is as if they have never heard of sexual freedom, with parents shying away from standing even half nude in front of their children. The body, whether female or male, is in chains."

Given the opportunity, and unlimited funding, the journalist asks, what photographic project would she be eager to embark on?

Bella smiled and shook her head. "I wonder if there is any point in answering your question, which I take to be nothing but a sort of a trap."

"Let me ask it in a different way," said the journalist. "Who would you rather be, a Sebastião Salgado or a Robert Mapplethorpe, given the chance?"

"A Sebastião Salgado any day."

"Why?"

"Because I would start my own series about the end of women's manual labor," Bella replied.

The truth is, Bella did photograph her lovers in the nude before she was intimate with them, but she will never discuss this. She believes this affirms her power over them. As she prepares them to sit for her, she watches them from behind the camera lens, intently waiting and deliberately making them nervous before her finger presses the shutter.

Nor does she share with her interviewer the shock and then the amusement she experienced when, in a hotel in New York where she was staying, she found a Mapplethorpe book of black male portraits in the nude where a Gideon Bible would normally be. Did she like what she saw? Did she think that what she saw was art? She wasn't sure. Of course, she wouldn't deny there was novelty in doing what Mapplethorpe did, and she admired the way he'd made his own niche, in both the market and the art of photography. But she wasn't so sure that what he was doing was any different from the titillating nude photographs so many photographers had taken of so many women.

"Who in your experience is the most difficult subject to photograph?" the journalist had asked.

"The eye of the camera sees what is in front of it, and it records the moment it captures truthfully," Bella replied. "However, it may have difficulties in fronting impossible situations. My mother hated being photographed despite knowing that there was nothing more pleasing to me than taking her picture. So I would say she was the most impossible subject to photograph."

"And who is the most delightful subject to photograph?" the journalist asked.

That one was easy. "Aar, my brother, and his children," Bella had answered.

4.

Bella knows that she is procrastinating, but she does not yet feel up to the enormous responsibilities that await her. She tells herself that until she has a better grip on her emotions she shouldn't make contact with her niece and nephew. The folly of mourning, and thus confusing love with loss, is so natural in us humans that it can leave us physically and mentally unable to perform any of our usual tasks, let alone look after anyone else.

She pulls her mobile phone out of her shoulder bag to ring Gunilla again. But she has scarcely dialed the long international number when the hotel phone on the bedside table rings, startling her. With her hand shaking and her head spinning with an array of conflicting fantasies—someone is ringing to tell her that Aar is injured but still alive; or it is Gunilla calling to tell her that Valerie has been released and is on a flight bound for Nairobi?—she finally finds the strength and the voice to pick up and say hello.

The hotel receptionist informs her that she is sending up a fax message that has arrived marked VERY URGENT. And because the woman gives neither the sender's name nor the country of origin, Bella again allows her mind to go wild, imagining all sorts of far-fetched scenarios. Perhaps the fax brings news that her niece and nephew have been in a car accident on their way from their boarding school on the outskirts of Nairobi. Bella sits down, her lips silently unleashing a salvo of Koranic verses she hasn't recited since childhood. The next minute her optimism is ascendant, the fax bringing a different kind of news about Aar: that his body was found in perfect condition, proof that he did not suffer much pain or trauma. She stands by the entrance to her room, ready to open the door to the bearer of the message. When she hears the lift doors open and then footsteps approach, she gives in to her eagerness and opens the door. But there is no one in the corridor. So she sits tight and waits, accepting her powerlessness to do anything about anything.

Bella tells herself that she has lived for years in a cocoon. With no child of her own and no steady partner, she hasn't had many worries to bother her. Healthy, young, and blessed with good looks, content with the professional niche she has made for herself, she has had few serious worries, at least until Aar's transfer two years ago to the UN office in Mogadiscio. From that day on, she paid more attention to the news coming out of Somalia. Even so, she was unmoved by much of what she read, even the suicide bombings and the constant deaths from IEDs planted by the terrorists. As long as the casualties were unknown to her personally, the tragedies felt abstract. Until now! As she said to Marcella—was it yesterday or the day before?—"Aar's death changes everything." What she meant was this: From now on, when the telephone rings in the middle of the night, she will imagine a car accident, a bombing in a shopping mall or restaurant in which someone dear to her loses their life. And while she will no longer worry herself to death about Aar, she will dread what might happen to her nephew and niece, the same way many a parent she knows has an ear cocked for a phone call when her teenagers are out at a party after midnight.

Bella is just at the point of wondering if she might have misunderstood the receptionist when she hears a gentle knock on the door. Now she takes her time before answering, searching for a little baksheesh, but she has found only euros when there is a second tapping and then a third. She opens the door and finds herself face-to-face with a handsome young man with big eyes and a fetching smile, in hotel uniform. Extending her right hand to receive the envelope he bears, she sees that it is shaking and stops. But the young man has no eyes for her trembling hand; he is ogling the slight opening where her robe has slipped a little. Suddenly amused, Bella relaxes and, no longer shaking, receives the envelope with both hands and thanks him.

"Why has it taken you so long to come up?" she asks him. "I'd almost given up."

"The receptionist twice sent me to the wrong room," he replies, shaking his head and smiling. "Maybe she was confused because your name is hyphenated on the fax, but you registered with only a single name." But he apologizes and she gives him a couple of euros for his troubles before she gently closes the door.

Her hand is trembling again as she takes a seat, her feet planted on the floor. Bizarrely, she looks left and then right, as if she expects someone else to be with her in the room or as if she were engaged in a conversation. Then she nods her head, as though giving an okay, and tears the envelope open and reads the name of the sender: Helene, in Kampala. But Bella knows no Helene in Kampala. The message is in legalese and brief. Helene introduces herself as an attorney who is writing at the suggestion of Gunilla, who provided her with the name of

Bella's hotel. She continues, "Since the matter I wish to discuss with you is of utmost urgency and its nature delicate and familial, I would appreciate it if you could contact me at your earliest." Helene provides two office landline numbers and a mobile phone number, each bearing a Kampala area code, and an e-mail address.

This must be an attorney representing Valerie and Padmini, Bella guesses. The thought that such a person exists relaxes her. She will not walk away from her responsibility to her sister-in-law, she knows, but she also knows that, once free, Valerie will carry on as if nothing has happened, except that she will blame the whole thing on anyone but herself.

Bella calls one of the landline numbers she has been given. As she waits for someone to answer it, she tells herself that she won't ever forgive herself if she does nothing to help Valerie, never mind the nature of the trouble the woman is in. And Uganda being Uganda, she thinks that she will be able to find the right officers to bribe. To get matters moving, Bella decides to insist that Helene not disclose to Valerie who is putting up the bail and paying all other expenses incurred.

Finally, Helene answers. After Bella has introduced herself and then acknowledged receipt of the fax, Helene says, "I'll tell you enough of what we are up against so you can decide whether you wish to get involved."

"I can't help it, I have to be involved."

Bella can hear papers being shuffled and then Helene says, "I must tell you this at the start. We do not represent Valerie as such."

"Please explain your meaning."

"We represent Padmini, her partner, in a property dispute between her and a Ugandan businessman," Helene says. "And then this."

"'And then this'? What's 'this'?"

Helene says, "A few days before Padmini and Valerie's arrest, we had received notice from the courts about a preliminary date when a judge would hear the property dispute."

"Are you telling me that this is why they are locked up?" says Bella. "Because the Ugandan has played a dirty hand?"

"Yes."

"What happened?"

"The Ugandan tycoon hired a private eye to dig deep into the dirt," Helene says. "He hopes to force Padmini's hand so that she will flee the country or at least withdraw her case."

"How much dirt did the private eye dig up?"

"The private eye sneaked in on Valerie and Padmini's privacy and left his hiding place with a rich harvest of sexually explicit photographs."

"How careless of them," Bella says.

"Their lack of awareness would be quite understandable if it weren't for the fact that Padmini comes from here," Helene says. "She was born here and her family is well known and well respected too."

"How do we proceed?"

"We need to get them out of prison. The yellow press is sniffing around, readying to run off with the story. This will do irreparable damage to their reputations. Somalis, as Valerie told me—as if I needed telling—will bay for her blood if it comes out that she is Aar's widow. We must do something quick, get them out, and put them on a flight to Nairobi."

"Why a flight to Nairobi?"

"According to Valerie, Nairobi has one of the largest communities of homosexuals, second only to Cape Town in the entire continent, and she says they will feel comfortable there."

"How can I help?"

"Can you come in person to Kampala?"

"As I said, I do not want her to know that I am her benefactor," Bella says, this time with great emphasis.

"We need to move fast," Helene says.

"How much will it take to get them out?"

"A couple of thousand dollars in legal fees, and a couple more to make sure that we grease the right uniformed palms adequately so they will be discreet in their dealings with us and the press," Helene says.

"What if I can't come in person?" Bella reminds herself that she is primarily in Africa not to solve Valerie's problems but to mother her nephew and niece.

"You can choose one of two options."

"I am listening."

"You can wire the funds. Or you can find someone residing in Uganda whom you know personally and whom you trust—a Somali, say, as there are hundreds of thousands of your nationals residing in Kampala, many of them very wealthy, and you arrange with them to settle the bill right away and then pay them later. This will be the quickest way of having them released. The money will be delivered to us in cash and we will act forthwith—very efficient!"

Bella doesn't like either option.

"What if I transfer it electronically?"

"We don't have that facility at our legal firm, I am embarrassed to say," Helene says.

Uganda has never figured in Bella's imagination in any shape or form beyond the revulsion she felt for Idi Amin when he was in power, in addition to being disgusted by the bloodthirsty Lord's Resistance Army sect led by Joseph Kony. "Let me come back to you shortly," she says to Helene. Then she requests that Helene supply her with all of the bank details and the address of her chambers just in case.

But she won't ring off until she understands how it is that a lawyer with her own chambers is in no financial position to have funds transferred electronically from a neighboring country. Maybe there is something not kosher about the deal. She asks Helene to explain.

"Recently, we've been victims of hackers," she says. "We suspect a former client of mine, a Nigerian, now in jail for drug-related crimes, has had a hand in this. Since then, all our accounts are frozen because of the ongoing criminal investigation. But trust me. We are legit." Helene goes on and then breaks into laughter, adding, "Listen to me trying to convince you to trust me! This is hilarious."

Whereupon Bella says, "I do trust you."

Helene says, "You do? How noble of you!"

And then Bella does ring off, promising to get back to her in an hour at most.

Next Bella rings Gunilla on a mission for more information. While she waits, she Googles Ms. Johansson, who is described as heading the forensic department for the UN office in Nairobi and who is charged with determining the disposition of the UN victims' assets as well as dispersing any additional support for their dependents.

"Gunilla," she answers, sounding clipped and purposeful.

This time, Bella, who has her wits about her, remembers to ask Gunilla for further details, not about Valerie's situation but about where Aar's body was discovered.

Gunilla confirms what the news reports said, that his body was blown apart by the blast of the bomb, unrecognizably mutilated, and that his head was recovered several yards away.

"Where is he buried?" Bella asks.

"At least he has his own grave."

"Not a mass grave, like the others share?"

"That's right."

In the pause that follows this, Bella joins Gunilla in crying herself sore. Then she remembers her first order of business, as well as the promise she made to Helene. "Where are you now?" she asks Gunilla.

"I am currently in Kampala."

"The children, where are they?"

"The children know you are expected."

"But no one is answering their phones."

Gunilla explains that people in Nairobi do not answer their phones if they do not know the identity of their caller, too many wrong numbers. "Have you sent text messages?" she asks.

"Why didn't I think of that?" Bella says.

Gunilla says, "I'll call them."

Then Bella says, "Speaking of Kampala, Gunilla . . ."

Assuming that Gunilla is in the know about Valerie and Padmini's situation, Bella fills her in on what has transpired with Helene. Gunilla then says, "Will you please allow me to act on your instructions and settle the attorney's fees and all other expenses, and you and I will go over it when we meet in a couple of days?"

The phone line carries Bella's hesitation all the way from Nairobi to Kampala—and Gunilla can sense it. Bella, in turn, can feel it, even though the two women have never met. But Bella says, "You've been of immense help."

Then Gunilla says, "Tell you what. I'll call on Valerie and her partner in the police holding cell in person and see if there is anything else we can do for them, including lending them money or taking them a change of clothes."

"I wouldn't ask that of you."

They ring off, agreeing to speak again.

———————

When Gunilla rings back in a couple of hours, neither of them is as emotional as before. She updates Bella on what she has achieved since they last spoke, which is to say a great deal: She has settled the attorney's fee and oiled enough corrupt police palms that Valerie and Padmini are in the process of gaining their freedom.

"What's their plan?" Bella asks.

"Helene tells me they are Nairobi-bound."

"Did you tell them I'm here?"

"Of course not."

Bella asks whether Gunilla has spoken with the principal of the children's school or his wife, as she has been unable to reach them or the children.

Their phones must be off, Gunilla thinks, or perhaps they are somewhere where there is no mobile coverage.

Bella hesitates before asking the other question that is on her mind, but she reminds herself of what Somalis say, being a hardy people with a great sense of pragmatism: The shoes of a dead person are more useful to the living than the corpse itself. "And can I get access to Aar's house and car keys?" she asks.

The children have their own keys to the house, and Gunilla tells Bella where a spare set of car keys is located in Aar's study. She invites Bella to stay at her house when she returns to Nairobi; she has a spare room with its own bath.

Out of politeness, Bella takes her time in answering, as if she were giving the offer serious thought, even though she knows that she won't accept it. Finally, she says, "I am okay where I am until I meet up with the children. And then, I think, we will go to Aar's house. But thanks all the same."

They say their good-byes, agreeing to talk before the end of the day and keep each other abreast of developments.

Bella telephones Mahdi and Fatima. As with Gunilla, Bella loses hold of her emotions as soon as Fatima lets loose with a bellow of grief. At last she hears Mahdi, the epitome of self-restraint, say to his wife, "Come, come!" From this, Bella gathers the strength to shut off the flow of her tears. And then Mahdi is on the line, saying, "Where are you now?"

She names her hotel.

He says, "Can we fetch you home? We would very much like to see you, hug you, hold you, be with you."

"Too exhausted," she says.

"Say the word and we'll fetch you home."

But she excuses herself and hangs up, more knackered than before.

Bella can't sleep. She changes into a pair of pajamas, draws the curtains, turns out the lights, and gets under the covers. But sleep won't come.

Her phone rings, but when she answers it, no one is there. When this happens several times, she clicks on the log of recent calls and, finding the number to be local, copies it out on the pad by the landline and then dials the same number. Bizarrely, there is a recording, both in English and Swahili, telling her that this number cannot be reached.

She decides to go out for a walk, convincing herself that the fresh air will do her good and that there is no point in staying cooped up, fretting and moping, in her curtained room in the hotel. She dresses again, this time in stylish jeans, as if intending to set herself apart from the large number of Somali women here who wear body tents. She has heard that lately, following terrorist threats linked to Shabaab, the Kenyan authorities have been harassing anyone who looks Somali, especially in

Eastleigh, the district with the heaviest concentration of Somalis. She selects one of her favorite DSLR compact cameras to take along, with the intention of capturing Nairobi by daylight.

Going out of her room, she puts the DO NOT DISTURB sign on the door. At the reception desk, she purchases Kenyan shillings with euros in case she needs to pay for coffee or something to eat in a café or for a taxi on the way back. As she prepares to step out of the hotel, she hesitates for a moment, uncertain if it is wise to leave her expensive cameras and other equipment in her room. But what the hell! she thinks. Hasn't she already lost her most precious Aar. Even though the cameras are expensive, they can be replaced. Not so her one and only brother. What a pity she hasn't a snowball's chance in hell to avenge him, sending every one of his murderers to the lowest place in Gehenna!

Having stayed at this hotel on multiple occasions, Bella is rather familiar with the neighborhood. The city center, she remembers, is at most twenty minutes' walk, a compact neighborhood not much bigger than the layout imposed on it in the late 1890s when a railway depot was built on Masai-owned land. Photographs from that period show tents pitched and shacks hurriedly erected for the railway workers. And from what she has read, confirmed by what Aar and others who know the city well have told her, Nairobi has never enjoyed much stability; right from the get-go, a concentration of British colonists occupied the best land and the Africans were pushed into the slums to live in shanties knocked together out of sheets of zinc, earning no standing in the colonial scheme as the city became a hub for business and, eventually, international organizations. The instabilities, which are of a piece with an African neocolonial city, have continued till this day, making Nairobi one of the most violent cities in the continent.

There is a greater agility to her stride now as she waves away invitations from a couple of the taxi drivers parked inside the hotel grounds and then walks past the uniformed security to the street. Once outside, she discovers that one half of the street has been totally blocked off to vehicular and human traffic. Presently, she observes that this is because the Israeli embassy sits directly opposite the gate of the hotel, a fact she had not remembered. Keeping to the open half of the street, she takes care to avoid twisting her ankle or falling on account of the many potholes. Eventually, the road widens, and it is lined with red-tiled, timber-framed villas on either side, as she remembers. Then there is an incline that makes her huff and puff, exhausted and out of shape as she is. She half regrets that she didn't take a taxi, but she soldiers on nonetheless, the camera slung over her shoulder knocking against her ribs as if urging her on and on, the way a jockey spurs his horse.

The road is a lot longer than she remembers, and she hopes she hasn't made a wrong turn. When it bends to the right, now in a steep incline, she comes upon a mass of unwashed commoners in dirty overalls, men with something scurrilous in their appearance who are gathered in huddles, smoking. They look to her like mechanics on their tea or lunch break, but the low way they speak is worrying. Her heart misses a beat in fright, and she is relieved when the men take no notice of her. Hurrying past without incident, she reminds herself why she is in Nairobi this time and remembers the responsibility awaiting her. When she spots a taxi, she flags it down.

The driver asks her where she is going. "Kimathi Street," she says, without a second thought. The price he names is far too much, but under the circumstances, she decides not to fuss about it. She gets in, remembering that Kimathi Street was named for a Kenyan warrior whose statue was unveiled there in 2007, the year she met Handsome-Boy Ngulu. She remembers with nostalgia the bar the two of them used to frequent, close to the Stanley Hotel.

Near the city center, the streets are too jammed for the taxi to proceed easily and she gets out. The sidewalks here are narrow and busy, and the shops fronting them appear to be Indian run, their customers nearly all African. She knows that a forest of eyes is trained on her, following her every move, taking in her jeans, her T-shirt, her upmarket sunglasses, her foreignness. She is used to Italian streets throwing up troublesome wet blankets in the shape of men wolf whistling at passing women. Here the local yokels ogle, their ceaseless staring bespeaking their desires. No harm in that, she thinks, only she wouldn't want to be in their company alone in a room or a dark alley. But as it is daytime and the streets are full of people, Bella allows her sense of mischief to get the better of her.

"May I take a picture of you, please?" she calls to a man undressing her with his eyes.

"On condition we have a photo together," the Ogler says.

And soon enough a crowd gathers as the Ogler poses. Others volunteer to be photographed. As Bella presses the button, now taking a photo of one person, now of a group, she rejoices in the charm of Africa, even as she knows that such a friendly crowd can just as quickly turn violent. Here one must be on one's guard at all times, she knows.

When some of the men suggest that she lend them her camera for a minute or so, Bella extricates herself from the engulfing mob. But as she tries to move away, the Ogler insists that she keep her word. She is reluctant to let anyone else handle her camera so as a compromise she suggests that someone else use the Ogler's iPhone to take a photo of the two of them standing side by side. That way he will have their picture together, she points out to him. And so the Ogler, his right hand mauling her side, poses with her as if he were the happiest man ever.

Finally, Bella decides enough is enough, as a number of other stragglers have gathered around her and are asking to have their photographs taken with her. Quitting the scene as fast as she is able, she enters a shop to buy a local SIM card and a hundred euros' worth of airtime for the spare mobile phone she brought along from Rome. Another minute or so later, with a train of lollygaggers still in pursuit of her, she hails another taxi, gets in, and says, in the assured tone of a local, "Take me to Village Market, please."

At the market, she finds a café and sits at a corner table, where she orders a latte and a croissant. While waiting for it, she eavesdrops on a young couple in their early twenties who look to be newly married and Somali—Bella judges this from the woman's palms, henna decorated the way Somali women do. Debating whether Bella is Somali, Ethiopian, or Eritrean, the man insists that she is Somali and the woman maintains that she isn't. As if to prove his point, he goes over to Bella's table and asks in Somali if she would take a photograph of them using his iPhone. Bella obliges and at first takes a series of shots with the iPhone, and then, given their permission—in fact, urged by the woman—takes more with her camera, at one point suggesting that they stand outside with the city's skyscrapers in the background. When the young woman says *"Mahadsanid"* in Somali to thank her, Bella answers, *"Adaa mudan."*

As they return to their respective tables, the man says to his bride, "My sweet, I've won the bet, haven't I?"

The woman introduces herself to Bella as Canab and her husband as Kaamil, and explains that the two bet on whether Bella was Somali or not. And they invite her to join them.

"But may I continue to take pictures of you?" she asks.

"Of course," the woman agrees, delighted.

The couple is so excited to pose for her that it isn't until the waiter brings Bella's latte and croissant that the man asks what her name is and what has brought her to Nairobi.

She is in no hurry to answer, not yet having decided how much of her story she can bear to tell to total strangers lest she burst into tears in front of them. She takes a sip of her latte and has a bite of her croissant, and just as she is about to speak, a young man comes to their table to offer her a wood carving of no exceptional quality. "Cheap, cheap, cheap," he says.

Canab, seeing Bella hesitate, says in Somali, "I know where you can get the best of this kind of wood carving, or better still, the best Zimbabwean stone sculptures."

Bella turns to the young seller of the wood carving and, apologizing, says politely that she isn't interested in buying his wares. The peddler is suddenly and inexplicably furious, and looks from Bella to Canab and back to Bella and asks, "Where are you from and what language are the three of you speaking? Arabic?"

"We are speaking Somali," says Bella.

Whereupon the peddler begins to shout, his rage, insofar as Bella is concerned, coming out of nowhere. He says, "Y'know what? My goods are not from a flea pit, where you come from and where you rightly belong. Terrorists, the lot of you, who have no right to be here! Blowing up our malls, terrorizing our nation. Go back where you come from!"

The outburst is so violent that it draws a few uniformed security officers. Meanwhile, Bella and the couple get ready to leave, and gather their things. Canab pays the bill, leaving a generous tip under a saucer for the waiters. Kaamil offers to take Bella to the craft shop, but Bella is too unsettled by the volatile outburst, which makes her uneasy. She

says good-bye to the couple, declining to exchange phone numbers and
e-mail addresses. She hurries off, catches a taxi at the stand outside the
mall, and returns to the hotel.

Back at the hotel, Bella finds a fax waiting for her at the reception desk.
"Valerie," it says, with a telephone number that has a Uganda exchange.
Bella puts it in her pocket without reading the rest and walks up the
stairs instead of taking the lift to her room. Inside, she starts to set up
her local mobile phone by inserting the Kenyan SIM card. She is eager
to reach her niece and nephew.

When there is no answer, she checks her e-mail messages and finds
one from Catherine Kariuki waiting. The message reads, "Please accept our condolences for the tragic loss of Aar. We feel a deep sorrow.
You are in our thoughts and our prayers." The message explains that
the Kariukis have taken the children to a nature reserve out of town,
intending to return to Nairobi in time to meet her flight. Bella checks
the date. Evidently, there has been some confusion over the timing of
her arrival. No matter. She is relieved to learn the reason for her inability to reach the Kariukis or the children.

And now that she can make a call from her newly rejuvenated phone,
she dials Salif's number and then Dahaba's number. When neither
answers, she calls Mrs. Kariuki. Catherine answers on the second ring,
and at once the two of them speak of their brutal shock and great loss,
for which neither can find adequate words. Then there is a brief pause,
when one or the other of them speaks Aar's name and both are choked
up with tears. Then Bella hears a man's voice—it must be James—
offering to pull over and give Salif and Dahaba a chance to speak to
their aunt. But Catherine insists on having a word with Bella first.

"We thought we would meet your flight tomorrow."

"My mistake. I must have confused the dates when I wrote to you," says Bella. And then she says, "Please let me talk to the children."

Salif takes the phone first. "This is terrible, Auntie," he says in Somali. "I can't believe it. I don't want to believe it. It is so unfair, so unfair."

Bella commiserates with him. "I am here now, my sweet."

There is a pause, and then Bella hears a sound she cannot identify, followed by an expletive from Salif. It sounds as if Dahaba has suddenly snatched the phone away from him. Without missing a beat, Dahaba asks Bella, "Where were you when you heard it?"

Bella tells her how she found out about it in the airport, from the newspaper, and Dahaba says, "How terrible. It's so unfair." They weep together, and then they speak again at the same time, exchanging languages and words of commiseration.

Finally, James comes on the line. Bella thanks him and his wife for looking after her niece and nephew and asks how they can arrange for her to come and take the children home to Aar's house. They offer to pick her up at the hotel and then bring her and the children to Aar's house, but she insists on going there herself in a taxi. James promises to e-mail her directions to their house the moment they get home and rings off.

It takes Bella a minute to bring herself to unfold the fax from Valerie even though she is aware that there is no way of avoiding coming face-to-face with her. She feels a flush of rage at the thought of having to behave not only civilly but also solicitously toward a woman who, unless she has changed, is not likely to show an ounce of kindness back. Even though it has been years since the two have met, Bella has not till this day forgotten the initial shock and anger she felt when she first learned of Valerie's sudden disappearance from Aar's and the children's lives without an explanation. Because of this, she is determined not to allow Valerie to take advantage of her, especially now that Aar is no longer in the picture. Still, Bella must steel herself for the worst, knowing how exploitative and naturally abusive Valerie can be. A blighter of a woman, Valerie does not know what is off-limits and what is acceptable. Valerie's loyalty is only to herself, never to any other person.

Bella thinks, what a pretty kettle of fish, cursing the day her brother met and then married this woman; she can't bring herself to open and read the message, annoyed that she has to do so. The cheek of the woman! Does the fact that she cannot keep her irritation in check mean that Valerie has her completely in her power, Bella wonders. Hurdo, she recalls, would have had no such doubts. She would describe Valerie as some peanut-brained la-de-da with no self-regard. As much as she loved her son, rather than see him as a gentle spirit and saint the way Bella did, Hurdo thought him a weakling and a pathological procrastinator who lacked the balls to square up to Valerie. Hurdo's words seem prescient now. "Imagine what a nightmare their lives, and everyone's, would become if something were to happen to him," she said, adding, "One day, he will regret his indecision." Now, it seems, such a day has come.

Finally, Bella reads Valerie's message. It fans the flames of her anger, recalling their previous associations as well as their unspoken acrimonies—unspoken because she had no wish to upset Aar. Even so, Bella knows she must accede to some of her sister-in-law's demands, including meeting up with her and allowing her to see Salif and Dahaba. She sends a text message to Valerie instead of calling her on the number she has provided, maybe because she doesn't wish to hear the woman's voice, which is bound to irritate her no end.

Valerie replies almost instantly, as if she had been waiting for a return message. She informs Bella that she will be in Nairobi tomorrow

74 ⬩ NURUDDIN FARAH

and looks forward to linking up with her there. She doesn't mention Padmini, and Bella wonders if Valerie will bring her too. Anyhow, Bella resolves that, escorted or unaccompanied, Valerie will be received with the welcome due a sister-in-law.

Bella is exhausted from all her inner tensions, some to do with Valerie's arrival, with Padmini and other untellable troubles in tow and others to do with her anxiety over the challenges awaiting her with Salif and Dahaba. Because she is too exhausted to spend more time and thought on Valerie and her doings, Bella concentrates on what needs to be done. And in a moment, she has the clarity of mind to call down to the reception desk and book a limousine to take her to the Kariukis' house first thing tomorrow morning.

Then she draws the curtains, darkening the room to such an extent that it feels as though it were night. She then prepares to take a well-deserved sleep. At first, she tosses and turns for a long time, apparently too tired, too jet-lagged to achieve her aim. However, when she perseveres in her desire to give to her body what her body needs most—a restorative sleep—Bella ultimately succeeds into dropping into the deepest of slumbers, from which she is awakened by a nightmare.

In the dream, Bella finds herself standing on a cliff, engaged in a heated argument with a woman who is unknown to her. The two exchange unkind words, and then a falling sensation from the cliff's great height causes Bella to wake up, and she screams in fright.

5.

After her long sleep, albeit one interrupted by the bad dream that was terrifying in the extreme, Bella feels restored enough to plan the day ahead. She gets out of the bed naked and opens the curtains wide to let the morning in. Instantly, she senses there is something open-ended about the African dawn, as if each day were a new offering, each hour a mystery unfolding. She takes a brief moment to watch as a couple of sparrows come to her side of the window, chirping, singing to her, welcoming her, her first dawn in Nairobi, a city that has the potential of becoming one of her favorite cities, except when she thinks worriedly about its violent nature. But that is not what she is thinking about now, the mayhem that is synonymous with this city, the bombings, and the reckless killings. Rather she is thinking about all the things that need doing—and there are legions of them, so many she would lose count were she to list them. Then with a frightening inevitability, she remembers why she is here: Aar's death in Mogadiscio and her nephew and niece who need looking after. And the ache in her heart, rapidly increasing, dampens her spirits and she moves away from the window, turning her back on the morning and on the birds whose chatter she no longer hears.

Her change of mood leads her to the bathroom, where, in hope of regaining a firmer foothold in the slippery realities that are claiming her attention, she takes a hot shower. The stream of water jets out, hitting her body from all sides as she soaps herself, as she shampoos her hair, as she watches the brownness of her dirt fleeing fast down into the waiting drain under her feet, and this helps her remain a little aloof for the briefest time possible.

Toweled, she emerges from the bathroom and runs a comb through her dripping wet hair, then uses the hotel dryer. She oils her body with moisturizing ointments and then changes into a custom-made power suit her favorite tailor in Rome, a half-Somali living in that city, designed for her. Bella is pleased with the suit, delighted she could afford to pay for it, as it is out of her league. She brought it along to wear on a day such as this.

Finally, she packs a medium-size bag, into which she puts her most expensive cameras, her cash, her passport, and her computer, from which she has downloaded the attachment to Mr. Kariuki's e-mail giving her the directions to their home and then copied it by hand since she has no printer in her room. But she doesn't go down to the lobby immediately, because she is caught in midthought, which unsettles her; she is thinking about where she and Valerie will meet when her sister-in-law arrives in Nairobi tomorrow, something for which she must prepare well in advance. And Bella comes to an instant decision: It would be better if she kept her hotel room for one more day. That way, instead of inviting Valerie (and Padmini, if indeed she is coming) to Aar's home, where she and the children will have been installed, she will have a neutral place to receive her. After all, you can never tell with Valerie.

Before leaving the room, Bella makes certain to secure all the locks on the hard cases and put the DO NOT DISTURB sign back on her door. And when a woman at the reception desk calls to inform her that her limousine is here, she realizes that she does not have ample time to eat breakfast and settles in her mind for a takeaway coffee in a styrofoam cup and some fruit, which she thinks will be sufficient, as she can't bear the thought of eating anything; she is antsy, her heart beating needlessly faster, as she thinks of all the possible skirmishes that lie ahead. She walks into the breakfast hall and helps herself to the coffee and grabs a banana and an apple and, smiling, waves away the attention of one of the waiters, who is eager to know if he can assist.

At the reception desk, she identifies herself to the concierge, alerting him that she will be ready to join the driver of the limousine soon. Then she cashes more euros, and with the key to her room safely in her bag, she goes out to meet the limousine. The driver turns out to be a very pleasant elderly man from Eldoret. Bella insists that he tell her the route he plans to take to get to the Kariukis' home before she gets into the vehicle. She compares the options he gives to the directions Mr. Kariuki has sent her, and when she is satisfied that he knows the route, she climbs into the back and settles in for the ride, anticipating the meeting with Salif and Dahaba with equal parts of joy and dread.

Traveling through the city in the back of the limousine, Bella feels almost in her element again. In recent years, her most obvious link to the African continent has been her brother and his children. Yet she is often happiest here. She feels connected to the soul of the continent, even though she knows that, almost to a man or a woman, any African would say that she is not of them. Playing the music of Baaba Maal, Cesária Évora, Toumani Diabaté, or Miriam Makeba calms her nerves and transports her to a world beyond memory, where sadness cannot reach her.

She is most conflicted when it comes to Somalia, her natal country, where bloodthirsty "nativists" claiming ancestral ownership of the land on which the city of Mogadiscio was sited ten thousand years ago have made the city ungovernable. According to what Aar told her when they spoke on the phone or met, the city had lost its charm under the repeated incursions of the clan-based militiamen recruited from communities in south-central Somalia. Then Ethiopia took it, at the behest of the U.S. And then came Shabaab.

It is the emphasis on what passes for clan, ethnic, or religious identity that makes her lose hope for the place. Just because she is a bit light-skinned and has a father from elsewhere is not reason enough to deny her the Somali identity to which she has legal and natal rights. That kind of nativist backward thinking reminds her of the American "birthers" who question Obama's right to be the president of the United States. For that matter, it reminds her of how some Zambians challenged Kenneth Kaunda's right to be the country's first president even after he'd been in power for twenty-six years because he'd been born, they claimed, a kilometer over the border with Malawi.

She hopes that her luck will hold and that she will not find Salif and Dahaba in worse shape than she has been. At the very thought, her eyes fill with tears again, her chest heaving. She pulls out a towelette, the type airlines supply their passengers with before serving meals. She doesn't want Salif and Dahaba to see her disconsolate. Or at least she doesn't want to be the one to lead off the wailing.

And then she finds it startling to be staring into the vehicle's side mirror. Mirrors have always had an immediate impact on her thinking, and seeing her face so unexpectedly reflected in it does not only surprise her but also imposes on her mind a humbling rationale: that she is alive and Aar is not. In an instant, her face, unbidden, runs with buckets of tears making their way down to her cheeks and staining her power suit. And her hand reaches up toward her eyes that are too un-handsome to behold. But when her wandering gaze encounters the driver's worried look in the rear mirror, a shiver having its origin deep in the seismic tremor that has occurred within her produces a brief muscle spasm. Several seconds go by before the shaking slackens and she is able to wipe away the wetness from her cheeks.

By then, she senses the car slowing down and she assumes that they have arrived at their destination. The driver, discreet as ever, does not delve into the matter in any manner or depth. Nor does he say, "We are here," even after he has stopped at a manned boom gate, where a uni-formed security guard approaches her side and asks her to fill in a form and wait. Bella pulls herself together and does as instructed and gives the clipboard back to the man, who goes into a cubicle and then emerges to tell the driver, "The principal's house is the biggest bungalow to the left. You can't miss it."

A few minutes later, they stop in front of a large bungalow. Bella gathers her thoughts in silence and then tells the driver to wait here, as he will take her and two other people back to Nairobi. But before step-ping out of the vehicle, she is suffused with a mixture of anxiety and foreboding, and in a momentary fit of delirium, she wonders if she has the mental strength and physical stamina to maintain her self-control and make sure she won't lose hold of her emotions and burst into tears the moment she sets eyes on Salif and Dahaba. Eventually, a woman Bella presumes to be Catherine Kariuki opens the door and waits. Bella, unsteady on her feet, somehow makes it out of the car and moves toward the woman holding the door, and her arms open to embrace her.

In spite of herself, however, Bella is sniveling again the instant Cather-ine says, "Bella, sincere condolences for your loss and ours," and wraps her massive body around her. Then both women let loose a torrent of damnations aimed at Aar's murderers, at which point the mention of his name brings forth a salvo of blessings. They stand like that, two grown women, one in flat shoes and a flowery summer frock, the other in a power suit and beautifully designed Italian shoes, each repeatedly pleading with the other to please stop crying, please, neither obliging until soft steps descending the stairs behind them make them go silent.

But it is not the children; it is the dog in playful but silent pursuit of the cat. Then the dog starts to bark and Catherine shushes her, saying, "Quiet, you silly thing. It is Bella." She fetches a toy for the cat to play with, and the two women pause in their grieving, as if attempting to recast their roles in the tragedy they are reliving. The dog disappears and then reappears, holding a leash in its teeth: She wants to go for a walk. Catherine pays no attention but the dog, as if seriously offended, barks fiercely. The cat then turns its back on the goings-on and strides into the inner part of the house. Bella waits, as if expecting that the cat might come back with something in its mouth too, maybe its bowl, to indicate its owner has forgotten to put food in it. Or maybe it will return with a dead mouse, not so much to feed its hunger but to receive a pat on the head. Meanwhile, Catherine holds the dog by the ears, pulling the leash free of its jaws and hanging it on a hook with the promise of a walk in a minute or so. Catherine says to Bella, "As you can see, I have my work cut out for me."

Bella is not unhappy that they are talking about ordinary matters. She is glad for anything that will occupy her mind and make her forget her pain. She says, smiling, "Now dogs insist on their rights? Dogs?"

"Normally, my husband takes her out first thing, but he had a family emergency in his village and he drove off as soon as we got back," Catherine says. "He hopes to be back in time to see you."

"I hope it's nothing serious," Bella says.

"Emergencies are a daily routine in our country," Catherine says, shaking her head. Bella knows what she's alluding to. In a place where violence is endemic, sudden death, car accidents, family feuds over land and other matters, witchcraft killings, and other deadly rituals are not uncommon.

Catherine says, "Do you mind if I leave you in the house with Salif and Dahaba while I take this dog for a walk?"

"Where are they?" asks Bella.

"Up in their rooms, both of them," Catherine says, "probably surfing the Net and catching up on text messaging with their friends."

"Are they already up?"

"I know Dahaba is. She came down when she heard James getting ready to leave. She thought it might be you. She and I had breakfast together."

"And Salif?"

"He said he wanted to wait and eat with you. He acts tough sometimes, but he's actually very sensitive. Deep down, he has a big soft center—you'll see."

"Just like his father," says Bella.

"Eggs and bacon and tomato ketchup, those are his morning essentials, he can't live without them. But perhaps he's gone back to sleep."

"Good for young people to sleep; that's how they grow so big these days."

And just as Catherine gets hold of the dog's neck to put the leash on her, Dahaba hurtles down the stairs in a precipitous headlong rush and throws herself into Bella's arms, her head finding familiar comfort in the curve of her aunt's neck. A tremor as quietly invasive as it is sudden runs through Bella's body and transmits itself to Dahaba, and suddenly she is crying out in pain. As if she can't bear the sight, Catherine slips out the door with the dog in tow; her presence now is redundant.

"I know, darling, I do know, I do," Bella whispers.

"Why should it happen to us?"

Bella thinks, why indeed? But she doesn't say this aloud.

Dahaba clings to Bella until at last she is calm enough for Bella to release her. But when she looks up into her aunt's eyes, a fresh sorrow touches off a new round of weeping. Bella kisses her niece on the cheeks. Dahaba says, "We don't have another parent."

Bella wants to say, "I know," but she thinks of Valerie's impending arrival and simply says, "You have me, darling, for one. I am here, to be with you and look after you."

"Thanks, Auntie," says Dahaba. But Bella pushes on.

"For another, you have a living parent, your mother."

At that, Dahaba pushes Bella away, and for the first time the two of them stand apart, Dahaba staring at Bella with a look of anger that she has insinuated Valerie into their conversation. Bella won't pursue the topic now; now is not the time. But Dahaba isn't quite ready to let it drop.

"Remember, Mum went on a walkabout."

"Regardless of what she did, she is your mum."

"We don't wish to see her," says Dahaba.

"She loves you, in her own way," Bella insists gently, remembering that Dahaba was especially close to Valerie at the time when she abandoned them.

"She called here last night," Dahaba says. "But Salif wouldn't talk to her."

"What about you? Did you speak to her?"

"He hung up on her before I got the chance."

"When did she call?"

"Yesterday evening, just after we got here."

"She called just the one time?" Bella asks.

"She called back again later."

"And they talked, did they?" Bella says, sensing that this is the case.

"They spoke a long time," Dahaba says.

"What about?"

"He won't tell me."

"And you didn't speak to her yourself?"

"I didn't want to. I'm still upset from before."

None of these goings-on surprise Bella, and she sees that Valerie's blowing hot and cold conjures a parallel pattern of anger and yearning in her daughter, and no wonder. Yet again, Bella marvels at the woman's narcissism, which seems to know no limits.

Dahaba dries her cheeks and leads Bella by the hand into the living room. Suddenly, she turns and says, "It's wonderful, wonderful that you are here."

"You are my only darlings," Bella says.

"We love you too, you know that."

"I do, my sweet!"

"So you are here for a week or something, right?" Dahaba asks, as if afraid to venture more.

"No, darling," says Bella. "I am here forever." And at the moment she says it, it dawns on her it is true.

"Forever, Auntie?"

"I am not going back to Europe."

"And you'll be our mum?"

"Yes, I'll be your mum and your dad too."

This time it is tears of joy that wet Dahaba's cheeks. She takes hold of Bella's hands, kissing each of them in turn. Not for the first time, Bella marvels at how easily a child's mood changes.

"And so we don't need to go boarding, do we?"

"No, you don't."

"Wait until I tell Salif!"

It strikes Bella only now how child rearing requires a sort of unconditional internal commitment to the task. Everything to do with raising children has its own rationale, she thinks, constructed along the lines of a minor and a major premise and a conclusion bizarrely drawn from neither. For every child is in a world of his or her own making, and everyone else remains outside of it until there is need to involve them, to invite them in—and then only provisionally, and for self-serving reasons. She remembers a Somali saying something to the effect that one's children are not one's parents. Which means, in effect, that we think far more often about our children than they are likely to think of us. Even if you are sick or having money problems or other troubles, she realizes, you must not expect them to respond to your needs in the way you've responded to theirs. You won't be able to sleep when they are sick, and you'll do whatever you can to alleviate their pain or allay their fears. But do not expect them to feel anyone else's pain the same way! Until, of course, they become parents themselves and have their own children.

"Is Salif still in bed?" Bella asks Dahaba.

But it is Salif who answers, "I am awake," and, turning, they see him: a gangly youth trying his best to grow a beard and not succeeding. His face is pimpled, his pajamas are missing a couple of buttons, and he is barefoot. Bella instantly suspects that while Dahaba will benefit greatly from her presence it is Salif who needs more care, however he might insist that he needs no one and nothing.

"Hello, my darling!" Bella says.

But Salif is not in a pliant mood, and he won't rise from where he is crouched on the bottom step of the stairway. Nor does he attempt to take the hand she offers to lift him up. At last Dahaba goes to him and whispers in his ear. He is not moved.

At last, he says to Bella, "When did you come?"

Dahaba, intervening, says, "Don't answer him."

"Yesterday," Bella replies.

"And why didn't you tell us you were coming then? We would not have gone away!"

Bella looks him in the eye, aware that this sort of conversation so soon after her arrival does not bode well. "There was a misunderstanding about the time of my arrival," she says calmly. "I was exhausted and upset, and I sent the wrong information."

"Have you spoken to Mum?" asks Salif.

Bella hesitates. "Not yet. But I will."

"About our future?"

Again Bella pauses, wondering how best to proceed. "Of course. That will need to be discussed."

"She gave the impression you did," says Salif.

Bella is fairly certain that the cold shoulder she is getting is the one he intends for Valerie. Or perhaps he is just going through a phase where he needs to assert his positions and know that he is being taken seriously. At any rate, her instinct tells her to let him bully her a little. She senses that Valerie is a presence in nearly every conversation Dahaba and Salif have right now, the children taking out their anger and uncertainty on everyone else. She examines her fingernails, as though examining them for structural weaknesses; lately, they have been cracking. Then she looks out the window and spots shadows and the shapes of birds high up in the trees. But she is too far away to hear their chirping. Dahaba joins her where she is standing and the two lock arms, the little one placing her head once again in the curve of Bella's neck.

"Would you like your breakfast, Salif?"

Salif's expression darkens with unspoken outrage that Bella won't engage with him in conflict. He has always hated it when adults change the topic of conversation to mundane matters, like food or sleep. When he was younger, he would create ugly scenes when that happened. He was notorious for his ill-timed tantrums, especially in public places—airports or the homes of his parents' friends. He seemed, in fact, to take great delight in embarrassing his father in front of his friends. As a result, Bella knows, Aar seldom brought anyone home, and until Gunilla, he had never brought home his women friends for fear that his children might behave badly or speak spitefully in their presence. Bella wonders if Salif will one day revisit these ugly confrontations with self-loathing. Just now, he is biting hard on his thumb, as if to keep himself from speaking.

Bella says to Dahaba, "Do you cook?"

"I can make spaghetti and sauce."

"And what can Salif make?"

"Nothing, not even his favorite bacon."

"At nearly seventeen, he should be able to make something, surely," says Bella, opening the fridge and bringing out the butter and then going to the cupboards to find a frying pan. She has difficulties turning on the gas, but Dahaba helps. Then Dahaba takes a seat, gazing at her auntie in delight, in contrast to Salif, who stands silently in the kitchen doorway, pretending still to be angry.

Bella says to Dahaba, "Do you eat bacon as well?"

"Yes, I do, Auntie."

"And yet you claim to be a Muslim?"

Dahaba nods her head and says nothing.

"We do eat it and are proud of it," Salif says defiantly.

Bella opens the packet of bacon and begins to separate the stringy rashers and lay them in the frying pan.

Salif adds, "Our father always insisted on us being Muslim, culturally speaking, even though he partook of the odd glass of wine at birthdays and other celebrations, and occasionally with his meals."

"How are Qamar and Zubair?" Bella asks, changing the subject. Qamar and Zubair are Fatima and Mahdi's daughter and son, who are close in age to Dahaba and Salif and not only go to the same school but also have similar interests. Zubair, like Salif, is into soccer to the point of obsession, and Qamar, like Dahaba, is a budding feminist.

"We haven't seen them for a couple of days," Salif says, this time not sulking at the change of topic.

"I spoke to Auntie Fatima and Uncle Mahdi," Bella tells him.

"Can we arrange to meet them?" Salif asks.

"As soon as you like," Bella says.

"Tomorrow?"

"I can't see why not," Bella says.

Bella knows that it is only because Mahdi was away in Somalia at the time of Aar's death, and Fatima had a medical procedure scheduled, that the children went to stay with James and Catherine rather than with these dear family friends. She also knows that Qamar and Zubair do not eat bacon and that their parents do not touch liquor at all. But they are tolerant enough of their friends' "un-Islamic" ways.

She also suspects that Valerie would go bonkers if she knew about her children's closeness to the family, who no doubt encourage them to identify primarily as Somali and Muslim. Valerie harbors an ancient antipathy to Islam, springing from a story about her grandfather being sodomized when he fell into the hands of a local militia in North Africa.

Bella puts a plate before Salif. "Here, done. Come and eat."

Salif drowns the bacon in huge spurts of ketchup, and despite the knife and fork she has set by his plate, he uses his fingers, mopping his plate with the last rasher.

Then he says to Bella, "About our father?"

"What about him?"

"In his will, did he ask to be cremated?"

"Not to my knowledge," Bella says. "But I have not yet seen his final will. Why do you ask?"

"Mum talked about cremation yesterday."

"She mentioned nothing of the sort to me," Bella says, reminding herself to stay calm.

"Where was he buried?"

Bella takes care not to give any more information than necessary, as it will serve no one's interest. So she does not disclose all that she has learned of the circumstances of Aar's death but says only, "In Mogadiscio, soon after he died."

Dahaba asks, "Why did they bury him so fast?"

"It is part of the Muslim tradition."

"No," says Salif, ignoring her and answering Dahaba himself. "They bury the dead within hours because it is very hot up there, being closer to the Equator, and unless the corpse is embalmed quickly, it will begin to deteriorate." Again that hostile edge!

He turns back to Bella. "Mum thinks it is stated in his will that he wants his body to be cremated."

For the first time in their presence, Bella feels her temper flare. But before she can speak, Dahaba chimes in, "Mum has no business here."

"As if she will listen to your advice!" Salif spits.

And just as the two of them face off, about to go at it, Bella clears her throat, making them turn to face her. Regaining her calm, she says, "Next time, please tell your mum to address any questions she may have about your father's will, his burial, or his estate to me directly."

But Salif isn't finished. "Is it legally incumbent on the living to follow to the letter the will of the dead with respect to their wishes for the disposition of their bodies?"

"From whom does this question come?" says Bella, not answering.

"Does it matter?" counters Salif.

"It does," says Bella. "And I don't know the answer."

Bella is more than certain that Valerie, whose nickname in some quarters is "Madam Confusion," is the source of this line of questioning. Bella has a copy of one version of Aar's will, and she knows it makes no mention of cremation, but she is not certain it is the most recent one. Still, she suspects that if there was ever such a stipulation it belonged to an earlier period, when Aar was interested in Indian philosophy, and to an earlier draft. A draft when Valerie and he still lived as husband and wife. She says to Salif, "What's your interest in all this?"

"We should do what his will says."

"And if it so stipulates, would you like your father's body exhumed?" Bella asks.

"Why not?"

"And what if people—living people—find the idea inconsistent with their beliefs and abhorrent? Do you think this would bring comfort to your father? What would be gained?"

"I want to honor his will."

"But that is ridiculous," Dahaba says.

To Bella's immense relief, at that very moment they hear a key turning in the lock. The dog enters and makes her way right for Dahaba and Salif, jumping boisterously on them. Catherine greets them and excuses herself to go wash her hands. The lucky arrival of the dog has defused a moment of tension. For the time being, the subject is dropped.

At the mention of the move back to their house, Bella offers to help Dahaba and Salif to pack. Dahaba says, "Yes, thank you," but Salif says, "I can do my own packing."

And they are ready to leave inside half an hour.

6.

Salif, standing little on formalities, is brief in his farewell, and he takes his leave and carries the suitcases to the waiting limousine. The driver, with his windows down, is half asleep but sufficiently alert to release the button controlling the trunk. Salif puts the cases beside his aunt's singularly heavy bag there—he can't help being impressed by what a light traveler Auntie is, if this is all she has come with; but he won't rush to make a judgment; he will wait and see.

Meanwhile, he hesitates, trying to decide whether to sit by the driver in front, which is his preference, or in one of the roomier rows in the back. If he is unsure where to sit, it is because he thinks that Dahaba is likely to make a hell of a fuss about whatever choice he makes. And for once, he does not wish to engage Dahaba in a squabble about seating. So he stays outside the vehicle, waiting and chatting to the driver, who is polite enough to turn off the radio news, which is in one of the local languages, most likely Kalenjin from the sound of it—Salif has sufficient Swahili and a smattering of Gikuyu. When he assumes he has waited long enough, he returns inside. Dahaba, from the look of it, is in no hurry to leave. As for Bella, she is hanging on out of good breeding, maybe because she is hoping that James will get here in time for them to say a proper good-bye. And so they waffle about something, which, in Salif's view, is of no consequence, even though he won't say it. Salif wants to avoid getting caught in Nairobi rush hour traffic. And so, leaving again, he says, "I'll be in the car, Auntie, waiting."

The pin dropping, Bella hugs and kisses Catherine, stressing how much she would have liked for the two of them to meet under different circumstances. Though she has no children of her own, Catherine clearly has both the maternal instinct and the disciplined oversight requisite to a boarding-school principal's wife. And not for the first time Bella is effusive in her praise of Catherine and James and thanks them for providing a safe and comfortable home to Salif and Dahaba in these difficult times. She adds she is sorry not to have met James, but that she looks forward to doing so in the near future and requests that Catherine please give him her kindest regards. "I am sorry he is not here for me to thank him personally and I pray that he meets with good news at his village and that there is nothing to worry either of you."

Eventually, Bella and Dahaba leave holding hands, and together they sit in the back, speaking today's language of choice, Somali. When Salif opens the car door to sit by the driver and finds there is a clutter of maps and other paraphernalia on the seat, he hesitates, and this time it is the chauffeur who apologizes and moves his stuff.

Bella says, "Catherine is lovely, isn't she?"

"Even though she has no children of her own," says Dahaba, "she treats the children as though they were of her own flesh and blood."

"I am sorry I haven't met the principal."

"There is plenty of time."

And during a pause, Bella remembers hearing on a past visit Salif's comparing his experience as a boarder to that of a prison inmate who knows all the ins and outs of the system. She had assumed that he hated being a boarder and was loath to return to it, but he had corrected her, saying, "On the contrary, I often have a different kind of fun when I am a boarder. The rules are clear. Mr. Kariuki is very strict but fair, and Mrs. Kariuki is very caring. What more can you want?" Now, Bella knows that the pair of them, one as the principal, the other as his spouse, have set the bar high. But she feels cut out for this sort of challenge.

And as if to put that confidence to the test, Salif and Dahaba begin to war with each other, as if on cue. He accuses his sister of dillydallying and telling stories of no importance whatsoever. "We are going to run into terrible traffic and will be lucky if we get there before dark."

"I was just being polite." Dahaba recruits Auntie Bella's support, adding, "That was okay, Auntie, wasn't it, and you were just being polite too, weren't you?"

Bella says she thinks it is time the two of them have outgrown quarreling, bickering about petty things, and getting on each other's nerves. "Especially you, Salif. She is your sister and is younger."

"I hope Salif doesn't think that by saying what you've just said you are taking my side on your first day here," says Dahaba.

"Listen to her!" Salif says.

Bella says, "Maybe there is much sense in silence if your sister says something provocative. Especially when you are a guest in someone else's house, someone who has hosted you and taken good care of you."

But her words have little effect, and the words that emerge from their mouths, as noxious as raw sewage, put an end to the sweet good-byes. Bella decides not to intervene again, reasoning that perhaps this rowing is at least a distraction from thinking about their father's death. She feels there is no point hassling them about their sibling rivalry, even if it is improper. Let them have their altercations. And in any case, their set-tos are nothing new. Bella remembers witnessing a terrible quarrel when she visited them a few years back. Aar had planned a beautiful day in the countryside near Naivasha, and Bella was packing a lunch for a picnic when the children got into a fight about whose turn it was to sit in the passenger seat. Salif insisted it was his turn first. In effect, Bella was partly responsible for the row, as she interfered with the smooth working of a system they had fine-tuned to a T: Salif or Dahaba would sit in the front seat beside their father on the way there, and the other one would have his or her chance on the way back. Aar, naturally, had suggested that Bella sit in the front for the entire ride, but she had foolishly offered to sit in the back because she wanted to speak privately to Dahaba because Aar suspected Dahaba was having "woman trouble."

Distressed by the conflict, Bella had asked Aar in Italian to step in. But Aar had explained to her, also in Italian, his belief that as part of growing up children had to acquire for themselves the skill of learning when to fight and when to accommodate. "It is something you can't teach them," he said. "They must come to this understanding by themselves." He quoted the Somali adage that with age children become good adults. Bella wasn't convinced, but she let go, saying, "Who am I to challenge you on this?" And to make the peace, she got them to toss a coin.

But today there is no one else to intercede or decide if intercession is warranted. They ride in silence, watching the view and each other, apparently living alone in their thoughts. Now there is a ravine to the right, now a clear blue sky as the highway bends to the left, now an eagle descending to catch its prey and taking off again with its victim in the clutches of its talons. But the beastly row has left an ugly feeling in the car, and it is difficult to enjoy these sights. It isn't until Dahaba begins to cry again, silently, that Salif reaches back and touches her shoulder in silent commiseration.

Then Dahaba asks, in much the same mode as Americans ask where people were when JFK was assassinated—or, for a new generation, where people were when the planes flew into the World Trade Center—where Bella was when their father was killed. This is a different question from the one Bella has been asked before. She did not learn of the death until she landed at Fiumicino, but she has done the math and she knows exactly what she was doing at the moment the bomb went off.

Bella is the first to believe in the therapeutic benefits to be gained from speaking openly about the circumstances around the death of one so close. But she is caught in a trap from which she does not know how to free herself. In truth, at the moment when Aar's life was ebbing away, Bella was with Humboldt, her Afro-Brazilian lover. They had made love and were taking a breather. Humboldt had already come, and he was just beginning to assist her toward the longer, deeper orgasm they both sensed she had in her when she glanced at the clock and realized she was in danger of missing her plane. She hesitates; Dahaba says, "The question upsets you?"

She is amazed at how many difficult questions there have been to answer from these two in less than twenty-four hours! Concentrating on the scenery, she decides that this is a private matter that she can't share with them truthfully. Giving Dahaba's hand what she hopes is a comforting squeeze, she says, "Nothing else matters more than the death itself. It is the saddest thing that has ever happened to me. Or to you."

Salif says, "But surely . . ." but Bella presses on.

"For days I have blamed myself for not speaking my mind when he called and said he was going to relocate to Somalia to work on the logistics of moving the UN offices to Mogadiscio."

She feels the tears filling her eyes and wishes she didn't have to expose either child to the harsh realities of life; for there is no merit in doing so.

They drive on, having fallen silent, the car engine hardly making any sound, the highway straight. Dahaba's eyes have closed and her breathing has slowed; she seems to be asleep. Salif is busy with his iPhone.

Bella asks Salif, "And you, my dear. What does your father's death mean to you, his firstborn?"

Salif says, "Uncle Mahdi told me that the death of a father is the making of a son. Not in quite those words, but something along those lines."

"And is that what you feel?"

Salif replies, "Yes, I think so. The surviving older offspring has to take on more of a burden of responsibility and offer help to the other immediate family members, especially the younger ones, who are in more need than he."

"Is that what you will be doing, helping Dahaba?"

She locks gazes with him in the side mirror into which they are staring from their respective positions. Neither looks away, as each holds the other's gaze. At this, he comprehends her meaning.

"But she is annoying," he complains.

"You haven't answered my question. Have you?"

"She is trouble every minute of every day."

"Still, have you shown her kindness?"

"I doubt it," he says grudgingly.

"How about you do it? There's nothing stopping you."

They are passing through a village now. An accident has occurred here—just a few minutes before, from the looks of it. The street is full of bystanders curiously looking on. Bella thinks of how one accident often leads to another; she has never understood why crowds gather around collisions. Are they there to share the gory details of what has occurred or get their hands on any available loot while everyone is distracted? Salif suggests that they stop to see if they can be of any help, but at Bella's urging, worried for their safety, the driver pushes on. After all, she has in the trunk of the car her photo equipment as well as her computer, her passport, and quite a lot of cash.

She returns to their earlier conversation. "Being the older sibling, in what way do you feel obligated to care for Dahaba, your younger sibling?"

"It should be a pleasure, not a duty."

"Do you find the weight of this responsibility—even if it is a pleasure—too heavy to bear at your young age?"

"No," says Salif thoughtfully. "After all, my father started helping you when he was even younger than I am, and he contributed to your life in some ways more than either of your parents, according to what you've both told me."

"Does it worry you that your father's death could be the unmaking of you?" Bella asks, and then she pauses before continuing, "You will have more freedom, which, if not wisely used, can be the cause of inescapable failure—yes?"

Salif says, "Dad as a single parent carried the burden of our absent mother. This means I have twice the weight my father carried."

"Are you man enough to meet the challenge?"

Neither speaks, but Bella observes that a touch of sorrow has entered his eyes. She asks, more gently, "Are you okay?"

"Why are we talking about all this?" he says.

"What do you think?"

"To be sure, I was out of order earlier," Salif at last acknowledges. "Can I rely on you to guide me and set me right when I go wrong?"

"Of course, darling," Bella says.

"It is a deal, then."

They are getting close to Aar's house—even Bella recognizes the neighborhood now. When they turn into a side street, Salif leans forward.

"Ours is the fourth house on the left," he says.

They stop in front of a green gate and honk. A man in a uniform—a day guard—opens the gate and they drive in.

Dahaba awakens. Salif gets out of the car but does not retrieve the bags from the trunk. Dahaba is woozy, deeply involved in her sleep or a recent memory of a dream; she sits on the front steps of the door, waiting to be told when they will go in or what they will do.

Meanwhile, Bella asks the driver how much she owes him. He takes a long time working this out and she waits patiently, watching his lips move as he calculates then decides on a sum then shakes his head, probably thinking he has totaled the fare wrongly. Such a sweet man, Bella thinks, and she decides to assist. And to make it all aboveboard, lest he should think that she is cheating him, they do the sum together, so much per hour, so much per kilometer—and then she adds a generous tip. He leaves a happy man, grinning from cheek to jowl and offering to come and get her whenever she needs a ride. In fact, for a moment, she even abandons the thought of driving Aar's car to the hotel and parking it there—and instead she thinks about requesting that he take her to Hotel 680 now. But she remembers that they have to settle in the house and get something to eat before she returns there.

As the limousine reverses, Bella observes that one of the day guards has come to offer to help carry the bags in. But Salif declines the offer, saying, "Thanks, but we can cope."

When he sees the question in Bella's eyes, he whispers, "It is always safer not to let any security personnel know the inside of your house.

Then they won't be able to organize break-ins if you fire them. You learn that by living here."

They wait for Salif to disarm the alarm. When he has done that, he comes out to help to bring in the bags, one at a time, leaving them on the ground floor for the moment.

"I'll take them all up later," he says.

Dahaba, now fully awake, is in her element; she says, "Just because we are women, it doesn't mean we can't carry our own bags upstairs ourselves."

Salif refrains from answering back, and Bella is impressed. Maybe their little talk has made an impression. Salif makes himself busy opening the downstairs windows then turning on the taps until the water runs clear. Not that it is drinkable unless it is boiled, Bella reminds herself.

With Dahaba trailing her every step, Bella gives herself time to take it all in: a big house with two floors and, from what she can so far see, boasting a sizeable kitchen, a lavatory, and plenty of secure windows with mosquito netting fastened between the outer safety glass and the inner blast-proof safety panes. There is a large living room boasting a big flat-screen TV of Japanese manufacture, and Dahaba is pleased to explain the complicated processes of how to turn it on, play video games, and go back to watching TV.

Bella is thinking of other practical considerations. She says to Salif, "Do you still have a maid in your employ?"

"We do," Salif says hesitantly.

"Dad didn't think well of her," Dahaba says.

"Why is that?"

"He used to say she had butterfingers."

Bella says, "Dropping things, breaking them?"

"We are still paying her though," Salif says.

Bella is so encouraged by the progress Salif has made in such a brief time that she wonders if she can train the children to help run the house without the services of a maid. For when she looks through the cupboards, she observes other signs of sloppiness or laziness: The forks don't match; the plates belong to different eras of the household, some going back to the day when Aar and the children lived in England and some from when they were residing in Vienna.

"Let's not call anyone yet," Bella suggests. She decides to talk to them about this later.

"Let's enjoy one another's company," Dahaba says.

"All right by me," Salif says.

Salif and Dahaba are in their element now that they are in their own home. They are more at ease, as if they feel unbound, unchained. Bella knows that their father's death will hit one or the other of them hard and knock them around. It is one of the challenges awaiting her, the revisiting of sorrows, the emptiness. But just now, they are cheerful.

Bella follows Salif up the stairs, helping with the luggage. As she remembers, there are four bedrooms, three of them en suite, one for each of them, plus a spare room, which served as Aar's study, the only one that was often locked in Aar's day.

They stop in the children's rooms first. Dahaba's door is painted dark purple and adorned with a couple of photographs of women singers, including Celine Dion. Dahaba says, "Meet my room," as if she were introducing her aunt to an entire world. Inside, the room is adorned with more posters of female singers. There is a messy unmade bed, and the floor is littered with dirty socks. But there are also books everywhere, and Bella thinks that this is a girl for whom reading will be the best defense against depression.

"Where do you borrow books from," she asks, "the school library or the public library? Or is there one in Nairobi?"

"She likes her books bought new," Salif says.

Bella says, "We'll have to talk about that."

"The biggest bookshop is in the Yaya Center."

"Prices are exorbitant, aren't they?"

"Quite often five times more expensive than a book costs anywhere in the UK or the U.S.," he says. "When you think of it, there is no way most people can afford to buy books at all here. Nor does Nairobi have any good secondhand bookshops. So many secondhand clothes stores, a number of which are run by the church, but no good secondhand bookstore."

Dahaba says, "For someone who seldom reads, Salif is making strange comments about the price of books, Auntie."

Salif still does not allow her comments to upset him. In his room, indeed, the bookcases are almost bare. In fact, there is hardly any clutter in the room at all. Everything seems to be in its right place except for the sports shoes that are arrayed on the lowest shelf of the bookcase. He does not seem eager for any of them to enter any farther. He closes the door to his room and says, "Auntie, let us show you to your room."

"Who has a key?" she asks.

"We both do," Dahaba says.

"He was a good dad," Dahaba says. She begins to weep again, but when Bella and Salif each reach out a hand to comfort her, she regains her composure, and they enter the room.

Dahaba says, "Our dad had no secrets from us."

"Except when it came to work," Salif says. Then they retreat to their respective rooms, Bella wanting to shower, Salif turning his computer on, and Dahaba starting to read a much dog-eared sci-fi novel.

Just as Bella is undressing, she receives a text message from Valerie, who has checked into the hotel and wants to know where Bella is and how soon she can visit her children. Before Bella can even think how to respond, Salif calls from his room, saying that he too has received a text message. And then Dahaba receives a message as well.

They meet in the kitchen and read the text messages they've received from Valerie, and Salif dictates a message, on which all three agree and which Dahaba is assigned to forward to their mum. "Just got back to Nairobi and we are too knackered to see you. But please come for dinner tomorrow evening at seven p.m., Mum." And she provides her mother with detailed directions on how to get there and tells her to call if there is need.

"Does that mean we'll have to cook tonight?" asks Dahaba.

"No, it doesn't," says Bella. "You can eat a takeaway of your choice here or I can take you to eat out and then I will drive you back home."

"What is your plan?"

Bella says to Salif, "Your dad's car keys first?"

Salif runs up and comes back with the car keys.

"We won't eat in tonight," she says.

Salif says, "Cool."

"I want McDonald's," says Dahaba.

"I want sushi," says Salif.

"Do you know the addresses of the restaurants?"

Dahaba says, "We sure do."

"Here is the condition," states Bella.

Dahaba is quick to say, "We won't fight, promise."

"Just wait. Do let Auntie tell us the condition."

"What is the condition?" asks Dahaba.

"Since I need to get back to my hotel to get my remaining suitcases, I will bring you home; drive away; do an errand or two, including perhaps meeting your mum for a drink; and then come home," says Bella.

Dahaba says, "I want to meet Mum too."

Salif is of a different opinion. He says, "I think it is best that Auntie meets her alone first. We haven't seen Mum for a very, very long time and waiting to see her for one more night won't kill either of us since we've invited her for dinner." Then he says to Dahaba, "What do you think, my little sister?"

"Okay, we'll meet her tomorrow," agrees Dahaba. Then she adds, "But I want a Big Mac, one huge tub of ice cream, and a Diet Coke. And I want us to go right away. And let there be no argument."

Bella goes to the car to get herself reacquainted with it. Dahaba sits in the front by her side, knowing that Salif is unlikely to make a fuss now because he sat by the driver earlier and because Dahaba acceded to Salif's demand that Auntie Bella meet their mother outside their presence so they could talk about matters of adult concern.

Bella turns the engine on while waiting for Salif to set the alarm. She lets it idle as she gets accustomed to where everything is. She engages the gears, pretending she is changing them, and then lets up on the clutch gently and moves forward half a meter—this startles Dahaba, who seems frightened by the suddenness of the move.

Bella says, "Sorry."

"It's okay, I know what you are doing," says Dahaba.

"I am trying to get a grip on how it works."

"Please don't mind about me. Do what you must do."

"I won't give you a fright, I promise," says Bella.

"I won't take fright now I know what you are doing."

Then Bella works the brakes, relieved that Dahaba has stopped yattering and promising she won't take fright. If you asked Bella how she feels right this instant or if she is scared driving back at night from her Nairobi hotel, she will admit that she is a little fearful. The car is new to her, this is the first time she has been behind the wheel here, and the city streets are unfamiliar to her, and from her previous memory, drivers in Nairobi are in the habit of using their full-beam lights and are very likely to blind the drivers in the oncoming vehicles. And you have to look out for pedestrians crossing the roads at any time and there are deadly obstructions on the sides of these narrow roads. You would be mad not to be cautious, very cautious.

Salif joins them in the car, and without the slightest fuss, he sits in the back and presciently says aloud, "Everything is under control," perhaps meaning that he has set the alarm and all is well. Bella, however, feels it is time she had a paper map and also wonders if either of them knows how to set up the GPS in the car. Salif says, "Do you need to set up a GPS on top of Cawrala?"

"Who is Cawrala?" Bella asks.

Dahaba explains that it is the nickname Somalis have given to the female voice of the GPS, which is beginning to gain currency here, just as it has in North America. And she shows Bella how to use it.

When Bella asks for the address of their favorite McDonald's drive-thru, Dahaba has no idea because she is bad with addresses and doesn't know the names of any of the city's streets, and Salif is about to start teasing her about this.

"Salif, dear, not a word more from you," says Bella, displaying a moment's irritability. "Just give me the address of the drive-thru." And he does so.

"Let us get your food," says Bella, moving.

And voilà, the GPS makes contact with the satellite, which is now ready to guide her and Cawrala, the woman whose voice she is familiar with, as she has heard it in a variety of cities, in different languages, and in different continents. The voice has a temper of such meanness that it reminds Bella of her first-grade teacher, who was often cross with her. Cawrala tells Bella to turn left and she does so, and then after a couple of hundred meters, Cawrala tells her to turn right. Because Bella is intent on testing Cawrala's patience, she takes a left turn, contrary to the woman's instructions. The woman's bad temper is back, albeit still in control, as she recalculates before coming back with renewed advice on how to set matters right so they can get to the mall where the drive-thru is located. Salif, irritated at Dahaba's yattering about things to do with GPSs and satellites, offers to lead Bella to their favorite McDonald's if only Auntie would silence Cawrala and tell Dahaba to "shut her gob too."

Bella pulls off the road, stops the car, turns to Salif in the back, and says, "I'll remind you again, my dear, of the promise you made to me earlier today that you would show patience, which you and I know would stand you in better stead in good and bad times."

"My apologies, Auntie," says Salif.

Dahaba says, "It's okay, Auntie, he can't help it."

Despite not liking what Dahaba is doing, always speaking in protective defense of Salif whenever she tells him off, Bella makes no comment and gets back on the road, with Cawrala taking a few moments to come back on. A left turn, followed by a right turn and a long silence, leads her to think about her upcoming encounter with Valerie in an hour or so. And Bella discovers that she cannot dislodge a worry about whether she will tell Valerie that she is driving Aar's car and then give her and Padmini a lift to the restaurant. Bella decides that it is unwise to complicate an uncomplicated situation; she won't say much about the children at this first encounter, nor will she offer to drive them to the restaurant; let the damn women get to the rendezvous their own way.

Bella decides she should be worrying about how she is going to make this thing get her to the hotel and back to where the children are. Having guided them to the drive-thru, Cawrala says, "We've arrived at your destination, to your right."

The service is fast and Salif and Dahaba are happy with their respective orders. On the way back to their home, Bella, with Dahaba's tutoring and Salif's insistent encouragement, masters how to make the GPS function, including feeding in the street name of the hotel and Aar's home address.

When they get back to the house, Bella goes upstairs, and having no other dress to change into, she brushes her hair, borrowing Dahaba's comb, which she has to clean on account of the girl's hair that is there from previous use. And before leaving for the hotel, Bella touches base with Dahaba and Salif, who are having their takeaway meal in the kitchen.

"Please remember to call me at the slightest worry."

"We will, Auntie."

Dahaba says, "We'll set the alarm if there is need."

"We can take care of ourselves," Salif assures her.

Bella remembers how too much unnecessary fretting takes one to an early grave and how anxious Hurdo always was about her children's well-being to the extent that she couldn't sleep when one of them was out of the house. She spoke constantly of her worries, which provided her with the partner she often lacked, what with the doubts about Aar's father's companionability and Bella's dad living far away in Italy. Bella mustn't be like that.

Then she leaves, saying, "Back in a couple of hours."

7.

Now that she has made it out of the gate alone for the first time since reuniting with her niece and nephew, Bella is overwhelmed by the sorrow she has given no release to in front of them. Her eyes overflow with tears, her chest heaving, her entire body trembling; she weeps loudly. She realizes, as if for the first time, that the loss is permanent. It isn't easy to fall back on her Somali hardiness—hardiness being practically the definition of Somaliness, Somalis being a practical people with sufficient backbone to pull through anything. While Bella admits there is no shame in being distraught or even suffering a total breakdown after the death of a loved one, she is aware that it is wiser to adopt a quiet dignity to ennoble Aar's memory and mourn his death with solemnity. Only then would he feel adequately honored and only then will he be proud of her.

Being back in Aar's house has reduced the children's anxiety, she could see instantly. She left them holed up in their respective rooms, Salif playing solitaire, Dahaba reading yet another novel. What follows, however, will not be easy, Bella knows. And she knows too that when she gets back to her hotel, there will be several messages from

Valerie already waiting for her under the door, where the DO NOT DIS-TURB sign still hangs.

Bella gets back on the road, driving with renewed confidence. She takes a few moments to think about what information about the children she is willing to share with Valerie, at least until she figures out what Valerie's aims are. She is not in the habit of lying, but she knows that there is nothing to gain by telling Valerie the full truth. If possible, she decides, she will be evasive, buying time until she figures out where Valerie's devious mind is headed.

She knows that she could do with all the help she can get from Gunilla, who knows the legal side of things, and, of course, from Mahdi and Fatima; the former affording Bella a guide through the troubled waters of UN bureaucracy; the latter directly and through their children providing her and the children with the support they require.

Finally, Bella parks the car in a public open-air lot after going through a boom gate and picking up a ticket. Once at the reception desk to inquire if there are messages, she asks the concierge to send a valet to take the car and park it in the section reserved for hotel clients. Then she goes up to her room and, using the hotel phone, calls Valerie's room.

A woman answers, but she doesn't sound like how Bella remembers Valerie, so she takes the safe option of asking to speak to Valerie. The voice says, "A moment, please."

Valerie comes on the line, and the voice is overwhelmingly, un-pleasantly familiar and abrasive. "Where are you? Where have you been? I've been calling and calling. And where are the children?"

Bella will not be rushed. When answering Valerie's questions, she takes her time thinking about what to say. One needs to compose and recompose oneself when one is dealing with Valerie. What's more, Bella wants to prove to herself and her sister-in-law that Valerie cannot exercise power over her. When Aar was alive, he was the focus of Valerie's maneuvering; now, Bella thinks, it is her and the children's turn to be the victims of Valerie's blackmailing ploys. Bella is no pushover; it is time Valerie came to accept this as fact and get accustomed to it.

"Come on, Valerie. You haven't even said hello or offered condolences." She asks where Valerie is staying, which turns out to be in one of the upmarket chalet-style accommodations the hotel offers nearby, and Bella ascertains that Padmini is with her. She gives Valerie her room number and floor and warns her to come alone. Then she hangs up.

Not fifteen minutes later, she hears a knocking at the door, but she does not answer immediately. When she judges that she has made Valerie wait long enough, she goes to the door and looks through the peephole. Standing there is a woman she no longer recognizes. Valerie is wearing a cotton hip sari, but her body has spread with the unforgiving weight gain of middle age. Nevertheless, her bulging midriff boasts a jeweled belly button, and her nose rings are further evidence of a taste that has been acquired since they last met.

When Bella opens the door, Valerie smiles up at her, but Bella simply meets her eyes, neither overtly friendly nor openly hostile. She doesn't immediately show Valerie into the room, but instead looks her up and down, as if measuring her for a coffin. As if Bella's stare literally undoes her, Valerie's sari starts to come undone, and in her attempt to pull herself together, she drops her handbag, which spills its contents on the floor—tampons, a packet of condoms, toothpicks, a hairbrush. Bella doesn't look away; she simply waits, saying nothing, as Valerie gathers her things. Then at long last Bella motions for Valerie to enter and closes the door behind her.

"How was your flight?"

Valerie pulls a face, as if unready to answer the question. Then after a very long pause, she says, "Not too bad, actually, considering it could've been a lot worse."

"I hear you were in Uganda," Bella says.

Valerie says, "Word travels fast."

Bella asks, "What's the story about Uganda?"

"It's a beautiful country."

"And they eat *mattock* every day, don't they?"

"Mashed plantain with peanut stew."

"Anything happen there?"

"They said you'd be mean to me," Valerie says.

Bella does not rise to the bait, does not even stop to wonder who "they" are. But she does wonder yet again what a man as gentle, loving, and generous as Aar found in such a woman and what held them together for so long. She remembers once asking Aar this directly. As he was prone to do, he took refuge in a piece of Somali wisdom, this one a caution against outsiders placing themselves between "the penis and the vagina of a couple."

Bella pressed him. "Not a good enough answer."

"Maybe sex holds us together," Aar said.

And at that, Bella had fallen silent, defeated.

Now Bella tries another tack. "Who gave you the sad news?" she asks.

"My mother did," says Valerie. She still does not offer her condolences, even when Bella says, by way of apology, "I had no way of reaching you." Yet Bella knows that she herself has been equally rude—she hasn't greeted her sister-in-law with any real warmth or grace, nor has she so much as offered her something to drink. Her words sound stilted to her ears. The English phrase that one closes a letter with, "Yours sincerely," comes to mind—a phrase that is not always meant to represent sincerity.

She watches with annoyance as Valerie looks askance at her, as if she wouldn't want to be seen in such company. And rather than feel sad at how their mutual hatred has blossomed over the years, Bella gives in to the impulse to be nasty.

"Why were you in Uganda?" she asks.

"What a question to ask!"

Bella is relieved to discover that neither Helene nor Gunilla seems to have shared Bella's involvement in paying Valerie's legal fees. "Did you mistake Uganda for Kenya," she asks, "and go there by mistake?" Valerie's ignorance of geography is legendary.

"I know better than that," Valerie says.

"Oh?"

"Yes," says Valerie. "It happens that Padmini was born there."

"Still, that doesn't explain why you were there."

"I went with her—to recover some family property in Nakasero, the center of the city," Valerie says. "Her family was among the Asians expelled by Idi Amin. Remember those Dukawallahs?"

Bella does. The Dukawallahs were small-business men and shop-keepers hailing principally from the Indian subcontinent. Many had originally come to work on the Ugandan railway. Often they set up general stores in hard-to-reach localities in the African countries where they settled—just as the Somalis in South Africa are doing these days—but as they thrived, they moved to the bigger cities. Idi Amin ejected them from Uganda in 1972, but in Kenya, they still account for ten percent of the population.

"And why are you here?" asks Bella at last, turning to the matter that must be on both of their minds.

But Valerie is evasive. "Here, as in Nairobi here?"

She seems to be stalling, and as Bella waits for an answer, unpleasant memories of their previous encounters surge up in her, crowding out her few pleasant memories of Valerie. Of course, she has little impulse to dwell on pleasant memories anyway, at a time when she is at peace neither with herself nor with the world at large.

"Yes," she says. "What brings you to Nairobi?"

"My husband's death," Valerie says.

"Aar's death has brought you here?"

"That's right."

"But he didn't die here."

"And my children, of course."

Bella waits, and Valerie continues. "And if I am honest with you, it's also about the guilt I've felt over these years, even though I pushed it back and did not attend to it; this brings me here too. I hope you understand where I am coming from."

Bella disregards this last—her sister-in-law, she believes, has no understanding of the concept of guilt and its ramifications and attendant responsibilities—and goes for the jugular: "How do you mean, you're here for your children? You haven't seen or communicated with them all these many years."

"I am their only living parent," Valerie says.

And before Bella knows it, she has lost it despite all her resolve. "Parent, you call yourself a parent? Not to these children you aren't, and you haven't been for many years."

But Valerie isn't backing down. "Now that their father has been killed and I am still among the living, it falls to me, as their mother, to have them come to me so I can look after them."

The woman is clearly insane, Bella thinks. Look at her, dressed as though she were on her way to a Bollywood party. Beware of the middle-aged woman who doesn't behave or think like one! It isn't going to be easy to do battle with Valerie, Bella thinks.

"When was the last time you spoke to them?" she asks. "The last time you sent them a birthday present or penned a letter or sent an e-mail to congratulate them on their excellent achievements in sports or school. When?"

Valerie pauses. "Still, they are my children from my own blood."

"Have you been in touch with them since you arrived?" Bella says. She does not divulge the fact that the children are in fact at home, where she left them.

"Mum has given me their numbers," Valerie says.

"You tried to speak to them, did you?"

"I did speak with them," says Valerie, not offering more.

Bella lets the half-truth stand. What kind of reception did Valerie expect when her own children haven't heard from her or set eyes on her for years? This madwoman does not seem to remember that just as infants look like one parent one day and then seemingly overnight change their features, as though at will, so that they look like the other, children aren't consistent when it comes to which of their parents they love more. And thanks to Valerie's absence from their lives, Salif and Dahaba have little reason to revert to their earlier intimacy with her. What chance does she have to win back their hearts—not in the courts, surely, having deserted her family, even if she is still technically Aar's wife—or, rather, his widow? But Bella is no legal expert, and she doesn't know what a judge in a Kenyan court would make of Valerie's situation.

"I'll do the best I can," Valerie says.

Bella stares at her in disbelief. "And what if they don't wish to see you?"

"I'll take my chances."

The two lock eyes, and for the first time since they began to talk, Bella really looks at her, taking in the face spotted with pimples—or are those mosquito bites?—and what seems to be an atypical paleness.

Has she had malaria? Bella wonders. Perhaps it's not that her skin is pale but that her eyes seem jaundiced.

"How long do you plan to stay in Nairobi?" she asks.

"It depends," says Valerie.

"On what?"

Valerie looks around, as though others might overhear her, and when she speaks, it is almost in a whisper. "On how things pan out."

"What things?"

This time Bella doesn't get an answer. Instead, Valerie asks a question of her own. "Do they know that you are here?"

"They do," says Bella.

With a touch of sarcasm, Valerie responds, "Lucky you!"

And Bella can't resist adding, "But then, I've invested in them and you haven't. I never lost touch." Bella doesn't like to hear herself speaking vengefully, rubbing more salt in Valerie's open sore. And so she adds, a little more softly, "Not that anyone can guarantee it will be smooth sailing with teenagers."

But her sympathy evaporates when Valerie responds, "I can't wait to see them, my treasures!"

Bella doesn't tell her what the children have said to her about their mother. She spares her this, not out of kindness, but because there is no point in getting into a scuffle.

Bella gets up, ready to show Valerie out, but just then the phone rings. It is Mahdi. She asks him to wait, then she says to Valerie, "Please see yourself out, if you don't mind. I must take this call."

At that, Valerie exits, slamming the door behind her.

After speaking briefly with Mahdi, Bella calls the hotel reception desk to ask that they prepare her bill since she will be checking out of the hotel in an hour or so. One less worry, she thinks, as she goes through the room, making sure she leaves nothing of hers behind.

Then she rings the concierge, requesting to please have her car brought to the front and a bellboy sent up to her room to take her luggage to the vehicle.

Valerie walks out of the room and turns left past a fire door. She takes a lift to the ground floor and slips out a side entrance. In the gathering dusk, she makes her way along a tree-lined path until she comes to a low-built two-room chalet. She knocks three times on the door, then, without waiting for an answer, inserts the key and enters.

"It's me, Pad," she announces. "I'm back."

Padmini has just stepped out of the shower, a towel wrapped around her head and another one around her waist. She stands not an inch shorter than six feet and is very proud of her height. At once serene, majestic, and beguiling, Padmini is ordinarily capable of stunning anyone, man or woman. But after two nights in a Kampala lockup being roughed up, humiliated, and bullied by corrupt police officers, she would not remind anyone of the famous actress for whom she is named. As part of their intimidation, the officers shaved her head with a dull razor in the basement of the jail. Then they made her sweep up her hair and take it back to the lockup to show to Valerie. Padmini will remember this mortification for the rest of her days. And it is compounded by the fact that Valerie was not subjected to similar treatment. Padmini knew the police goons had singled her out for this punishment in accordance with the Ugandan stereotype that Indian women take excessive care of their hair. Seemingly to go with her new look, she wears no makeup at all. Still, she is gorgeous—"to die for," as the phrase has it.

Padmini struts to the standing mirror and examines a reddish spot—maybe a mosquito bite—between her breasts, each the size and shape of a plantain. The spot is sensitive to her touch and turning redder by the second. She is incensed, uncannily angry. She utters muffled curses, damning Africa and its malaria and wishing to get rid of everything to do with the continent. Padmini finds her handbag, fumbles in it, and brings out a tube of antibiotic ointment, which she applies to the spot. Then she swivels her head in Valerie's direction.

"How have things panned out?"

"Let me see." Valerie moves toward Padmini.

"Was she hostile?"

"What do you expect?"

Padmini turns to face her. "Surely the children are more yours than hers."

"She was friendlier than I expected."

"I wonder why."

"Maybe she is up to one of her tricks."

"And what might those be?"

"She knows something I don't."

"Something to do with her brother's will?"

"Bella is no fool."

"She is very smart. I'll say that."

"She hasn't struck me as devious."

"But she isn't as straightforward as Aar."

Valerie says, "Aar was an angel, the best man any woman could hope to find among the pack. Not an ounce of badness in him. I can't say that about Bella."

In the abrupt silence that follows, Padmini starts to turn her interest to another insect bite just below her right buttock. She relaxes her grip on the towel and cranes her neck, but she is unable to catch sight of it. She utters a salvo of damnations aimed at every insect that bites and then curses Africa, which has reared the lot, willing them to torment everyone who visits the damned continent.

She turns angrily on Valerie. "Look at what they've done. I tell you that Africa is out to disfigure my body."

"Come, darling," Valerie pleads.

"Take a good look. I am done for."

Valerie parts the towel and sinks to her knees, as if in worship of a temple deity. She touches the swollen red spot and, going still redder herself, kisses it.

But the instant Padmini's eyes clap on their bodies in the mirror, she snaps, "Don't you start!"

"What's with you lately, Pad?" Valerie says.

"I feel as if I'm being watched."

"I'll protect you!" cries Valerie. But when she follows Padmini's gaze, she sees a man with a hose watering a neatly trimmed patch of the garden opposite, and she realizes that he is not so covertly staring at them. Stiffening, Padmini gets up to draw the curtains. They stare at each other, Padmini with a look of reproach and Valerie with a look that says, "So what, who cares? Let them look." In India, Valerie remembers, it used to be the other way round. She should never have come to Uganda with Padmini, she thinks.

"You are in one of those moods," Valerie says.

The two of them have been through a lot together, first as classmates at their boarding school in Ely, in East Anglia, then as friends enjoying a secret liaison while each of them was married. The question now is: Will their partnership survive the current challenges? No doubt, Kampala was a disaster. But will Valerie's attempt to reclaim her children meet with success? It is too early to tell. In the company of those of similar sexual orientations in Europe and North America, Padmini and Valerie delight openly in their union and speak of their partnership as being on a par with marriage. Not so in India or Africa. When Padmini mentioned that she would love to mother Valerie's teenagers, whom she's known from birth, she added a caveat: that they move back to Britain, where they can live as a lesbian couple with full rights. Of course, who knows how Dahaba and Salif will react to this proposal.

Now Padmini holds Valerie's gaze and they look deeply into each other's eyes, eyes flooded with worry. Padmini's parents relocated to Britain when she two; she was brought up in a very strict household. Their homes, both in Uganda and England, had a small Hindu shrine off the kitchen, where incense burned day and night. When Padmini was fifteen and still at school, her mother "found" her a husband—a very handsome boy two years her senior, the only son of a family that lived next door in Kampala before the mass expulsion; his father owned a chain that distributed newspapers all over Britain. Padmini became distraught at the thought of marrying a man she barely knew. "You don't know what I am like," she sobbed to her parents, "and any man who marries me isn't going to like me when he gets to know the real me." No one bothered to ask Padmini what she was really like. If they had, would she have dared to give her love a name? Her parents thought she meant to say that she was not going to be a typical Indian wife. They let that match go, but it never crossed their minds that their daughter was partial to women.

She was an outstanding student and represented her comprehensive school in many interschool competitions. It was in the finals of one such competition that she encountered an equally exceptional student, Valerie Wilkinson. Padmini won first prize, and Valerie took second. They began writing letters to each other, and a friendship grew. Both were accepted to the University of East Anglia, where they roomed together and exchanged stories of their crushes and previous amorous encounters. Valerie was keener on boys, while Padmini already knew that she was only attracted to girls. One summer, they traveled together to France because Valerie was majoring in French and Padmini harbored the ambition of one day running a Michelin-starred restaurant.

After completing their studies, they went their separate ways, but they stayed in touch. Valerie was very surprised when Padmini entered into an arranged marriage. Rajiv was okay, but he and Padmini were nothing alike. Meanwhile, Valerie went from boyfriend to boyfriend until she met Aar, her first long-term affair. He was five years her senior and based in Geneva as an employee of the UN. He traveled a lot, which was part of his appeal for Valerie. He would go to London for weekends, where he would share her room at the hotel where she was a deputy manager, mainly in charge of the bars, the restaurants, and the catering service. She spent a wonderful week with him in Senegal in a beach house he borrowed from a colleague who worked with him in Geneva. Back in England, she brought him along to a party at Padmini's. That night, Valerie became pregnant. When she informed Aar, he sought Bella's counsel. Bella was not in favor of her brother's having a child with Valerie, nor of their marrying. She said, "I have a visceral dislike of the woman and would advise against your marrying her."

But Aar and Valerie were married anyway, in Mali, at a ceremony where the country's most famous band led by Salif Keita performed. Several local notables had been invited and everyone had a good time, especially the marrying couple. And during the first few years of their marriage, it was universally agreed they were a happy couple. They had Salif, who was named for the bandleader, and then Dahaba.

After that, things seemed to change. Aar was loyal to her, and Valerie was hospitable to their friends, but at home he took more care of the children than she did; she seemed relaxed only in the company of other adults, especially when she and Aar were giving dinners. Aar felt,

Bella remembers, that these gatherings gave Valerie's life purpose. When they were living in Geneva, she set up a catering business for the foreign embassies, consulates, and UN bodies. But she was always fighting with her employees and firing them.

Padmini remained a frequent visitor, staying away from Rajiv for longer and longer spells. During Aar's protracted absences from home, Padmini and Valerie slept in the same bed; the children, especially Dahaba, were unsettled by this and complained to Aar about it. But because Valerie seemed happy again and complained less, he stayed quiet. By then, Valerie had abandoned all pretense of running the catering business. It was equally obvious that Padmini's marriage was doomed, but she hadn't the heart to bring it to an end, reasoning that in her culture such things were not done.

The first time Aar caught Valerie and Padmini in bed was when Valerie fell asleep in Dahaba's bed after reading her a bedtime story and instead of joining Aar in the conjugal bed, she went to Padmini's room, sneaking back to Dahaba's bed before sunrise. Good breeding forbade Aar to speak of what he saw. But when Bella came for a brief visit, he talked about what was going on. To his surprise, Bella refrained from giving him advice. Perhaps, he thought, she'd decided it was too late to give her opinion on Valerie.

And so Aar bided his time until an opportunity presented itself. There was an opening in the Nairobi office. Padmini was on one of her many visits. He told Valerie he had to go to the New York head office for an interview, and by the time he returned, he would know if he had the job in either Vienna or Nairobi, with a possible secondment to Somalia. When he got back, Padmini was there. He told Valerie he had been offered the position in Vienna. Eventually, he said, he hoped to be transferred to somewhere in Africa, preferably closer to home.

Valerie did not appear to be enthusiastic about moving to Vienna with him. Unlike Aar, who had already acquired Italian in Somalia, English in Canada, and French in Geneva, she was not proficient in languages and had no intention of learning German.

Valerie smiled when her eyes met Padmini's but frowned when her gaze encountered Aar's knowing grin. He guessed that Valerie and Padmini needed time alone to talk things through. A furtive glance at his wristwatch supplied him with an excuse to depart. "I'll pick up the children from afterschool," he said. "Let us talk later after dinner."

When he returned home with the children, he found a note from Valerie. The note simply said that she and Padmini had gone to the gym for a workout and were not coming home for supper that night. They did not return until about one o'clock in the morning; a light sleeper, Aar woke to the sound of Valerie's key in the lock and then their footsteps.

A couple of days later, Padmini left, and things seemed normal between Aar and Valerie, even if she didn't return to the conjugal bed or accept any of his physical approaches. As he was not the type to force a woman to do his bidding, especially his wife, Aar acceded to her request that they remain physically apart.

Aar was not due to begin the job in Vienna until the fall. With the end of the school year approaching, Salif and Dahaba talked of how eager they were to visit a game park in Africa. Aar said, "What a brilliant idea." He suggested a family trip to Nairobi in a bid to work on the marriage and mend his rapport with Valerie without the presence of Padmini. All four of them had a wonderful time, above all Valerie, who was equally delighted to see wild game galore and sample some of the sixty-four types of meat served at the restaurant Carnivore, which Salif adored and Dahaba, who was in her vegetarian phase, hated. Taking long walks and long drives, staying up late and rising early to watch wild animals in their habitat, everyone enjoyed the visit to the game park. But as the trip progressed, Valerie began to run a high fever, especially in the evenings, apparently because a tick bit her.

When they were back in Geneva and ready to move to Vienna, Valerie's fever persisted, but she still refused to see a doctor, until she developed massive headaches as well, whereupon Aar insisted she see someone. She was eventually diagnosed as suffering from the aftereffects of a tick bite. Most of her physical symptoms came under control, but others—the obvious volatility to her behavior in particular—persisted.

Three months later, just at the end of the school year, Valerie was suddenly gone. She left Aar not even a note saying where she had gone or when she would be back. He called her mother, who didn't know any more than he did. He tried contacting Padmini, but she didn't answer either his e-mails or his phone calls. When September neared, Aar relocated himself and the children to Vienna, arranging to move their belongings and enroll the children in a new school.

"We were meant for each other," Valerie now says to Padmini. "That is the long and short of it. And although we failed in Uganda, I am optimistic that we'll be successful in our effort to reclaim my children. I can't imagine them not wanting to be with us and staying with Bella instead."

"Yes," Padmini says, "Bella doesn't have the patience to look after teenagers, I reckon. Here one week, Brazil the next, then Mali and back to Rome, the life of a sailor."

Valerie yawns and looks away, eyes closed. She is thinking about Bella and the appetites she senses in her. Yet Bella is so discreet that in all the years Valerie has known her she never worked out where Bella was with sex. With whom did she do it, if at all? Was she frigid or merely discreet?

Valerie asks Padmini what she thinks. "Of course there are lovers," Padmini says. "There have to be."

"Some women who hide in plain sight?" says Valerie.

"You reckon she is in the closet?" says Padmini.

Valerie says that she once asked Aar directly about his sister's love life. "He looked at me, amused. Then he said, 'For crying out loud, she is my sister.'" That was Aar, proper in every way. And that was Bella, a mystery. "In all the years I've known her," Valerie says, "I haven't detected any flicker of an intimation of what excites her."

Padmini says, "Maybe, being Somali, she doesn't have it in her. Maybe they chopped hers off, all of it."

Valerie laughs. "How about if we ask her?"

"At the first opportunity."

Valerie says, "I wonder what circumcised female genitals look like." She imagines something like the hollow cheeks of an elderly person, a cavern.

"In Uganda," Padmini says, "they stretch the labia."

"Ideal for self-stimulation, I hear," Valerie jokes. She knows they are having fun at Bella's expense, but the two of them are roaring with laughter when the phone rings. They fall instantly silent, as if suddenly aware that someone has been listening in on their indiscretions. The ringing goes on and on, but neither dares to answer it. Finally it stops, but then it almost immediately resumes. "Maybe my children," Valerie says. "Hello!"

It is Bella, inviting them to dinner.

"Give me a sec," says Valerie. She consults with Padmini, who nods.

They settle on an Indian restaurant called Tandoori House at eight.

Bella says she has some things to take care of first and that she will meet them there. She doesn't elaborate. "The reception desk will tell you where it is," she says.

After Valerie hangs up, she discovers that a new worry has crept into their conversation now that they are no longer saying terrible things about Bella's privates. Padmini says, "Why is she inviting both of us?"

"Maybe she wishes to take your measure," says Valerie. "After all, you're the one who led me astray, made me into a lesbian."

"You're too long in the tooth. She won't believe that."

And suddenly there is joy on their faces as they prepare to go out. They resolve to ask Bella about her love life at dinner. They shower together and take their time dressing. Valerie chooses a multicolored silk sari that Padmini suggests. And Padmini, not feeling Indian with her shorn head, puts on a pair of jeans.

8.

Bella, her stomach churning not so much with anger but with anxiety about what Valerie is about, packs the rest of her belongings and checks to make sure that she has her point-and-shoot in her shoulder bag. That camera, she thinks, will be adequate for what she has in mind. Bella has a plan that she thinks will work in her favor and that she hopes will take the edge off her interactions with Valerie. Into the same shoulder bag she also packs a few photographs she has brought along of the children soon after Valerie left—only the children, never ones with Aar or herself. She checks to make sure she has the car keys.

Just before she leaves the room, she grabs the book she is reading—Camus's *Lyrical and Critical Essays*—so that she will have something to read if Valerie and Padmini are late. She remembers that Valerie likes to make a point of her importance by a tardy arrival. More than once she has showed up for a flight after the gates had closed. What used to bother Aar was not so much her lateness but the gloating that came after. "Let them wait and let the world be damned," she would say. For her part, Bella would get her sister-in-law's monkey up by spelling "Valerie" with a *y*.

Bella takes the lift down to the lobby, looking as if she has just stepped out of a bandbox.

The drive takes half an hour despite the short distance. The night is starry, the sky cloudless, the streets no longer crowded with peddlers but now teeming with pedestrians on their way home and fifteen-passenger *matatu*s—minibuses that stop wherever they please—being driven at reckless speeds. Bella knows that she is taking a more circuitous route to the restaurant than necessary, but this does not disturb her in the least. In fact, she needs to kill some time. She parks the car and walks around with her Polaroid, taking photos.

The waiter shows her to a table. As she waits for Valerie to arrive, she thinks back to the time when they had their one and only overt row. Bella, visiting the family while Aar was away on business, had gone to a supermarket with Valerie and the children in tow—for some reason the supermarket was a place where the children were especially prone to behaving abominably. At some point, the staff felt it necessary to summon the manager because Salif had turned an entire shelf of the chocolate row into disarray, dropping more than half its contents onto the floor and trampling on some of them. When the youth responsible for stocking the shelves pleaded with Valerie to make her son desist, she just shrugged her shoulders and, acting nonchalant, said, "Just tell me how much destruction he has caused and I'll pay it as part of my grocery bill."

Bella had seen quickly what Salif was up to; in the process of creating mayhem, he was deftly removing the wrappings of the chocolate bars in such a way that the scanning machine would not have prices to read. That way he could slip a couple of bars into his satchel and get away with it. He undoubtedly knew Valerie wouldn't allow anyone to question or search him. And indeed, the young manager of the supermarket chose to let them go rather than call the police, saying, "Just go, madam. These are black kids and I do not wish to give them a bad start in life by accusing them of theft. But I worry what will become of them if you do not do the proper thing by them."

In the car, Salif had boasted of what he had done, and Valerie had said, "How rascally clever of you!" Rather than blow her top right there and then, Bella had waited until she and Valerie were alone. Then they had an epic fight, in which she tried to insist that Valerie speak to Salif about the consequences of his behavior.

And Valerie went ballistic. Pumped up by rage, she seemed to grow an inch taller in her chair. Her voice took on a hoarse tone, and her gestures went operatic in their movements. "How dare you accuse my son of theft," she shrieked.

Bella very calmly said, "Salif must know how to distinguish right from wrong. And now is the time to teach him, during these tender years."

"And you'd call what he did a theft?"

"Is there another name for it?" Bella said.

"An eight-year-old boy having a bit of fun? Where is the harm in that? Just a bit of mischief making, that's all."

"Is that what you call it, mischief making?"

"Salif is learning how the world works."

"The world doesn't work that way, Valerie."

Valerie said, "I encourage my children to learn how to get away with things. In my book, that is not theft. You call it theft, I call it being smart!"

Bella said, "There is an ancient wisdom, Italian, I believe, which purports that a mother can teach her child only the good morals by which she abides."

Valerie said, "I find that offensive."

"I don't mean to be offensive."

"And anally moralistic, if I may say so."

"I'd do anything for my nephew and niece," said Bella.

Valerie hit back. "With none of your own, you have no more idea how to deal with children than you know how to live with anyone, man or woman."

Bella refused to be diverted. "I don't want my nephew to steal from anyone at any time," Bella retorted. "Theft is theft, not a bit of fun. Thieving small things is morally wrong because one may develop the habit of stealing bigger things. I won't condone it and neither would Aar, nor will any sensible person in any society anywhere."

At the mention of Aar's name, Valerie cringed. Then she said, "Relax, my dear Bella. Relax."

"How can I relax?"

"Salif will outgrow this childish habit. It's like having sex with other boys, something natural and not to be frowned at as long as nobody else finds out."

Bella, who was brought up in a tradition in which in-laws did not discuss certain taboo topics, told herself that Valerie had no sense of actual shame or privacy. Uncertain how a talk about theft had led to one about sex, however, she said, "I don't want him to end up in a police station."

"They are my children," Valerie said.

"And I am their aunt."

They faced off, on the brink, and then Bella decided to let things be. She decided not to speak of it to Aar. What would be the point? She wouldn't want to be accused of creating a rift between man and wife. A few days later, she took Salif for a movie and a treat—Dahaba had gone with Valerie for a swim—and the two of them had a talk, Bella impressing on her nephew the importance of respecting others in the way you would like them to respect you.

She approached the topic in subsequent conversations, coming at it from different angles, until Salif promised never to do such a thing again. "Touch my heart, Auntie," he said, "you can trust me." And he seemed to mean it.

Bella makes no comment when Valerie and Padmini arrive forty-five minutes late and don't apologize. She is used to Valerie's ways and is certain that it won't help matters if she fusses about them. There are many other gauntlets to run in the coming days, after all. She'll save her ammunition for the battles worth fighting.

"Hello," Valerie says, towering over Bella in her chair.

"Hi," Bella says, the Camus dropping to the floor as she gets up to give Valerie a hug. "A bonus to see you for the second time in a single day."

Padmini keeps her physical distance and greets her from the other end of the table, but Bella, out of exaggerated politeness, almost tips over the entire table reaching to shake her hand.

"I am glad you could join us," Bella says.

"Delighted to be here."

Even with Bella standing, Padmini towers over her. She is wearing a headscarf in the elegant way Somali women wear theirs, with the knot in the back.

Bella and Padmini have held each other in mistrust ever since they first met years ago on some simultaneous visit to Aar and Valerie's in Geneva.

"What book are you reading?" Padmini asks now, as Bella bends down to retrieve it, nearly knocking her head against the table in the process. Bella shows her the cover.

"Camus." Padmini pronounces the *s*. "I used to love him as a student."

Bella pushes a bottle of sparkling water toward them. Valerie fills her own glass and then Padmini's. Then the waiter comes and Valerie orders a gin and tonic, and Padmini orders a bottle of South African red, even though Bella insists she is happy with the fizzy water.

"Please accept my condolences," says Padmini.

Bella nods and mumbles her thanks.

Padmini looks around, her eyes following the waiters. "I bet there aren't many Indian restaurants in Italy," she says.

Valerie asks, "What makes you say that?"

"Indian, Chinese, and even Ethiopian restaurants do well in countries where the cuisines are by their nature less sophisticated," Padmini says. "In Italy or France, there are sufficient excellent regional varieties of cuisine, and the locals have no time for foreign cuisine."

"In England, we have regional varieties and we also have plenty of Indian and Chinese restaurants," Valerie says.

Padmini continues, "It is no wonder too that in Holland, where the cuisine is as awful as it is in England, there are many Indonesian and Malay restaurants."

Bella contributes to the debate. "It is for the same reason that I doubt there are many Italian or French restaurants in India."

Valerie is visibly annoyed. "Remember how you used to love fish and chips, Padmini?"

"Because I was young and I had more than I could take of Indian food, cooked by my sister every single day of the week," Padmini says.

"That's not how I recall it," Valerie says.

Bella thinks that Padmini and Valerie are behaving like long-term partners edgily exchanging put-downs, and she stays out of it. She changes the subject. She asks, "Are South African wines readily available for your restaurant?"

Padmini says, "I loved what we sampled in Cape Town when we went there for the Gay Pride parade last March. Loved Cape Town too, for that matter. Everyone who is anyone goes to Cape Town for that event! It is like Sydney's or San Francisco's."

"What do you know?" Bella says neutrally.

The waiter brings Valerie's drink and the wine bottle. He has difficulty uncorking it, and Padmini takes it from him and uncorks it with professional ease. She pours out glasses for the three of them, and they raise a glass together without uttering a toast. When the waiter returns, they let Padmini do the ordering. When the food arrives, they tuck into it.

"You haven't aged at all," Padmini says to Bella.

"Nor have you," Bella says.

Valerie says that she is not sure she could pick Bella out from a lineup with absolute certainty. She adds, "I am good with voices, not with people's faces."

Bella knows that not all women age alike. African women make less of an effort as the years go by. Women elsewhere spend more time and money consciously grooming their bodies, taking pills and applying antiaging creams.

"What was Kampala like?" Bella asks Padmini. It is time to get a little more serious.

"Not likely to return there ever."

"Why?" Bella asks.

"Obviously, we made a mistake."

"In what way did you make a mistake?"

"We thought that with Amin dead and gone the new guy would be different. You see, I went to repossess our family property. But once they discovered that we were gay in a country where it is a criminal offense to be gay, the man we were in litigation with hired goons and spies to amass sufficient forensic evidence to have us put behind bars. At first we did not even have the possibility of bail. Fools that we were, we hired a lawyer, who unbeknownst to us was also on a retainer from the very man I was in dispute with."

Bella pretends she is hearing all this for the first time and asks, "Then what?"

"We spent two nights in a lockup smelling of years-old urine and a rotten history of sodomy and rape." Valerie steps in to explain. "On the next day, our photographs were in some yellow rag and our story made it onto YouTube. Then our lawyer, without consulting us, came with papers she drew up not as our advocate but as though she were a mediator, playing one side against the other, all the while she was taking our money."

"How humiliating!" Bella exclaims.

Padmini says, "The deal on the table was that we should sign the legal documents she prepared, giving him all the rights to the property, in exchange for our freedom."

"Was that what you did?"

Padmini says, "Wouldn't you?"

The dark rings around Padmini's eyes have become more prominent, and Valerie holds her head between her hands. Bella decides to withhold judgment until she has the whole story from Gunilla.

They eat in silence. A waiter inquires how they are doing. They nod their heads and, still not speaking, they eat some more.

"And you, Bella, how have you been?"

"I am well, considering. If it wasn't for what happened to Aar, I would say I am happy in my job, on the road a lot, excellent friends everywhere I go. What else can one ask for?"

Padmini says, "Sex, good sex."

She says this so loudly they can feel the shock waves hitting the next table, and the waiter, who has moved on, turns and stares.

Bella says, "Who says I don't have good sex!"

"Do you?" Valerie asks.

Padmini says, "Who gives it to you?"

"What do you mean, who gives it to me?"

"A man or a woman?"

Bella remembers the last time she made love, that day with Humboldt, the day Aar died. She can't believe she is being asked about this twice in one day. But she only says, "I view sex as a private matter."

But Valerie has her blood up, and she isn't done. She says, "Ask her about the other thing."

The waiter is whispering something to one of the other waiters behind the counter, and the two begin to laugh.

Padmini says, "Do you enjoy sex?"

"What a stupid question to ask," says Bella.

"Haven't they chopped yours off?"

Valerie adds, "That genital thing, she means."

"What are you talking about?" Bella says.

"She means genital mutilation."

"Or female circumcision," Valerie says, "which has to do with the removal of the entire clitoris, if I understand it correctly. Is that what you meant, Pad?"

Padmini nods her head and falls silent.

"What is your question?" Bella asks.

"Do they feel anything?"

"I can't speak about what others feel or not."

"Can I ask you a question?" Padmini asks.

"Go ahead and ask."

"Were you circumcised?"

Some people are insensitive to the point of being ridiculous, Bella thinks.

"No," she says.

Valerie says, "I thought you were."

"Well," says Bella, "then you are wrong."

"I imagined every Somali woman underwent infibulation," Valerie says.

Bella now remembers what Aar said after Valerie's sudden and unannounced departure. "You never know what you know until you realize that you've known it all along. One day the pin drops, and you see you had the knowledge all along!"

"Were you spared because you were special?"

Bella doesn't bother to answer the question. She should never have invited them to dinner, she thinks. But she keeps her cool, reminding herself there will be many more skirmishes along the way until they fall on their backsides and receive their just deserts. She now says, "Would either of you like another drink, dessert? Shall we ask the waiter to bring the menu again?"

Padmini says, "No, thank you."

"Shall we share the bill?" Valerie says.

"You are my guests," Bella says. "I invited you."

She motions to the waiter to clear the table and prepare the bill, but Valerie stops him. She wants doggy bags.

As she signs the bill, Bella says to the waiter, "Lovely food. My friends here and I have enjoyed the food and the atmosphere."

"But where are you from?" he says to Bella.

"I am Somali," she says.

"I wouldn't have thought so," he says.

"And why not?"

He says, "Somalis frequent the restaurants near the main mosque in the center of town or the eateries in Eastleigh. Also . . ."

"Go on. Also . . . ," she encourages him.

"Somali women don't go to restaurants."

She is not at all surprised that this young Kenyan holds nothing but generalizations about Somalis, who form about six percent of Kenya's population. After all, Valerie, who was married to a Somali man and gave birth to children who are part Somali, has just demonstrated that she knows next to nothing about Somalis. How she wished they had talked about Aar and not about so much other disillusioning nonsense.

"What are you doing now," Padmini asks. "We would like to sample the nightlife in Nairobi, go to a jazz joint or something, or to a gay bar."

Bella declines—she wants to get back to the children, but she doesn't want to go to Aar's car until they are gone.

Padmini asks, "You wouldn't know of any gay bars since you know this city well, would you?"

"No," says Bella.

Outside, Padmini and Valerie engage in some quick brainstorming and decide to ask a taxi driver where they might find some nightlife. A driver in the queue, overhearing them, waves furiously at them. "Ladies, I am your man, here to take you where you want." He offers to take them to a dance spot he knows, "where there are plenty of men, big and strong, and you ladies can have a good time."

Padmini says, "We're not into men, thank you."

The driver is unfazed. "Nairobi is a big town, especially at night. I know a couple of places you would like."

"Now you are talking," Padmini says.

Valerie turns to Padmini. "But before we go."

"Yes, dear. Any problem?"

The driver takes a renewed interest in the way they are looking at each other and discreetly touching, and a knowing smile crosses his expressive face.

"Let me have a word with Bella," says Valerie.

"About what?"

"About tomorrow evening's dinner with the children."

"I thought that was done and arranged," says Padmini.

"You see, I am eager to see them, that is why."

Bella watches all the goings-on with amusement, especially the expression on the taxi driver's hatchet face, a lit cigarette dangling from his half-pouting lips as he trains his full attention on Valerie and Padmini.

Valerie, meanwhile, is a foot closer to Bella and says in a half whisper, "We're all set for tomorrow, are we, the children, you and I, for dinner?"

"We are and they are looking forward to seeing you."

The sound of jollity wafts across from a group of young men and women in a festive mood after several hours' drinking; their noises are happy and everyone is in character. In fact, one of them, a young man who is too far gone to know what he is doing, opens the taxi Padmini is now sitting in, waiting for Valerie to join her. Padmini shoos away the young man and tells Valerie, "Time to go and party. Come."

They go, and Bella feels a terrible sense of relief.

Bella picks up Aar's car from the parking lot. However, she is aware of the late hour and drives with unprecedented alertness, keeping a keen lookout for any suspicious vehicle following her home. In addition to being concerned about the valuables in the trunk of the car, Bella is worried about driving at this hour in a city that she associates with terrible violence. But since she won't allow fear to dominate her life, she will trust her luck in hopes that all will be well.

And in fact, everything turns out to be okay. And when she gets home and lets herself in—Salif had the wisdom not to set the house alarm, for she wouldn't know how to disarm it—she can sense movement in their rooms. She wishes them good night before turning in herself.

9.

Bella wakes with the sun in her eyes. She revels for a moment in the tropical warmth that she always relishes here, the open-ended feeling of the hour. Then the alarm of her iPhone goes off. At first she thinks it is someone else's, someone with something urgent to attend to. Here, there is no worry that she might oversleep. So what is the hurry? She tries to go back to sleep.

And then she remembers where she is, and why—in the master bedroom of her dead brother's house, the children in their respective rooms. A line from a poem by Dylan Thomas comes to her, uncalled: "After the first death, there is no other." Of course, a great deal has happened since her arrival, some of it heartening to her, especially when it comes to her nephew and niece; some a little harrying, particularly when it comes to Valerie and her intentions. She remembers her evening with Padmini and Valerie, and how, ultimately, it disintegrated. Her throat feels tight as she wonders how much of Valerie and Padmini's life she should share with the children, to whom it will probably be news that there is more to the two women's partnership than business. She is sure, because he told her more than once, that Aar simply never bothered about telling the children more than they needed to know, especially because there was no way of knowing how they would react if they knew the truth about their mother's sexuality. He once explained his difficulty dealing with this dilemma, saying, "At times, a child may direct undeserved hate toward the bearer of a message rather than toward the person the content of the message is about." And because Valerie never communicated directly with Aar or the children, it was erroneously assumed that worrying about what to tell the children about their mother's sexuality was unnecessary. Now—now it is up to Valerie to deal with it, Bella decides, as she has other matters of grave consequence to worry about. The children are now grown—and they and their mother can sort things out between themselves as articulate adults. Even so, Bella is aware that indiscretions such as last night's will in no way bring them closer.

She gets out of bed naked and moves about the room soundlessly, as if there were someone else asleep in the room. And now she remembers her dream as well, a dream in which she shared a bed with Handsome-Boy Ngulu and they lay in each other's embrace, her heart beating furiously, as if it wanted to break out and flee. She walks into the bathroom and stares hard into the mirror, berating herself for having such thoughts so soon after Aar's passing. What sort of a person is she, giving in to desire when there is so much at stake, when there is a lot to be done?

The sight of her reflection surprises her. Her eyes are swollen and bruised looking, and she wonders if she cried in her sleep. She looks roughed up and sad, off-kilter on a morning when she needs to be efficient and at her faultless best. Despair is not an option. She scolds herself, speaking directly into the mirror, getting closer and closer until she can see a cloud of breath on the mirror's surface.

She takes a selfie, a habit that dates to long before she had an iPhone.

Whenever she was in a fix and unsure of how to proceed, she'd place herself at an angle to a mirror and take a photograph so that she could talk to it. Sometimes she would even tell herself folktales. It's working, she sees, as she looks at the photo on her iPhone. There's a little relief in her face, as if she's starting to have faith in herself again.

Bella slips on a robe. In preparation for Valerie's visit, Bella puts her belongings all around Aar's room. She doesn't want there to be any mistake about who's in charge here. She puts her clothing in the closet and dresser, pushing aside Aar's to make room and leaving her suitcases on the floor. She opens every drawer in the room, taking a quick inventory of the contents. Some things she buries away from Valerie's prying eyes; others she locks away in Aar's study, the key to which the children have given her and she stashes in one of her camera cases.

It strikes her how flat-footed sudden death catches its victims. Hurdo used to say that a woman must always be prepared for life's surprises—her toenails trimmed, her hands manicured, her underpants clean, nothing left to chance. She may have had an exaggerated sense of preparedness, but Bella has to agree now that perhaps her mother had a point. She sees Aar's unpreparedness everywhere—in the open documents in his study, in the packed suitcase he didn't take with him.

It does not take her long to open the larger suitcase. She is pretty certain that he uses variants on her name, nickname, or date of birth as his secret code for almost all locks, bank accounts, and other such things, just as she uses his. Inside, she finds several shirts, jeans, and underwear, along with his extra Mac, a wallet bursting with cash in dollars and several credit cards, and next to it is a printout of an e-mail addressed to Gunilla and signed "With love." In the letter, he explains that he is going to be in Mogadiscio for three months and asks Gunilla to please prepare all the legal documentation they've been discussing and have it initialed and then sent to him for signing before departure. He also requests that she make two copies of his "important documents," keeping one set and sending the other to him. Bella can't follow all the particulars—if anything, the state of affairs mirrors a general sense of lack of urgency—a man behaving as if he had all the time in the world and that he will be around for some time. These signs are what his belongings convey. At the same time, the discovery mirrors a sense Bella's had since Istanbul that he'd been confiding in someone else. That someone else appears to be Gunilla. Bella has come to Nairobi prepared with all the legal documentation that she might need to prove her identity. On top of all this, she has a signed and notarized document attesting to the fact that she, Aar's sister, is also his one and only executor. But it is Gunilla who has in her possession the items he deposited with the liaison office in Nairobi, and for those, she must await Gunilla's return. Bella reminds herself to ring the Swede, who is supposed to be returning tonight, first thing tomorrow morning to arrange a meeting.

When Bella questioned Aar during their time in Istanbul if it made sense to sink all his savings in a house of stone in a volatile country like Kenya and not in Mogadiscio, where, even though things were bad, there was the possibility of peace returning and property starting to appreciate again, Aar told her that he no longer thought of Mogadiscio as home. "Home," he said, "is where my children are, where they live and go to school and love to be. Besides," he added, after a thoughtful pause, "I am uncomfortable affiliating myself with a country broken into fiefdoms, where there is no room for someone like you or me."

They were at the Blue Mosque, where they admired the elegance of construction and the colorful tiles and silk carpets. They continued their talk while visiting the nearby Topkapı Palace. Aar said, "I am not comfortable in a Mogadiscio run by a confederacy of clans that are in cahoots with religious renegades. There is a great ache in my heart every time I drive past the cathedral and the oldest mosque, both of which lie in ruins."

A knock on the door gives Bella a start. Then she calls, "Come in," and Dahaba walks in, leaving the door ajar. Bella realizes that she is instinctively blocking her niece's view of the rest of the room, perhaps because she doesn't want anyone else to know about the broad sweep of her own intentions.

Dahaba asks, "What are you doing?"

"N-nothing!" Bella stammers.

Dahaba walks farther into the room and looks around, as if checking that everything remains as her father left it—except for a half-open drawer, which she now goes to.

"You looking for something?" Bella asks.

"Do you have any tampons, Auntie?" While Bella rummages for some in her travel case, Dahaba says, "What is the word for tampons in Somali?"

Bella chuckles. "I doubt we have a word for it." Then she remembers how in her youth, when tampons were not yet available in Somalia, women back home had to make use of strips of cotton, which had to be washed several times a day. In the Mogadiscio of the late eighties, they were again difficult to obtain; in those days, pharmacies would run out of all manner of daily necessities.

"Here," she says, giving Dahaba several.

Dahaba dashes out of the room, and Bella pushes the door gently shut on the pretext that she will be changing. Then she resumes searching the room, albeit with consummate caution. But she doesn't lock the door, not wanting either Dahaba or Salif to suspect her of foraging among their dad's things. Bella is certain that even Aar had secrets somewhere, but this is not something the offspring of a beloved parent find easy to believe.

Another knock on the door puts a stop to Bella's search.

This time it is Salif. "Would you like me to book a table at a restaurant if Mum and Padmini are joining us?" he says through the door.

Bella opens the door, but he is too timid to look at her because she is not yet decently dressed. What a charming, sweet boy, she thinks, as he stares at his fingernails.

"Which would you rather do, go out or bring in takeaway?" she asks. "For me, either is fine."

"Let's eat in," he says. "There is more privacy here."

"I see your point," she says.

"And they may be late."

She wonders if she should mention that their mother was close to an hour late yesterday evening. But all she says is, "Fair enough. The food can wait if they are late, and we can warm it up in the microwave."

He says, "You know that whatever we decide either Mom or Dahaba will fuss about it. But you know what?"

"What?"

"Fuss or not, they always eat the food you place before them."

Salif suggests sushi and claims to know where to get the best in Nairobi.

After allowing Salif and Dahaba computer and TV time, Bella decides to be a taskmaster for a change. In the sweetest way possible, she reminds them of their mother's first visit here, and she says that given they haven't as yet been in touch with the maid and that the corners of the rooms have been gathering dust and fluff wouldn't it be a good idea for each of them to clean their room? Bella offers she will do her room,

two of the four bathrooms, and all the areas that are of common use—
today, at least.

They each do their part, Salif playing heavy metal, Dahaba fussing
a little and then playing her choice of rock, and Bella saying nothing
to either of them. They take a break at about four and shower, readying
mentally for Valerie and Padmini's visit. And since Bella has no idea
what either woman would tell either child about her sexuality, Bella
decides not to bother, much less worry about the matter.

Dahaba wants to know if she can invite friends home to meet her
mother this evening, and Salif is of the view that the best way to welcome a person home is to cook—and maybe they should cook instead
of bringing a takeaway. But when neither Bella nor Salif thinks that
Dahaba's suggestion is good, and when neither Bella nor Dahaba is of
the opinion that Salif's idea to cook will fly, Dahaba is the one who
sulks briefly, retreats to her room and showers, then reemerges as if
nothing has happened.

At six, it is time to pick up the sushi, but Dahaba doesn't want to go.
"What did I tell you?" says Salif. He puts the alarm on downstairs and
tells her to stay up in her room while they are out.

She says, "You think I am stupid?"

He promises to get her a Big Mac, just the way she likes it. He turns
to Bella. "She has the woman's thing, I know," he says.

Bella thinks about how the world has changed. As a young woman
growing up in Somalia, she would never have told her brother about
her "woman's thing," as close as they were.

In the car on the way to pick up the food, Bella debates how much of
her own suspicions about Valerie she should air to Salif. But they have
been gone barely five minutes when Dahaba telephones, asking how

soon they will return. "Just stay put," Bella assures her, "and we'll be back before you know it."

Salif says, "Dahaba hates being alone."

The food court offers an assortment of fast food, but also a variety of international cuisines, mainly non-African: Indian, Chinese, and Japanese. Salif swears by the Japanese place despite the unlikely location. Bella gives him a wad of cash for the sushi and goes to order Dahaba's Big Mac and some Indian food for good measure.

"I hope she doesn't change her mind when we bring her what she asked for," says Salif. "She can be a terrible brat."

Within the hour, they return, bearing a variety of dishes—far more than they can eat today even if Valerie turns up with half a dozen Padminis.

By a quarter past seven there is still no sign of Valerie. The children are hungry, but Bella is happy to see that their banter has lost its sharp edge.

"Here, Chipmunk," says Salif, offering Dahaba a chip.

"Give it here, you beastly thing," she says.

They have a taste of the tikka, eating with their fingers, and put the rest of the food in the oven to stay warm and in the fridge to stay cool. Then they go back upstairs—Bella to put Aar's room in order, Dahaba to continue watching a movie on the Internet, and Salif to learn the result of the Champions League game between Bayern Munich and Arsenal.

At eight-thirty, they reassemble in the kitchen and eat at the table. Salif says that eating at the table makes him miss his dad, who was a wonderful cook and made dinner for them whenever he was in town.

Bella recalls that Valerie can't cook to save her life, although she is a stern critic of other people's cooking—the food is always too salty, too spicy, the steak too well done, the rice undercooked. But she refrains from badmouthing Valerie in front of Salif and Dahaba.

Salif offers to wash the dishes, Dahaba to dry them. Salif says to Dahaba, "Since you have a visitor, I don't mind if you go up to your room. I'll wash and dry."

Dahaba, a bit slow, says, "What visitor?"

But Bella sees where he is going with this joke and berates him for not keeping the promise he'd made regarding his treatment of his sister. Where does he get this macho thing, which is nothing like Aar? Helping Salif to grow into a young man who treats women with due respect is going to be work, Bella can see. She puts the leftovers away in plastic containers and says to Salif and Dahaba, "Help yourselves whenever you wish."

They wish each other good night without referring to the guest who did not show up or call, and they head back to their respective rooms.

Bella sits up in a stupor, woozily unsure where she is and whether she is dreaming or awake. She hears a girl loudly weeping and a man's voice comforting her. She puts on her nightgown and goes out to check. She stands in the doorway of her bedroom, trying to determine where the sounds are coming from and who is making them. She can see that the doors to the two rooms opposite are ajar. She finds the first room empty, but when she taps on the door of the second, the speakers fall silent and she pushes in without waiting to be invited.

Dahaba is sitting on the bed and Salif is sitting on a chair next to her, holding her hand, although he drops it when he sees Bella.

"What time is it?" Dahaba asks.

Bella has no idea; she is barely aware of where on earth she is.

Dahaba says, "Are you alright, Auntie?"

Salif gets to his feet and, as if he were dealing with a child who has awoken from a nightmare, takes her hand and leads her back to her bedroom, where he sits on the edge of the bed. "It is only ten o'clock at night," he says, looking at the clock. "You're in Nairobi, and you're jet-lagged still. You've just awoken from a brief sleep. It's been a long day. So please take it easy and get some rest."

He offers her a glass of water, but she takes his hand to stop him from leaving. She doesn't think she can bear being alone, what with this cocktail of troubling ingredients that she is gradually remembering roiling in her—Aar's death, so much travel and dislocation, this sudden new role, Valerie and her lover hovering with probable malicious intent just outside the frame, and even the children not entirely to be counted on, as surely they will want to see where things stand for them before they throw in their lot with one side or the other. It is not in Bella's nature to give up at the first obstacle, but she also knows there is no point in forcing children against the grain. Or maybe this is an early indication, if she needs one, that she is not ready to assume the role of mother all of a sudden.

Dahaba joins them, and Bella taps the mattress on either side of her, indicating that they should sit. "What woke me?" she asks.

Dahaba says, "Salif and I were arguing, and we raised our voices. We are sorry."

"I upset her and she was mad at me," says Salif.

Dahaba says, "You see, I'm easily upset."

"Were you crying?" says Bella.

"Yes, she's a drama queen," says Salif. "But I admit I had a go at her."

Just talking like this about a mundane sibling squabble is calming Bella down. She goes into the bathroom to throw cold water on her face, although this time she does not dare to look at her face in the mirror. She whispers a line from Robert Benchley to herself: "Tell us your phobias and we will tell you what you are afraid of." She stands with her back to the mirror and feels how fragile she is. In her current mental state, she can't even tell what she is afraid of. But she has no desire to free herself of her new responsibilities either.

She flushes the toilet for effect and runs the tap again, washing her face and her hands with cold water once more. And when she comes back to the bed, she discovers that she is once again the adult and they the children.

Dahaba expresses her unhappiness with her mother for not showing up for dinner, and Salif condemns Valerie's "unpardonable rudeness," which he sees as of a piece with her generally undignified attitude toward others. Bella does her best to comfort Dahaba and reasons with Salif, reminding him that Valerie has other worries on her mind. They don't know the whole story, she reminds him. They just have to wait.

Bella wonders how much of Valerie's jerrybuilt maneuverings are in store for her. Shoddy as they are, they can be difficult to dismantle. How can she keep Salif's and Dahaba's allegiance and also protect Aar's honor and interests?

First thing tomorrow, she'll confirm her appointment with Gunilla. And with that in mind, she gets out of bed. Dahaba and Salif go back to their rooms, and Bella begins to gather the documents she will need for tomorrow's meeting with Gunilla—her passport, her Italian ID, her driver's license, her birth certificate, and the most recent copy she has of Aar's will. Bella puts all these in a satchel, locks it, and places it under the bed. She pictures Valerie using the upstairs bathroom, making an unsuspected entry into the room and ghosting out with this booty in her possession. It is not beyond Valerie to plan this sort of stunt. In the past, she has helped herself to Aar's credit card, forging his signature until she got caught. Greed coupled with opportunity can make a thief of the best of us, Bella thinks.

Her preparations done, she takes an enjoyably long shower and gets under the sheets with a mystery novel by Philip Kerr that she has discovered on Aar's shelves.

Bella has been reading for about an hour and, having grown pleasantly sleepy, is just about to turn out the lights when she hears the dull sound of the doorbell ringing downstairs. She throws on her nightgown again and a robe as well. Outside of her bedroom, the hallway is dark, and the children's doors are closed. She tiptoes down the stairway, but there is no peephole so she calls through the door, "Who is there?"

And sure enough, Valerie answers. "Bella, it's us, Padmini and I."

Bella turns on the entryway light and opens the door. Valerie walks right past her. "Not bad at all," she says, taking in the house.

"We should've called," Padmini says to Bella. Valerie continues to take a measure of the house, as if imagining what it would be like to live in it and hold big parties. She paces back and forth, now staring at the parquet floor, as if she were inspecting it for dirt. She turns to Padmini. "Not bad at all, eh?" she says again.

Bella almost laughs.

Padmini says, "We ran into some friends. We only meant to have a drink with them, but somehow . . . Our sincere apologies for disturbing you."

Not knowing what else to say, Bella asks, "What would you like to have?"

Padmini says to Valerie. "What are we having?"

But before Valerie can answer, they hear a squeal of joy, and Dahaba runs down the stairs, shouting "Mummy!"—a word she somehow stretches to three syllables—and throws herself into Valerie's arms, just as she had done with Bella at the Kariukis'. She is still dressed, Bella sees.

"My condolences, my sweet," says Valerie, softly maternal now. "I am so sorry."

Watching as Dahaba wraps her young body around her mother's middle-aged girth, Bella is touched despite herself.

Dahaba says, "How many years has it been?"

Valerie says, "Well, let's see—how many years?"

Then they hear Salif's baritone from the top of the stairs. "When you say you'll come, you must come," he says, the man of the house.

"It's hard to explain, so we won't try," Valerie says. "Anyway, my sincere condolences for your loss. We may not have got on, your father and I, but he was at heart a good man."

Salif doesn't acknowledge her words of sympathy. "And if you don't come when you say you will, then you must ring to say you'll be late."

Now Bella sees the Aar in Salif, and she can see that Valerie sees it too.

"Look at you, all grown and full of blame!" cries Valerie, but there is a touch of pride in her voice. She turns to Padmini. "My son. Isn't he handsome?"

Salif looks from his mother to Padmini, as if meeting her for the first time—which in a sense he is. He looks her over, taking her measure. "And who is this?" he says.

Valerie says, "You know Padmini. This is your auntie."

"No, but who is she really?" says Salif.

"She is like a sister to me," Valerie says.

Dahaba is standing next to her mother, their flanks touching. She says, "She is lovely, Mummy."

"That's my girl," Valerie says encouragingly.

Salif takes his time descending. He hugs his mother briefly then offers his outstretched hand for Padmini to shake with a look that challenges her to do anything but take it. "How would you like me to address you?" he says.

"Address her as Auntie," Valerie says.

"Mum, please, I am talking to her, not to you."

"She and I are as close as sisters," says Valerie.

"Mummy, you said that before," says Dahaba.

"And we are, in addition, business partners."

Salif lapses into Somali, addressing his words to Bella, but Dahaba dutifully translates for the benefit of Valerie and Padmini: "That's cool, I've just acquired myself an auntie, how wonderful."

Bella can see that Valerie is torn between irritation at her son's discourteous behavior and admiration for his ability to speak Somali so fluidly—not that she can understand him.

Dahaba is playing peacemaker. "He doesn't mean ill."

Valerie says, "It's good that you too speak it."

"Our best friends are Somali," says Dahaba.

Valerie says, "I hope your Somali friends here do not teach you to use guns and stuff!"

Bella recoils at the stereotype, but Dahaba says only, "Actually, they're very nice."

"What's this world coming to, knives and guns?" says Valerie. A long, awkward silence ensues. It is Salif who breaks it, surprisingly enough. It's as if, having made his point, he decides to make amends. He turns on more lights and gestures the guests to the couch. He sits beside Padmini and engages her in conversation, leaning graciously toward her. Valerie relaxes, and she and Padmini exchange a smile, which Bella catches in the net of her wandering gaze.

Dahaba says, "Mummy, you know Salif is always difficult."

"Yes," says Valerie. "But he is my son and I'll always love him."

Everybody falls silent again. Then Bella offers drinks again. Valerie opts for a gin and tonic, and Padmini asks for a double shot of vodka with ice. Bella locates a tray and a bucket for ice, and brings the gin and vodka and tonic. For herself, she pours only a glass of water, and the children get themselves soda.

"So, in a word, what have you been up to, Mum?" Salif asks. He sounds as if he is on the attack again. Actually, Bella realizes, he sounds like his mother at dinner last night. "Where have you been all this time, and why haven't we heard from you? And why are we hearing from you now?"

Valerie says, "I've been in India. You know that."

Salif looks from her to Padmini and back again. "I like that phrase, 'business partners.' It has an all-inclusive feel to it, rather more accommodating than, say, 'sexual partners.' You know what I mean?"

Valerie's discomfort is obvious and this makes Bella ill at ease too. She grabs one of her digital cameras, which is on the coffee table. "A photograph of the three of you," she says, "just the way you are. Salif on one side, Dahaba on the other, Valerie in between." She looks at Padmini, and hesitates. "Oh, wait. You too." Padmini flashes her a look of gratitude and joins the tableau.

Dahaba says, "Like a family for the first time."

Valerie says, "My loving children."

Salif says nothing, but he allows himself to be photographed.

Bella brings down more of her cameras and poses everyone in different combinations. They are more relaxed now. Valerie and Padmini want the photos sent to their e-mail and there is a pause while they all get their phones and enter addresses. Dahaba is the most excited of all.

Only Salif remains cool. "I don't want them," he says. Bella upbraids him in Somali, and Dahaba says, "Why must you be a party pooper?"

Stealing a glance at her wristwatch, Bella sees that it is long past midnight. It will be impossible to get them a taxi back to the hotel, she realizes, unless they have made prior arrangements with the driver who brought them here. Knowing Valerie, this is unlikely. And as reluctant as she is to have them stay overnight, Bella is not about to drive them back to their hotel; it is simply too dangerous.

Valerie is deep in conversation with Dahaba, who is eagerly telling her about a recent incident at school—a classmate with pimples all over her face had used her soap, and Dahaba has been scared to use it since. But Padmini seems to be reading Bella's mind.

"It's late, Val," she interrupts.

Bella looks around with a level gaze, waiting.

"What's the plan?" Valerie says.

Bella pauses a beat before asking, "Did you arrange a taxi to take you back?"

Padmini says, "I'm afraid we didn't."

"Not to worry," Bella says, because what else can she say? "I don't think you can get a taxi at this hour, and it's too late for me to drive you. But there is a spare bedroom down here, with a shower next to it. You're welcome to stay."

"Are you sure?" Padmini asks.

Bella says, "There is plenty of space."

Dahaba wedges her body between Valerie and Padmini, and takes their hands, delighted with the new situation. "Please stay," she begs. "Pretty please!"

Salif watches from nearby, looking amused.

A discreet nod from Padmini confirms her firm acceptance of the offer. And that settles it all. Dahaba issues a joyous call to order, announcing to the room that Mummy and Auntie Padmini are staying in the spare bedroom for the night.

Padmini corrects her. "One of us will stay in the spare room, the other here in the living room if Bella gives us some bedding for it."

Valerie receives this news with haughty indifference. Bella thinks that maybe in this partnership it is Padmini who organizes all the pedestrian details. Just as Aar did when he and Valerie were together.

Bella gets bedding and even a spare pair of pajamas for Valerie, who receives them with the insouciance of someone who can't be bothered. Bella stifles her annoyance—not tonight, she thinks, definitely not tonight.

They say their good nights. Dahaba is the last to go upstairs to bed.

10.

Today Bella does not wake with that lovely open-ended feeling. She wakes with a start and instantly remembers where she is, who is in the house, and what the day ahead holds. She slept fitfully, dimly aware of movement downstairs and up and down the stairs during the night, the sound of the refrigerator opening and water running. Not wanting to intrude, she resisted the urge to go down and see that the food was put away or even to get herself a glass of water. When she slept, she had an exhausting dream in which a man instructed her to sit in one side of an industrial scale while he placed a heap of stones in the other. They repeated the process several times, but somehow no one could tell if the stones were heavier or if she was, or whether the experiment merited the attention they gave it. In the end, she threatened to walk away, no longer caring what might be done to her by way of punishment.

She is too thirsty to stay in bed any longer, so she goes down to get herself a glass of water, soft-footedly cautious. She holds her breath as her right foot touches the creaky lowest step, anxious lest she disturb Padmini on the sofa bed in the living room. But the sofa bed is empty of Padmini.

Now she has a new worry: What will Dahaba think when she discovers that their mother and Padmini are more than business partners? Will she find her mother's "business partner" still so "lovely"? Bella suspects that Salif has a better idea of what is going on. The guest room door is closed, so Bella switches on the kitchen light. She pours herself a glass of water and then notices that there are crumbs all about. Opening the fridge, she sees that someone has helped themselves to a portion of a hamburger, and the uneaten portion is unwrapped and smeared with ketchup, which is also on the refrigerator shelf. Bella uses a wet cloth to wipe off the ketchup and finds the box near the trash bin with a couple of chips in it. She places the uneaten burger in it and returns it to the fridge then, glass of water in hand, calls to one of the security guards at the gate and asks him if they can please get a packet of fresh eggs and sliced bread. She gives him more money than he needs to purchase these two items and then returns to the house more emboldened than before.

She knows that Aar, unlike most Somalis raised in the urban centers in the south of the country, had no issue with male homosexuality and couldn't be bothered about lesbianism. As for herself, while the platitude is true—many of her best friends are gay, and some are in openly gay marriages—she acknowledges that maybe she is not quite as advanced in her attitudes as she likes to think. But with her three lovers, she knows that she lives in a house of glass and cannot afford to throw stones at anyone in a similar position. Many Somalis would think there was something wrong with her, would see her as worse than a whore, because no cash exchanged hands.

Freedoms are a package deal, she thinks, useless unless you value them all. Freedom of expression, freedom of religion, freedom to associate with whom you please—all of these are as important as the right to education, to food, to clean water. In Africa, gay men and women are seldom open about their sexual preferences. In many countries homosexuality is a crime, and even where it is not, people talk as if it were alien to the culture of the continent, even though, of course, there are gay people in every society everywhere. In South Africa, the most democratic nation on the continent, vigilantes organize "corrective rape" rampages on known lesbians in the absurd belief that such actions will keep women from desiring relations with anyone besides heterosexual men.

There must be a premium placed on truth-telling in a household with children, she thinks. Discretion—being economical with the information you share—is fine. But your actions must match your words, and you must not describe your relationships as other than they are. There are no hiding places from the young for liars. Valerie and Padmini might think they are being discreet, pretending to sleep in separate beds and then coupling quietly behind closed doors. But it was Valerie's decision to cut off contact with Aar and the children for all those years, and it has been Valerie's decision not to speak openly to her children about the choices she has made: "Sisters" and "business partners," indeed. If you can't stand the heat, as they say, get out of the kitchen.

It doesn't help that Valerie and Bella have never gotten on, even when Valerie was living with Aar. But Bella doesn't want the children to get the impression that her disapproval of Valerie has anything to do with Valerie's being gay. She realizes she has to make this clear. And she must also remind Salif privately that he must show respect for his mother and accept her choices, no matter what he thinks about her behavior.

Bella reads a bit more to kill time, then showers, the hot jets of water waking every pore in her exhausted body. She rubs lotion all over her skin, combs the kinks out of her hair, and puts on her power suit again. She puts her documents in a special pouch and replaces it in her shoulder bag. At seven, hungry, too anxious to stay in her room alone and needing to collect the eggs and the sliced bread from one of the security guards, Bella goes down and steps out, noticing that the fresh eggs and sliced bread bought from the corner are at the door waiting for her. She will have to remember to give the change he returned as a tip later. Back in the kitchen, she makes breakfast for herself and for anyone else who might turn up.

She notices that someone has been in the kitchen since she was last downstairs because there is a sealed packet of bacon on the windowsill. She thinks that Salif, who is so partial to bacon, has possibly been here. Bella likes to breakfast on Spanish omelets or muesli with berries, plums, raisins, or other dried fruits, with a few dry sliced bananas thrown in. She likes to have tea first, very dark with milk, and coffee afterward, the stronger and darker the better.

She finds eggs in the refrigerator, but they are long past their eat-by date. But there are all kinds of teas, including a number of Kenyan ones and a couple of brands imported from South Africa, and she boils water to make a pot. She finds a packet of muesli and, checking the date, is delighted that it is edible. In the refrigerator is also an open carton of UHT milk, which she puts to her nose. It smells all right, but she has no idea when it was opened or by whom. Just to be on the safe side, she looks in the cupboard and finds another container of milk from Germany that is unopened. A country with so much milk potential importing milk from Europe—that's Africa for you.

But what can she offer Valerie and Padmini for breakfast? The truth is that she doesn't quite think of them as her guests. It's not her fault they missed the meal they were invited for, and she didn't prepare for overnight guests. Searching in the pantry, she discovers cans of tuna, tomato, and onion. She rummages in the freezer and finds frozen peas and chips of every variety. Relieved that she will be able to feed her guests—or, rather, Salif and Dahaba's guests—she turns to her own breakfast, enjoying her crunchy muesli and mouthfuls of her dark, dark tea. When she has finished, she brews a pot of Kenyan coffee, which is among the best in the world.

Salif is the first to dawdle in, wrapped in a colorful robe with a pair of pajamas under it. Barefoot, he has on a big grin of the sort that prompts you to ask a leading question, and next to it there is a smudge of toothpaste. He kisses Bella good morning and says, "What a night!" Bella can tell that he wants her to ask him to explain himself, but she pretends not to notice.

"Breakfast," she says, as if it's his name, while she roots in the cupboards.

He points at the bacon on the windowsill.

She asks, "What will you have with it?"

He opens the freezer and takes out a loaf of sliced English-style bread, hard as rock, the type she can't stand after her years in Italy. But she tells herself that it's good for Salif to learn to look after himself. He finds a pan for the bacon and puts it on to fry.

Padmini walks in and greets them both.

Bella asks, "Have you slept well?"

"Yeah, I did," she says. "And you?"

Again Salif says, "What a night!"

And before they can say anything more, Valerie ambles in. "What's for breakfast?" she says. And then Dahaba arrives, making a beeline for the fridge before she greets anyone. "For my breakfast," she says, "I am having the leftovers from last night, and I won't share it with any of you. I am starving."

She gets out the rest of the hamburger and puts it in the microwave then turns to the others. She greets her mum and Padmini, rubbing cheeks with both. To Bella she says, "You're up and dressed early. Where are you going?"

The whole scene reminds Bella of the movie *The Dirty Dozen*, where the twelve characters straggle in one at time, each speaking his piece.

Valerie says, "Yes, Bella, where are you off to?"

Bella tells her and Padmini what there is for breakfast, but Valerie refuses to be diverted. "Is it something to do with Aar?" she asks. "I've a feeling I must tag along."

Dahaba, lapsing into Somali, asks Bella if there is any truth to that. Bella tells her patiently that politeness demands she speak a language intelligible to the whole group. Dahaba apologizes to her mother and Padmini, and repeats her question in English.

Valerie is not one for politeness, however. "Why are you shoving me to the side like useless furniture?" she demands of Bella.

"How am I doing that?" says Bella.

"You are trying to keep me from being involved," she cries, "that is how!"

Salif says, "Mum, you made the choice to disengage yourself from Dad and us many years ago. You can't now accuse anyone else of denying you the right to get involved."

"I've had enough," Valerie says, and stands up.

But Salif isn't finished. "And let me add this, for what it's worth, Mum. You haven't asked us anything about Dad, what he was like as a father to us after you left. All you have done is create confusion in my head about the circumstances of his burial, urging me to act without even bothering to ascertain the legal and logistical implications."

Valerie is at a loss for words. She stands there, looking too shocked to sit, too weak to remain standing. Padmini says, "What's all this about?" Finally, Valerie, her face pale, pulls out a chair and sits. Dahaba takes her hands. "Salif doesn't mean to make a monkey out of you, Mum," she says in an attempt to placate her mother. "He is just like that sometimes. You know he loves you more than he can say."

Bella plates the omelets and waits for the kerfuffle to die down. Placing a plate in front of Padmini and another in front of Valerie, she says, "Please. Here. Eat."

Valerie hesitates, but Padmini starts to eat heartily. Bella slips out of the kitchen at last and goes upstairs, patting Valerie on the shoulder as she passes. She comes back downstairs with her bag and the keys.

"What's in the bag, Auntie Bella?" says sharp-eyed Dahaba.

"Not much," Bella says. She lets Dahaba lift the bag to see how light it is.

"Are you going shopping, Auntie?" Salif asks.

Bella looks at Valerie and Padmini. "I'd offer you a ride," she says, "but I have to get going now."

"For your appointment, right?" Dahaba asks.

Bella says to Padmini and Valerie, "Please allow me to treat you to a taxi back, as your host." She opens her wallet and puts several bills on the table in front of Padmini.

Valerie's nose twitches, and she hesitates. But Padmini takes the money, thanking Bella effusively for her offer and her hospitality in general. She apologizes for all the inconvenience they have caused.

Bella says, "Don't worry yourself. I am glad that you came in the end. I'll let Dahaba and Salif speak for themselves, but I can tell you that I enjoyed the visit."

"But we haven't even had a chance to talk about Aar," protests Valerie. "I have so many questions."

Bella thinks, why won't this madwoman let go? But she only says reassuringly, "It's still early days, and there are many things I am only just beginning to understand. I shall share what I know as I know it."

NURUDDIN FARAH

Of course, she thinks, she won't share everything. She will tell each of them what they need to know, what is appropriate for them to know.

More quietly, Valerie says, "You won't even tell us where you are headed and whom you are meeting dressed up like that?"

Salif, looking mischievous, says, "You're out of line, Mum. What if she is meeting a lover?"

"Darling, don't be daft," says Valerie.

"What's daft about meeting a lover?"

"It's not the right time of day!" Valerie exclaims.

"There's a right and wrong time of day?" says Salif.

Even Dahaba has had enough. "For the love of heaven, Mum, who are you to demand total transparency? How about telling us what you and Padmini were up to last night?"

Valerie's eyes narrow into slits. "What are you on about, silly girl?"

But Dahaba sails out of the kitchen in a fit of pique, leaving them all on tenterhooks. "Ask Salif," she says in parting. "He knows." Then she runs up the stairs, and they hear the door to her bedroom slam shut.

Valerie turns to Salif. "What is Dahaba on about?"

"I don't wish to get involved," he says in Somali.

Bella shakes her head in disapproval, reminding him to repeat in English what he has just said in Somali to his mother and Padmini. When he does, Valerie's eyes widen in shock.

Bella, looking away from Valerie, reprimands him for not remembering what his father taught him: to be forever polite and remain considerate toward adults—"More so now to your mother," she stresses.

Like the good boy he is, he apologizes to his mother.

It is obvious to everyone that things have got off to a bad start between Valerie and the children, and that it is time she made amends and spent quality time with Dahaba and Salif to set matters on a safer course. Bella asks Valerie, "What are your plans for the day? Maybe you would like to spend more time with Salif and Dahaba." And then before Valerie has reacted, Bella says to the children, "What about you? Wouldn't you wish to see your mum and Auntie Padmini for a longer time? They live in a continent you've never been to. Wouldn't you want to know more about their lives in India, what young people of your age are up to in the subcontinent, maybe even plan to visit one day?"

"Yes, I would, Auntie."

Bella say to Salif, "On a topic of housekeeping."

"Yes, Auntie?"

"Please remember to get in touch with the maid and ask her to come as soon as she can. This house needs serious cleaning."

"Yes, Auntie. I will do so."

"And one more thing."

"Yes, Auntie?"

"Please look after your mum and Auntie Padmini while they are here. Don't forget they are our guests. One honors one's guests always."

"Of course."

"Now here is cash for a taxi to wherever you are going and back again," she says, handing him a wad of cash, which she knows to be far more than they will ever need for a taxi and a meal at a decent restaurant for four persons.

"What about Dahaba?"

"Let her come with you. That way both of you will get to spend time with your mum and Auntie Padmini," Bella says.

On second thought, she fumbles in her shoulder bag and brings out a credit card. "Call me if there is a problem, any problem."

She turns to Valerie and Padmini and speedily walks the short distance separating them, and she hugs now one, now the other, and then says to both, "You are welcome here. Please come visit again."

Valerie says, "Thanks. That is kind of you."

"You have both my numbers?" she says to Salif.

"You mean your Kenyan and the Italian? Yes."

"Call me if there is need," she says, and turns to go, then stops. "Remember to be here when I return," she says to Salif. "There is only the one set of keys."

And off she goes to meet Gunilla.

11.

Within a few minutes, Bella finds herself in heavy morning traffic, the GPS notwithstanding. Above all, she does not know the shortcuts to avoid getting rush-hour madness, as local taxis might; nor does she know how to predict Nairobi traffic, where five minutes this way might make a great difference if you know the mood of the place. The traffic is utterly unpredictable though and very untidy, and this would tax anyone's nerves, but it is also, she knows from Aar, a drag on the local economy in both obvious and hidden ways. She remembers that he told her that the city authorities were at long last waking up to the challenge, and a couple of Chinese and Japanese firms have been enlisted to find a solution to the problem, but their efforts plainly have yet to bear fruit. The problem, Aar liked to say, wasn't only the large number of vehicles plying too few roads. It was the obstreperous drivers, each of them thinking themselves smarter than the others and behaving in the most undisciplined way with no fear of penalty. And Nairobi traffic is such a chronic condition that people have grown accustomed to it and in a sense rely on it. You can blame it for your lateness; you can catch up on your phone calls and texts; you can do your shopping from the peddlers making their way between the slow-moving cars. Incidents of road rage are rare because, while everyone is impatient, the opposite is equally true: Everyone is at the same time tolerant of everyone else's wayward ways.

Bella is annoyed but not anxious. She has left ample time to get to her appointment, and if by some miracle she is early, she has brought along the Kerr novel to read, which she is certain to prefer to the journals or glossy magazines that likely await her.

She dashes into an opening in the traffic, making a quarter of a kilometer gain before she has to brake suddenly behind a truck emitting black smoke that has created another jam. As she inches forward, she thinks about the evening and the morning, and how encouraged she feels by Salif, who has been so steadfast with her. Even Dahaba did not abandon her, divided as her feelings obviously are.

The down side of it is that they seem to have it in for their mother now, to the point of being cruel. Yes, Valerie is irresponsible and insensitive, but the world was not as kind to her in her own tender years as it was to Bella. She knows that Valerie's father, an actor, was often out of work, and the family mostly survived on Wendy's paycheck. Worse, Valerie's father was a drunk who sexually abused his daughter from the age of sixteen. When at long last he began to find steady work in Hollywood, he would often fly Valerie over to join him. That came to an end when a paparazzo took a picture of the two of them in a compromising position and this made it into one of the tabloids. Wendy brought all her wrath down upon his head, demanding an end to the matter on strict terms: Valerie must go to boarding school, and he must pay all the fees. Even that wasn't the end of the liaison, which continued in secret until Valerie met Padmini at school.

Aar knew none of this until Valerie was pregnant with Salif, and he revealed none of it to Bella until Valerie left for India with Padmini.

Perhaps, Bella thinks, this is why nothing Valerie does ever shocks her and why in some sense she cannot forsake her, much as she dislikes her. It is something she learned from Aar: Only those to whom the world is kind are truly able to be kind to the world. This history is not something she can explain to Salif and Dahaba, not yet, at any rate. But she resolves to teach Salif to be fair in his judgments and to encourage Dahaba to be moderate in her efforts to assert herself. And she resolves to make every effort to amicably work out the legal matters that await them without bringing in a scavenging herd of lawyers alien to the cause, whose primary aim will be lining their own pockets.

The traffic is once again at a complete standstill, and the driver of the vehicle in front of her gets out of his car and comes to her window, apparently wanting to speak to her. Visitors to Nairobi are often advised to beware of potential violence, which can strike at any hour of the day or night. Bella looks in her rear mirror to be sure that others are watching and checks that her door is locked before she lowers her window a few inches.

"Eh?" she says.

"I've run out of fuel," he says.

She shrugs her shoulders, acting the part of the Italian, making exaggerated gestures with her hands like a terrible actor in a B movie. *"Ma non capisco!"* she says.

But the man does not move, and Bella, taking pity on him, lowers her window a little farther so she can lean out far enough to see what sort of shoes he is wearing. Bella is certainly enough of an Italian to be superstitious about footwear. If you are good at heart, she thinks, you tend to have shoes of good quality, or at least ones that are polished and looked after. This man has on an excellent pair of shoes. In fact, they look unquestionably Italian.

"What would you like me to do about it?" Bella says.

"Do you have an empty jerry can in your trunk?" he asks.

Bella says, "I doubt it," but she pushes the button to open it so he can make sure. They all wait while he pushes his car off the road, then he pockets the keys and sets off, presumably in search of a petrol station.

She calls after him. "Come. Get in."

He tells her there is a gas station less than a mile away, and he knows how to get there. He tells her his name and offers her his card.

"What about you?" he says. "Where are you from?"

"I have no card to give you," she tells him.

"But you do have a name?" he teases.

She gives him the absolute minimum, her first name.

"How did you come by an Italian name?" he asks, and despite herself, she volunteers a little more.

"My father is Italian, my mother Somali," she tells him.

At the gas station, she waits while he borrows a jerry can and pays for fuel to fill it. She brings him back to where his car is parked and waits until he has it running. Once again, he comes to her window. He thanks her and says, "You realize you haven't given me your number."

She says, "Maybe I've none to give."

"Or an e-mail address to write to?" he says.

"Maybe I don't wish to."

"As you like," he says. "You have already done so much for me."

"Maybe you can do me a good turn," she says.

"Anything," he says, enthralled.

She gives him the address of the UN offices in Gigiri. Does he know a shorter way to get there? she asks. She explains that she has an important appointment for which she cannot afford to be late.

The Kenyan gentleman with the shoes to die for tells her she has been needlessly sitting in traffic—Cawrala, the GPS woman, has sent her on a most indirect route. He gives her a quicker way, carefully writing out the directions on a pad she gives him while he talks her through it. As a result, she arrives at the UN offices with half an hour to spare.

Which turns out to be a good thing because the security measures at the gate are draconian. It's as if she were waiting to board an El Al flight to Tel Aviv, she thinks. The blue-clad Kenyan guards manning the gates are rude beyond belief, barking instructions. One of them, waving what looks like a wand as if it were a scepter, directs her to turn off her engine, leave the key in the ignition, get out of the vehicle, and take all of her personal effects with her. She approaches the gate on foot, joining one of the two queues. When she gets up to the gate, a man sitting in a cubicle extends his hand through a small window to take her passport; in return, he passes her a long form to fill in.

As she does what she is told, she wonders whether similar measures were in force at the UN office in Mogadiscio where Aar was killed; if they had been, perhaps he would still be alive. The report was that the bomber simply walked into the compound and detonated his device, but this has not been confirmed. She used to hear from Aar how corrupt the Ugandans were. They provided the largest contingent of soldiers for the African Union, otherwise known as AMISOM, a mainly U.S.- and EU-funded force numbering close to twenty thousand. The Ugandans, being the first to arrive in the country and the strongest, were assigned to guard the international airport and several major government buildings, including the presidential villa and the National Parliament. Rumors circulating among the Somalis that were picked up and published in the foreign press say that some of the Ugandan top brass serving under AMISOM were making lucrative deals selling weapons to the Shabaab terrorists. On Aar's penultimate trip out of Mogadiscio, he told Bella, he had gotten through all the checkpoints and into the VIP lounge without anyone so much as opening his suit-case or even putting it through a scanning machine because he was in the company of a young man whose family owned one of the biggest and most expensive hotels near the airport. All the guards knew him and greeted him by name; the young fellow was so brazen that he men-tioned the name of the bar in the city where he would meet them later that evening.

Bella finishes filling out the form then watches while a couple of men place some sort of device in the shape of a huge shovel—a metal detector, she presumes—under the belly of Aar's car and another one gets into the car with a gadget that looks like a small vacuum cleaner to check the interior for explosive devices.

Then she loses sight of the car as she passes to yet another cubicle, where yet another blue-clad officer asks for her name and then slides her document out of a pile. He checks that her passport photograph matches her face. Bella is aware that she seldom looks like her official photograph, which tends, like everyone else's, to look like a mug shot. But she seems to pass muster, and he gestures for the form. Now a young woman asks her to look into a lens, and then she is fingerprinted.

"There is one more hurdle," the blue-clad man standing outside the second gate tells her. He directs her to walk through a body scanner after putting her shoes, her belt, jewelry, and mobile phone in a bin, just like at an airport. And just like at an airport, she is admonished to take out any laptops and liquids and put them on the conveyor belt as well.

Bella is relieved to see that Aar's car has made it through as well. "Triumph!" she says to herself. After the scanner, a woman administers a thorough body frisk, pointing out to Bella that she must open her fists. "You are an adult," she chides Bella, "not a baby. What are you holding?"

Bella is about to say, "Nothing," when to her great surprise, she discovers that she is, in fact, holding something—the card given to her by the stranger with the exquisite shoes. "Kenneth Kiplagat," she makes out, the card still in the tight grasp of her hand, as if she is loath to let go of it. Then she relinquishes the card and the female guard, who puts it through the scanner, says, "Just in case," before she completes her pat down.

Bella retrieves the card and puts it in her wallet. Then she gets back in her car and drives the hundred and fifty meters or so to the visitors' lot. She waits there until it is time for her appointment, preparing herself mentally as best she can. Then she steps out of the car, pulls herself together the same way she has seen gymnasts and other Olympic athletes do just before they compete—puffing out their chests, pumping the air, and mouthing silent encouragement to themselves. "*Coraggio,*" she says to herself. Then she walks into the building.

The receptionist says immediately, "Our commiserations, Bella. We all loved your brother, and we will be missing him. He was a gentle soul, genuinely friendly and good at heart."

Bella feels the tears beginning again; it is only natural, she thinks. But she is grateful when a second woman says to her in a businesslike way, "Gunilla is waiting. Immaculata will come down to escort you to her office shortly. Please take a seat and wait for her here."

Bella does as she is told, wondering whether the receptionists have been rehearsing these speeches the entire time she has been standing in the queue. Immaculata, she muses, what a name.

Bella follows Immaculata, high heels clicking, tight miniskirt hugging her knees and high bum, into the elevator and down the hall. She remembers wearing and loving miniskirts as a long-legged young girl in the Somalia of her day, but alas no longer. Not only because a woman her age isn't expected to show off her wares, but also because Somalia has fallen victim to the terrorizing dictates of religionist renegades, and her beloved Mogadiscio is no longer a cosmopolitan city. Lately, "secularist," once a term of approbation, has become a dirty word. Somali society has taken a giant step backward, not only as a consequence of the long-running civil war but also because it lags far behind most other countries in education and the other parameters that measure social progress.

"Are you a good Catholic girl?" Bella asks Immaculata.

"I never miss Sunday mass," the younger woman answers, but something about her expression encourages Bella to say, "I suppose you are regular about your weekly confessions as well?"

"Are you Catholic?" Immaculata asks. Now that they are walking side by side, Bella can see that Immaculata is heavier than she thought and that her skin is not very good. Her hair has been lengthened with extensions, which don't seem to agree with the dryness of the air-conditioning.

"I was brought up a Muslim," Bella says.

"I wouldn't have thought so, looking at you. You're not wearing body armor."

Bella thinks that such exchanges are getting boring, and she is tired of explaining. But Immaculata persists.

"Where were you born and brought up, really?" she asks.

"Mogadiscio, Somalia," Bella says.

"You are teasing me."

"I am not."

Immaculata says, "We have Somalis everywhere in our country, millions of them in refugee camps, and they've also taken over parts of our country. Have you been to Eastleigh? You don't look like them—you have beautiful skin, too light for a Somali. Nor do you carry yourself like them, walk like them, or behave like them."

"How do they behave?" Bella says.

"They are full of themselves, madam," says Immaculata.

Bella does not wish to get into an argument with anyone, here above all, but it disturbs her to let a half-truth go uncorrected. Kenyan Somalis, who account for nearly six percent of this country's population, have remained third-class citizens here, disenfranchised and marginalized. If they behave badly, that is undoubtedly in part a result of their poor treatment by other Kenyans. But the refugees in the camps are recent arrivals from Somalia, driven out by the collapse of their government. But what is the point of trying to correct this woman?

"Guns, lawlessness, and daily murders of their kith and kin, you name it," Immaculata says. "They've brought guns into our country across the border. They bomb our churches and they bomb their mosques. But of course, you are not like them. And I'm told that Aar, your brother, was such a gentle soul."

"He was," says Bella.

"Thankfully, there are several battalions of the Kenyan Defense Force currently stationed in Somalia to bring order to your country," Immaculata says.

At this, Bella has to respond. "Have you ever had occasion to meet or speak to a Somali other than me?" she asks.

"Never," Immaculata says.

"Why not?"

"They're too arrogant to talk to the likes of me, a tea girl," Immaculata says.

She stops before a closed door, on which she taps. They wait, and then a woman's voice says, "Come in." Immaculata steps aside deferentially and Bella hesitates, then goes in.

A well-built woman of Viking stock, big boned and blue-eyed, gets to her feet, smiling. She waits with her hand extended while Bella makes her way around a huge escritoire. Gunilla Johansson's grip is firm, her self-confidence immense. There are elements of generosity and joy on her face as she and Bella shake hands, then hug and let go. "Welcome," she says.

The desk is cleared of everything but a couple of files. Bella wonders if it is always this way or if Gunilla has prepared it so for this encounter. Were the circumstances different, she would describe the encounter as a joy, she senses—but tragedy has removed such a word from her current vocabulary. And it would be in her character to be a lot warmer to Gunilla as her potential in-law, which, sadly, did not come to be.

"Thanks for making the time to see me," Bella says. "And before I forget it, I must thank you for the help you've provided in having Valerie and Padmini released from their lockup in Uganda. I very much appreciate your sense of discretion in such a delicate matter. Thanks to you, Valerie and Padmini are now in Nairobi, but they are none the wiser about your invaluable contribution. All because of your friendship with Aar, who was most dear to us all."

At that, Gunilla's eyes well with emotion. She takes half a step back, saying, "Sorry," then reaches for the box of tissues. She pulls out a couple and then touches them gently to just below her eyes, blotting carefully so that her makeup remains unaffected. Bella can't help thinking that Gunilla has practiced this move countless times—maybe with Aar nearby, watching, overseeing.

Gunilla says, "We'll miss him. I loved him."

What Bella suspected has become obvious. She remembers back

to that last time in Istanbul with Aar—his aura of happiness, the two necklaces he purchased—one for her and the identical one, she thought then, for Dahaba, but now she knows for sure. He behaved like a teenager with a secret to treasure, and now she knows what it was.

Immaculata is still standing in the half-open doorway. She wants to know if either of them would like tea, coffee, or water.

"Coffee, Immaculata, and thanks," Bella says.

Gunilla says, "Same for me and some water too."

Gunilla closes the door behind the tea girl for privacy. An instant of indecision wrinkles her brow, and then her features relax.

Bella knows that as one of the most senior of the UN staff here Gunilla would be privy to a great deal of what goes on in the upper-level bureaucracy. But it is of private matters that Gunilla now speaks. "I believe I was the last person he spoke to," she says. "He rang me from his apartment complex to confirm that he would be on the UN OCHA flight, and we agreed that I would pick him up and that he would spend the night at my place. This was not always the case. Often his driver would fetch him and then he would come straight to the office or go home and report for duty the following day."

"What did he sound like when he called?" Bella asks.

"On edge."

"What was the reason?"

Gunilla tells her about the death threat and the visit from the security team, and Aar's suspicions and subsequent change of plans.

"Why did he make that detour to his office?" asks Bella.

"I don't know," Gunilla says. "Maybe he felt he was a marked man. He knew he would be asking for a transfer to Nairobi immediately after he flew back. Knowing he wouldn't be back, maybe he wanted to get his things."

While Gunilla rummages through a filing cabinet, Bella hears some humming in her ears. The humming goes on long enough to worry her. And then she has a momentary headache, her vision blurs. When the humming clears and she can see better, she starts to pay attention to what Gunilla is saying to her.

Gunilla apologizes. "I'm sorry," she says, "but I need to have you fill in some forms. Are you up to it? I can help you, if you like. That way it will be quicker."

Bella hesitates.

"Why don't we start with you?" Gunilla says.

"How do you mean, start with me?"

"For starters, did you bring along all the forms of identification you need to fill in the insurance forms and collect his personal effects?"

Bella provides these. Gunilla scrutinizes the documents, and when their eyes meet, she smiles a little. Then she inspects the notarized copy of Aar's will. Gunilla opens it page by page to study it, checking it closely with her eyes and then feeling the stamped bottom corner, as if examining for its authenticity. When Bella asks her if the version of Aar's will that she has now submitted and that nominates her as his executor is the most recent and therefore the valid one, the Swede checks it against the copies of the documents that are on file.

Then Gunilla reads part of the will out loud, pointing especially to Aar and Valerie's "out of community of property marriage in England." She consults the will on file against the one Bella has brought along: same working, same provisions, same signatures, including Fatima's and Mahdi's. "Yes," she says, "I met them even before I met Salif and Dahaba."

Gunilla and Bella now hear a gentle knock on the door and Immaculata enters. A tray on which there are glasses of water and coffee precedes the tea girl into the room. When Immaculata has set the tray down on the low table, Gunilla says, "Thank you, that is all for now."

When the young woman has left, Gunilla pours out two cups and asks if Bella takes milk or sugar. Bella shakes her head no and then, nodding and mouthing the word "Thanks," receives the cup with both hands. She waits until Gunilla's cup is poured before she takes a sip.

At last they get to the final form. "This one is difficult," says Gunilla. "It gives you the right to receive his personal effects."

Try as she might, Bella can exercise no more self-restraint. And Gunilla joins her in weeping. Eventually, she pulls herself together and says, "How about I put the questions to you and I write down what you say?"

It is easy for Bella to make room in her heart for Gunilla.

The questions are easy to answer: date of birth, place of birth, current nationality, profession, address, marital status, Bella's relationship with the deceased, date and place of death, date and place of burial.

These last questions give Bella an occasion to ask some of her own, questions she has been dreading and yearning to ask. "What do you know about how he died?" she asks.

"According to one of the survivors brought to a Nairobi hospital for his serious wounds that proved to be fatal," says Gunilla, "Aar is believed to have died immediately from a bullet that penetrated his heart. He was hit, execution style. And according to unconfirmed reports in the Mogadiscio press, he knew the man who struck him, the Shabaab mole working in the UN office with him who not only knew him but also had threatened him."

"And his burial," Bella asks, repeating the version she has read in the papers.

Gunilla replies, "The explosion soon after the Shabaab mole shot him fragmented not only his body but also the bodies of several other victims who could not even be identified."

"Do we have any idea if the forensics folks know if his body suf-

fered a second, more severe trauma following the latter explosion?"
Bella says.

"We're waiting for the FBI report."

"How is it that the FBI is involved?"

"Because some Americans were among the dead," explains Gunilla,
"and in any case, there are no Somali forensics teams available—you
know how things are in that country better than I do."

All of a sudden, Gunilla catches Bella's eyes and this time her burst
of emotion becomes uncontainable. Bella is equally in a delicate state,
and although she finds it hard to desist from joining Gunilla, she doesn't,
telling herself that she has done enough weeping. Gunilla says, "I miss
him terribly."

"We all do," Bella says.

"How are Salif and Dahaba faring?" Gunilla asks.

"It's been difficult, but they are strong and lovely."

"I met them twice, the first time on a camping trip."

Bella says, "Their mother has been visiting. We met two nights ago
for dinner—she and Padmini, her partner, and I—and she is now with
Salif and Dahaba."

"Since Valerie and Aar married out of community of property, the
law is clear, from what I gather," says Gunilla. "I've consulted a UN
colleague who is British. Therefore, you have no worries there, legally
speaking. But if the children were to declare strong loyalties and if she
filed her papers here in Kenya, then you have some untidiness to deal
with. Even so, the deciding judge must take her situation—that of being
an absent mother for years—into account. Any idea how likely it is for
the children to declare loyalty to her?"

"I doubt it, from the little I know since getting here."

"And then, of course, it depends on what your intentions are."

"What do you mean, what my intentions are?"

"Are you willing to take on the responsibility of parenting them? You are Aar's executor of his will, and as long as they are with you, there is nothing to worry about."

Gunilla turns several pages one at a time and then she talks to herself in a low voice in self-reprimand. Eventually, she says, "Valerie has been in touch with me too."

"Has she now?"

"Her expectations are unreasonable."

However much Gunilla pretends to be following the UN rules and acting neutral, Bella is aware that love and the memory of her affection toward Aar will sway her mind. She will exploit the play in the rope. "Valerie rang me at Padmini's insistence, she assured me, to see Aar's last will."

"What was your answer?"

"It is out of the question."

Bella is determined not to prod.

Gunilla goes through moments of nervy dithering. "Then a man claiming to be her lawyer rang me just before you came, wishing to know if this office had a copy of Aar's will on file and if his wife and the mother of his children could see it. I replied that I would get back to him about it after I had the chance to look into the matter further. Meanwhile, I consulted a Kenyan who is well informed about who is who in the legal fraternity and who happens to be a good friend of Aar's. I gave him the name of the lawyer representing Valerie. Apparently, said lawyer is Ugandan, with his chambers in Kampala, not here."

Bella says, "They are married out of community of property and the two of them have not lived together or shared a conjugal bed for a number of years. Does she have any legal legs to stand on?"

"Chances are she won't file."

"Why do you say that?"

Gunilla narrows the blue hardness of her eyes into slits because the sun is in them. "Aar was of the impression that Valerie doesn't have the patience to pursue any matter, especially a legal matter, to its conclusion. According to him, she would never do anything of the sort."

"There is always a first time."

"Aar used to say to me that Valerie would start on a project with great enthusiasm but wouldn't follow it to its end. Even having the children was such a project, embarked on with passion but abandoned in the end. This has been her downfall: the inability to stay the course; the refusal to pay up when a bill is presented to her unless Padmini steps in to help. Now tell me," she says, "how have Salif and Dahaba responded to her presence?"

"They are hostile to both Valerie and Padmini."

"And how does that sit with you?"

"I want no friction if I can have it my way."

Gunilla again opens one of the files, which she studies for a couple of minutes. She nods in silence in the manner of someone who has finally gained an understanding of a complicated matter. She says, "Please sign these forms using your name as it appears on your birth certificate and your passport."

Bella signs the forms without reading them. Gunilla has earned her trust.

"As the children's mother, what are her chances of convincing a judge to grant her custody now that she is back in the same country as they are and since she is the only living biological parent and they are under the age of majority—are there any good legs she can stand on?"

"The law is not favorable to her side."

"Besides, Valerie has a way of spreading vitriol the same way one spreads butter on one's toast," says Bella, and she tells Gunilla about

Valerie's trying to convince Salif that his father had wanted to be cremated.

"But that is absurd. She hasn't seen the will."

The telephone on Gunilla's desk squeals. She picks it up gingerly, as if it might burn her fingers, and holds it away from her ear, speaking rather disinterestedly into the mouthpiece. "Yes, who is it?"

A moment after the speaker on the other end of the line identifies herself, Gunilla indicates to Bella that she wishes to take the call and makes as if she is leaving her office. Bella motions to her, waving, and mouthing the words, "I'll step out for a moment," then does so.

She tiptoes out of Gunilla's office and then takes the opportunity to call Salif and Dahaba, who don't answer. Then, remembering how the young are more fond of text messages, she sends one to Salif, who responds instantly with three comforting words, "All well here." Even though she is tempted to ask where "here" is, Bella restrains herself from doing so.

She hears her name being called and sees Gunilla waving to her from the doorway of her office. "Please pardon the interruption and let's resume our conversation where we left off."

Bella says, "I would rather not know what Valerie said."

Gunilla agrees. "Fair enough. I won't tell you."

They sit opposite each other. Gunilla spreads the relevant papers on a low table and asks Bella to bring out her documents. Gunilla purposefully states what they are as if their conversation were being recorded. Gunilla reads the list aloud: an original copy of the will and statement. She receives the stapled document consisting of three pages and studies it with care, comparing it for the second or third time to the notarized and witnessed copy she has on file.

Gunilla rises to her feet, opens a cupboard, and brings out a folder with the name AAR on its cover. The documents in this folder have been brought from Mogadiscio and they include several personal papers found in his apartment and office.

"And here is Aar's passport," says Gunilla.

Bella receives it, her hand shaking.

"Please open it and check," says Gunilla.

Bella does as told.

Gunilla then rummages in her briefcase and brings out a one-page document—Aar's death certificate issued by the UN office in Mogadiscio. Again, Bella scrutinizes the document, saying nothing.

"Please come with me," Gunilla says to Bella.

"Where are we going?"

"To photocopy every single piece of paper, including the notarized and witnessed documents, which, I understand, are also with Aar's attorneys in England."

Gunilla leads the way after locking her office.

"Why are you making photocopies?"

"The originals will be stored here as reference."

When they are back in her office, Gunilla replaces the documents in their correct folders and puts all of these into a drawer, which she locks with a key. Then she returns Bella's originals, her passport, and the copy of the will she had come with, saying, "Please keep them in a safe place in case somebody wants to see them."

Gunilla then warns Bella to prepare mentally for a great shock. She says, "I am now going to hand over to you Aar's personal effects that were found in the taxi, including the shoulder bag he was intending to bring along to Nairobi, as well as his personal computer. You are a strong woman, and you will understand if I don't preface this ordeal further. I see you have come prepared for it," she adds, noting Bella's carryall.

It is Bella's turn to break down at the sight of Aar's favorite pair of jeans, his jogging shoes, his sunglasses, his Yankees cap, his T-shirts. Then Gunilla hands over a small plastic-covered shoulder bag, which she says contains Aar's Mac computer and his two mobile phones, which Bella knows are one for Somalia and one for Nairobi.

Bella says, "Do you know whether anyone has his passwords?"

"Ask Salif. He never gave them to me," says Gunilla.

But Bella knows there is no need to involve Salif for now. Unless Aar has changed his practices, she believes that, as with his suitcase, he will have come up with a password based on her name or nickname or birth date. She will try these when she is back home.

"And here is something else," Gunilla says.

Knowing Aar, Bella is not at all surprised that he has entrusted the passwords to his Kenyan bank account to Gunilla. She has all the passwords to his euro accounts. Aar was in the habit of trusting people— and it is not out of character for him to have trusted Gunilla to wire funds to him in Mogadiscio, as credit cards did not work there. He needed an active account in Nairobi, where the children lived. Every now and then, he would telephone to wire transfer large sums from an account he held in Switzerland from the time he worked there or from another account in Vienna. He led a messy life, one that was trusting, loyal, and orderly in its own way. Bella once asked him how he could trust his accounts and all his secrets to others. And he responded, "Because secrets are not everlasting and you can trust most people with your money as they will take it upon themselves to honor the faith you've put in them."

Bella can't think of what to say. When there is time and the opportunity presents itself, she will ask Salif to tell her what he knows about these things. Salif acts more grown-up than most youths his age; his father trained him that way. He is self-confident, and his self-regard is of a high quality.

Gunilla says, "I would very much love to see Salif and Dahaba. No rush, though. There is all the time in the world."

"It'd be inappropriate to do so now."

Gunilla agrees. "We'll arrange to meet in due time."

"Once the legal matters have been settled."

Gunilla says, "Very wise. Just like Aar."

"Take care. We'll be in touch," Bella says.

"We will indeed."

12.

Bella is exhausted when she returns home. She has an atrocious pain in the lower reaches of her pelvis, which, for want of a better explanation, she ascribes to her terrible posture as she drove back to Aar's house from Gigiri, pitched forward as if that would somehow make her go faster. She parks the car and, stepping out, places one hand on her back, pressing it hard, and the other on her midriff, squeezing it. It doesn't help. This, she guesses, is the price she pays for not taking good care of herself and not adequately resting for the past few days. She also ascribes some of it to the overwhelming grief over her loss, and the worry, and the exhaustion from all this travel, and the dislocation, and the determination not to display any signs of the stress to Valerie and Padmini. Finally, she blames all the driving around she has had to do looking for a camera store and then negotiating the price down, which in the end was not worth all the bother.

There is no denying too that her unceasing thoughts about the children and their continued presence in her mind and life have contributed to her general anxiety. Good as they have been with her, she senses a chasm in her knowledge about them. They have not yet truly tried her patience, but in time, she knows, they will. The gap between what she knows about them and the things she has yet to know reminds her of something Aar said to her about Somalis and their relationship to their language. Somali remained an oral language for a long time, acquiring a written form using Roman script only toward the end of 1972. Aar argued that those who had known the language only in its spoken form felt a great disconnect between the tongue they spoke and the one they were beginning to learn to write. Bella perceives such a lack in what she knows about the children, but she can't quite identify what she is missing. She also has few close friends here to provide her and the children with additional support and someone to fall back on. It would be a different story in Rome, where she has a host of old friends. Still, meeting Gunilla, whom she not only likes but also finds impressively competent, has cheered her. The woman knows her way around Nairobi, knows how things work here. She is sure to cultivate Gunilla's friendship, in whom she sees a link with Aar, someone both of them loved.

Bella brings in the bags of groceries she has bought but leaves the carryall containing Aar's personal effects in the trunk of the car when she parks. Before bringing them in, she wants to know what the state of affairs is here.

She remembers she has no key and rings the bell at the same time as she knocks hard with her knuckles on the solid wooden door. But there is no answer. A worried second later, she thinks she should have called from the shopping mall to alert them when to expect her. Then her instinct leads her to lean heavily on the door and turn the handle in an instant of optimism. And the door opens. Now all sorts of worries invade her mind: Have they forgotten to lock it in the first place? Have burglars broken the door or somehow found their way in? And given that there is no one downstairs, she allows other fears to prey on her thinking until she hears the soft whirring of the fan of a computer coming from upstairs and then an instant later a faint human humming, most likely Dahaba singing along with one of her favorite tunes.

Laden with the shopping, she closes the door gently, not wanting to frighten Dahaba. In the kitchen, her gaze falls on a heap of dishes, saucepans, and utensils piled up in the sink, still waiting to be washed. Evidently neither Valerie nor Padmini helped clean up the breakfast mess before leaving—unless they are still upstairs with Dahaba or Salif. Bella's mind now retrieves a memory pertinent to the occasion: Aar saying he had three children to look after.

She opens the fridge, in which there are half-eaten packets of sweets and a couple of cans of half-drunk soft drinks. Another empty can is abandoned on the windowsill. She puts away the groceries, pours herself a glass of water, and sits at the kitchen table, which is equally messy. After a couple of sips, she gets up and empties the fridge of the abandoned items, wipes the surface of the kitchen table, and discards the empty can. Then she sits back down, feeling instantly less exhausted. She calls out to Salif and Dahaba, and when they welcome her back, she suggests they come down and help her prepare a light midday meal.

As Bella seasons the chicken she has brought, Dahaba is the first to speak as she shows off a silver bracelet her mum bought for her. "Isn't this the most gorgeous thing you've ever seen, made, of all places, in Mogadiscio?"

"Made in Mogadiscio?" questions Bella.

Dahaba assures her that the Indian jeweler who sold it to them swore it was handmade in Tangaani, an arts-and-crafts place in Mogadiscio. Excited, Dahaba jumps around in joy.

Bella corrects the place name. "*Shangaani* in Mogadiscio."

Because Salif remains silent, Bella asks, "And you?"

He sounds dismissive of the whole exercise, and then, when least expected, he says, "Same boring stuff, as always. You are unhappy, you are bored, Mum buys you a present. You see, I didn't want to ask her, or either of them for that matter, questions about their life, but I hoped they would bring me into their life, what it is like to be where they are, what makes the two of them tick. What do you get? Presents. A new iPhone, if you want."

Bella can't think of what to say so she doesn't even try to reason with him, maybe because he has a point, his point, the point of a teenager who meets his mum and who wants to be no longer thought of as a child.

"And he was rude to Mum," Dahaba says.

Bella asks, "Rude? Why rude? How rude?"

"She gave him cash," Dahaba says, "since Salif wouldn't accept a present from her. And he threw the money back at her, in full view of everyone."

"Then what happened?"

"We left and took a taxi home."

Bella feels powerless to do anything about what happened and she is at a loss for words. And of course, she understands that Salif was hurt and had the right to feel that way. She senses the best thing to do is to leave things the way they are and revisit them another time. And with no one speaking, Bella deliberately lets the subdued manner dominate, convinced that something of monumental significance has occurred during her absence.

Dahaba says, "It was just terrible."

Salif, surprising Bella, comes to the rescue. He goes over to where Dahaba is standing and he hugs her to him and he says, "Nothing to worry about. I told her she is welcome to visit whenever she pleases, didn't I?"

"That was sweet of you," says Dahaba.

"See. Nothing to worry about."

A phrase from Samuel Beckett, "a stain on silence," springs to Bella's mind as she thinks how best to move on.

Salif again comes to the rescue. He is adept at changing the thrust of a conversation, helping to veer it away from controversy. He says, "Let's help put the groceries in the fridge and then let's prepare a light lunch."

While he puts the shopping in the fridge, Bella, happy to do so, chops onions and puts them to brown in a frying pan then begins slicing mushrooms. Something tells her that there is something else brewing—and that Salif is not the culprit, the author of whatever devilry they're not telling her about. He is staring at his fingernails, grinning in triumphant mischief, and Dahaba, nervous and dying to say something or revisit a scene, bites hers to the quick. Salif and Dahaba are looking away from each other in a bid to avoid eye contact. Bella will give them a few minutes, and if neither tells her something, only then will she ask. She pretends that everything is okay and stirs the mushrooms and onions, then adds spinach to the pan. She turns the chicken over, poking it with a fork. She washes the salad thoroughly, making sure there is no sand in it.

To keep Salif busy, Bella asks him to please make the dressing and, to this end, hands him half a lemon, some mustard, balsamic vinegar, and oil. He gets down to business, enlisting Dahaba to crush some garlic and find the pepper grinder. They all fall silent, but Dahaba can't seem to relax; she seems to need to say more about last night. "How dare they do it here, in our house?" she bursts out.

Bella says to Dahaba, "What is it? Tell me."

But Dahaba won't speak, it seems, until she receives the go-ahead from Salif. Bella plays the waiting game. Finally Salif gives his sister the signal, subtly indicating that she can go for it.

"I came upon them doing it," Dahaba says.

Bella acts as if she doesn't follow.

Unbidden, Dahaba continues, "The door ajar, their noise breathy, you know, and their bodies shapeless. Does that make sense to you?"

"Why did you come downstairs last night?" asks Bella.

"I was hungry," Dahaba says.

"Did you find something you could eat?"

"I couldn't bear the thought of eating anything after seeing them."

"You are not making sense."

"I was no longer hungry; I was angry and returned to my room."

"I can't make sense of what you are telling me."

There is no look sadder than the look of innocence in ruins, Bella thinks, as Dahaba sits apart, sadly remembering the scene involving her mother last night.

Then Salif says to Bella, "Then she came to wake me."

Abandoning the making of the dressing, he joins Dahaba where she is because he can't bear the thought of his sister being so sad; in this moment, he is in a protective mood, and he caresses Dahaba's hand reassuringly, as if saying to her that all will be well. They are in a world of their own, a world to which Bella has no access. This is the chasm in her knowledge about them, the gap in her understanding of them—the cause of her anxiety, her exhaustion.

"Did you go down to see for yourself?" asks Bella.

"Of course not," Salif says.

"He didn't have to," says Dahaba.

"I know what is what," he says.

"You do, eh?" says Bella.

"And have eaten from the Tree of Knowledge too."

"I needed to speak of what I saw," Dahaba says.

"I can see that," Bella tells her.

"I felt lost."

"I understand."

A sudden wildness enters the look in Dahaba's eyes. And she bursts out, "How dare they do it here, in my father's house? How dare they, so soon after his passing?"

"What did Salif say when you told him?" asks Bella.

"He didn't want me to disturb his sleep."

"I bet that upset you too," comments Bella. She catches a ghost of a smile around Salif's mouth. "Up in Lapland, little Laps do it"—the line comes to her, unbidden, and she finds herself grinning too.

Bella dishes out the food and they all sit to eat.

Years ago, she remembers, Salif used to delight in hiding Dahaba's favorite toys and then telling her that burglars had taken them away. After she had cried her heart out, Salif would give them back, claiming to have saved them from the thieves. One April Fool's Day when Valerie was out for the afternoon, Salif gave Dahaba a fright. Pretending to be weeping, he told her that he had just received the sad news that their mother had died in a car accident. When Valerie returned to a hysterical Dahaba, Salif laughed it all off, saying, "Don't you know it was just a prank?" Nowadays, whenever he tells her a fib, Dahaba retorts, "You can't fool me; it's not the first of April."

Bella says, "But what is it that happened today?"

Dahaba says, "Because he knew about it."

"Darling, you are not making sense," Bella says. "What did Salif know? Tell me from the beginning and do it slowly so I can follow you."

Bella reasons that Dahaba is a tabula rasa girl. Assuming that what she knows is known to others, she always begins stories somewhere in the middle.

Salif steps in. "Dahaba came to my room, upset at what she had seen. She woke me up. I told her to let me sleep. She wept. Unable to go back to sleep, I told her about a YouTube video our cousin Dhimbil had come upon and forwarded to me. It shows Mum and Padmini in some compromising positions. So there we were: Dahaba upset with Mum and Padmini; and Dahaba furious with me because not only wouldn't I wake up and hear her out but I also hadn't shared what I knew about Mum and Padmini. That is the long and short of it."

"Yes, I was angry that he hadn't shown me the YouTube," says Dahaba.

"I meant to spare her the agony of knowing," says Salif.

"I'm not a baby," Dahaba protests.

Salif says, "With some folks, you can never win."

"Listen to him gloating," says Dahaba, getting angrier.

For a while, they eat their meal in silence, even though Bella fancies she can hear the thoughts turning in their heads. It doesn't rain in this household, she thinks, it pours.

Bella says to Salif, "You still haven't told me how you got into a row with your mum? What was that about?"

"Mum came into the row later," Salif says.

"How do you mean, later?"

He replies, "Dahaba told Mum how upset she was over seeing them doing it. Mum tried to explain things to her calmly. Everything was cool until Padmini had the gall to refer to Dahaba as an evil little ghoul roaming the house in the night in hopes of finding fault with how the world works."

"Then what?"

"Then I lost my cool."

"Did Padmini use those words?" Bella asks.

"No," Dahaba says.

"Be a good boy and tell it in her words."

Salif speaks with care and precision. "She described Dahaba as an evil owl wandering in the darkness on the pretext of locating what evil there is in the world we inhabit." He seems pleased with himself, his attitude that of someone who has passed an endurance test. Dahaba nods her head in support of him.

"Imagine thinking I am evil," she says.

"You're not evil and you know it," Bella says.

"An evil owl," Dahaba says.

Bella assures Dahaba, "You are a wonderful girl, and you do not possess even an iota of wickedness."

Dahaba shrugs. "Why did they blame me?"

"Maybe they were shocked themselves," Bella says. "You mustn't take any of this to heart. These sorts of misunderstandings happen in families, but you have to let them go."

"It's all Mum's fault," Salif says.

"How so?" asks Bella.

"She didn't have to stay with Dad," he says. "And it would even have been okay if she left him for a woman. But couldn't she have partnered with a woman good enough for us to accept into our family? She chose a basement bargain! And you know what they say, you get what you pay for."

Bella knows she can't afford to comment.

Dahaba says, "Padmini should've stayed on the couch where we left her. You took the trouble to make it up for her."

"Or the two of them should've shown patience until they were in their own private hotel room," Salif says. "Even cigarette packets carry warning signs."

Is he trying to be hilarious? Bella thinks, taking a mouthful. But she keeps mum. She must let them speak their minds.

Dahaba now says, "After they went to jail for it, you would think that they would be more careful the next time."

"I've nothing against Mum going gay," Salif says.

Dahaba says, "It just gave me a shock, seeing them and all."

Bella looks at one and then the other, and speaks with extra caution. "In much of Africa, being gay is considered an abomination. I hope you are more advanced in your own views and are more tolerant of other people's choices. What people do and who they do it with is their own private affair."

"I agree with you on that score," Salif says. "But there is a *but*."

"Let's hear it," says Bella.

"You must tell the truth, no matter the fallout," he says. "Why lie and say that Padmini is like a sister to her when it is clear there is something else going on. You see what I am saying?"

Bella does. Indeed, she is astonished to find that he is thinking just as she thought.

"What about you, Dahaba, darling?" says Bella.

"I am not against her being gay," says Dahaba slowly.

"But you were shocked," Salif reminds her.

"Because I didn't expect to come upon them," she says. "And because Padmini called me evil."

"And what do you think now that a little time has passed?" Bella asks.

But Dahaba is unwilling to say.

"What's your position, Auntie?" says Salif.

Dahaba says, "Auntie lives in Europe, where they accept such behavior, where they tolerate it."

"What are you saying?" Salif challenges Dahaba.

"In Europe, being gay is no big deal."

"Why don't you let Auntie answer?" he says.

Bella says, "People everywhere should be in a position to make their God-given choice and to be with those they choose to be with. We

Africans lag behind the rest of the world, and we waste valuable energy putting our noses in people's private lives. We have no business there."

"Did living in Europe change your views," Salif asks, "or are those the views you held before you left Africa?"

"I've always appreciated differences," Bella says. "My mother had a lot to do with that. She appreciated the things that set people apart. She was never one for monotony."

"Why are most of us so wrong about this?" Dahaba asks.

"We are ill informed about the world, ill educated, intolerant of the views of others when they do not agree with ours," Bella says. "We are undemocratic, just like our governments. But sex is a personal matter that our societies and governments have no business with."

The children are proud of her strong statement, she can tell. Especially Dahaba, who makes as though she might applaud.

Salif says, "Have you ever fancied women?"

"Never," Bella replies.

"Not even tempted?" Dahaba asks.

"Never."

Salif asks, "Did it ever cross your mind that our mother was inclined that way before you discovered it to be the case?"

"You never know what you know until you come to know that you know it," Bella says. And then she gets to her feet and starts gathering the plates.

"Auntie is smart, isn't she?" Dahaba remarks.

"Smart in her evasiveness," Salif says.

Bella adds the plates to the mess in the sink. But she doesn't speak of the tedious business of dishwashing. Instead, she says, "Any plans for today?"

"We'd like to visit Auntie Fatima and Uncle Mahdi and their children," Dahaba says.

"I can you take there."

"Can we sleep over?" asks Dahaba.

Bella thinks that Aar would not object. And she would love to see his dear friends again too.

"I'll ring them," Dahaba says. "And then we'll do the dishes."

Salif says, "We'll make our beds."

Bella goes up to her room to collect the presents she has brought for them. She has always wanted to share her knowledge of photography with them and regrets that she never found the time until now. She brings down two identical digital cameras, each with a manual. But Bella shows them the basics herself, along with a few shortcuts she knows.

"Can we show them to Zubair and Qamar?" says Salif.

"Of course you may."

Dahaba takes a selfie and says, "How exciting!"

Everything is quiet, save for the clicking sound of Dahaba taking photos, now of Bella or Salif, now a selfie, and now of objects around the room. She is getting more excited by the second. But Bella's mind has gone in a very different direction. She is imagining Death entering the scene again, depriving her and others of those they love. She remembers reading Roland Barthes's prophetic answer to an interviewer: "If photography is to be discussed on a serious level, it must be described in relation to death." She remembers vaguely that Fatima was having a medical procedure. What kind of procedure? she asks herself now. It is not the type of question to put to Dahaba at this very moment when she is enthralled with capturing life. She will ask Salif when the two of them are alone; maybe he will know. She says to Dahaba, after she has taken yet another photograph of her, "Now what did Auntie Fatima and Uncle Mahdi say when you rang the house?"

"They said we are most welcome," says Dahaba.

"Only for an afternoon visit or for a sleepover?"

"Sleepover," Dahaba insists.

"I want to hear one of them confirm it," says Bella.

"Would you like to ring them now?"

"There is plenty of time before we go."

Dahaba practices with the cameras a bit more, taking photos of Bella, then of Salif. They pose in ones and twos, and then take a selfie of all three of them.

Bella starts on the dishes. Salif, unasked, puts away his camera and begins to dry the plates. Bella remembers wanting earlier to tell him about not leaving the door open the way she found it when she came in with the shopping. But she is content to talk about this on another occasion. And, with him helping, they are soon done.

Bella leads the children upstairs and they help each other to make the beds, to turn off their computers, to draw the curtains, to put the wet towels on racks, and to flush the toilets. Then Dahaba and Salif pack their shoulder bags with a change of clothes and their toothpaste and toothbrushes. Dahaba gets Uncle Mahdi on the phone to confirm that she and her brother are welcome to stay the night.

Bella makes a call of her own in the privacy of her room: She telephones HandsomeBoy Ngulu, the lover who lives in Nairobi. They chat briefly, the first time they have spoken since her arrival. Of course, he has heard the tragic news, and he offers his condolences.

"If you are free this evening, maybe we can meet," she says.

As soon as the words leave her mouth, alarm bells of worry ring in her head. She wonders if she is ready to meet a lover so soon after her brother's death. But her heart's quickened pace at the thought of it is pleasurable too. They agree to meet in the café of the Nairobi Serena, a five-star hotel.

13.

Bella hides the papers she has brought home under the mattress in the master bedroom, just as her mother used to do, but she doesn't yet dare bring in the carryall with Aar's personal effects among which she found a set of house keys, which she will keep. She is glad the children are going to see their friends. It will be good for them not to be obligated to defer to an adult the entire time; she imagines this must be exhausting, like speaking a foreign tongue in which one is hardly proficient. It can't have been easy to live in the house of your school principal and his wife, she thinks, no matter how kind they are. With their peers, they can be uninhibited and speak frankly, with everything up for open analysis and hearty discussion.

Still, she thinks, they've been lucky to be raised by Aar rather than in a traditional Somali household. And Aar, in turn, was lucky to be raised by Hurdo, who not only tolerated differences between people but also appreciated them. Aar's playmates would be beaten at home by their parents if they talked back and the children seldom got a kind answer if they questioned an adult. In such a household, a child inevitably resorts to lying, sneaking around, and being evasive. Bella remembers the story of a boy whose father struck him in the face as they passed each other in a hallway of their home even though he had done nothing wrong. When the son asked him why, the father replied that the blow was "for the wrongs you will surely commit in the future." Aar, she knows, never raised a hand to a child in his life.

Dahaba brings her mobile phone to Bella, indicating that Uncle Mahdi is on the line. Fatima and Qamar are out shopping, he says, but he hastens to add that they will be back by the time Bella and the children can drive there and that they are welcome to sleep over.

And so they set out, the car keys in Bella's hand, and a set of house keys for her and Salif in the event the children get back when Bella is not in the house. Bella reminds herself to have a set made for Dahaba, who has never been trusted with keys because she has a habit of mislaying them. But Bella intends to make Dahaba more responsible for herself.

But when Bella wonders aloud if they should set the alarm and Salif concurs, Dahaba goes into an inexplicable panic. "Why set the alarm?" she says.

Bella says, "Why not?"

Dahaba says, "What if I come back alone and I can't remember the code?" Her teeth are clenched, and her features are contorted with anxiety.

Bella reminds herself that there is now a before and an after in these children's lives and that this new phase requires compassion. There is no sense in upping the ante, especially as Dahaba has a tendency to make a drama out of everything.

As a sibling, Salif is harsher, refusing to fall for what he calls Dahaba's "exploits," and it annoys him no end when tears get her what she wants from adults. Aar was well aware of her tactics, but worried that a heavier storm was brewing, he sometimes gave in to her demands. Bella too is familiar with this side of Dahaba, and while she thinks it is too soon to get confrontational, she knows that sooner or later she will have to face the challenge if she doesn't want matters to get out hand.

"Will someone answer, please?" Dahaba says.

"When have you ever had a problem with the alarm," says Salif, impatiently. To Bella, he says, "Please let us set the alarm, Auntie."

Now Dahaba's voice begins to rise. "If the alarm is set, I panic and have no idea what to do. If the alarm goes off and armed security arrives at the gate and the guard lets them in and they find me alone, imagine what may happen—me alone with four armed men!" Bella senses that Dahaba knows how ridiculous she sounds, which only makes her more shrill and defensive.

Salif says, "Dahaba will be the death of us."

Dahaba throws her hands in the air. "Do what you want," she says, "if your conscience doesn't tell you that you are doing something wrong."

Bella tells Salif to set the alarm and turns to Dahaba. "As for you," she says, "you may phone me at any time of day or night and I'll be here to let you in or drive you back. Let this be the end of it." She tells herself that all children benefit from a firm, fair hand.

It is Dahaba's turn to sit in the front. Bella leaves Cawrala silent and gives Dahaba the task of guiding her to keep the children from arguing and keep their anxieties of whatever nature at bay. Bella is remembering her last encounter with Fatima, who took her to the airport on her last visit on a day when Aar was too busy to take her himself. Mahdi is five years Fatima's senior. In the late seventies, he served as the editor of a Somali weekly before incurring the dictator's wrath. He quit the country before he was detained and, together with a few close friends who had similarly fallen out of favor, set up a trucking business in Zambia. The business, which specialized in transporting everything from grains to vehicles to landlocked Zambia and Zimbabwe, did very well. Along the way, he met Fatima in Lusaka, and they married. Eventually, they relocated to Kenya, where the business did even better and where their children were born. Qamar and Zubair have never really known their parents' country of birth, but Mahdi still publishes pieces on Somalia in the Kenyan press or for one of the many websites that have lately flourished. Now and then he toys with the idea of returning to Somalia and setting up an independent daily newspaper, but Fatima isn't keen on throwing their hard-earned income into such a shaky venture. She wants her children to attend one of the best universities in the UK or the U.S. Bella is partial to Fatima, but she respects Mahdi's sharp mind and generous heart.

Dahaba directs Bella onto a new four-lane highway that the Chinese have recently constructed. Then Dahaba looks at Salif in the rearview mirror and says, "Do you remember why we ended up with the Kariukis instead of with Auntie Fatima and Uncle Mahdi?"

Salif is shifting uncomfortably, but he replies, "It was bad timing. Auntie Fatima had to go into the hospital for a procedure. Qamar and Zubair were sent to stay at their cousins' house for a few days."

"How come you knew about that when I didn't?"

A deadpan expression spreads itself like melting butter over Salif's features. He says, "I don't trade in gossip."

Bella thinks about this. It's true, she knows, that Dahaba has been accused numerous times of trading on family secrets, especially with Qamar and Zubair. She tells them both plainly that she hopes that neither of them will speak to others of what happened last night. "This is a family matter," she says, "and I don't wish you to spread it or trade in it."

"Padmini is no family of mine," Dahaba says.

"She is family as long as she is your mum's partner," Bella says, "and you must respect her as such. Nothing that occurs in the house gets repeated outside of it. Is that understood?"

"I won't talk," Dahaba remonstrates.

"Are you sure?" Bella says.

The question stings, and Dahaba falls into a stubborn silence. At length, she says, "Why don't people believe me when I promise I won't talk?"

Salif says, "He who tells his secrets will hardly keep those of others. Somalian proverb," he adds, looking pleased with himself.

Bella says, "We believe you, darling. Relax." She reaches over to pat her niece's hand, but Dahaba moves it out of range, her expression sour.

Bella has just finished honking to attract the attention of the day guard when Dahaba is out of the car and banging on the gate, calling to the guard on duty to let them in. Bella shakes her head, amused by Dahaba's suddenly reclaimed assertiveness. She glances at Salif to see if he shares her amusement, but he is absorbed in his mobile phone. Salif seldom reads, she notices, except when consulting the results of the latest soccer matches. When Dahaba was younger, Bella remembers, Aar used to tussle with her about reading in the back of the car in bad light. So far, her eyesight does not seem to have suffered. It just goes to show, Bella thinks, that adults worry themselves unnecessarily about children's health and behavior.

The gate opens, and Dahaba runs into the complex, shouting her thanks to the guard, and Bella and Salif follow in the car. Inside are twenty or so semidetached houses, each with its own small patch of garden where the residents grow vegetables or roses. Bella halts to let a child collect an errant soccer ball. His mother takes him by the hand and pulls him out of the way, apologizing to Bella and berating him. This time Bella catches Salif's eyes in the rearview mirror, and they both smile. The boy reminds them of Salif, who lived and breathed soccer when he was that age, dribbling and bouncing his ball against the walls of the house, inside and out, every waking moment, and falling asleep each night with the ball clutched to his chest. A proverb Hurdo often quoted, usually in reference to Bella's own behavior, returns to her: It's not the parent who chooses to favor a child, but the child who behaves in a way that compels a parent's love. In this shared moment, Bella feels that she and Salif are confederates, coconspirators, working in tandem to look after Dahaba.

Bella likes the community feel to this complex, she realizes, as she brakes again to let two elderly Asian women cross to the other side of the road with the help of two African women. The scene reminds her of a family of elephants on their way to a watering hole, a sequence recalled from a nature documentary. Then that image gives way to a caravan of camels being led by a Somali herdsman. Ten meters on, her eyes fall on a white woman in the doorway of one of the houses, bending down to tie the shoelaces of a dark-skinned child, who is fidgeting and raring to be off.

Dahaba has already disappeared into Fatima and Mahdi's house, which is at the end of the complex, a stand-alone two-family structure bigger than all the others. Bella parks in front, but she does not immediately get out.

"Who told you that Auntie Fatima was having a medical procedure?" she asks Salif.

"Dad did," he says. "In fact, he left me a message saying it was the reason he was coming back from Somalia so suddenly. He said he planned to go straight to the clinic to visit her there."

"And what was the procedure for?" Bella asks.

"Something to do with high breast density."

"You even know the term for it, I am impressed."

Salif hesitates. "I did a bit of research about it on the web too."

"Any idea about the result?"

"I understand that the results of the tests were worrying enough that she's lined up a specialist in England, at Barts, for a second opinion. She's going there in a few months' time."

"And your dad told you all this?"

Salif nods, his look humbled in memory of his father.

Bella wonders what else he knows, remembering what Gunilla told her: that Aar trusted Salif with everything, including the passwords to his computers. She gives Aar credit for his trust and foresight, which have helped to prepare his son for the unfortunate position he now finds himself in. It's a great pity that Valerie hasn't the character or the humility to appreciate the traits Aar instilled in Salif.

"Do I understand that you have your father's computers' passwords at your fingertips?" she asks Salif with care.

"Have they found his computers?"

"Please don't answer my question with another," she reprimands him gently.

"I'm sorry," he says. "I do."

"Every single one of them?"

"Every single one of them."

She looks at Salif, as if with a new pair of eyes, and sees Aar in him vividly now: astute, caring, trustworthy, levelheaded, with an unerring sense of what matters. It's the first time she has understood the meaning of the saying, "The child is father to the man." She prays she can aspire to achieve a fraction of what her brother achieved as a single parent.

Mahdi is waiting for them in the doorway. He hugs Bella warmly, his whole body trembling, his tears flowing freely. Bella hasn't had a cry since her encounter with Gunilla, but now she gives in to the impulse again. Salif doesn't permit himself to get carried away, however, giving Mahdi only a brief hug and muttering, "Yes, we'll miss him terribly," in response to Mahdi's outpouring. "You're a big, grown man yourself," he concludes, sizing Salif up. "You're your own man. But I want you to know we are here for you." He turns to Bella. "We could have picked them up, you know."

"I did not think to ask," Bella says. "Besides, you have your own worries." She wants to let him know that she has an idea about Fatima's state of health even though this is not the right time to discuss it, and she can see that he is touched by the delicate way she has let him know. He takes Bella's hand in his left and offers his free one to Salif, and the three of them enter the house.

"We've been grieving, following the loss," Mahdi says, as if standing here where Aar so often stood has brought him back even more vividly. "He was our great friend, and no commiseration or sorrowing words spoken will replace him. Nor am I fond of the words of condolence we Somalis often invoke—that we are all headed in the same direction, toward our graves. That's no consolation. Me, I don't like this kind of talk."

It is these words that at last bring tears to Salif's eyes, and he moves to embrace Mahdi, but just at that moment, Mahdi turns and shouts up the stairs for Zubair to come join them. Zubair careens down the stairs,

Dahaba with him, and the young fellow offers his formal condolence, hugging Bella and then standing apart, head bowed and looking sad. But as soon as they have satisfied the demands of politeness, Zubair and Dahaba bound back up the stairs to reenter the world of the young, where sorrow is held at bay for as long as possible.

Mahdi says, "Where are my manners? Please forgive me." Bella doesn't quite comprehend why he says this. Not until he turns to her and asks, "What will you have?"

"Tea is fine, if that is no bother, thanks."

They follow him into the kitchen. Bella sits as he pours water, but Salif, who has brought his camera, wants to take photos of them, and he asks them to pose for him, his first photo of two adults outside his home.

Mahdi insists on seeing the camera before posing, and after receiving it, he admires it. "Nice camera, must be expensive." Then he asks, "Where did you get it, I never knew you had such a beautiful camera?"

"A gift from Auntie Bella," says Salif.

"Well, well, a grand camera for a lucky boy."

"She got one for Dahaba too."

"But that is wonderful."

Bella listens in silence, happily beaming.

Mahdi and Bella obligingly pose for Salif and he takes a couple of photos just to be sure, and then goes upstairs to join the others, a fresh spring in his gait and a broad, joyful smile covering his features.

The two adults are now alone in the kitchen. Mahdi brings out a tray and teacups and the ubiquitous UHT milk and sugar. Bella notices that his hands are shaking, and wonders if he is very, very sad not only about Aar's early tortured death but also about Fatima's cancer.

Mahdi says, "When a country like ours goes to ruin, it takes our best too." He sighs. "We go back a long way. Your mother taught me at the law faculty, Aar was a schoolmate of Fatima's. His name was on every girl's lips, but he took very little notice of any of them because he was hardworking, always thinking about schoolwork, competitive, the best in everything, soccer, chess, games, you name it. Later, at the university, they went to different faculties, he to economics, she to agriculture, but they still kept in touch and we reconnected when they both graduated and he came to our wedding and then he often visited our home for the odd meal. We would tease him about women and Fatima even tried to set him up with one of her girlfriends. Not interested. Fatima would say Aar was meant for greater things, certain that he would do well at whatever he set his mind on, for he was talking of doing his PhD. Then I was in political trouble, the dictator threatening me with prison, and we left Somalia. Then came the civil war and we lost touch, but we were happy to reunite with him here. You were much too young for all this."

"I remember Fatima," says Bella. "Her beautiful dresses above all. I recall these bright dresses with great envy as a young thing, touching, feeling with my hands the material they were made from. She would bring me marzipans and I would follow her and Aar to the door as they left, hoping they would take me with them wherever they were going."

"We loved him," says Mahdi.

"My memories of those days are still with me and they remain sweet in my mouth and I feel as though I can taste their ambrosial residues," says Bella. "I too was sweet on my brother, as were many other girls."

"We loved him and now hold you and his children very dear."

Even though they are standing apart, it is as though, with their reminiscences of Aar safe in their memory, Bella and Mahdi are wrapped in a single cloth woven out of their sorrows. And they fall silent, neither wanting to add to what has been said.

Then the sudden entrance of a cat startles them out of their stupor.

The cat rubs against Mahdi's legs, and then Bella's, meowing. Then they both hear a key turning in the lock and see Qamar barging in, excitedly lugging a huge shopping bag too heavy to lift. Fatima brings up the rear, admonishing her, "Do be careful, my sweet." Then she catches sight of Bella and, the door still open, the key still in her hand, she exclaims, "Oh my God, I had no idea." Fatima sweeps her up in an embrace, her joy at the sight of Bella quickly giving way to fresh grief over Aar, but not before Bella takes in the headscarf that Fatima has on, the first Bella has seen her wearing, the headscarf meant to hide Fatima's loss of hair from a combination of chemo and related treatment. Also, Fatima's skin looks pallid, with a worrying patchiness, which Bella associates with the taking of drugs. Bella's own sorrow grows more acute with the awareness of this new sadness, and it is doubly painful to be able to speak of the one but not the other.

Qamar is waiting patiently for them to finish their hugging before offering her own commiserations to Auntie Bella. Fatima, noticing this, gradually releases Bella from the tightness of her embrace. "My sincere condolences, Auntie," Qamar whispers.

Bella says, "Oh, my sweetness, thank you."

"We must stay strong," Mahdi says.

Bella says, "Thanks for all your support."

"What else is there to do, what else to say?" says Fatima.

There is a serious struggle all round and Bella is unable to stay on her feet, struck afresh by the reality of Fatima's illness, and she sits down, exhausted. Mahdi, Fatima, and Qamar surround her, watching in perturbed silence until Mahdi gestures to the others to give her space.

"Tea?" Mahdi says to Fatima.

"I could do with a cup," Fatima says.

"What about you, Qamar?" her father asks.

"Not now," she says, and then she bolts up the stairs.

Bella longs for something a lot stronger than tea, but she is not sure there is such a drink to be had in this house, and she doesn't want to discomfit her hosts by asking for it. She hasn't felt the need to take strong liquor since leaving Rome—not even in the plane. She will have sufficient time to make the cultural shift and knows not to expect to be served wine or other liquor in the homes of Somalis, and she reminds herself that she hasn't been around her fellow nationals in a long time.

Mahdi says, "How would you like your tea?"

"Black, strong, no sugar, please," Bella says.

Mahdi and Fatima are staring intently at Bella, who finds herself unable to recall how she got from the kitchen to the couch in the living room. She realizes she has been daydreaming of happier days, when Aar was alive and the children were young and all of them looked forward to a future uncomplicated by deaths, diseases, civil wars, and other sorrows. Her eyes closed tightly, she balls her hands into fists and sits still for quite a while, conscious of Fatima and Mahdi still watching her. The instant she sees them both standing, her fists unclench, and she pats the couch on either side of her, and the two of them take the free spaces she has indicated.

Bella says, "You give me strength. Thank you."

As they take the time to contemplate the ruins of the world around them, Dahaba, prancing down the stairway with her camera in hand, breaks their reverie. Fatima looks up, amused by the girl's expression, as serious as if she were ready to announce an important event.

Dahaba says, "I would like you to pose for my first picture of the three of you with the first camera I've ever owned, a gift from Auntie Bella."

"How would you like us to pose?" Fatima asks.

"Please stand up and smile for the camera."

Bella thinks it is an odd request to make of them at this point in time, but she decides to let it pass because Dahaba is unfamiliar with the etiquette of taking photos at a time such as this. The three of them stand and let her arrange them until she has taken the photos to her own satisfaction.

Then Mahdi brings the tea and, spoon clinking against saucer, Bella tries to think of the best way to broach the subject of Fatima's cancer. She gets her moment when Mahdi takes his leave with a bow, on what she is fairly certain is a pretext that he needs to complete a piece of writing. He takes his tea and sets off up the stairs in the direction of his study.

"Would you like some biscuits?" Fatima asks.

Bella shakes her head no, wondering if Fatima is loath to burden Bella with her illness when she is already grieving.

"I hear their mother is here," Fatima says.

"Yes, she is."

"And I hear you hosted her last night."

"Yes, we did indeed."

"And I hear she is trouble."

"We won't let her cause disruption in our lives."

Fatima says, "If marriage is heaven and hell, then Aar was heaven, where he now must be residing, and his widow—if she is entitled to such an office, which I doubt—is hell, from what my children have told me."

Bella is a little miffed that someone, most likely Dahaba, has shared family secrets with either Qamar or Zubair, who must have passed them on to Fatima, the very thing against which she has been inveighing.

Fatima can tell Bella looks put out, and she guesses the reason. So she says, "Our children are very close, and they talk their hearts out to one another, especially at moments of great sorrow."

"I understand," Bella says, "but don't we Somalis say that a secret known to more than one person is no longer a secret?"

"Aar guarded his privacy and so does Salif."

"Not so Dahaba."

"There is in each of us a secret chamber whose key we offer to those we choose—a husband, a wife, a brother, a sister, a lover, or lovers known to no one but ourselves. I am sure there are personal secrets that Dahaba won't divulge to anyone, and with age, she will learn to know how to treasure more secrets, keep them hidden."

"I do hope so."

"If I may be so bold, might I ask who is the custodian of the key to your secret chamber?" But when Fatima sees the hesitation on Bella's face, she says, "Consider it unasked."

"I am no different from Aar, say, who entrusts a password to his computer to Salif, the details of his banks in Europe to me, having also given me power of attorney to them, and who then makes you and Mahdi serve as witnesses to his most recent will. We guard our secrets in different ways and entrust some to those we feel close to."

"We've always wondered why you never married."

"With a brother like Aar, how could I?"

"I can see where you are coming from," says Fatima. It seems to be confession time. "Mahdi never tires of telling everyone that Aar was every girl's favorite boy. But I can tell you he was very hard to get to know, and it was difficult to plumb his persona, a smart, lovely guy like him. It is sad that he ended up with a woman who walked out on him."

"I may have fancied him too," says Bella.

Fatima pours Bella more tea, and then asks, "So what are your current plans?"

"I am thinking of moving here," Bella says.

"There is nothing standing in the way, is there?"

"How do you mean?"

"A love, a mortgage, a professional commitment?"

"Nothing I can't clear away."

"It'll be great for all of us to have you here."

Ill at ease, knowing what she knows, Bella shifts her position as if awaiting a blow. She stretches her hand to touch Fatima's, and then tears well up in her eyes and, with words failing her, her Adam's apple moves up and down and, her breathing agitated, she seizes her opportunity to take Fatima's hand, which she kisses. Then she says, "Do I hear cancer?"

"Yes," Fatima says. "We didn't discover it in time, my fault. I was never in the habit of self-examining. With me, it all started with an unusual swelling of the breasts as well as a lump in the underarm. I consulted my GP, who, after examining me physically, sent me to the breast clinic. The results of the initial biopsy came back showing that mine was in an advanced stage. I was put on a chemotherapy with a drug called Doxorubicin. I am feeling a great deal better, but you can see how the combination of the chemo and the drug has caused my loss of hair, and I am weak and sweat frequently and am moody. Mahdi has been very supportive, my other friends also. We are going to England to see a consultant at Barts, and maybe we will go to France or America later."

"This is most sad."

"Aar knew about it even before I told Mahdi, in fact."

What a touching tribute to their friendship! thinks Bella.

Fatima continues, "He was sorry he wasn't here with us. He tried to bring his return forward, intending to visit me at the cancer clinic where I had gone for a minor procedure. In a way, I am to blame, though, because I kept postponing my mammogram until it was too late."

"It's good you're getting a second opinion," says Bella. "When are you off to Barts to see the consultant?"

"In a month or so," replies Fatima.

Bella clears her throat and says, "I'll want Zubair and Qamar to stay with us when you do go. And if there is anything else I can do, please let me know."

"Qamar and Zubair would love that, I am sure."

"It would excite the children to be together," says Bella.

"And I hope for their sakes and everyone else's that Valerie doesn't cause further upsets in the existing harmony," says Fatima.

"I'll make sure she won't," promises Bella.

"What are their mother's prospects in the new setup?"

"None, legally speaking."

"Is she going back to India or moving here with her partner?"

Has Dahaba been speaking again? Bella asks herself.

"I doubt they will move here," ventures Bella.

"But it is true that they are trouble?"

Bella changes her position. "They've been indiscreet."

"With movement in the small hours of the night?"

Bella then tells an edited version of the events as they occurred. "For all we know, Padmini may have gone out for a smoke when Dahaba saw the unoccupied couch. Not that it matters in the end."

"Is it true that Valerie wants Aar's corpse to be exhumed, brought here, and then cremated? Because in the will we signed as witnesses in London, there is no mention of cremation or where he should be buried."

"Valerie has the habit of creating confusion."

"But that's madness," Fatima says.

They sit in silence, not knowing how to move on.

Fatima is the first to speak. "What are your plans?"

"I am here to mother Salif and Dahaba."

"You are relocating—completely?"

"At some stage, I can envisage setting up a freelance photography business when I feel things are more settled," says Bella. "But not now. I want them to attend universities here. I feel very comfortable in Africa and I am glad I am back on the continent and delighted that I can be of some help to my nephew and niece. It's been traumatic, a great deal chaotic—but calmness will reign and we'll all be happy to be together."

"These are challenging times, aren't they?" asks Fatima.

In a flash, Bella remembers everything she has done since coming here, but remembers nothing of what happened before that. She thinks there is something amiss and the only way to cope with this sort of personal crisis is to take the tea things into the kitchen and then go to the bathroom, wash her face with cold water, and have a moment of quiet all to herself.

She then takes leave of everyone, shouting to the children upstairs, "I have things to do, my dears."

14.

Older but not necessarily a great deal wiser, Bella telephones HandsomeBoy Ngulu as soon as she sets off from Fatima and Mahdi's house. The thought of postponing their meeting until she is in a less delicate state of mind crosses her mind, but this strikes her as a cop-out, and she dismisses it. When Ngulu answers, she pulls over to talk to him.

"Hello, sweetness," he says. "What is up?"

It takes all her self-control not to tell him that in her current state of mind there are only two people she considers entitled to address her with such an endearment: Dahaba and Salif. True, Ngulu has in the past been in the habit of using that term of affection, both in person and in his texts and e-mails. And indeed, each time he used it ("Is that you, sweetness?"), it seemed to dispossess her of some inner strength, robbing her of the power she always assumed she had over men, quickening her with feelings from the past. Which is all the more reason why she doesn't want to hear it now. Another day, perhaps, but not today. But how is he to know how fragile she is?

She asks if they are still meeting.

He says, "I've been looking forward to it all day."

"The Serena, right?"

"Right, the Serena."

"It'll be good to meet and talk."

"I'll be waiting in the back of the café bar, my dearest."

She wonders if she should call off the tryst. Despite the verbiage, she isn't picking up the kind of feeling she expects from a lover she is seeing after so long an absence. She senses stress in his voice, maybe dread; he sounds like an unhappy man. Nor, she notices, does he go the extra mile to express his sorrow for her loss. But she says nothing.

The first time they slept together, she was putting up at a three-star hotel, the Meridian. It was a rainy October night, and she'd come from Rome to do a bit of camera work for Oxfam. She recalls that night with amusement now. He'd climaxed before he even entered her, without so much as bothering to knock on her door. He wasn't much good as a lover at first, but he was so young and handsome that, ogling his naked body and touching him here and there, her eyes at least felt fully satiated. Hence her nickname for him, Bell'Uomo.

As she drives, she lets Cawrala tell her where to turn while memory leads her by the hand. The second time they'd met, it was by chance, in Edinburgh. Bella had gone to Scotland to spend a romantic weekend with Humboldt. But Ngulu, who was there for a seminar on the causes of famine, spotted her walking in the rain holding hands with the sculptor. He followed them into a restaurant and sat at the bar in the corner, keeping an eye on them until they'd ordered their drinks. At which point he presented himself in a here-I-am sort of way. Bella was startled, but she felt relieved when it became clear he wasn't going to make a scene. Speaking in Portuguese, she introduced him to Humboldt. He picked up the basics of what she said about him: that he was a Kenyan, working in Nairobi for Norwegian People's Aid. He made as if to sit and almost pulled up a chair to join them at the table, but when they resumed their conversation in Portuguese and he couldn't make sense of what either one of them was saying, and with Humboldt staring at him like an undertaker deciding the size of the coffin to put him in, Ngulu withdrew. Bella flew back to Rome that night and Humboldt went to London, where he was having an exhibition of his works.

Amazingly enough, she met Ngulu by chance again the following year in New York. This time she was with Cisse Drahme, her Malian lover, who was doing some research on African astronomical systems at the New York Public Library. They had just checked out of their hotel on a side street near the UN when Ngulu appeared before her and said, "Hi, fancy meeting you here." On this occasion, Bella walked past him without a look. And when he caught up with her and said, "It is me, Ngulu," she pretended she didn't know him and asked him to repeat his name. If he was stalking her, she was determined to put an end to it.

Cisse took possession of Bella's arm and the two of them walked away from Ngulu with their arms linked. He stood where he was, staring at them pulling away and wondering if he had mistaken another woman for Bella, for a time a woman of his heart.

But the next time she went to Nairobi, she was in a low mood, a big EU-funded project of hers having fallen through. She was again staying at the Meridian. Restless and in need of temporary entertainment, the kind tourists from the moneyed parts of the world enjoy when they are visiting Africa, Bella discovered she still had the landline telephone number Ngulu had given her when they first met, and on a whim, she tried it. A woman answered—his wife, his mother? She left a message with the woman, giving her name and the name of her hotel.

To her surprise and delight, he rang her from the lobby at six. When she came down, he was all spruced up. He was flaunting a well-maintained moustache, had a sports jacket on, a pair of jeans too tight in the crotch, and a silky shirt unbuttoned to display the tuft of hair on his chest. The handsome smile she remembered played around his eyes, his mouth forever parted in a grin. She knew right away that he would not mention either of their two previous encounters, as though he had wised up to the fact that reminding her of them would piss her off. And he didn't. They talked briefly about what each had done since their last meeting, and in giving an account of his activities, he didn't refer to either of her two prior putdowns.

At seven, she noticed he was looking ravenous. She took him to the Carnivore, where he ordered a plateful of meats—beef, ostrich, and hippo—which, according to him, had been cooked to perfection; in fact, he suggested she try it. Since she found the idea of a restaurant making an offer of some sixty types of meat revolting, and she had only a salad, there was a moment when she felt ambivalent toward a man who could bear to consume so much meat—and she thought maybe she should terminate her interest in him. But there was a strong feeling toward him and she stayed with him, paid the bill, and he took the rest of the food in a doggy bag, maybe because he could live on it for a few days, given that his salary as an NGO employee wasn't high.

They jumped into a taxi and she took him back to her hotel, still uncertain whether she wanted anything more than a nightcap with him. But he was still handsome and young, and she was lonely, and when they got to the lobby, she took him up to her room and they made love.

The sex this time was scarcely better than the first. As a lover, Ngulu clearly was no Humboldt. Unhandsome as the sculptor was, rough in manner and uncouth in his comments, Humboldt lived for sex and art. Ngulu has no strong ambition of any sort. Moreover, he fell asleep soon after the evening's one and only round of lovemaking, stirring only to spread his legs, raise his pelvis, and release a silent malodorous fart then yawning and stretching his limbs one at a time, all the while remaining asleep. And his penis is small. Still, Bella longs to see him. For the first time, she admits to herself that she admires him for what he is: a youthful angel of extraordinary beauty. And with Salif and Dahaba away, what is the harm? If she plays her cards right, she will get what she wants and still have a delicious evening to herself.

And yet she can't help thinking about the questions Fatima asked about Aar and his attraction to Valerie. What would make an intelligent, loyal, loving, and attractive man link himself to such a woman? "What does he/she find in him/her?" is a question asked the world over. And the answer is "Nobody knows." Still, she would not marry a man like Ngulu or have children by him. But knowing what she knows about the pull he nevertheless exerts on her, she is more generous toward Aar for having chosen Valerie and by extension toward Valerie, despite all her failings.

Stalled in traffic, she glances in the mirror, unable to decide whether she is any the worse for wear. But what about Ngulu? She wonders if experience has made him any better as a lover. Although the pay for NGO workers like him is modest, the demand for a handsome companion like him is high among the many unattached British, European, and North American female employees, for whom there are few good marriageable men. She is familiar with some of these women, including a former classmate from university she sometimes stays with when she is traveling. In fact, it is that classmate who told her that Ngulu had been taken up by a Canadian woman old enough to be his grandmother, a sugar mummy of exceptional stature, quite literally—a redhead more than six feet tall, with a voice as many-tempered as Paul Robeson's. How does he address this elderly Amazon, she wonders—"Sweetness"?

Thinking of the unhappiness in his voice just now, she wonders again whether she should have canceled. The idea of being taken for granted makes her uncomfortable. And truly, it is time the man figures out what he wants in life and moves on. She will impress this upon him, she thinks. And at any rate, it is too late to cancel; a few minutes later, she is at the hotel.

He is waiting for her in the back of the café bar, just as he said he would be. And if Bella needed confirmation of her feelings, she gets it as she approaches him—his exquisite features no longer stir things up in her, which is how she used to describe his particular appeal to herself. He is like the favorite toy a child holds close to him for years as he falls asleep, touching, kissing, and holding it, drawing physical comfort from it. And now, it seems, the toy is broken or she has tired of it.

But as she comes closer, she sees that he seems eager indeed. He is up on his feet and waving enthusiastically to her. He takes a few steps toward her, meeting her before she reaches the table. They embrace awkwardly, and when their lips meet, his mouth is open and wet, in a more intimate kiss than she is prepared for. She frees herself quickly, saying, "Okay, okay, okay." She allows him to lead her by the hand back to his table. He's been drinking. There is an almost empty whiskey glass—not his first, she guesses—and a couple of empty beer bottles and a can of Coke.

"How have you been doing?" she asks.

"I've been doing very well, thank you."

Bella squirms. She flags down the waiter. Ngulu orders another whiskey with ice, and then the waiter turns to her.

"What about you, madam? What can I get you?"

She says, "I have had a long day, and a longer night is waiting for me. Please get me a bottle of mineral water with a slice of lemon."

When the waiter leaves, Ngulu takes the hand closest to him and, with a smile in his eyes, says, "Good. A very long night, I like it."

She doesn't even bother trying to set him straight.

He says, "My sincere condolences for your loss. Often, I ask myself what this world is coming to. Innocent people getting killed when they are just going about their business and working for an honest living." He shakes his head and tells her about some of the casualties they've suffered in Nairobi at the hands of terrorists acting in the supposed name of religion, nationalism, or ethnic loyalty.

"And did you lose any friends or family in one of those incidents?" she asks.

He shakes his head, but says, "We're all affected by it, every one of us."

She knows that a million and a half Kenyans lost their lives in such violence around the elections a couple of years ago, and close to three million joined the ranks of the internally displaced. But she is in no mood to hear her specific, personal loss glibly lumped in with so many others. Granted, she agrees that in a general sort of way we are all affected at least momentarily by the footage of a bomb blast and the grisly carnage that results. But that is no different from coming across the collision of two vehicles in which passengers have died or been injured. We drive with extra caution for another kilometer or two then return to our habitual careless ways. Only when we are affected personally, when a family member or close friend loses his or her life, do we really feel the pain and cruelty in our guts, in the marrow of our bones. That is why in Somalia people pray that God spares those one loves while taking those one does not even know.

The waiter brings their drinks and then tots up their bill, scribbling the total and leaving it on the table.

"How are Aar's children faring?" Ngulu asks.

"They're having a difficult time," Bella says.

"They go to school here, right? In the suburbs?"

Bella is not inclined to give him any more information than she needs to. She senses that their relationship is dying a natural death, although she is not sure this is the right moment to end it definitively. She will bide her time. What is the rush?

Ngulu asks, "Have you a plan for this evening?"

"I am planning for a very long night."

"With me, I hope."

"And what do you have in mind?"

He brings out a room key. "This is the plan I have in mind. I've paid for a suite for the night where I hope we will frolic and love and remember."

Bella's gaze shifts from the room key he has shown her to the mineral water, which she has not even touched. She weighs her words carefully before she speaks. She knows that she is in a more privileged position than the vast majority of women. She is economically independent, she has a profession in which she is well respected, she knows what she is passionate about, and she has friends on whom she can rely. Most important, she is not beholden to any man. She has had the run of her own affairs for much of her life, and it is not only in her nature but also in her means to withdraw unequivocally from any situation where she is not treated with the dignity she deserves. Life is tough on women, and Bella thinks she has been well prepared for it. If, as Sophie Tucker is thought to have said, a woman needs good looks between ages eighteen and thirty-five, a good personality from thirty-five to fifty-five, and plenty of cash thereafter, Bella has had all that she needs to make herself happy with her lot. So why should she permit this boy toy to behave badly toward her?

She says, with the calmness of Lot addressing his betrayers, "I wish you had let me know because I've made other arrangements. In future, always tell people what you have in mind. I might not have come if I'd known you expected me to spend the night with you. In fact"—she looks at her wristwatch—"I really must leave. Will you pay for my water, or shall I pay for it myself?"

And with that, she walks out of the café bar.

Bella is not proud of what she has done, but she feels that she had few options. She couldn't let Ngulu get away with such insulting presumption. But she is angrier with herself than with him, for it is she who put herself in a position to be treated with so little respect.

It will do her good to spend an evening by herself, relaxing and eating leftovers or making herself an omelet. Then she can set to work cracking Aar's e-mail and other accounts. Realizing that there was no way of knowing what personal secrets she might find once she cracked the computer's code, Bella had decided not to seek Salif's assistance in puzzling out his father's passwords or bank details. It wouldn't be fair to him, she thinks, nor would it be fair to his father. The living who happen to have access to the secrets of the dead must deal with them as though they were sacred.

She doesn't recognize anything she is passing, and wonders if Cawrala has led her astray, but then she spots a familiar landmark and knows that she is on the Uhuru Highway. She knows the way from here. She silences Cawrala and drives the rest of the way home feeling calmer. Next time, she thinks, she will bring along some CDs, music to feed her soul. Jazz, in particular, has always nurtured and sharpened her creativity, bringing out the best in her.

She is only a few streets from Aar's house when she hears her phone somewhere in her handbag. She decides she won't bother to answer it. Likely it is Ngulu calling to apologize, and she has nothing more to say to him. In any case, she has never liked the idea of being on call like a medical doctor, obliged to answer every time the phone rings, and she disdains the habits of the text-messaging generation, who seem to think of their iPhones as extensions of themselves. On the other hand, what if it is Salif, or Dahaba having a difficult time and needing to be comforted or picked up? Didn't Bella tell her to call her at any time of night or day?

By the time this thought occurs to her, she is home. She parks and deactivates the alarm, then goes into the house, turning on the lights in the kitchen. She pulls out her phone to see who has called. Gunilla!

Bella dials her back. They chat for a few minutes, and Gunilla asks after her and the children, speaking as a friend rather than as Aar's colleague. Bella tells her about the sleepover at Fatima and Mahdi's and her plans for a solo dinner of leftovers and a quiet evening of work. She makes no mention of her encounter with Ngulu, needless to say.

Gunilla says, "Of course, you haven't had time to do a proper shop! In fact, you probably don't even know your way around the neighborhood. You know, I'm not far from you, and there is a big mall close to my house that doesn't close until about nine in the evening. I know how difficult it can be to figure out daily life in a city that you are not familiar with. Would you like to give me your shopping list, and I can get the items for you and bring them over later? I have to do a shop myself."

"I don't want to trouble you," says Bella.

"Or how about this? You have a bite to eat. I'll come for you in an hour or a little less, and we can go shopping together. I'll take you home, and if you have the energy, we can have a chat and a cup of something."

Bella's heart surges with pleasure, but still she hesitates. "Are you sure you have the time to do all this?"

"I do," says Gunilla, "and I'd love to see you."

"Brilliant," says Bella. "I look forward to it."

As soon as she hangs up, Bella realizes that she has forgotten to tell Gunilla the address. She is about to ring her back when she remembers that, of course, Gunilla knows where it is. She has been here with Aar. Bella smiles to herself—she's not the only one with a secret life.

Bella brings the carryall with Aar's personal effects into the house. She puts the laptop on the desk in the study and plugs it in so that it can charge. She puts the rest of his things back in the carryall, which she hides under the bed. Then she goes downstairs and makes herself a bowl of spaghetti with plain tomato sauce.

When she is finished, she goes back upstairs and sits down in front of the laptop. She guesses at the password, trying various combinations of Aar's pet names for her, Gacalisissima1, Nuurkayga3, Gabar, Gu', TobanKaroon! She tries the date of her birth. After a few attempts, she hits on the right combination.

As she waits for the desktop to appear, something inside her goes very quiet. For a moment, she feels as if her heart were about to stop pumping blood to her head. It's as if she has crossed the boundary between herself and Aar by accessing his private life without his permission. This is an infringement she would never have allowed herself while he was alive. What makes it kosher now that he is dead?

Bella hears a quick rat-a-tat knock downstairs. The time has passed more quickly than she thought. Gunilla is at the door, her idling car behind her. She says she will wait for Bella in the car. As she turns to leave, Bella notices that Gunilla is wearing the necklace that is the twin of her own, the one Aar got for them both.

She goes upstairs and turns off the computer, puts it in her room under the mattress. Now that she knows how to get in, there will be time to venture further later. She locks the bedroom door, shuts off the lights, sets the alarm, and locks the door to the house.

On the way to the shopping center, Gunilla speaks of her own delight at having met Bella. "Only I wish the circumstances were different," she says.

"It can't be helped."

Indeed, Gunilla says, they almost met once.

"When was that?" asks Bella.

"Remember when you came to spend a few days with Aar in Istanbul?" Gunilla continues without waiting for a confirmation. "I was due to arrive from Stockholm two hours after he escorted you to the airport for your departure. He dropped you off and waited for me to arrive."

Secretive Aar! "I was there when he bought that necklace," Bella says.

"And did he tell you to whom he was giving it?"

"I didn't ask him."

"You were not curious enough, you mean?"

"He was a very private man, Aar," Bella says carefully. "I think you too would have found it unbecoming to ask him questions of that nature if you had known and loved him as much as I knew and loved him."

There is a silence, a silence that indicates that they have arrived at a sort of T junction in their conversation, no way forward, only to the sides.

Gunilla says, "How have the children been?"

"We're okay when it's just us," says Bella. "But as Sartre says, 'Hell is other people.' When others are around us, there is turbulence."

As if intuiting which "others" Bella is referring to, Gunilla says, "By the way, we had a three-way conference call at Valerie's insistence, involving me, Valerie, and the Ugandan lawyer representing her. She wanted to enlist our help in a new idea she has: a trust in the name and for the benefit of the children, to be set up with UN help. Naturally, she suggested that she, as the surviving parent, be appointed as the trustee. She spoke at length about her business savvy, managing what amounts to millions of rupees—not that millions of rupees is that much."

Bella says nothing, wondering to herself why Gunilla thinks this will be of interest to her. But, as a Swede and a UN bureaucrat, she is just being thorough. Or at least Bella hopes that is the reason.

"And you know what I also found out today?"

"What?"

Gunilla is pleased with herself. "The penny has finally dropped. Valerie has no legal right to the children or to Aar's estate. One: because their marriage in England was out of community of property. Two: by abandoning the family, Valerie did not share a conjugal bed with Aar for several years, which is one way of defining matrimony. Three: you and the children, as per the will in the files, are the only heirs—and her name appears nowhere in it. Valerie knows it too. So this is her new iron in the fire, this trust fund. Apparently, she has charged the Ugandan with the task of getting it up and running."

"Need we bother ourselves with any of this?" asks Bella.

"Not really," says Gunilla. "Unless out of generosity you wish to involve her in a trust fund for the children—and I see no reason why— or you allow her as co-custodian, which I doubt is wise, given what you've told me so far. This is what I think personally."

At the entrance to the mall, there is a police checkpoint. Gunilla's vehicle is subjected to a thorough inspection by several plainclothesmen and some armed men in army uniform. When at last they park the car and enter the supermarket, it is getting near closing time. They divide Bella's list, and Gunilla goes to get produce and drinks, while Bella gets everything else. Bella gets to the checkout counter in twenty minutes, as planned. Gunilla arrives a few minutes later.

"I know," says Bella, "that it is never easy to shop on behalf of someone you do not know well. And we have the additional burden of shopping for two teenagers whose habits neither of us knows well either."

As they drive away, Bella feels triumphant, as if she has accomplished a great feat. Gunilla says, "Having no children of my own, I can imagine how daunting it is to have this new responsibility."

"Believe me, I've gone shopping with them when they were younger," Bella says, "and without them was easier! At least when Valerie was around. Later, Aar set stern terms with them before they so much as entered a shop. Children are easy when they know where the boundaries are."

"Have you checked in with them at Fatima and Mahdi's?" Gunilla asks.

"I am working on the assumption that if there are calls to be made then they should be the ones making them," Bella says. "As a child, I discouraged my parents from meeting my playmates, believing they would embarrass me. So unless I hear otherwise, I won't call. They'll call me when they're ready to come home."

"They are lovely children," Gunilla says.

"I hope you'll get to meet them," Bella says.

"I have met them twice," says Gunilla. "The first time when I went camping with them and Aar."

Bella had forgotten. "I'm sorry," she says. "Of course you did. Forgive me for having forgotten. Maybe we'll do that again," she adds softly. "I mean, camp."

"I'd like that very much," says Gunilla.

Bella feels that if the difference between formality and familiarity is made obvious by a speaker's use of *tu* or *vous* in French or *tu* or *Lei* in Italian, then she and Gunilla have now gone beyond addressing each other formally and can assume they share amity, a closeness born out of mutual trust and potential friendship.

And suddenly Bella's imagination is flying ahead into a future with the children—one in which Gunilla reencounters the children, but not at a restaurant or on a trip, but at a proper meal in that kitchen, where no one has cooked regularly for months. Surely Aar, who had to look after his children on top of traveling a great deal and often working late into the night, had neither the energy nor the desire to entertain. Her mind races with plans to explore the country with the children and learn to love it with them and think of it as her own. She will organize camping trips, visits to places of interest in the suburbs of Nairobi. She'll encourage them to improve their Swahili and think of themselves as citizens of Kenya.

Her thoughts come back to the present as the car comes to a stop at the gate. The guard waves them in, and they park and bring their purchases into the house, sharing the intimate mundane task of putting them away in the fridge and pantry.

When they are finished, Bella offers Gunilla a drink. Compared to many Swedes Bella has known—and even compared to Valerie or Padmini—Gunilla is a modest drinker. It takes her a whole hour to finish her one glass of red wine. "I've learned from Aar to enjoy the pleasures of life and delight in the mercies that life has afforded us, always remembering that while we have plenty millions of others have nothing," she says. "So what's the hurry? Take it easy. Life is in no rush, so why rush?"

Bella recognizes her brother through and through in this sentiment. "How true!" she says, finding herself once again near tears.

"Since I met Aar," Gunilla continues, "I no longer drink hard liquor, and I no longer take even wine when I am alone; I do that only in company and only after work. This modest drinking is rather uncommon among Nordic expatriates, you might have noticed," she says with a smile. "Those among the UN staff who have seen me in Aar's company say, 'What next?'"

"What do they mean, 'What next?'"

"They are wondering if the next time we meet, I'll be wearing the hijab," Gunilla says. "I tell them, 'Don't be daft,' because they are daft. After all, Aar was a thoroughly secular man, cosmopolitan in his temperament, very modern in his thinking, soft-spoken and unassumingly humble."

Now it is Gunilla's turn to tear up. She rummages in her handbag for a tissue but finds none. Bella looks around, frustrated at how difficult it is to find even ordinary things in an unfamiliar house, especially one in which teenagers live. Gunilla says, "Pardon me," and she is gone for a few minutes. When she returns, she is carrying a large packet of tissues.

"And here is something for you, Bella, dear," she says.

At first Bella thinks Gunilla means the tissues. And then she sees that she is holding out an intricately wrapped package firmly sealed with tape. Bella receives it with both hands.

"What is it? What's in it?" she asks, thrilled and surprised.

"It is a gift from me to you," says Gunilla. "Open it."

"I love gifts," says Bella.

She is so eager to see what it is that she tugs at the tape impatiently. But the tape is stubborn, and she is about to resort to her teeth when Gunilla has the presence of mind to get up and fetch a pair of scissors, whose mysterious location she clearly knows well.

Bella gazes down at the gift, remembering a line from a poem by

Apollinaire: *"La joie venait toujours après la peine."* It's a collection of photographs: Aar with friends at a party; Aar with Gunilla and the children camping; Aar in Nepal, India, Bangladesh, and Burma; Aar with Gunilla in Istanbul. Bella has never seen any of them before. And they are good, very good, every single one of them.

"They're Aar's," says Gunilla. "I've put them together for you and the children."

"Grazie, carissima Gunilla!"

She receives the present with out-and-out joy, appreciative of the time and thought Gunilla has put into arranging them in an album and giving it to her and the children.

Bella embraces Gunilla, who says suddenly, "That reminds me. We had a phone call earlier today at the office from an elderly Italian lady. She said her name was Marcella and that she'd been ringing every UN office in Nairobi trying to reach someone who knew you."

Bella sits up with a worried look. "Maybe Marcella called me on my Italian mobile number, which has been turned off since my arrival here. And Marcella hates e-mails so we've never communicated that way. We always use the telephone. That is typical Marcella, seventy-five and still volunteering in a Rome hospital. And you know what? She delivered me. Anyhow, what message did she leave?"

"She said to tell you, *'Come mai ti sei perduta?'*"

Bella asks Gunilla, "Do you know what that means?"

"My Italian isn't perfect, but I thought she was telling you that you should be getting in touch with her. You're lost or something, *perduta?* No?"

Relieved, Bella relaxes. She will call Marcella in the morning. And now Gunilla reverts to more Swedish ways. They chat and drink some more as if one or the other of them were going to go away at the break of dawn, never to be seen again. Gunilla promises that each glass will be her last, but they keep unearthing memories and anecdotes about Aar that they want to share. They page through the album together, Aar's photos inspiring further recollections.

Eventually, they are too exhausted to talk, and Bella offers Gunilla a place to sleep, but Gunilla declines. "No," she says. "I'm sober enough, and tomorrow I have to work. I'll call you to let you know I got home okay."

"Till tomorrow, then," says Bella.

Later Bella starts to retrieve Aar's computer from under the mattress, but she can't bear the notion of any more incursions into his privacy tonight. Granted, she knows many things about him that no one else knows, but it is also increasingly evident to her that there are many, many things he did not tell her and that there are even things he didn't want her to know.

She leaves the laptop where it is and goes into the bathroom to brush her teeth. Just as she comes out of the bathroom, Gunilla rings. She has arrived safely, thank you. And with relief in her mind, Bella sets the alarm and goes to sleep.

15.

Today, things are not going swimmingly for Valerie. She is not getting anywhere with her plan to ease her way back into Salif's and Dahaba's hearts. She speaks to Dahaba, when the girl is at Fatima and Mahdi's, and makes an attempt to woo her with the pleasant-sounding idea of a trust in her and Salif's names. But Dahaba says she doesn't understand what "trust" means in this context or how it works to her and Salif's benefit, and suggests that Valerie discuss the matter with Salif, "who is smart and bound to know the legal and other ramifications." She then adds, "And please remember to talk about the matter to Auntie Bella, who, so far as I know, is our legal guardian."

It is evident from Dahaba's choice of vocabulary that she has a better grasp of legal matters than she claims. It's also evident that she is not keen on taking a position on what her mother is suggesting. She signs off with a quick and unconvincing "Take care, Mum, I love you," then runs off to join her friends, and gives her mobile phone to Salif.

Salif is very short with Valerie when she speaks to him, partly because it is the second time she has interrupted him during this visit with his friends. The first time she interrupted his chess game with

Zubair, and when he went back to the game, he could not regain his focus and he lost to Zubair—Salif hates losing a chess game to Zubair, of all people! This time he is even more annoyed as he immediately suspects that his mother's latest move is nothing short of a ploy to cheat him and his sister out of their rightful assets. "You are scheming to sabotage the smooth running of our lives in any way you can," he tells her curtly, "and we won't buy into it." Then, just as Dahaba did, he makes kissing sounds into the phone, saying, *"Arrivederci,* Mum," and hangs up.

Padmini, who stood by yesterday afternoon listening in on Valerie's conference calls with her lawyer and Gunilla, is of the opinion that both the lawyer and Gunilla were less than enthusiastic about the idea of creating a trust. In her view, Gunilla, in fact, seems biased in favor of Bella. Padmini suggests that it was foolish of Valerie to suggest herself immediately as the trustee. In her opinion, Valerie should have made no mention of the trusteeship at all at the outset.

"I have to be the principal trustee," Valerie insists.

"Why?" Padmini asks.

"Because I am the only living parent."

"If that is what you are trying to do, then you better get the children on your side, especially Salif, who is no fool."

Now, with the telephone dead in Valerie's hands after Salif has rebuffed her, Padmini says, "This is not working out, darling, so give it up." And as if in accordance with Valerie's sense that the hotel room has started spinning, a glass precariously balanced on the edge of the nightstand falls to the floor, spilling the dregs of last night's liquor and shattering on contact with the hard wooden floor.

But Valerie is as dead to the world outside her head as she is alive to the obsession that has taken hold within it, the idea that she believes will allow her to play a part in her children's lives, giving her a chance to make up for her earlier failings. Padmini says nothing, because she knows from experience that when Valerie is in the grip of an idée fixe there is no convincing her of anything she doesn't wish to hear and that Valerie, being Valerie, will not give up the hope of achieving her ambitions until either success dances attendance upon her or she stares into the ugly face of defeat.

Padmini comes from a traditional background of the Southeast Asian variety—never mind that she was born in Uganda and raised in Britain. She was brought up in a monogamous household—never mind if her parents' arranged marriage was a happy one or not. The fact is that the idea of unknotting the marriage ties linking her and her husband together was not only shocking but also unthinkable to either of her parents.

Valerie's background, Padmini knows, is different. The lifestyle in which she was raised is of the European—that is to say, British—variety. Add to this her father's career as an actor, his drunkenness, his infidelities, and his predatory sexual behavior, imposing himself on his young daughter. Valerie is unlike most women Padmini has known. She is a woman apart, a woman who sets her own tradition, different from everyone else's, while claiming to be continuing that tradition into which she was born. Valerie had left Aar and her children to be with Padmini and before that had done the same to a number of other lovers, abandoning each as she started a liaison with another. So Padmini knew from the beginning not to be surprised if Valerie erred in her ways, whether with a man or a woman.

And yet Valerie and Padmini have always seen their rapport as special. Not for them the rows over betrayal that have caused several of the couples they know to go their separate ways. Or so it was until a few years ago in Cape Town.

They were visiting during Gay Pride Week, staying with like-minded friends in Simon's Town. Padmini was so much in love with life in Cape Town that she suggested to Valerie that they consider relocating there. Valerie seemed to be falling in love with Cape Town too. She'd discovered a gym in Claremont that she liked, and she started going every day, returning later and later with an air of something different about her. When Padmini asked what was going on, Valerie had no explanations to offer. She said only, "We aren't married, are we?"

Padmini went off her rocker. Such was her anger that she threw her mobile phone at Valerie. When she missed and hit the wall, shattering the phone, her fury reached epic heights. The fight escalated, with unforgivable words exchanged until finally Valerie shrieked, "You know what I like about her? Her cunt doesn't stink." She meant to inflict pain, and she did. Then words were not enough, and Padmini tore into Valerie, the two of them struggling like bitches in heat.

When their hosts returned from work, they found themselves staring at broken chairs, tables with no legs, splintered mirrors, and doors without handles. They couldn't make out what had happened, since neither Padmini nor Valerie would tell them. Maybe their hosts worked it out on their own or maybe they didn't, but they stopped asking.

For Padmini and Valerie, what happened during that week in Cape Town remains the elephant in the room, and neither will admit to seeing it. From that day on, they've avoided any kind of conflict that might lead them back to such a precipice. Sometimes, when it threatens, one or the other of them will say, "Cape Town," and the reminder is enough to check their rage. But the rift that happened there has never fully mended, and it has left Padmini with the suspicion that Africa itself may not be good for them.

Already they have approached acrimony on this visit over who is to blame for the fact that Dahaba came upon them on the night they were Bella's guests in what is still, technically speaking, Aar's house. Was it

Padmini's fault for not staying in the sofa bed or was it Valerie's for inviting Padmini into her bigger, more comfortable bed?

Padmini, for her part, has been trying to support Valerie however she can, even though she does not wholly agree with the way Valerie is going about things. After all, Valerie stood steadfastly by her side through all the difficulties in Uganda, which stemmed from an ancient dispute involving her family. And she is sensitive to the difference between her mission there, which was purely financial, and how much is at stake for Valerie emotionally with her children.

Still, the ups and downs are hard to weather. Valerie's conversations with Dahaba and Salif have sent her into a dramatic oscillation between frantic busyness approaching mania and almost total inertia, accompanied by a significant increase in alcohol intake. Meanwhile, their plans for the future—whether to return to their restaurant business in Pondicherry or relocate to Nairobi if Valerie finds a footing in the lives of her children—hang in the balance. Each time they make love after one of their quarrels, they talk and talk before they fall asleep, and Padmini reassures Valerie that she is innocent of blame, and as Padmini drifts off, she hopes that the morrow will bring peace back to their lives. But nothing of the sort has happened—and Valerie is all the more obsessively driven in her pursuit.

Now Valerie is gathering some of her things, as if readying to go out: wallet, room key, and body lotion.

"Where are you going, love?" Padmini asks.

"I am not going anywhere."

But despite what she says, Valerie continues to pack her handbag, putting into it combs, a hairdryer, a change of underwear, a pair of pants, and a couple of shirts.

"Why are you fretful?"

"Because I am getting ready."

"Cape Town" threatens.

Valerie is on the edge. And no wonder. She has slept and eaten little and drunk a lot as she schemes about how to lay her hands on the treasures that appear close, within reach—if only! There is nothing that would delight Valerie more than to forge some closeness with her children, and after that, oversee a trust in their name. And if Padmini is unhappy because Valerie closes a deal in which the children become her own again and the problems with the trust are hammered out the way she likes, then it is just too bad, she thinks. Padmini can go where she pleases. As a matter of fact, Valerie believes that since Padmini has never been a mother, there are certain maternal instincts that evade her comprehension. The same is true of Gunilla. And if only Bella were not here to spoil things and deny Valerie's ambitions—ambitions that are for the good of the children, she is sure. She says to Padmini, "Blame it on Bella and Gunilla, dear."

Padmini has been intent on averting disaster, but at this she cannot help but say, "I wonder who Adam would blame if there were no Eve?"

Valerie takes her handbag and heads for the door.

Padmini asks again, "Where are you going, love?"

"To the bar in the hotel to have a stiff drink."

"Isn't it a little early in the day?"

"You are most welcome to join me," says Valerie.

She closes the door behind her and runs down the flights of steps, not pausing until she takes a seat in the bar. Her back is to the wall as she waits for someone to take her order and watches men and women coming and going, white-shirted, khaki-trousered, well-primed specimens every one of them. How Valerie hates them; they remind her of her father.

A waiter sporting a well-tended hairdo, yellow lips, and a nervous smile asks, "Anything, madam?" He smells of Lifebuoy soap.

"Two whiskies, three tots in each, plenty of ice on the side, and two glasses of water, please." She adds, "My friend is joining me shortly," even though she knows this is untrue. She will drink everything, just as she has done every day for the past few days in secret binges Padmini has not detected.

"Yes, madam," he assures her.

"We can put the drinks bill on the room, right?"

The waiter leans down to whisper as if he were sharing a confidence with her—how his body smells, despite the Lifebuoy, she thinks. "I'm sorry, madam, cash up front. That is the hotel policy for hard liquor."

"You go and get it," she says.

"Cash up front, as I've just said, madam."

Valerie can't decide with whom she is angrier, the waiter, Gunilla, Bella, or the children, the multiple sources of her troubles. And to top it all off, she discovers that her wallet is bereft of cash. Enough. She is sober still, sober enough to decide she won't be bullied by a Kenyan smelling of soap.

When she gets back to the room, Padmini is reading and doesn't even bother to look up from her book, pretending she hasn't noticed Valerie's return. It is broad daylight, but Valerie gets under the covers and, weighed down with depression, goes straight to sleep.

Qamar and Salif are lying side by side on the bed with their shoes on, their heads on huge cushions, passing a cigarette back and forth. The windows are wide open and the two ceiling fans are doggedly running, producing scant air. Through the wall, they can hear the sounds of Zubair and Dahaba shrieking with laughter as they play computer games. Salif's phone rings.

"Are you having a good time, darling?" Bella asks.

"Yes, Auntie, we are, thanks." Indeed, they have been having a splendid visit, eating too much chocolate, smoking, gossiping about their friends, and taking turns telling tall tales to one another. Salif is aware that Dahaba is stiff with worry about their mother's unscrupulousness. But he will assure Dahaba, when they are alone in their house later, that he knows a lot more than his mum does about the existing will, his father having confided this to him. Their father was more worried about the legion of his so-called Somali relatives who, like vultures, would descend to make their clan-based claim on his children and Bella's inheritance were he to die without a will. This is why the will names Bella, his closest living blood relative, as their legal guardian.

"Will you be ready if I come to pick you up in half an hour?" asks Bella.

"Is it okay if you come in an hour instead?"

"Yes, it is. See you in an hour." And Bella hangs up.

"I've been wondering," Qamar says, trailing off.

Salif teases. "Keep going; keep wondering."

Qamar asks, "How binding is the will of a dead person?"

Qamar has probably spoken to Dahaba, who is understandably worried about their mother's talking the way she did about trusts, with Bella seemingly unaware of her machinations. He can imagine why Dahaba would want to know if their father's will would protect them.

"Wills are more than a word given, they are written and signed in the presence of witnesses," says Salif. "And they are binding. Otherwise, not honoring them might create avoidable frictions within family units, and nobody wants frictions."

Qamar draws long on the cigarette and waits for him to continue speaking. She holds the cigarette away from her face until he passes her the ashtray. Then she brushes the ash off and passes the cigarette back to him.

Salif takes a puff, and as he blows rings of smoke out, he thinks about cremations and what the Zoroastrians do: construct a raised structure on which the recently dead is exposed to scavenging birds. He cannot determine which is worse: to be interred in the ground, cremated, or become food for scavenging birds.

Qamar says, after having a toke on the cigarette, "How do you know all this, about the enforceability of wills, I mean?"

Salif replies, "My dad explained it to me."

"Why would he tell you that sort of thing?"

"It is as if he knew that our mum would one day turn up and make unenforceable claims. So he warned me about it and said to rely only on Bella, whom he would make our legal guardian in the event he preceded her."

"My dad never spoke about this type of thing to me."

"Maybe your situation is different and he needn't do that."

"Or maybe . . ."

"You see, Dad hoped I'd become a lawyer," says Salif.

Salif receives the cigarette now that it is his turn to have a puff, then closes his eyes after drawing on it, holding the smoke in his mouth and releasing it gently.

"I think your mum has her madcap ideas," says Qamar.

Salif has a hungry long draw on the cigarette for a second time before passing it to Qamar. And then he feasts his eyes on the well-presented series of photos of a young and an old Nina Simone and of Miles Davis playing a gig in a dive in Japan. Salif prefers African music in all its forms to American or European music. He has a stash of records from all over the continent and is disinterested in rock, country, or any music from elsewhere. And he doesn't make a statement with his choice of music. Qamar is a statements girl and declares that jazz is the music to cherish. Curiously, when the two talk about jazz, literature, or

anything serious, they speak in English, in which they feel more comfortable. They lapse into Somali when the topic is one of immediate concern: cigarettes, food, cinema money, or cash for more mobile
phone minutes. At present, they are speaking in Somali interspersed
with English words.

"Ever listen to Somali music?" Salif asks.

"I've had Somali music up to here." Qamar touches her throat. "I
had to listen to it as a child every time I got into the car, being picked
up from school or taken shopping. Also, if I want to hear Somali music,
I go downstairs: My mother has it on all the time. Except we seldom
hear it in the house lately because Mum is in no mood to play music, any
music, these days."

"But you are your own person now, or so you think."

"Where are you going with this?"

"You become more tolerant of the choices other people make when
you are your own person. A girl your age with your background should
allow others to make their choices and not take things in a personal
way, as one does when one is a child. Wouldn't you agree?"

The cigarette is finished. Qamar picks up the ashtray, steps into the
adjoining bathroom, empties the ashtray into the toilet, and flushes it
before she returns to the bed.

She says, "Have we become our own persons?"

"Listening to your parents' choice of music and fussing are run of
the mill experiences during the transition from the person our parents
want us to be and the person we eventually become. Along the way,
one loses a few things and gains others."

"Life is boring, life is exciting."

Qamar takes a sip of water from the glass on her side of the bed.

Salif says, "I bet it would be tedious to eat caviar in the morning, caviar in the afternoon, and caviar in the evening. In the end, you would want to eat anything but caviar."

As the children of Somali parents in exile, they have each been drilled in Somali identity. Yet Qamar remembers when she once asked one of her uncles in English to pay for an ice cream cone and he answered that he would do so only if she made the same request in Somali. She refused to oblige, choosing to forfeit the treat rather than be forced to do something against her will. When she repeated the anecdote to Salif, he said she was being foolish. Qamar retorted, "I am not someone's project. Speak Somali or else? I won't. And I can live comfortably without ice cream, thank you."

Salif now says, "In Somalia, a woman is not thought of as a complete person in her own right. She has become male society's project in the making, which is why we refer to 'women's organizations' as 'mothers' organizations.' The same is true of Kenyan society, in fact, more so than in Somali society. You will notice that every older man is addressed as 'Father,' which I see as part of the project. In short, I think that African societies view having children as an integral part of project making."

"I won't think of myself as part of anyone's project."

"Will you have children or not?"

"Supposing I do?"

"Then you will be complying with society's wish."

"No, I won't."

"Yes, you will."

"Don't you talk like that to me," Qamar said.

"Anything that requires advance planning is just a project by another name. If, from the look of things, children do well, then the project has been a great success. Look at you and me: We are but seeds projected from our ancestral Somali tree. It's too bad we Somali off-spring are unable to have direct knowledge of the country and its cultural nuances. The very parents who want us to become and remain Somali tell us it is unsafe for us to go there."

"They have a point," Qamar says.

"Don't I know it?"

"You've no business putting your life at risk," says Qamar.

"Yet the European passport on which I travel is to me a mere document permitting me to legally board flights, fill in forms, go into and out of other lands—and have some form of identity."

"Why do you have a European passport?" Qamar asks. "Was it via your mum?"

"No," says Salif. "Our EU passports were granted to us thanks to my dad's working for the UN. Another way of gerrymandering the boundaries of identity."

"Hence the question," Qamar says.

"Question, what question?"

"What does it mean to be Somali in this day and age?"

"What about your Kenyan papers?"

"Our father obtained Kenyan citizenship through bribery after living here for decades as an undocumented refugee."

"I had no idea."

"Yes, they were declared stateless when they first arrived, along with all the other Somalis fleeing the civil war. Eventually, they got Kenyan papers, but I do not think of myself as a Kenyan since I am not welcomed as such. I am Somali, and my loyalty is to Somalia, which I've never visited and do not know. My attitude toward Kenya will change the day the people of this country accept me as Kenyan and do not tell me to go back to my own country!"

Salif says, "Our hearts are not where our papers are."

He lights yet another cigarette, but when he passes it to Qamar, she shakes her head no.

"Who knows what will become of people like us?" she says.

"We are difficult to define, aren't we?"

Dahaba calls to Salif. He stubs out his cigarette and Qamar hides the ashtray before Dahaba appears in the doorway, leaning against the jamb.

"Do I smell what I think I smell?" says Dahaba.

"What's your beef, Dahaba?" says Salif.

She furrows her forehead and holds her nose in disapproval. "You promised!" she says.

"Promised what?" challenges Salif.

"You promised our father."

"Were you with us when I promised?"

"No, I wasn't, but you told me."

"Anyway, what is your point?"

"You swore you'd quit smoking."

A sudden unease dominates the room. Salif gets out of bed and stares at Dahaba, annoyed; Qamar looks sheepishly away.

Dahaba says, "I'll tell on both of you."

But just as Dahaba prepares to leave the room, looking as if she might indeed report them to one of Qamar's parents or make a phone call to Auntie Bella, Salif says, "Listen, Dahaba." He has a look of mischief on his face. "You may tell on us to anyone you choose as long as you don't tell Qamar what happened last night, since you've already shared it with Zubair."

"How do you know I told him?"

"Something tells me that you have."

Salif has Dahaba's total attention and Qamar's too.

"What happened last night?" Qamar asks. She looks from Dahaba to Salif and back.

Salif is trying to rattle Dahaba's cage, but he hopes she realizes that telling on him won't help anyone.

Qamar says, "Will someone tell me what happened last night?" She turns on Dahaba. "I thought we shared everything, you and I?"

Dahaba tenses. "You tell her," she says to Salif.

"No, you tell her. You saw what happened with your own eyes. I didn't."

Qamar says to Dahaba, "Let us trade secrets."

Dahaba says, "It all started with a YouTube video that Dhimbil, a distant cousin on our father's side who lives in Kampala, forwarded to Salif. Salif, being mean, wouldn't share it with me."

"Cool. And then?"

Dahaba tells what she saw at their house, her mother and Padmini "doing it." And then her phone rings. It's Bella, who says, "My darling, I am waiting in the car outside the door. Since I do not want to disturb Fatima or Mahdi because they may be napping, would you give them my best and thank them and come to where I am parked?"

And before Qamar can say anything, Dahaba and Salif run off to join Bella in the car.

Driving away from Fatima and Mahdi's house, Bella is in a good mood and so are the children. She is getting the hang of how Nairobi works, and she is also getting the hang of how these children work. She prods them less about what has been said by whom because she is beginning to realize that the young are like sieves when it comes to secrets, which they share as readily as they would share a sandwich.

Salif has forfeited his turn in the front seat to Dahaba, who jumped at it and thanked him. Nevertheless, Bella smelled cigarette smoke on

Salif's clothing when they hugged, and she plans to have a word with him on the subject when the time is right. It's a waste to speak to the young when they are not ready to hear you, she is learning; you need to speak to them at a time and in such a way that they think they are the ones who made the choice.

Back at home, they assemble in the kitchen and Bella first shows them the big album she made out of the photos she brought from Rome. And then she shares with them the album that Gunilla presented to her. She must call Marcella, she reminds herself, but right now she is enjoying what the children are doing, sitting side by side, delighted with what they see: photographs of Bella; of Hurdo, their Somali grandmother in Canada; their father back when he was writing his dissertation. A photo of baby Salif and one of baby Dahaba, Bella with Salif in a kindergarten in Geneva, learning his alphabet in French. Padmini with Rajiv, whom neither child remembers.

Salif says, "How long did it take you to collect these photographs, and where did they come from? They are quite something, very much worth the effort."

Bella asks them both if they remember Gunilla.

"But of course we remember her," Dahaba says.

"She was our father's lover for a time," Salif says.

Bella pretends not to have heard his assertion.

"Gunilla brought many of them last night in an album of photographs that she gave to me, and the other album I brought with me to give to you."

Salif says, "That is brilliant."

Dahaba says, "I'd love to see Gunilla again."

"What about you, Salif?"

"We both liked her. Gunilla was fun."

"I'll ask her to come to dinner," Bella says.

"That will be great."

Then the children retreat to their rooms, text messaging or consulting websites of one sort or another or listening to music of their choice until dinner is ready and Bella shouts to them to come down and eat.

Valerie's mobile phone squeals, breaking into the late-afternoon silence in the hotel room. It rings on and on, and Padmini does not pick it up. Valerie has been in the bathroom forever, doing who knows what. Eventually, the phone stops ringing, and Padmini thinks, what a relief.

Today, Padmini has been finding Valerie more difficult to deal with by the hour. The time has come, she thinks, for them to question whether there is any point in staying on in Nairobi. Padmini hasn't yet shared her worries about their mounting expenses with Valerie because her partner has the pie-eyed look of someone who has been in her cups for days. Padmini is coming around to thinking that it is time they cut their losses, just as they did in Kampala, and return to Pondicherry, where, according to the sign they put on the door, they are due to reopen their hotel and restaurant in less than a week.

Valerie's phone rings again, and again Padmini lets it ring until it stops. But when the ringing begins again, with still no sign of Valerie, Padmini picks it up and answers.

"Is that Val?" The woman on the other end of the line has a heavy Teutonic accent, and she sounds supremely self-assured. "This is Ulrika Peters. Remember?"

Padmini explains that she is answering Val's phone. A short pause follows as Ulrika absorbs this information.

Ulrika says, "You met us, you and your English rose, Val, last night, remember? She said to call and maybe we could meet up and have a little more fun."

"Where would you like to meet?" says Padmini. She is playing for time as she tries to figure out if this is the beer-guzzling Oktoberfest-type giant with the iron handshake who so impressed her and Valerie last night with her heroic drinking abilities and her carrying on with the women on either side of her. Nipple pinching and toe sucking in public! The things some people go for, thinks Padmini. But maybe Valerie would like that sort of thing.

"At Bar in Heaven again," says Ulrika, "the friendliest bar in all of Nairobi. The best bar on the entire continent, except perhaps for a couple of bars in De Waterkant in Cape Town."

Do not mention Cape Town again, please, prays Padmini to herself. But to Ulrika she says, "And when?"

"Tonight, why not?"

"Just a second, please," says Padmini. "I need to consult with Valerie." She knocks on the bathroom door.

"Go ahead," says Ulrika. "I will wait."

"What's happening?" says Valerie, heavy-tongued, emerging from the bathroom with toothpaste on her chin and her hair carelessly brushed.

"An invite is happening," says Padmini.

Valerie says, "Tell me more!"

Padmini tells her. "What say you?"

"I say let's go! Let's drink and be merry."

Padmini hesitates, her hand over the phone, taking in Valerie's condition. Then she tells Valerie that she will accept, on condition that Valerie rests up and refrains from drinking until they get to the bar. Into the phone, she says, "What time do we meet there?"

"Ten o'clock."

"See you at ten."

Padmini calls room service and orders a club sandwich for them to share and a glass of milk for Valerie instead of her usual sundowner. Then they sleep until just past nine.

They rise and shower in turn, and then Valerie calls the concierge to order a taxi for ten-fifteen. "Let's get there half an hour late," she says to Padmini by way of explanation. "We don't wish to appear too eager, right?"

"Okay by me," says Padmini. But she can see that Valerie is wide-eyed with anticipation.

"We're going to enjoy ourselves, you'll see."

Padmini is not so sure about that. But she is glad for an excuse to get out of their stifling, expensive room.

"This calls for a celebration, I'd say." Valerie brings out a bottle of chilled champagne, and Padmini, conceding defeat, gets two glasses. Valerie opens the bottle and Padmini puts out some French cheese, her favorite, on a low table, along with a baguette wrapped in the front page of *The Independent* and a stash of white and dark chocolates.

As they eat and drink, Padmini reads a news story to Valerie from the front page of *The Independent*, which is a week old. The article cites a letter from an eight-year-old English girl to a British MP who was quoted as saying that gay couples are not fit to raise children. In her letter, the girl describes herself as the happy daughter of a lesbian couple and tells the MP that she is "perfectly fine . . . a real child with two mothers, who are real people with real feelings." The girl closes by writing, "You can be brought up well by anyone who loves and cares for you and who makes sure that you are happy."

The paper has withheld the identity of the girl and her parents. Padmini and Val now debate the merits of this. Padmini questions whether it's right to withhold the name of the girl while publishing the MP's. Valerie retorts that no newspaper in Britain would dare publish the name of a minor without the approval of a parent or guardian. "She could be bullied at school or worse. And maybe it's out of deference to the mothers' feelings."

Padmini asks, "Do you think they care what others might say about them?"

"Their situation is unlike ours."

"How so?"

"We are in Africa."

"And your children are not only half African but also Somali and Muslim," says Padmini. "Somalis are bigots, every single one of them. They would delight in burning us at the stake. They see us as deviants, worse than devil worshippers, and they believe we deserve commensurate punishments."

"And you think the West is so much better?"

"There is no depth to the commitment, despite the laws on the books. But at least we can go to sleep at night confident that we won't be arrested just because we are gay."

Valerie says, "You know, Pad, Aar came to accept our relationship in the fullness of time, and so did my mother, especially after knowing what my father did to me. But not your parents."

Padmini says, "And Bella?"

"Neither she nor Aar is your typical Somali or typical African," Valerie says. "I think it's because their mother was ahead of her time."

Carried away by the prevailing positive mood, Valerie wonders aloud, "I wonder whether we can persuade Salif and Dahaba to throw in their lot with ours."

"You mean, come with us to India?"

"Why not?"

"Who knows?" says Padmini. "The idea might excite them. The subcontinent is a much bigger world than either of them has known. Don't they say, 'See the elephant; see the world'?"

"And if living in India doesn't much take their fancy, we should be open to the idea of moving to Britain. You wouldn't mind if we did that?" Valerie asks.

"Not if it is the only option open to us," says Padmini. Her straying hand touches Valerie's cheek, and before long, they are making love in a way they haven't for a long time. Then they go down to the waiting taxi and head off into the night to join Ulrika.

From the outside, the nightclub looks uninviting. The building is composed of a ground floor constructed along utilitarian lines that can accommodate any use: workshop, fitness center, or a place of worship. Inside, however, a lick of paint and a raised ceiling have transformed it. At one end of the floor, there is a bandstand where a group of women is playing. At the other is a long bar with stools and tables and chairs, for which there is an extra charge. Tonight all the tables are taken, and the dance floor is full.

As soon as Padmini spots Ulrika sitting in her own special corner, a little away from the other tables and farthest from the music, she recognizes her as the big-boned but well-honed woman she remembers. She also remembers her suddenly as the woman who made a pass at her the other night and had the gall to call her the "brown beauty." But she lets Valerie lead her by the hand through the melee of drinkers and dancers and busy waitresses. When they get to Ulrika's table, she welcomes them with a hug and kiss, and then introduces them to two African women who are sitting with her. What a promiscuous woman you are, Ulrika, thinks Padmini.

Ulrika explains that the owner of the club is a Kenyan, a former lover of hers, and Ulrika was one of the first investors in the venture, which has been a roaring success. The special table is her perch. She turns to Valerie. "Dammit, I forgot to bring the two books I promised you."

Valerie looks as if she can't for the life of her remember anything about any books, but she says, "No worries. Maybe next time." But Padmini says, "What books?"

"Jeanette Winterson's *Why Be Happy When You Could Be Normal?* and Jackie Kay's most recent novel, which is set in part in Nigeria, where her birth father hails from." Ulrika flags down a waitress and asks what they want to drink. "You are my guests," she says, with the same Teutonic certitude Padmini heard on the phone. "The first round is on me."

"What is a giant German woman doing in Kenya?" Valerie asks. "I am curious."

Ulrika tells them that she makes her living as a masseuse. Well over six feet tall, with a laugh to match, she also has a larger-than-life generosity of spirit that leaves her open to new ideas and new ways of having fun. Her business is booming too. It's adjacent to her home, in several thatched huts, each with its own Jacuzzi. There's also a swimming pool of Olympic proportions, a bar, and a small gym. At the extreme end of these structures is the well-appointed apartment where she lives, often alone.

"How do you mean, often alone?" Valerie asks.

"Sometimes I have guests, family, friends. And at other times, I entertain my lovers."

She is close to her parents, she says; they helped her to establish her business.

"How often do they visit?"

"Twice a year," Ulrika answers. "They spend the whole European winter here."

"And who helps you run it?"

Ulrika tells them she employs two young men, one from Cape Town and the other from Sydney, along with several African women, for the running of the business, plus a couple more that she has trained as masseuses. She adds, "I grew up in South Africa, where my father was West Germany's consul." She explains that her father always insisted on sending her to the same schools as the locals and not, say, to the German school in Cape Town, so Ulrika has always felt more comfortable in the company of Africans.

"And whom do you cater to?" asks Valerie.

Padmini can see that the idea of Ulrika's working on her body turns Valerie on, and, sure enough, Valerie says, "Can I book a session?"

The band launches into a cover of a popular song by a Congolese group, and the two Africans sitting next to Ulrika invite Padmini to dance with them. By the time they return to the table, Ulrika and Valerie are deep in conversation.

"I've always dreaded what would become of my body," Ulrika is saying, and Padmini guesses they are talking about pregnancy. Ulrika tells one story after another, and Padmini has just about fallen asleep when she hears Valerie ask, "An indiscreet question, if I may?"

"Go ahead and ask," Ulrika tells her.

"Do African women do it too—woman to woman?"

"Of course," Ulrika answers.

"Who did you have your first experience with?"

"An African girl who was several years older than I—I was nine, she fifteen, and from that day on, I've never looked at a boy. In Africa, because no one suspects women to be interested sexually in other women, people leave you alone. The idea of two women doing it is basically alien to African men. But they abhor the idea of men doing it with other men. You can see their disgust in their expressions. And yet I know many African gay men."

"Maybe it is like the Muslims and drinking."

"How do you mean?"

Valerie says, "When they come to functions at European embassies where the drinks are flowing, they ask to have their wine and other *haram* drinks put in coffee mugs so no one can see what they are drinking."

"But since Allah sees all, why bother?"

"It is for show."

"You mean saying that we have no gays is for show?"

"That's what I think."

"Maybe you are right."

"Maybe I am."

Now it is time for Ulrika and Valerie to go to the dance floor. At first Ulrika pulls Valerie close, her hands wandering all over Valerie's body. But Valerie disengages, and they dance a meter apart. For once, she is doing her best not to upset Padmini.

16.

Something goes wrong with the alarm, which insofar as anyone can tell has gone off for no reason, since no one set it when they turned in for the night. Bella is the first to emerge from her room. Then Salif comes out into the hallway too. "What the hell?" he says. They stand there, Salif in his pajamas, Bella in her robe thrown over a gown she suddenly realizes is missing the top button, listening to the alarm without talking and without the slightest sign of panic. Then, just as mysteriously as it started, it goes off.

Bella says, "What was all that about?"

Salif waits a beat, as if to be sure the alarm is really off, and then he gives a "Search me" shrug of his shoulders.

"Well, what do we do now?" says Bella.

"You want me to go downstairs and check?" Salif looks furtively around and cranes his neck over the top of the banister. "See if there is someone else in the house apart from us?"

Bella says, "Of course there is someone else besides us in this house. There is Dahaba."

"Nothing wakes her," says Salif. He picks up the phone and calls out

to the cubicle to the right of the gate outside, where the watchmen jabber away in the daytime and sleep at night even though they are supposed to be awake and on guard. When no one answers, Salif says, "I
always wonder if there is any point in hiring night guards. They never
answer the phone because they are too busy snoring."

However, as if to prove him wrong, down the stairway they see the
moving shadow of a man in uniform outside the front door, and before
either of them speaks, they see him waving up to them and then hear
his loud banging on the door. Salif goes halfway down the staircase to
ascertain that it is one of the night guards, even though he has no intention of opening the door and letting him in. He knows the man by face
and name, and they wave to each other. Relieved, Salif rejoins Bella,
who tells him, "Go now, check your sister's room, please, and see if she
is asleep, despite so much seismic racket."

He pushes open the door and vanishes for a few seconds, then reemerges to say, "Why don't you believe me, Auntie? She is asleep, her
head under her pillow."

"I was hard to awaken too when I was young."

"She reads till very late. That's why she can't wake up."

"Maybe she finds it difficult to sleep, as I did. I used to read or draw
figurines, faces of humans, or animals. I fought with our mum when
she came in and turned the lights off."

Salif stares away in the distance, as if in discomfort. Maybe he
doesn't like her to compare her younger self to Dahaba, Bella thinks.

It's the sudden silence of the house once the alarm is off that wakes
Dahaba, who, rubbing her eyes red, joins them, asking what has happened. Bella and Salif look amused, and Bella says, "Not to worry."
Dahaba and Salif are thirsty and want water to drink, and Bella wants
to have tea, so they gather in the kitchen.

Bella asks them about their conversations with their mother the previous day, and Salif tells her about Valerie's plans to found a trust. Bella knows that Valerie hasn't the wherewithal to fund a trust, or even to set one up, without Bella's tacit approval and backing, but knowing that Valerie's ploy is no real threat, she is sorry that it has backfired on her. How, Bella wonders, can she give the children and their mother a chance to arrive at a rapprochement?

Instantly it comes to her: How about inviting Valerie and Padmini along on an outing to Lake Naivasha today? They'll stop to have a picnic by the lake, and if there is time, they'll venture farther up the Rift Valley. Even better if the children are the ones who invite them.

Dahaba is enthused about the plan, but she insists that Salif make the call, not her. After all, it's Salif who was so rude to Valerie when she called him at their friends'.

"I will do it with pleasure, Auntie," says Salif, "first thing in the morning."

It is after three in the morning when they retreat upstairs, and still later when Bella leaves two presents wrapped in pretty paper outside of their bedroom doors. Then she too goes back to bed.

The alarm goes off again a couple of hours later, coinciding with the muezzin's call to prayer. As before, Bella is the first to come out of her bedroom, and once again she is joined by Salif, who, cursing, comes to her aid and turns it off.

Bella says, "We need to have the alarm serviced."

"I'll see to that, Auntie."

"Don't alarms put the fear of the Almighty into you?"

"No, because I know how to disarm ours."

"Clever boy," she says, and she asks if he wants to join her for breakfast. He accepts, and she goes downstairs to get the meal started while he takes a shower and dresses. When he walks into the kitchen after his shower, Salif is carrying the wrapped present. She pretends not to notice it until he sits at the table and unwraps it and exclaims in delight. He walks over to the stove and gives her a hug and a kiss. "How could I have missed this?" he asks. He is effusive in his thanks, although he struggles to find the words with which to express his gratitude.

"You weren't expecting it."

"I must've been exhausted too."

"Glad you like it."

"Am I ready to roll?"

"You are."

"Is there film in it?"

"Of course."

"Is it color?"

"There is a roll of color film in it, but I also bought one that is black and white from Nakumatt when I went there for last night's shop," Bella says. "I prefer the traditional in most things, and the memory of holding my first camera, putting a roll of film in it, taking photos, and then developing them is indelible. There is something hauntingly beautiful about the process itself: the feel of the photo paper, the smell of the chemicals, the anticipation of the details that will be revealed. There is none of that with the immediacy of digital photography."

Salif has already aimed the camera at her and begun to take his own pictures of her during this soliloquy, capturing the eyes she narrows as though she were focusing on an unreachably distant image. She is remembering a couple of lines from a Rilke poem—Rilke, who began to mean something to her when she visited the Castello di Duino near Trieste, where she spent three months after Hurdo's burial in Toronto. Afterward, she'd learned sufficient German that, with the help of an Italian translation, she could read the master's elegies to that beautiful place. In the poem titled "Turning-Point," Rilke alludes to the fact that even looking has a boundary and that the world that is looked at so deeply wants to flourish in love, yearns to "do heart-work / on all the images imprisoned within you."

Bella shakes herself out of her reverie. "You'd best call your mother now to see if she and Padmini will be able to join us today."

Salif dials her, looking apprehensive, but from the change in his face it is obvious to Bella that her plan has worked. Salif has woken Valerie, but once she understands why he is calling, she accepts eagerly. She says they will be at the house as soon as they can dress and shower and arrange a taxi.

"Excellent," says Bella. "Now what would you like for breakfast?"

"What are the choices?"

"I did a big shop," she says. "Come, open the fridge."

"Bacon, with bread and two eggs sunny side up if that is no problem," he says, taking out the ketchup and closing the fridge.

"Why do you say, 'If it is no problem'?"

"I thought you might disapprove, seeing that you were brought up in a Muslim household."

"I got it for you and Dahaba," she says.

"But you don't eat it yourself?"

"Not because of religious reasons."

"Why then?"

"Too salty and too fatty."

"You know what Dad used to say?"

"Remind me."

"He found the idea of eating pork abhorrent."

"But not for religious reasons, right?"

"Same as you on that score."

She places the bacon in the pan, overlapping the slices, and then puts some porridge for herself to simmer. She breaks the eggs into the pan and asks Salif to put the bread in the toaster. She doesn't turn the eggs but leaves the yolks golden and runny, just as he'd asked. She stirs her porridge and turns the bacon with a practiced hand, making her meal and his almost at the same moment so they can eat together. *"Bismillah,"* she says, and he wishes her *"Bon appétit!"*

Barely has either of them taken a mouthful when Dahaba appears in the doorway, groggily focusing on the camera next to Salif's plate.

"Why did you give it to him, Auntie?" she asks.

"Give what to whom?"

"The beautiful camera."

Bella looks at Salif in a manner that makes it clear that she does not want him to rise to Dahaba's provocation. Then she says to Dahaba, "First a good morning greeting, my darling."

"Good morning, Auntie."

"Did you sleep well?"

"I did, only I thought I heard a loud noise going off, and some people speaking in the landing above the staircase. But I was too exhausted to get up to see if any of it was real. Now it is the smell of frying bacon that has woken me. Can you make some for me, Auntie?"

"Of course, my darling," says Bella, and she gets up and gives her niece a hug and a loving kiss.

Salif speaks up. "Why don't you eat your porridge while it's nice and hot, Auntie, and I'll offer my bacon to Dahaba. I don't mind waiting a few more minutes for my own."

"Thanks, darling, but I'll make her own," Bella says. "What else would you like with your bacon?"

"Same as Salif's, except I don't like the yolks liquid. In the mean-

time, I'll pop a slice of bread in the toaster if there is some to be had."
Dahaba makes as if she will do as she says, but she moves half-heartedly,
as if hoping that someone else will beat her to it. She looks tired.

Salif makes a point of not looking in her direction as he dip slices of
his bacon in ketchup and yolk. His habit of eating his bacon this way is
part of family lore. Wendy could never abide it and thought it unre-
fined. "What are knives and forks for if not to be used, and why would
anyone bother to place them on your table if you are going to end up
behaving like some savage from Africa?" Bella can hear her saying.

Dahaba looks as if she can hardly bear the thought of waiting for her
own breakfast, but in a little while it is ready, though Bella's porridge is
now cold. She puts a lump of butter in it and microwaves it until it is
hot again, then eats it. When Bella gets up to make herself a *macchiato*,
Dahaba asks, "What is your answer, Auntie? Do you have another
camera like the one you've given to Salif or not?"

Salif can't restrain himself anymore. With a touch of sarcasm, he
says, "Yours is right outside your bedroom door, wrapped in the most
beautiful wrapping paper."

Dahaba abandons her breakfast and darts up and down the stairs
with remarkable alacrity. Yet she unwraps the present with surprising
delicacy, like someone removing a Band-Aid. Salif, impatient, offers to
do the dishes before Valerie and Padmini arrive.

Bella says, "I'll give you both a brief demo of the art of nondigital
photography. I hope you will appreciate the cameras and look after
them with great care. My hope is to train you to do your own printing
here in this house, where there is plenty of space to set up a darkroom."

Dahaba's concentration falters as she fingers the knobs on the
camera. This is the first time she has held such a camera, and it frus-
trates her that it doesn't react to her touch the way the digital camera

did. "What is the difference between digital and nondigital cameras, Auntie?" she says at last.

"Good question," says Bella, pleased. This is as good a place to start as any. And she begins to speak, picking her way through a minefield of data and information that she knows won't make much sense to novices such as Dahaba and Salif.

"Nondigital cameras differ from their analog predecessors in that they do not have film inside them, is that right, Auntie?" says Salif.

"What are analog predecessors?" Dahaba cries. "I have no idea what you two are talking about." She pleads with them to use words she can make sense of. "Analog predecessors? I know what 'predecessor' is, but not what 'analog' means. Please."

While Bella is thinking of a way to explain these concepts, Salif adds to Dahaba's confusion. "In place of having black-and-white or color films in them, digital cameras save the images they capture on a digital memory card or cards, in addition to some form of internal chemical storage."

Dahaba screams, "Stop showing off, you fool."

Bella falls sadly silent, knowing that in this, as in so much else with these children, it is not going to be easy to negotiate the obstacles. She will need time to work out a course of action that will allow Salif and Dahaba to grow into who they wish to be—not into what she wants them to be.

Valerie and Padmini's taxi drops them at the gate more than half an hour early. They are waiting to be let in. Bella suggests Dahaba put away the cameras while Salif goes and welcomes their guests. Dahaba seems to be torn between greeting her mother and partner and going upstairs to shower and get ready. Bella encourages her to do the latter, saying, "We don't want to get a late start."

Padmini enters, and she and Bella hug and exchange kisses on their cheeks. Bella observes that Padmini is a touch warmer than before. In fact, it occurs to her that the two of them have never been alone in a room before—and therefore have never had the pleasure (or displeasure) of exchanging their views on matters of common concern, namely Valerie and the children. Maybe the time has come to cultivate Padmini.

"How are things?" asks Bella. "It's lovely to have you here. You and Valerie should come and spend more time with us. Chill out, play cards, watch movies together, and get to know one another. We would all enjoy it, especially the children."

Something is making Padmini a tad uncomfortable. Bella entertains a suspicion that Padmini does not want Valerie to see them conversing or to overhear them. Bella cranes her neck, trying to see where Valerie is before she says anything. "Not to worry," she says to Padmini. "We'll have plenty of time to talk, you and I."

Then in they come, Valerie and Salif. Valerie embraces Bella, and after exchanging cursory greetings, asks, "Where is my daughter?"

"She is showering and changing," says Bella.

"Was she late in waking up as usual?"

Bella says protectively, "She was up early."

"And we all had breakfast together," adds Salif.

Bella washes her hands and dries them and offers to make coffee or tea. Padmini opts for coffee and Valerie for tea with milk and sugar.

Salif, in the meantime, goes upstairs and discovers that his sister has decided not to bother with showering. She is in her bedroom wearing a pair of many-pocketed safari pants, but she has decided she isn't happy with how they look or feel. She takes them off and puts on a pair of jeans, but they are too tight. She complains that it is all the eating they've been doing lately that has made her gain so much weight. Salif, still standing in the doorway, looks from the clothes on the bed to Dahaba and back. He urges her to get on with it. "We're going on an outing, not on a photo shoot."

But this only throws her into more of a muddle. She takes off the jeans and puts the safari pants back on. But now she can't undo the knots in the laces of her tennis shoes. Salif also observes that she has on socks mismatched in both color and size.

"I'll go ahead if you don't mind," he says.

"Give me another minute."

Salif cannot figure out why she is so nervous, nor why she is fussing about what to wear, especially in a country where outdoor clothing is an all-year affair. He importunes her to get moving when he hears their mother shouting from downstairs. "Where are my darlings?"

Bella says, "What has become of you two?"

He goes downstairs to find everyone waiting. "Dahaba will be here pronto," he says. But when she does ultimately join them, Dahaba is back in the jeans and has on a pair of sneakers different from the pair whose laces she must have failed to untangle. Salif fights back a fledgling grin forming around his lips at the memory of the many occasions when Dahaba couldn't decide what to wear, what to eat, or whether she was a friend or foe to this or that person.

Valerie says, "Are we all set?"

Dahaba nods her head. "Yes, Mummy."

"Auntie Padmini, who I understand has motion sickness, will sit in the front," says Bella. "And I will drive."

"And where is Mum going to sit?" asks Dahaba.

"In the back, between you and Salif."

Valerie wraps herself around Dahaba, and the two of them walk ahead in the direction of Aar's car. Salif hangs back to set the house alarm then locks up and hurries to join them. When they are all seated, Valerie, sandwiched between her son and daughter, whispers, "Are you okay?" to Dahaba. Dahaba says that she has an upset stomach. But when Valerie asks if she is well enough to come on the outing, Dahaba waves her away.

Salif attributes Dahaba's discomfort to nerves and her lack of control over the seating arrangements, which have deprived her of the front seat. Well, if she wanted to be present when that matter was being decided, Salif thinks, then she should have made up her mind which pair of pants she wished to wear a little sooner.

Dahaba wants to know if the restaurant where they will have their lunch has been decided on.

"I prepared all kinds of finger food yesterday when you were with your friends," Bella says. "We have drumsticks, salad, pita bread, and a couple of baguettes from that French bakery opposite the Nakumatt supermarket. Plus we have all manner of soft drinks and bottled water. I was thinking we'd have a picnic near Lake Naivasha."

Dahaba says nothing, even though it is obvious from the expression on her face that she doesn't like this either. Salif leans forward, as though he might reprimand her, but just then Bella turns on the engine, and he sits back. She adjusts her seat and programs the GPS, then voilà, bad-mannered Cawrala awakens, her voice gruff and impatient. "Out the gate, make a right." No please and no sweet words from today's grumpy guide.

At the exit, the guard opens the gate for them, smiling broadly, and then they are off on the eighty-seven-kilometer drive to Naivasha, much of it uphill.

"What would we do without GPS?" says Bella.

To everyone's delighted surprise, Dahaba is soon her usual feisty self. "We'd rely more on maps, no problem. Years ago we read maps. There was even a time when maps didn't exist, not the way they do in this day and age. Every generation finds its own answer to the questions life and its sidekicks pose. Now there is GPS. In a decade, there will be something else in its place."

"And before city maps existed, what did people do to help them go places?" asks Bella, looking into the rearview mirror, her eyes meeting Dahaba's.

"People traveled less," says Dahaba. "They were less adventurous and stayed within confined areas that they were familiar with."

Salif, presently finding his tongue, says, "Dad told me that Somalis are hardly the ideal tourists. You don't find them exploring the flora and fauna of a new place and few of them set foot in a museum. They visit their relatives or friends, that's all. If you have a Somali visiting you and you go to work in the morning, it is possible you will find him still sitting there in front of the TV when you return, waiting for you. It doesn't occur to many of them to venture out on their own, to buy a metro ticket, and to experience life in the city to which they've come until you are there to be their guide and mentor."

"You're aware he was generalizing?" says Dahaba.

"Of course he was," concedes Salif. And in the silence that follows, he points out the Muthaiga Country Club, Muthaiga Road, and Limuru Road, which will take them up the steep hill toward their destination. Everyone seems relaxed because the stop-and-go traffic they were anticipating has not materialized.

Only Salif seems unsurprised. "It's a public holiday," he informs them.

Bella asks, "In commemoration of what?"

"I forget which one, there are so many of them."

Dahaba gives her two cents' worth of theory. "One can't remember what the holidays are for when one is not entirely in sync with the national psyche."

"I don't follow your meaning," says Padmini.

Salif picks up where Dahaba has left off. "Somalis, even those who are to all intents and purposes Kenyans, do not feel part of this country. I saw a moving documentary on Al Jazeera the other evening, an original documentary put together and narrated by a Kenyan Somali, a well-respected journalist. He says that as a minority Kenyan Somalis feel politically disenfranchised, alienated from the country's body politic."

Padmini says, "Maybe it is Jomo Kenyatta Day."

Valerie asks, "Must we talk politics?"

"This is not politics, Mum," says Dahaba.

"If it is not politics, what is it?"

"It is the history of this country."

"Reminds me of the conversation I've often heard whenever two Somalis meet and, like the Irish, can't avoid talking politics—the Troubles, the massacre of year so-and-so, the IRA and who was in it and who wasn't."

"Know why the English talk less about politics?" asks Dahaba, speaking too loudly for everybody's liking because she feels she has a valid point to contribute to the conversation.

Valerie turns to Dahaba, "Why, my darling?"

"Because you don't need to talk much about politics when you have so much power you don't know what to do with it."

Although Bella is not displeased so far with the way the conversation has gone, she is also relieved that there have been no tantrums, no lost tempers. So far everybody has been making his or her point civilly. But like Valerie, Bella has had enough of this type of conversation. It's one reason she does not always like socializing with Somalis; they talk politics incessantly, cutthroat clan politics. They live and breathe it, and they never agree on anything.

To get everyone's attention, she makes the unilateral decision to turn off the GPS. There. Silence. Then she says to Salif, "What would you say are the major formations that the East African Rift has evolved into over many tens of millions of years? I know you did a class project on that."

Valerie says, "Now that will interest me."

Salif becomes self-conscious and stays silent for a second. He breathes in and then out as he thinks about the answer to the question. He says, "There is the rift known as the Gregory Rift, then there is the Western or Albertine Rift. The peoples that inhabit these formations are vastly different from one another and so are the flora and fauna, as are the great gatherings of wild and not-so-wild animals found on its grasslands, each with its own particularities. The variety of landscapes are astounding, from the Afar Depression, where the land is some five hundred feet below sea level, to snow-capped mountains that reach almost to seventeen thousand feet."

Padmini asks, "How was the rift formed?"

"Volcanic eruptions gave it its form, the same kinds of eruptions that have shaped many of the world's iconic volcanic regions."

"Have you been to the Serengeti, to the Mountains of the Moon? Have you seen the volcanoes there that are still emitting heat and smoke?" asks Padmini.

"Dad took us to all those places," Salif says.

"So you know a lot about the Rift Valley?"

Salif gives them a brief rundown of facts and figures, how the valley served generations of Ethiopians from the highlands and people from the wetlands of the Sudan; and how, during the British presence in this area of Kenya, the Masai people were pushed out of their lands into reserves, the entire landmass becoming royal property, given at will by the governor of the colony to white men to do with it what they pleased.

They are nearly there. Salif guides Bella to his favorite place. Bella finds a spot with a good view. They get out of the vehicle, and young men selling touristy merchandise surround them with frightening speed. Valerie and Dahaba snap pictures of each other, then of the spectacular scenery down below. And Salif describes from memory the various features—the huge rocks down in the valley smoothed by centuries of passing water; a body of water appearing miragelike in the distance; a forest of trees so green they appear turquoise; a volcanic crater rising from the depths of the water and resembling a tiny cave; and, of course, the beautiful islets, each unto itself.

Salif doesn't go far from the vehicle. Bella observes that Valerie and Padmini admire the knickknacks, turning them this way and that, but neither one of them purchases anything, maybe because they have no extra cash to spare.

Dahaba wants a group photograph. Everyone obliges, and they stand side by side with the vista behind them.

When they get back into the car, they fall silent, as if in awe. The valley falls away on either side of the road, which is lined by the hardwood groves the farmers use to carve their plows.

Salif says, "There are many standout spots along the way, but none is as formidable as the Rwenzori Mountains in Uganda, known to the ancient Greeks as the Mountains of the Moon, or those in the Serengeti savannah in Tanzania. And nothing is as hot or harsh as Lake Assal, in Djibouti. This is really a poor aspect of the rift's uniqueness, even if it is breathtakingly impressive."

"Did Aar become more religious in the last days of his life?" Bella blurts out the question unexpectedly, eliciting surprise from her listeners.

Valerie's expression hardens, but Dahaba is venomous. "He did no such thing."

Salif takes it easy. "Why do you ask?"

"Because I read it in a Canadian paper."

"You've never told me this," says Valerie.

"It doesn't matter," says Bella. "Let us drop it."

Salif says, "I don't think it is proper for you to say to drop it now. You've raised the issue and you said you saw mention of the claim that he became more Muslim toward the end of his life. Tell us what you meant so we understand."

"His last words were words of prayer, it was reported," Bella says. "Specifically, a verse from the Koran."

"Well, he was culturally a Muslim," says Salif.

"And very proud of it," says Dahaba.

"But he wasn't religious."

"If anything," Dahaba goes on, "he was spiritual."

"He was decidedly secular," says Bella.

"Spiritual and secular," says Dahaba.

Salif says, "But he was respectful of other people's faiths, just as he was of their way of life: Muslim, Christian, Jewish, Hindu, and the lot. He was a good example to all who knew him."

Valerie is not so much ill at ease—as she was when they were talking about politics—as irritated. "How could you say that when in all the years you and I knew him we never saw him enter a mosque and pray?"

Padmini says, "I was born and brought up a Hindu, but I seldom go to a temple to worship. Ought I to call myself secular?"

Bella stays out of it, saying nothing. She has lost interest in the discussion, which doesn't appear to be going anywhere. And lest she miss the upcoming turn, she switches on the GPS. Again she has everyone's full, undivided attention when she says, "Time to take a break. What say you?"

"Is this Naivasha?" Valerie asks.

"We are close to Lake Naivasha; it's to the left," says Salif, "about twenty minutes' drive from here. Let us go there. You'll like it."

"I like the name Naivasha," Padmini says.

"What do you like about it?" asks Dahaba.

"It has a Sanskrit feel to it."

"In what way?"

"Like, I don't know, on a par with 'nirvana.'"

Dahaba says, "Cute."

"What does it mean in the local language?" asks Padmini.

Salif replies, "The name of the lake is Anglo corrupted, which was typical of the Brits, savaging native names by anglicizing them. The Masai word the Brits bastardized is *nai'posha*, which means 'rough waters' or some such. Now everyone including Kenyans know it by its anglicized version."

"Nirvana means 'extinguish,' as in extinguish the lantern, doesn't it, Padmini?" asks Bella.

"I am not so sure, now that you've asked," confesses Padmini. "But most likely you are right."

"There is a likeness of sound," says Dahaba.

"Not meaning," says Salif.

Dahaba singsongs "Naivasha" with "nirvana," and likes what she hears.

The car is going up a hill when a truck emitting a billow of black smoke struggles up the incline and passes them, and they all shut their windows quickly until they are clear of it. Then they open them again to the welcome fresh air of the valley and Bella continues.

Cawrala tells Bella to make a left, and she does.

Dahaba says, "I can see we are in Naivasha."

This is not quite true, but it will do. They are at a spot where they have a good view of the lake, and up and over the bridge they imagine the presence of fresh water and plenty of birdlife, not to mention several escarpments.

Bella maneuvers the vehicle around potholes. They pass a low building that looks like a local watering hole, its walls festooned with ads publicizing guitar entertainment at night for its clientele. Farther down the hill, they pass several more bars. They are happy when the nefarious odor of beer is no longer in their nostrils.

About fifty meters from the lake, Bella parks the car. She stops the engine and gets out, happy they've made it all the way to this place without a quarrel. They disperse in silence in different directions, some wanting to pee, and others to enjoy the view, to stretch their legs and welcome the peaceful air into their lungs.

Dahaba hangs close to the car; she is hungry. Bella and Padmini spread out picnic mats on the uneven ground. Valerie opens the bottle of red wine she and Padmini have brought and pours a paper cupful for Padmini.

Valerie and Salif find two tree trunks close to each other and take their food and drinks and sit together. Dahaba joins them. She says, "Last time we came here, we were four. And Dad was with us. And we seemed happy. We took delight in one another's joys and laughed at the same jokes. Then Mum left. And now Dad is murdered."

Maybe because Valerie is no state of mind to hear any of this, she wants to walk away. But Salif, as if by coincidence, blocks her way and gently lays his hand on his mother's elbow. After all, knowing Dahaba well, he senses that his sister has something heavy on her mind, a weight that she wishes to rid herself of right this instant. Valerie, having no choice, sits down and listens as though she were cornered.

Dahaba asks, "Why did you leave?"

"I wish I hadn't," Valerie says, weepily.

"Was Dad awful to live with, violent?"

"No, he was gentle, too gentle."

"Was he seeing another woman?"

"No, I was the world to him."

"Why did you leave then?"

Salif listens, saying nothing.

"One day I would like to know why," says Dahaba.

And all Valerie can manage is "One day." Then she resumes weeping, her head in her hands, as though she has just this minute received the news of Aar's death.

Still Dahaba persists. "There must have been a reason, Mum." She keeps insisting, and Valerie keeps weeping, neither of them able to move on.

Salif reflects on how much more he knows than his sister. One thing he knows is that his father was not the person making his mother miserable, even though Salif suspected that Aar felt she was a lost cause. Whenever Salif relives those terrible final days together, he remembers his father going about his business as if Valerie's problems were not his concern. He recalls waking up in the wee hours of the night, his mother by herself in the kitchen, the lights off, the cap of the whiskey bottle on the table and the bottle three-quarters empty, the ashtray full of cigarette butts, the smell of the liquor heavy on her breath. And then there were those other bottles, the bottles that once contained the tablets she took morning, afternoon, and evening.

Salif doubted his father was unaware of the demons preying upon his wife. Maybe he couldn't do anything to placate them.

"Did your father tell you why I left?" Valerie says at last.

"He always said to ask you," Dahaba says.

"I don't deserve your forgiveness," Valerie says, "and I am not asking you to forget what I did, which was foolish and selfish. But I love you, I truly love you."

Meanwhile, Bella and Padmini converse in low voices, their faces turned away from each other. They fall silent when Salif approaches. Padmini suggests they pack the uneaten meal, get into the car, and leave.

Bella asks, "What is the rush?"

"We must return to the hotel," Padmini explains. "We have to start packing up."

Salif is unhappy about departing this instant, but he is a well-brought-up young man and he restrains himself. Bella acquiesces too and whispers to him, "An hour this way or three hours the other way won't matter because we can come back to this very spot whenever we please, darling."

He shrugs his shoulders and starts to pack up. When the car is loaded, Bella bangs the trunk closed and takes her seat. Padmini gets in front, seething visibly but not saying anything. They drive back to Nairobi, the mood darkened by the silence no one dares to break.

17.

Padmini is anxious to get back to the hotel, but Bella insists they all stop at the house for something to drink. She promises to drive them back later so they won't have to call a taxi.

Valerie wants a sundowner, and she makes herself comfortable on the couch, cutting the figure of a memsahib accustomed to being waited on hand and foot. Padmini offers to help make tea, though she remains tense and fidgety. Bella assigns Salif and Dahaba the task of bringing in the mats and picnic supplies and uneaten food from the car. Salif avails himself of the opportunity to suggest that Dahaba apologize to their mother.

"I can't think of a reason to apologize. Why must I?"

"Because there is nothing to be gained from cornering Mum with questions she can't answer. And in any case, what is there to say? She was in the grip of a 'love supreme,' as the John Coltrane lyric goes."

"What if I don't want to?"

"Think about it. What do you gain?"

She thinks about it, then says, "I agree with you. There is no gain."

His hand, by its own volition, touches the small of Dahaba's back.

At first the girl tenses, and then she starts to relax. She says, "I felt a need to have a showdown, to get it all off my chest."

"Now that you've done it, what then?"

"I'll do as you say, apologize."

She goes into the house and Salif stays behind to finish clearing out the trunk. He throws the rubbish in the bin and brings in the rest. He stores the unused paper cups and paper plates in the pantry and stands the mats against the wall. When he goes into the living room, he finds Dahaba nestling up to Valerie on the couch and the two of them whispering amicably in each other's ears. He heads up the stairs toward his bedroom to commune with his iPhone and his computer.

The tea made, Bella serves it to Padmini and is surprised and relieved to see mother and daughter getting on so well. She sneaks upstairs and Salif fills her in on what has transpired. "We had a word, she and I, that is all."

"Well done," says Bella.

They are still cuddling and cooing when Bella comes back downstairs, but she notices that Padmini seems more uncomfortable than before. Is it the newfound rapport between Valerie and Dahaba that is causing her current discomposure? Does it make her feel like an outsider?

Bella mulls over what she can do to help. Should she offer to settle their new heap of debt for the hotel and the lawyers to make sure the two of them make their flight and return home as scheduled? Can she persuade Padmini to allow it?

Dahaba suddenly says, "I am hungry, Mum."

"Oh, my darling, are you really?"

"Please make something," pleads the girl.

"What's to your liking, my sweet?"

Just as Valerie rises to her feet, Padmini says, "Honey, I would like to get back rather urgently to the hotel."

"What's the matter?"

"My period has arrived unusually early."

Valerie looks helpless and indecisive. "What do you want to do?" she asks.

Padmini says to Bella, "I really want to go back to the hotel to shower and change my clothes."

Bella sees how reluctant Valerie is to leave Dahaba, and she is reluctant to break up their easy rapport. "I would really like you both to stay the night," she says. "Why don't I give you a lift to the hotel and back? At this hour there will be little traffic."

"Would you mind?" says Padmini. "I would be grateful if you could."

"Would you?" says Valerie. "You don't mind."

"Of course not," says Bella.

"And I'll feed my hungry angel here," says Valerie.

Bella goes upstairs to tell Salif what she is doing and gets her wallet, grateful that the ride will give her a chance to speak in private with Padmini.

They get in the car and Bella speeds off as though they were boarding school students in danger of missing curfew.

Without prompting, Padmini opens up just as Bella had hoped. She tells Bella that her and Valerie's return tickets to India via Kampala will become void unless they use them as scheduled; they are neither extendable nor refundable. And she says that she would leave, given the choice.

"And what or who is forbidding you to?"

"Our hotel bill is enormous and we haven't the funds to settle it," Padmini explains. "We receive messages from the management on a daily basis. In short, we are in terrible trouble. But Valerie pays no heed, unconscionably running up the bill and acting as if she were impervious to these difficulties."

Bella does not tender an opinion.

"I don't know what to do," says Padmini. "Valerie's moods keep changing. More and more of the time she is sullen and depressed, and she is drinking heavily. And she can't seem to give up the hope that she will resume what she imagines to be her role as a mother."

"But given the choice, you would go?"

"Yes, I would," Padmini says. "Don't misunderstand me. I still love her, but you know!"

Bella nods her head and says, "I do. Is there anything I can do to help?"

"I would be embarrassed to ask."

"Why?"

"Valerie won't countenance the idea. And as it is, you've already been generous beyond anyone's expectations, a wonderful host. But our debt is such that it is too big a favor to burden you with."

"Let me see what I can do."

"I pray daily that the same benefactor who spared us the humiliation of the lockup in Kampala will come to our aid. I've even been to the Hindu temple once in secret to offer my devotions to that end."

With no traffic to speak of, they have reached the hotel. Padmini says to Bella, "Please give me a few minutes," and she walks away, her stride faltering.

Bella goes to the reception desk and strikes up a conversation with the clerk, who recognizes her from her own stay. After a few pleasantries have been exchanged, Bella gets to the point. She explains that she wishes to settle Valerie and Padmini's account on her own credit card.

"But of course, madam," says the clerk. Bella pays for two more nights to cover the time until their departure for India, and she demands that the receptionist not divulge the identity of the benefactor, and she gives her a tip to ensure her silence.

On the drive back, Bella's conscience weighs on her. Ought she now to open her heart to Padmini and offer her own confidences? But already Padmini seems more relaxed, thanks not only to her shower and fresh change of clothes but also perhaps to the opportunity to confide her woes to a sympathetic ear, and Bella, not wanting to disturb her mood, stays silent.

They arrive back at the house close to eight in the evening and Bella goes upstairs, buoyed by a feeling of optimism, as she replaces her wallet and passport in their secret place. Then she has a quick shower and goes downstairs, ready to eat the food Valerie has cooked. Padmini's good cheer holds, and Valerie too seems to feel more at home in the house now that she has cooked a meal in the kitchen. Dahaba shouts to Salif to come down and they sit down together.

At the dinner table, the conversation is free-flowing. Padmini is sitting at the head of the table, serving the food and solicitously asking everyone if they want more of the chicken, the sauce, the salad. Bella sees Padmini with new eyes, as an ally. The woman is no quitter, and her patience and tenderness toward Valerie seem to know no limits, even if Valerie is less constant in her loving. How will they react when they find out that someone has settled their hotel bill? Maybe gratitude is not a notion that Valerie is familiar with. Or maybe she won't be able to accept the gesture without suspicion.

Dinner over, Salif volunteers to do the washing up, wearing his headphones so he can listen to music as he does so. Valerie and Dahaba take their leave and go up to the girl's room, voices low, still engrossed in each other. Bella puts on a CD of Miles Davis playing in India, and Padmini, who is not familiar with it, seems to enjoy it. And when Salif has done the washing up, he observes that their glasses are empty and brings the wine bottle to refill their glasses.

"Thanks, my darling, for the washing up," says Bella.

"I didn't cook or serve, so I must wash."

"He's a considerate young man," says Padmini, and Bella agrees.

He smiles sweetly and says, "I've been thinking, Auntie Padmini!"

"Tell me, what have you been thinking?"

"Wouldn't it be a very wonderful idea if Dahaba, Auntie, and I came to visit you and Mum in India and stayed in your hotel in Pondicherry?"

Padmini, surprising even herself, pulls him over to where she is sitting and she gives him a kiss on the cheek, her warmest and most genuine gesture yet. "But that would be wonderful," she cries. "And it'll make your mum full of rejoicing too."

"What do you think, Bella?" asks Padmini.

"I had no idea he was thinking along those lines, but what a brilliant idea," says Bella. "Of course we would love to visit you in India and stay in the hotel." Then, the cautious adult in Bella resurfacing, she says, "Such visits benefit from early planning. Yes, that would be stupendous."

Salif adds, "We are now old enough and travel savvy enough to come on our own if Auntie Bella is unavailable to come with us."

"But we would really love for her to come too," says Padmini.

They take a collective breather, as each of them imagines the context in which this scenario might take place. For Padmini, the prospect is particularly sweet, as nearly all of the visitors to their hotel and restaurant are strangers. To have "family" visit them in India for the first time is a very exciting prospect.

Happy in themselves, Valerie and Dahaba come down and join the rest. They sit next to each other, but not in a way that excludes the others. Salif, attentive as ever, brings a soft drink for Dahaba and the wine bottle, and Bella has the honor of refilling Valerie's glass.

Valerie senses that the silence is charged with meaning and so she asks of no one in particular, "Has anything I need to know about taken place since I was last here?"

"There is news that will delight you," says Padmini. "Your son here has been speaking of his wish to visit us in Pondicherry and stay with us in our hotel, darling. Isn't that fabulous news?"

And before Valerie has had the time to react to the news, Dahaba lets out a squeal of joy, "This is what I've been thinking the past hour and a half."

"Have you, darling?" says Valerie.

Dahaba, enthused albeit rueful, now says, "My brother always steals my best ideas and passes them off as his own. What am I to do about that, Mum?"

Valerie looks as if someone has stolen her thunder and she doesn't know what reaction to give. But Dahaba is so taken with the idea that she is bouncing on the couch, her feet catching the weight of her body and pushing off again. "When?" she says.

Salif says, "We need to plan ahead, Mum."

"What do you think, Mum?" asks Dahaba.

Valerie scrambles for an enthusiastic response, but it doesn't come easy to her. Bella thinks she knows what Valerie is thinking: Since the idea was not hers, then Bella must be behind it all. "Sweet, very sweet," she says, but her body language says something else. Still, while she doesn't appear exactly enraptured with the idea, neither does she throw cold water on it. "We would love them to come, wouldn't we, darling?" she says to Padmini, feeling everyone's eyes trained on her. Then she deflects the attention by saying to Salif, "Give us a kiss now, why don't you, darling."

Salif does as he is told. Then more drinks are poured, Valerie switching back to hard liquor—whiskey and water, which Padmini makes for her the way she knows Valerie likes it.

Valerie says, "As a professional photographer, have you taken pictures here in Kenya?"

"I did take photos before on commission, photos that were published in magazines in Italy and France—not of animals, but only of people and landscapes. This visit, I have been too busy to take any, but I plan to do so soon," says Bella.

"Have you taken pictures of the Somalis here?"

"I did so on my last visit a couple of years back from the vantage point of an attic two flights above an Italian restaurant on Mama Ngina Street. My subjects—three Somali men, each more handsome than the next—had no idea I was taking their photos. I also took pictures of Somali women in all sorts of outfits, some as striking as they were mysterious on account of their self-exclusion."

Bella takes a sip of her water and then waits with the studied patience of an angler for someone to comment on what she has said. When no fish takes the bite, she tells them about the Italian owner of the restaurant, who made a subtle pass at her. "What nerve!" she said.

Salif seems uncomfortable and changes the subject. "Tell us more about the subjects of your photographs, Auntie Bella."

But Valerie interrupts, "It always amazes me how good-looking Africans generally are compared to other peoples. Smooth skins, broad features, gorgeous eyes, statuesque, the palms of their hands as pale as the stones at the bottom of a lake, shiny and clean. They are gorgeous people, the men as well as the women. I would love to see some of your photographs."

Padmini says, "I can't stand the veiled women."

"If you want to know the women, you must visit them in their private spaces," Bella says. "There is a falsity, a sort of subtle theatricality, to them when you view them in public spaces."

Valerie says, "They strike me as pretentious."

Padmini says, "How can a country blessed with so many of the world's most famous models, the world's most stunning women, deny us the pleasure of feasting our eyes?"

Dahaba remembers Aar telling her that there was a time when the only veiled women in Somalia were the Arab women, Yemenis. "Covered from head to toe and all in black, as if in mourning."

"I recall our Somali neighbors in Uganda," Padmini says, "and after we relocated to England, we had Somali neighbors in our area of town too. In Uganda, they struck me as the most colorful people, their clothes far more beautiful than any sari. In England, however, where there is a growing population of Somalis, they are unsmiling, their expressions dour, and they dress all in gray."

"What do the two lots of Somalis have in common?" asks Salif, "the Somalis of your childhood in Uganda and the Somalis in England?"

Padmini says, "They are all a noisy lot."

"What else?" Salif asks.

"In Uganda, their daughters are irresistibly fetching, unlike any I have seen. In fact, I can trace my fascination with women's faces and bodies to this period of my life. I envied them their irresistibility! But they had no time for me. Look at Bella, and look at Dahaba, both of you lookers in your own ways. It would be criminal to deprive us of the pleasure to see either of you."

Valerie asks Bella, "Are veiling and infibulation linked in any way?"

"No link whatsoever."

Padmini says, "Is there a difference between infibulation or female circumcision and genital mutilation, which seems to be the term these days?"

"None," replies Bella. "Both terms describe the total removal of the clitoris, a most terrible barbarity to which our Somali society subjects women."

Valerie makes as if she has to choke, as if she can't bring herself to ask the question she means to ask. Then she takes a large sip of her drink so as to gain the mad courage to speak, and she says to Bella, "I've always meant to ask but haven't dared to. Did the brutes do it to you too?"

Salif is shocked into silence. Padmini looks up at the ceiling. Even Dahaba disapprovingly says, "Mum, how can you?"

But Bella coolly answers, "My mother spared me that."

"Just as Aar spared our daughter, right?"

In the silence that follows, Bella watches with no small shock as Salif brings out a cigarette pack and a lighter. Holding a cigarette between his thumb and forefinger, he rolls it and turns it and sniffs at it. Bella can't tell if he is trying to provide a distraction or provoke a reaction from everyone present, especially his mother. Will she rant and rail, advise him against smoking? But Bella won't say anything, given that Valerie is here.

Bella remembers when she was Salif's age, maybe even a year younger, and she lit her first cigarette at a friend's party. Later at school, she and her classmates would hide and puff away, doing all they could to avoid detection or punishment. At home, she would pilfer the odd cigarette from Aar, who by then was a heavy smoker. Despite his disapproval, Bella's habit grew, and she smoked on and off until eight years ago, when she kicked the habit with considerable difficulty, not because she wished to please her mother or brother and not for health reasons, but because once antismoking laws began to be passed, she hated belonging to the smokers' parliaments huddled outside bars and buildings, puffing away together to feed their nicotine cravings.

In any event, Salif doesn't light his cigarette. After playing with the cigarette for a while, he replaces the lighter in his shirt pocket and lodges the cigarette above his right ear.

Valerie says nothing about the incident and then changes the subject altogether. She says to Salif, "Apropos of visiting us in India, would you like it if we found you a school in our town?"

"As things stand now, we wouldn't," he says.

"We've been uprooted enough times, Mum," says Dahaba. "We would like to complete school here."

"What about schooling in the UK?"

"We are happy here, Mum," says Dahaba.

And Salif says, "We don't want to live in the UK."

"Why don't you think you would be happy in England?"

"Black boys my age have big problems in England. Often, they run into trouble with the school authorities or with the neighborhood police. I'd be viewed as a threat to the established order run for the benefit of those of a color different from mine."

"Would Dahaba be viewed with the same lens?" asks Padmini, and she looks at Bella, as if willing her to say something.

"Girls fare better," says Salif.

"Why is that so?" Padmini asks.

"Because they are not seen as a threat."

"Who have you been talking to about England?" asks Padmini.

Salif gives the matter serious thought. Then he says, "I follow the news. In England, I could easily end up in a detention cell for being black, male, young, and for bearing a Muslim name."

"You speak with clarity," says Padmini. "I am impressed."

And with that, they are all ready to call it a night.

18.

Bella is up very early, while the rest of the household is still asleep. She enjoys the quiet as she sits at the kitchen table and writes the phrase "home processing" on a pad and then underlines it. She is designing a very simple darkroom where Salif and Dahaba can learn to process film and have a bit of fun. Later, she can modify it so that it will serve her professional requirements. Since before dawn, she has been moving about with stealth, taking measurements. She settled on the spare room as sufficient for this purpose. Ideally, she would have preferred a basement or a room directly under the stairway, or an outbuilding or a stand-alone garage, as these are easier to black out using masking tape to block the light entering through any cracks. But none of these exist, and the bathrooms are too small for the purpose she has in mind. The spare bedroom will do, with an extractor fan installed to provide adequate ventilation. In addition, she will need an electrician to install more outlets for the enlargers and the dryers, and a plumber for the water supply needed for washing prints. Mahdi will know the right people to hire; she writes his name on the pad and then underlines it twice to remind herself.

Over the years, she has overseen the construction of many darkrooms, starting with the simple black-and-white processing setup Giorgio Fiori's colleague helped her to make in that closet back in Rome, when she was twelve. It is such an arrangement that she intends to start with here.

Before digital cameras came into vogue, darkrooms were fairly common, and most photo shops had one in the rear. As demand grew, though, little shops tended to outsource processing to larger, more sophisticated ones of industrial size. But remembering those simpler setups, Bella adds more items to the list she is drawing up: enlargers, three large trays, an eight-by-ten easel, a red lightbulb.

She hears the soft tread of someone approaching the kitchen, and when she looks up, Salif is there in his pajamas and robe. He looks surprised to find her already dressed and writing lists on a notepad.

"Morning, Auntie."

"Morning, darling."

"What's up?"

"A darkroom, that is what's up, today's priority."

A sweet smile later, he sits down. "That's good, bright and early," he says.

Bella pushes the notepad aside. "What would you like for breakfast?"

"I can make my own if you are busy."

"Good. Will you make my espresso for me too?"

"I would love to."

Salif busies himself making the espresso for her and an omelet and toast for himself. The household seems to be at peace with itself since they all went to their rooms last night, although Bella slept fitfully, listening for Dahaba's movements and reflecting on all that has happened so far. On the whole, she feels reassured about Valerie, who now seems much less in a position to muck matters up. The image that comes to her mind is of a hurricane, once strong and menacing, losing its ferocity as it hits land.

Salif asks, "Is it very complicated to organize a darkroom, Auntie?"

"It's not rocket science. I just need the help of an electrician and a plumber. And I'll need to go to a camera shop to purchase a supply of chemicals and paper."

The espresso is not to her liking—a bit watery—but she makes enthusiastic noises when she takes her first sip. She looks up when Salif's toast pops up but says nothing when she observes that his omelet is a little burnt. She clears space on the table for him to join her with his breakfast. When she sees that he has emptied the remainder of the ketchup onto one side of his plate, she adds "tomato ketchup" to the list on her notepad.

"Which room will we use as the darkroom?" Salif asks.

"The spare room is ideal," she says. "It is a corner room, set apart from the other rooms, it is spacious, and it has its own toilet so it already has a water supply."

"Super," he says. "Can't wait for it to be built."

Padmini is at the kitchen door. "Morning, dears," she says to them. "Did I hear the word 'build'? Build what, if I may ask?"

"A darkroom," says Salif.

"How forward looking," Padmini says. "Where?"

"In the spare room down here."

"Brilliant," Padmini says. "How exciting!"

Salif is up on his feet. "Breakfast?"

"Yes, please."

"What can I offer you?"

"Tell me the available options."

"Tea or coffee to begin with. And then you can tell me whether you would like oatmeal or an omelet."

"I would like tea with milk and oatmeal," says Padmini.

"I'll make the tea, then, and Auntie will make the porridge."

"You surprise me, darling," says Bella. "Making oatmeal porridge is a lot easier than making an omelet."

"I'd be happier if you made it," he says all the same.

Just as Bella rises to oblige him, Dahaba walks in with Valerie not far behind. "Morning, everyone," says Dahaba. Valerie silently waves and then slumps into a chair. She says, "I had an almost sleepless night, my daughter kicking me every time she turned. And when I tried to get away and return to my bed, she wouldn't let me."

"Mum snored as loud as a coal train," says Dahaba.

"How did everyone else fare?"

"Very well," says Salif.

"And you, Pad?"

"Slept well, thank you."

Dahaba is leaning against the back of Bella's chair. Bella says, "Come sit, my sweet, and I will make breakfast for you and your mum."

Valerie asks for bacon and eggs, and Dahaba opts for the same. Bella shoos Salif away and brings Padmini her tea and then her porridge. She steals a furtive look at her watch and reminds herself to call Mahdi soon. Once she has served breakfast to the stragglers, she goes upstairs for her credit cards and wallet, and then takes her leave of everyone, saying, "I'll be back soon." She gets into the car and turns on the engine; then, while waiting for Cawrala to respond, she rings Mahdi. He promises he will call her back with the name of someone who can get the job done quickly.

He calls her back when she is in the process of leaving the camera store with her purchases. He tells her the name of a contractor he recommends and says the man will call her shortly. And he does when she is on her way to the supermarket to buy more milk, fruit, soft drinks, sugar, tomato ketchup, and bacon and eggs. He says, "It's your lucky day today because, as it happens, we've just had a cancellation of a big job; the building where my electricians and plumbers were working collapsed. We can have an electrician and a plumber at your place in the next couple of hours if you give me your address."

"I'll be there," she says.

"Mahdi is a good friend," he says. "We'll look after you."

When she gets back home, she is delighted to see that she has hardly been missed. The four of them are playing cards, Valerie and Dahaba as one team and Padmini and Salif as the other, their rowdy noises reaching her even before she comes through the door.

She takes some of her purchases into the spare room and stores the rest in the pantry and fridge.

She says, "Anybody need anything?"

Dahaba asks, "Like what, Auntie?"

"Tea, coffee, some other drink or food?"

Salif says, "We're okay, thanks."

"We're not okay," says Dahaba. "I would like a Diet Coke."

Valerie says to her, "Can't you get it yourself?"

They stop playing cards while Dahaba gets her drink, and then Valerie's mobile phone squeals. She looks at the identity of the caller and then she says, "I must take this call." She leaves the room for privacy, and when she returns a few moments later, she is wearing the expression of a mourner. "Something terrible has happened," she says. And then she says to Padmini, "That was Ulrika. We need to get back to the hotel pronto."

"What's happened?"

"BIH has been raided and there have been arrests."

It is as though the two of them were speaking another language that the others cannot follow.

Bella offers them a lift.

"Can I come with you?" asks Dahaba.

"Not this time, darling," says Bella.

But Valerie and Padmini decline her offer and insist on calling a taxi instead.

The electrician and the plumber show up half an hour or so later, not only the two of them but the contractor himself and two additional workers. Bella gives them the sketch of what she wants done, and the men unload their tools. The plumber and the electrician write up the list of what they will need, and the contractor takes off to get the materials. Before long, the sound of hammering and male voices brings Dahaba and Salif down from their rooms. Before nightfall, Bella tells them, they will have a darkroom.

"Super," says Salif. Bella begins to explain the process to them, but Dahaba loses interest in the technical difference between pre-digital and digital photography, and the mention of landmark names such as Kodak does not excite her. "It sounds like the difference between typewriters and computers," she says, before she drifts back upstairs.

Bella tells Salif about the darkroom Giorgio Fiori's friend built her, and how Fiori taught her the basics of photo development.

"He wasn't a photographer, was he?" asks Salif.

"My father taught jurisprudence, and his specialty was the theory of law, or rather the principles on which Roman law is based. Photography was just a hobby for him. But what got him initially interested in photography was his enthusiasm for the history of image making and his interest in the reproduction of images in a variety of forms: in photography, in drawing, in painting, and in design patterns borrowed from African traditional societies. He had an early hand in the design of the fabrics that would become fashionable in West Africa."

"He was a brilliant man, your father?"

"He was indeed."

"I thought he taught in Somalia, where he met your mother," Salif says. "How did West Africa figure in his life?"

"He taught in Mali before coming to teach in Somalia," Bella explains, "and it was in Mali that he developed his interest in Dogon art."

"Dogon? What is Dogon? Who is Dogon?"

Bella answers the question with exemplary patience, as if she were a teacher. "The Dogon are a people known the world over for their exceptional wood sculpture, and their art revolves around their high ideals. Theirs is an art not meant for public viewing, so it can be seen only in private homes and sacred places. Dogon society puts great value on the symbolic meaning behind every piece."

Salif nods his head in appreciation, and Bella recalls how Aar spoke in an adult, sophisticated way to his children even when they were tiny. He would say that it was important that you talk to children the same way you talk to grown-ups. Children have the ability to catch up to you faster than you can imagine, he believed, and they remember tomorrow some of the things you speak about today.

Bella says, "So my father was the first to show me sculptures from the Dogon in Mali, sculptures whose forms excited my young mind. I decided then to become an artist. At first I thought I would pursue my ambition as a sculptor or painter, but finding my pursuit of these two modes of artistry challenging, I lowered my expectations and tried my hand at photography."

"And he built you a darkroom?"

"He taught me to treat the darkroom as both a sacred space and my own domain, my secret place," says Bella. "He discouraged me from allowing anyone else access. He spoke of the darkroom as though it were a tomb, a secret space not to be exposed to the eyes of others, lest it should be compromised."

Just then the doorbell rings. It is the contractor, who has come back with the items needed for the darkroom. Now the noise the men are producing increases tenfold. Bella hears the contractor shouting, "What have you been doing all this time? I don't want to disappoint Mahdi, who will be expecting a good report from her on our work. So get on with it."

Salif asks, "What do you think happened that made Mum and Auntie Padmini go into panic mode this morning?"

Bella tells him she has no idea.

"I hope they are okay."

"I hope so too." And she means it. She doesn't wish Valerie and Padmini to be subjected to further harassment of the sort they endured in Kampala. On the other hand, she will not be sorry if this turn of events makes them hasten their departure for India. After all, her motives in paying their hotel and legal bills were not entirely altruistic; she had hoped to get them closer to the exit door. Not that Padmini is likely to let Valerie know who their unnamed benefactor is. Pleased with her own discretion, Bella can't help but allow herself a smidgen of mischievous curiosity at how things will pan out. You never know if a given development will pique Valerie's rage or elicit the grace to admit defeat, say "thank you," and then depart.

The contractor enters the kitchen, rubbing his hands together and looking happy.

"We are done," he says. "Please come see."

At first the room is too dark for them to see. Then the contractor, who is behind them, turns on the light. Bella likes what she sees: plenty of room for their immediate purposes, as well as for improvements for her professional purposes. The contractor says to Bella, "Give it until tomorrow for the putty to harden and the grout to set, and then it will be ready for use."

Bella pays in cash, giving each of the workers a generous tip. The contractor gets Mahdi on the line. "Listen," he says to him, "there is a happy lady here who wants to have a word with you." He passes her his phone.

Tears well up in Bella's eyes unexpectedly, and her voice is tender with unreleased emotion. She tells Mahdi how delighted she is with the result his contractor has managed in such a short time.

Just as the men are leaving, Dahaba comes back downstairs. "Is it done, the darkroom, done, done?"

"Yes, it is," says Salif.

"What's it like?"

"Amazing."

"Can I see, Auntie?"

Salif tells her, "Not until tomorrow."

"Auntie, let me have a quick peek, please."

Bella allows Dahaba to stand in the doorway but no farther, lest she ruin the work before everything sets.

"A celebration is in order," says Dahaba.

"How do you want us to celebrate?"

Bella makes herself some tea and they toast each other with tea and soft drinks. Then Bella, exhausted, goes upstairs to bed.

She dreams that she is dressed to the nines, but the heels of her shoes are broken and she can't find a cobbler anywhere to repair them for her. It is raining very hard, so she shelters in a low shed with huge cracks in its zinc roofing. Wet and miserable, she sets out to seek better shelter, but her way is blocked by several stray dogs that bark viciously at her then attack her. She defends herself the best she can, but the harder she fights, kicking away at them, snarling, cursing, and screaming for help, the more dogs join in the attack. Eventually, she employs the shoes without heels as a weapon and hurls them at the dogs.

She retreats back into the shed and her bare feet come into contact with a bag. It seems to have been pushed into a corner and abandoned. She hasn't the time to investigate, however, before one of the smaller dogs makes its way past her, snarling, as likely as not to lead the attack from the rear, she fears. But when she kicks at him, she misses and kicks the bag instead. It breaks open, revealing bones. Is it possible, she thinks, that it was the bones the dogs were keen on instead of her?

She makes the opening in the bag bigger, then takes a handful of bones and scatters them over a large area outside the shack. The dogs fight fiercely over them and tear hungrily into them. While the dogs are busy fighting over the bones, she tries to scuttle away, unobserved. But a big bloodhound seemingly uninterested in the bones impedes her progress. Scared stiff, she searches for something to defend herself with—a stone, a stick big enough to strike with. She finds nothing. She lives on the edge of her nerves for a few minutes, trying frantically to imagine what it is about her that is drawing the hound's attention. Via a process of elimination, she focuses on the necklace of bones she is wearing. She unclasps the chain and throws it at the bloodhound, and at last he lets her leave.

She wakes up, heavily perspiring.

A couple of hours later, after a hot shower, Bella comes down to the kitchen. She makes herself some porridge and brews some strong coffee. The children aren't yet downstairs, but Bella has an appointment with Gunilla at the UN office this morning. Before long, Salif wakes and comes down to have his breakfast, and eventually Dahaba saunters in, holding a toothbrush aloft.

She says, "Somebody give me toothpaste, please."

Salif scoffs at her. "You're in the wrong room."

"Who says this is the wrong room?"

"A kitchen isn't where you want to be."

"But there is none in the bathroom," she says, and then she issues an abysmal groan, supplemented by a blob of phlegm that she spits into the kitchen sink. "Did I ask you to give me toothpaste? Please stay out of my way and keep your nasty comments to yourself."

Bella rises from her chair in anger then dispossesses Dahaba of the toothbrush, takes hold of the girl's wrist, and leads her out of the kitchen and back up the stairway toward her bathroom, where Bella is certain there is toothpaste.

When Bella returns to the kitchen, Salif says to her, "Why must you give in to every one of her vagaries, Auntie? This is no good. She will never grow out of it, you are spoiling her rotten."

"I know what I am doing, darling," says Bella. "Trust me."

She sits down to resume the notes she was making, but her millet porridge has hardened. She adds a lump of butter to it and microwaves it, but just as she takes a spoonful, Dahaba reenters the kitchen. Without asking for help, she sets about making her own breakfast this time. Bella wonders which of them is right. She's certain Salif believes that it's the pressure he has been putting on Dahaba that will ultimately pay off. And Bella thinks he may well prove right, although it is too early to determine how consistently Dahaba will do anything. She remembers that Hurdo used to say that raising a child is a long-term project, the nature of the child's needs changing as the child grows, but not the need itself.

Dahaba brings out the bread and puts two slices in the toaster. Then she takes out the marmalade and margarine, and when the toasts pop up, she picks them up with her forefingers. Although she flinches, giving the impression that her fingers are burned, she is pleased when she sits down with her toast. You would think she is expecting applause, so delighted is she with her achievement. She spreads large dollops of margarine and marmalade on the two slices and eats them, getting food all over her mouth and chin.

She says to Bella, "You going somewhere fancy?"

"I've an appointment."

"Where and with whom?"

"With Gunilla, at your dad's place of work."

"What's going on?"

"We need to sort out a few things."

"Would you like to tell us more?" Dahaba says.

Salif says to Dahaba, "Are you mad?"

Dahaba carps, "What have I done this time?"

Salif says, "Next time you'll ask Auntie to tell you how much money there is in Dad's bank account and how much of it is coming your way and how much my share is and how much, if any, will go to Auntie Bella."

"There is no harm in knowing any of these details, is there, Auntie?" Dahaba says. "Or asking questions of this kind?" Then she turns on Salif. "Why do you mouth off at me? What right have you got to talk to me like this?"

Bella says, "Please," to no one in particular.

"Am I out of line wanting to know, Auntie?"

Bella replies, "No, you're not." And to Salif she pleads, "Let it be."

The dream of last night has suddenly come back to her, and she feels despondent. She remembers now too that BIH is shorthand for a lesbian bar called Bar in Heaven and that Ulrika is a German active in the gay community in Nairobi. She has read all this online—the recent raid of the bar has been all over the news. She considers whether to call Padmini and ask if all is okay, but she thinks better of it and, opting for inaction on that front, turns her mind to matters closer to her heart.

She glances up and sees that Salif is looking as disturbed as she feels. His shoulders are hunched and he is clutching a knife in his right hand while his glassy eyes stare at a bit of uneaten omelet attached to the end of his fork. There is something blank about his gaze that puts Bella in mind of a mirror that has lost its quicksilver backing. He doesn't have much self-restraint: You annoy him and he will come after you until he unsettles you. Maybe he is the sort of person who believes that when you are bad, as bad as Valerie, say, you deserve to get your comeuppance. Like Salif, Bella finds Dahaba's occasional unpleasantness tiring, and often she doesn't know what to do about it. But Salif needs to learn that he doesn't have to show his ugly side so quickly and that he doesn't need to zero in on other people's weaknesses, as if he were a dog chasing the fear in those who are afraid of him.

Just before Bella goes out the door to meet Gunilla, Dahaba comes back downstairs, holding her phone. The girl is shouting, "Mummy, where are you?" An instant later, Dahaba passes the phone to Bella, saying, "Auntie, it's Mum, she wants a word."

What follows is so bizarre and happens so quickly that Bella will be confused about it for a long time to come.

Bella's first words are "You were in my thoughts. In fact, I nearly called you half an hour ago to ask how you both were."

"Cut the crap," Valerie says. "I want you to go upstairs and close the door to your room. I have questions to ask you and I want true answers. I don't wish the children to hear what I am saying."

Bella is in suspense to learn whether all this is provoked by the payment she made yesterday when she settled the bill at the hotel. Or could it have something to do with the raid on BIH and the resulting arrests? Is Valerie in deep trouble and in dire need of help again? She remains silent until she is in her room and then she says, "What is this about, Valerie?"

"Do you know—have you ever known—a Ugandan woman called Helene Nsembemba, with legal chambers in Kampala? And have you ever wired funds to her in your capacity as the Good Samaritan, working miracles and setting free two women in a Kampala lockup?"

"I've never met this Helene you speak of."

"I know you know Gunilla the Swede and that you've met with her a couple of times, so don't tell me you don't know her. Tell me what role the Swedish woman played in all this."

"I suggest we talk about this another time."

"Here you are fobbing me off again. Tell me truly, did you pay to have us released?"

"I've no idea what you are talking about."

Valerie says, "I'm told you paid the bond, wired the funds to pay off the Ugandan police and paid for our ticket, all through your lackey Gunilla. Is that true?"

"You are imagining things, Valerie."

"I have it from reliable sources that you are involved in much deeper muck than you are prepared to accept," says Valerie.

"Who is this reliable source?"

"A gentleman in the Ugandan legal fraternity."

"I insist I have no idea what he is on about."

There is a pause.

"Padmini and I are coming over to see the children. And I never want them to know about this terrible thing you've done, paid secretly and maliciously a bill you did not incur," Valerie screams into the phone.

There is a knock on the door. Dahaba says, "Is everything all right? I hear some shouting, are you shouting?"

"Dahaba, darling, I didn't mean to shout. Okay?"

Valerie asks, "What is happening?"

"Dahaba is at the door to my room, wondering why I am shouting and asking if everything is all right," Bella says.

"I want you to listen to me carefully, very carefully. Not a word to Dahaba and Salif about this. You hear me?"

"I hear you."

"Not to a living soul, you hear?"

"I said I hear you."

"No shouting, because you are still shouting."

Bella chokes on her words of self-explanation, thinking that one can never win when one is at war with Valerie. She is adept at turning the tables and making you sound silly and forcing you to apologize even though you have no idea why you are apologizing or why you got yourself into tangles and your tongue into knots.

"I'll see you soon enough," says Valerie, and she hangs up.

With the phone now dead in her hands, Bella opens the door to her room and finds she is face-to-face with Dahaba. Bella has no idea what to do or what to say. Dahaba is too young to understand all this. So Bella only says, "Thanks, here. Your mum called to tell us she and Auntie Padmini are coming over in a bit," and holds out the phone. But Dahaba notices and so does Bella that her outstretched hand is trembling and that she is shaking all over. Bella returns to her room and washes her face and hands, but she is still shaking.

When she comes out, Dahaba is still waiting for her. Bella embraces her and then says, "Let us go downstairs and see how the darkroom is doing."

Dahaba says, "Wait. Tell me what's happened."

"There has been a misunderstanding, that's all."

And Bella leads Dahaba by the hand, virtually pulling her, and doesn't stop until they are in the darkroom, where it is still night.

"May I turn on the lights, Auntie?" says Dahaba.

"Of course, my darling."

Bella moves around, taking note of what else needs to be done to make the darkroom operational. But everything will have to wait until she gets back from her appointment with Gunilla.

Bella, still a little shaken, is unhappy being alone with Dahaba. The girl has a way of unsettling her with her questions, and Bella needs time to think of what and how to answer. She calls out to Salif several times. More and more she realizes how comforting she finds his presence. It's not just that he is not antsy like Dahaba, who is demanding and unsure, but somehow being around him neutralizes things, balances them out. He makes problems bearable and often comes up with solutions to them, just like Aar.

Now he says, "Is it ready for use, Auntie?"

In his calming presence, Bella regains her composure. With her arms around Dahaba, whose small body is trembling against her, she says, "Between the items I purchased from the camera store and a handful of others I brought with me from Italy, the darkroom will be functional today. Later today, after I get back."

Salif smiles. "Must be an important meeting. Because you are in your power outfit."

"Wish me luck," Bella says, hugging Dahaba a bit tighter.

"When will you be back?"

"I'll return as soon as I am done. Your mum should be here by then."

Then Bella heads out of the front door, gets into the car, and drives off, reminding herself that she will not allow Valerie or anyone else to deter herself from the tasks awaiting her.

19.

Bella arrives at the UN offices in Gigiri almost half an hour late, and then, of course, she has to go through the series of checkpoints and scannings and screenings. She recalls Aar's comments about the corrupt Ugandan security forces at Somalia's international airport, but on reflection, she thinks that the blame lies squarely with the Somalis and especially with the current president and his regime. After arriving on a tide of great enthusiasm, he quickly proved incapable of steering the ship of state through disaster. He has been accused of unconscionable favoritism, of massive inefficiency, of unparalleled personal dishonesty. In the more than a year he has been in power, he has accrued more enemies than friends, both locally and among the international community. There is no one, it seems, he has not disappointed. UN investigators have uncovered corruption of immense proportions, reaching all the way up to his office and beyond. Two governors of the Central Bank later—one was sacked for impropriety, the other (with impeccable credentials) resigned—there is still no mechanism in place that can guarantee that the government kitty is safe from the pilfering of the president's associates and clansmen. A member of parliament, a former premier, has accused the president of enjoying an unhealthy rapport with "terrorists," and deny this as he might, the allegation keeps echoing in the media, especially on Somali-language websites.

Finally through the gauntlet, Bella is shown to Gunilla's anteroom by one of the assistants. She takes a seat, opens her briefcase, and takes out the Camus essays, which she hasn't found the time to concentrate on in the unpredictable emotional climate of the past few days. But after a few moments, the receptionist's intercom sounds. "Yes, madam," she says, then she informs Bella that Gunilla is ready to see her. Bella replaces the Camus in her handbag and, her knees creaking from lack of exercise, rises and knocks on Gunilla's office door.

They shake hands, they hug, and they kiss, touching cheeks. Not long after they sit, Immaculata the tea girl comes in without knocking. Bella can tell Gunilla isn't happy about this, but she lets it pass without comment.

Bella brings Gunilla up-to-date, starting with how much she and the children have enjoyed the album of photographs she gave them. Then she tells Gunilla about the cameras and the darkroom.

"How did the outing go?" Gunilla wants to know.

"Good until the last few minutes."

"Then what happened?"

"Salif and Dahaba took turns putting unpleasant personal questions to Valerie," says Bella, making sure that she doesn't portray Valerie in a way that may prove counterproductive.

"What were the questions like?"

"Dahaba asked first and Salif followed suit, the two of them working her like those little dogs that go for your feet and bark nonstop," says Bella, not wishing to reveal more than necessary.

"How did Valerie take it?"

"She was less worked up than I expected. But today was another story."

"What happened today?"

Bella asks if Gunilla has had any recent contact with Helene Nsembemba. Gunilla replies, "Yes, we spoke a couple of days ago because I called her to make sure that we go over her billing."

"Did you give my name and details at any time?"

"I didn't."

"Well, somehow Valerie found out more than she should have. She discovered that it was I who settled the bill, and she knows that you have been functioning as my intermediary as well. My guess is that someone at your bank provided her with the information, not through Helene, but through the other lawyer Valerie has been using since she regained her freedom."

Gunilla reflects on this then says, "In my capacity as a UN official, I must abide by the banking laws of the countries I visit. My primary base is Kenya, but we have accreditation in Uganda. It is very possible that a banker there was able to trace both your name and mine. I am sorry; I meant well and did what I could to process the transaction as quickly as possible, but I can't control everything."

"No blame is intended," says Bella.

"Anyway, was she grateful that you settled her and Padmini's affairs so they could regain their freedom and leave Uganda?"

"No! She said that she could do without my charity."

"How very ungrateful."

"There is something else besides. In our Somali culture and also in Islam, if you give someone a gift, you don't boast about it to others. If you do, then your present is deemed worthless."

"So she is saying thanks but no thanks."

They fall companionably silent and mull over their situation as Immaculata brings them their tea. Then Gunilla tells the tea girl to tell the receptionist that no one must disturb them again.

It has been increasingly obvious to Bella from each of their encounters that Gunilla had fallen under Aar's spell, abandoning herself to his abundant charm. He could work wonders when he set himself to pursuing a woman with interest, and maybe his interest had grown keener after so long a time without a serious female companion. To see Gunilla savoring her memories of him is a novel way of appreciating Aar. But Bella reminds herself not to mix the official business that has brought her here with her increasing affection for Gunilla and her longing for Aar; there is time enough to explore both outside these walls when time and circumstance permit.

So Bella turns her attention to the papers Gunilla has placed before her, crossing and uncrossing her legs as she concentrates on the thick file in her lap. Bella reads in silence, noting questions and comments here and there with a red pencil. Gunilla has explained that Bella must sign the documents, which include important insurance papers, in the presence of an outside lawyer, Godwin Wamiru, once her questions have been answered. He is expected to join them shortly, but just now he texts to say that he is going to be very late. "I hope that doesn't put your schedule out of joint," says Gunilla. "Do you have other business you need to get to today?"

"No," says Bella, "I cleared the day for this." Then she adds, as an afterthought, "For you, I have all the time in the world."

"There is no worry then," says Gunilla. "Let us go to lunch."

"Do we have to go back through security when we return?" says Bella.

"You're with me," says Gunilla. "I can sign you in. Just bring along your passport, and I'll lock the rest in my office."

A flush of affection sweeps over Bella. She is looking forward to spending time with Aar's lover, not only to hear about him but also to get to know her better for herself.

It takes them a few leisurely minutes to walk to an Italian deli nearby, where they sit apart from everyone else at a corner table with an umbrella. Gunilla is known to the staff here and the manager, a Sicilian with heavily accented English, comes round to greet her.

Gunilla sits across from Bella and, as if for the first time, Bella takes her in. She knows that Aar's lover is soft of voice, pleasant of face, and sweet-smelling, especially for a Swede in the tropics. On the matter of scent, Bella harbors a personal and unscientific theory: If you are the kind of person who bears grudges or is given to unfounded mistrust, she believes, your body will betray that in the sour odor it emits. Gunilla, for example, seems to produce less sweat than, say, Valerie. Bella has noticed all this before, but now she is struck as if for the first time by how gorgeous Gunilla is. Bella can hardly take her eyes off her, admiring her every move. Bella cannot recall feeling this way about another person, male or female. The only person who came close was Aar, with that beautiful face she knew better than her own almost from the moment she opened her eyes upon the world. Somalis say that you love the jinn of the person you adore. Maybe what she is seeing and adoring in Gunilla is the Aar both of them adored, if that makes sense.

Gunilla is wearing a dress and heels, her blond hair long but kempt, her makeup light, her skin evenly tanned wherever it shows except for a paler bit at the neck. Bella watches her chest rising and falling as she breathes, her fingers fondling the necklace Aar gave her, Bella's twin. Bella is sorry she hasn't worn her own today. It brings to mind a story she heard, about a poet who, fearing that he would die at the hands of a neighboring foe, composed a couplet and taught it to his daughters. If he was murdered, he told them, they should recite the first line to anyone who called on them; whoever knew its mate would also know who his murderers were. Is there some secret about Aar's last days on earth, some uncovered mystery, Bella wonders, that only Gunilla knows? A pity he died in Mogadiscio, not in the arms of this woman who loved him dearly.

"It is lovely, isn't it?" Gunilla says, fingering the necklace.

Bella thinks of telling her that what makes the necklace lovelier is its proud wearer, but she refrains, fearing it will seem crass to speak that way to a woman she hasn't known for very long. Besides, what if Gunilla misinterprets this and thinks she is making a pass at her! So Bella says only, "Yes, it is lovely."

"And you were with him when he bought it?"

"I was there."

Bella recounts how he bargained with the Turkish jeweler but, failing to persuade him to lower the asking price, gave in even though Bella thought the necklaces cost too much and could be had for a quarter the price in Mogadiscio, where he was due to travel in a month. When she insisted she didn't need it, he said, "I am buying two. The second is for a close friend in Nairobi."

That was the first time in a long time that Bella thought he might be seeing someone. The news gladdened her heart, but she didn't press him to give her the details, imagining that sooner or later he would tell her of his own volition. After all, she had gone to Istanbul a week ahead of him to spend several nights in the company of Humboldt, a liaison that she had never breathed a word to him about, nor had she mentioned her other two lovers.

But now it is Gunilla who is forthcoming, by a larger margin than Bella had ever expected. "We had plans afoot," she says. "Serious ones!"

Bella pictures a wedding party—friends gathering, Salif serenely welcoming the guests, Dahaba ecstatic—and she, the groom's sister, playing the role of host. "Tell me more about your plans," she says.

"They were in a rather advanced stage."

"A pity you didn't let anyone know about them," Bella says, as though to herself. Then she adds, "Why was that?"

Gunilla's expression darkens as she enters this sad world where death now reigns and grabs whatever it wishes. She says, "Aar wanted to prepare Salif and Dahaba for the news. He was worried about what they would think, how they would behave toward me. He said they could be difficult when they chose to be. And there was the matter of Valerie—technically still his wife as they'd never divorced—to deal with. But he worried much less about Valerie. The children were uppermost in his mind; he wanted them to be happy; he wanted me to be happy; he wanted everyone to be happy. No rush, he kept saying. Everything will fall into place."

Suddenly Gunilla looks bewildered, as if the world has become a mystery, as if death were all the more calamitous when it takes away someone with a plan. Bella remembers how Dahaba had called Aar's death "unfair." Why must death take away her father and not someone with no job, no life, and no love? Gunilla weeps gently, and when Bella goes around the table to console her, she cries harder. Bella hands Gunilla a tissue and the Swede wipes her tears dry. They sit in silence for an appropriate period of time and then resume sipping away at their coffee.

Then Gunilla's mobile phone, which is in her bag, tinkles and she brings it out and reads the text to herself. "It is Godwin. He says he is just round the corner from the office."

Gunilla pays for the coffees, apologizing to the waiter for not being able to order lunch, and they walk back to the office in some haste. Since Bella is with Gunilla, the security guards at the gate take only a cursory look at her passport and they are about to wave her through when another officer, evidently more zealous, makes her go through a more detailed check. Almost as soon as they get back to Gunilla's office, the receptionist rings to inform her that the attorney is waiting. Gunilla says, "Let him come in, please."

A knock on the door heralds the entry and then the imposing physical presence of Godwin Wamiru, who turns out to be a broad-shouldered, wide-jawed, long-limbed man. He is wearing a generously cut suit, his tie loose, his stride expansive and his self-regard high. He shakes hands with the attitude of a man on top of his game. Before he takes a seat, he says, "My name is Godwin Wamiru and I am a forensic expert in legal matters for the UN offices in Nairobi. One of the things I deal with is the complexities of wills when someone dies in UN employ. Now, let us get down to business so that we can wrap things up quickly for the sake of you and your family."

He sits down, opens his briefcase with panache, and brings out a pile of papers, which he consults only once before he recites the facts known to all parties in the case: that Aar was killed while on a UN tour of duty in Mogadiscio, in circumstances that lead one to believe that terrorists murdered him in cold blood; that he is survived by two children, both in their teens, an estranged wife who has lately turned up and whose intentions have been unclear, and Bella, his sister, who is present here.

Gunilla raises her hand as if she were a pupil in a classroom. "If I may ask you a question?"

"Go ahead, please."

"What's the latest with Valerie? You told me that she had initiated a claim. What have you made of it?"

"It's definitive," he says. "She and the deceased were married out of community of property, and Valerie is not legally entitled to anything. End of story."

"So it was all a lot of hot air and a waste of time?"

"All that I am prepared to say is that it was unwise on her part to pay those two lawyers," Godwin Wamiru says. "She is not entitled to the dust from two of Aar's shillings rubbed together."

Bella likes this lawyer, who doesn't sound like one. He has a severe, intelligent face, which he uses to great effect, and occasionally he raises his voice a touch for emphasis, as if to convince any skeptics. After he's spoken, you feel there are no grounds that you can challenge him on.

Now he says, "I took the deposition myself, in the presence of Valerie's attorneys. Here is the notarized document she signed, two copies of it, one for each of you. In her deposition, Valerie declares that she has withdrawn all claims and that the case is closed. In a codicil, she forfeits the right to make any further claims regarding the custody of the children."

"Why has she withdrawn her case?"

"She is indigent, unable to pay her legal fees."

Bella receives the information with mixed feelings: relief, because she has been worried about the effect that a drawn-out legal dispute might ultimately have on her relationship with the children on the one hand, and on Valerie's relationship with the children on the other. Still, she wonders how Valerie's concessions might have affected her. A lioness is at her most dangerous when injured.

Bella reads the deposition, made all the more satisfying because Valerie has signed it and was fingerprinted for it.

Gunilla says, "Out of curiosity, did Valerie and her attorney come into your office to have the document signed or did you go to her attorney's?"

Godwin Wamiru says, "The woman is broke. She and her attorney came to me because he wanted to put a stop to the clock running and the bill mounting since she was in no position to pay what she already owes."

"How does he intend to recoup what is owed to him?" asks Bella.

"Maybe he will have her arrested."

"And how much are we talking about?"

"Several thousand dollars."

Gunilla takes down the details of Valerie's Kenyan attorneys, aware that she needs these men to wrap up the case and leave no loose threads hanging. Then Godwin Wamiru takes his leave.

Not wanting to part yet, Bella and Gunilla extend their time together and go back to the Italian deli for the lunch that Godwin Wamiru interrupted, feeling more relaxed than before. And while neither is ready to celebrate victory yet, they admit to each other that Valerie is in a very weakened position, especially given her failure to pay her newly accrued legal fees.

All eyes follow their entry into the open-air restaurant, where they are led to a corner table. After they've ordered their meal, Gunilla remarks that something seems to be troubling Bella. "What is it, dear? A kroner for your thoughts."

"I can't bear the thought of having Valerie arrested for nonpayment of the attorney's legal fees. And yet I would have difficulty justifying my own action if I paid for it."

A sort of nervous energy descends on the two women as they assess the situation in their heads. The waitress brings sparkling water in bottles and some bread in a basket. Bella mixes balsamic vinegar with olive oil and then dips the bread in it and, as she chews in silence, wonders if Gunilla can bear to get involved in Aar's affairs again on her behalf.

"I am afraid that, having lost her shirt now and her marbles many years before, Valerie may do something desperate," Bella says. "She is mad, bad, and positively dangerous; and I am worried that we are back where we started: Valerie under threat of being locked up and needing to be bailed out."

"What are you thinking?"

"I am thinking of discreetly settling this bill too."

"I see where you are coming from, and I believe I can work out something with the two attorneys she owes legal fees to."

"How?"

"They can forward their bills to me and we will tell them that we will settle their fees from Aar's estate to save his good name," says Gunilla.

"How wise you are, Gunilla."

They are silent for a minute or so. When their meals come, they eat, neither speaking because Gunilla knows a couple of people sitting at the next table and she doesn't want them to hear her confidential conversation with Bella.

Gunilla says, "I'd like to see the children."

"Let me see what I can organize."

Gunilla reaches for the bill. Bella says "the children" as if it is synonymous with "my worry," the same way she says Valerie's name as if it is a euphemism for "trouble." They walk back together, Gunilla to her office and Bella to pick up her car from the parking lot.

All is well when Bella gets back home, lugging takeaway for an army. Valerie, Salif, Padmini, and Dahaba are in the living room playing Scrabble. Salif is the quickest at word games, and to give himself further advantage, he has imposed a time limit on each player's turn, regulated with the kind of timer professional chess players use. He has put himself in charge of the clock, on occasion declaring that a player has lost a turn because he or she is late in making a move.

Bella heads straight for the kitchen, avoiding Valerie's icy stare. As she unloads the food—curries, sushi, Thai veggies—onto the kitchen table, Bella hears Dahaba challenging a call, bawling, "I was just about to make my move!" Then Valerie shrieks, "No more time wasting, please!" And Salif calls out, "Cheaters!"

Bella goes up to her room, carrying her briefcase, determined to enjoy what peace she can find there. She changes into a housedress and finds a pair of flip-flops for her feet, remembering vaguely that Mahdi has offered to take the children to see a movie tonight. Truth be told, she is longing for some time to herself, but it is Valerie she no longer wants to spend a moment with, unlikely as that possibility seems. Indeed, even from up here, she can hear Valerie berating Salif. What has the poor fellow done now? she wonders.

She catches up on her e-mails, many of which contain belated condolence messages, including a few from Aar's colleagues. When she sees a long one from Ngulu, she deletes it right away. Then she boots up Aar's computer and opens his e-mail.

She skips the newer messages in his in-box for the time being, most of which appear to be junk mail, and starts with the messages from before he died. Nearly a third of the messages in his in-box are from Gunilla. Many of them are of an intimate nature, but a great number of them have to do with the management of his Nairobi account and other work-related ones. Bella checks his sent mail and finds many e-mails to Salif and Dahaba, about two a day to each of them, and others to Fatima about her cancer. In one Aar even offers to help financially if there is need.

After shutting down Aar's computer, Bella calls to invite Gunilla to dinner the next night, making their vague plan for a get-together definite. Then she thinks, why not make it a party? and she rings Catherine Kariuki. After updating her on how Salif and Dahaba are faring, she says, "If you are free tomorrow evening round about eight, we would like you and your husband to join us for supper. Please accept my apology for such short notice. We've been meaning to have you over, but the children's mother is here, and it has not been easy for me to get the household in order."

Catherine says, "Hold on, dear," and then comes back in a moment to say, "My husband says he would love to come, but it will depend on whether his chauffeur is available as we don't normally drive ourselves home at night."

"I hope you can come," says Bella. "That way we will be able to thank you properly for hosting Salif and Dahaba. And you will meet two or three of Aar's friends along with Valerie, the children's mother."

Catherine says, "In the meanwhile, kindly send us directions to your house. And I'll ring you tonight or first thing tomorrow to let you know whether we are coming."

Downstairs, the game is over. "Who won?" asks Bella.

Salif says, "I did. And Padmini came in second."

"Because you and Pad cheat, that's why," says Valerie. But she doesn't sound very miffed, and the current state of her feelings is a mystery to Bella.

It's Dahaba who begins to unpack the cartons of food and to ask who wants to eat what. Then Valerie takes charge, yammering away, ordering people about: Salif is to bring the cutlery; Padmini the napkins and plates; and Bella the drinks. Bella does as instructed and makes herself useful by serving everyone's drink of choice, although she begs off lunch on the grounds that she has already eaten.

"And where did you have lunch?" asks Valerie.

Bella thinks hard before answering the question, which, innocuous as it is, reminds Bella of how peaceful demonstrations turn to violent riots. Answering "Where" may invite "With whom?" she fears.

"Where?" Valerie insists.

"Just some little deli, you won't know it."

Bella observes that Dahaba is liberally dropping food on her place mat and wiping it up halfheartedly with her curry-stained fingers, which she then licks. "Dahaba!" she admonishes.

"Sorry," says Dahaba.

Valerie inquires, "Why are you sorry?"

Salif explains why, but Valerie answers, "Big deal. Just wash the place mat, it is made from cheap cloth anyway."

Now that the animation of the game is over, Valerie looks to Bella as if she hasn't had much rest; in fact, she looks like a street cat caught in the rain. Padmini seems subdued as well. Bella wonders if Valerie has informed Padmini that she has withdrawn her case and is no longer contesting the will or filing for child custody. Will their relationship come to grief when Padmini learns this, she wonders, or will Padmini see it as tit for tat for Padmini's ruinous attempt to recover her family's property in Uganda? And has Valerie told Padmini about her anger over Bella's rescuing them? Bella stands on the periphery of the circle and listens.

Dahaba is asking, "Mum, have you read much gay literature?"

"Gay literature, did you say?"

"You see," says Dahaba, "my friend Qamar has told me that nowadays you can take queer literature courses in America and the UK at universities. You can even do a PhD on the subject, it is so rich."

Salif makes threatening pistol-shaped gestures with his fingers at Dahaba, warning her away from this topic, and even Bella tries to catch the girl's eyes to suggest that she rein it in. But even when Salif kicks Dahaba in the shin and Valerie says to Salif, "Please. Where are your manners?" she doesn't stop.

"I can give you a list of classic gay authors that my friend Qamar says you'll enjoy reading," Dahaba says.

"Have you read any of them yourself?" asks Valerie.

Dahaba replies, "No, I haven't. But Qamar has."

"Give the list to Padmini."

Padmini says to Dahaba, "Give them to me. I am partial to such writing. Your mum likes thrillers and crime fiction. I can't bear reading any of that."

"Because murder has a built-in narrative structure," Valerie declares.

Padmini says, "I just love gay classics like *Nightwood* by Djuna Barnes; *The Picture of Dorian Gray* by Oscar Wilde; *Death in Venice* by Thomas Mann; *The Color Purple* by Alice Walker; *Zami: A New Spelling of My Name* by Audre Lorde; and *Oranges Are Not the Only Fruit* by Jeannette Winterson. They are wonderful."

Despite her worries that this discussion will lead the conversation back to areas that are best avoided, Bella is relieved that the topic of sexuality is now on the table. Nevertheless, she takes the opportunity to change the subject before too much more can be said. "We are having a dinner party tomorrow evening," she announces. "What do you say to that?"

"It depends on who is invited," says Dahaba.

"Your mum and Auntie Padmini for starters," says Bella.

"Oh, that's wonderful. I love parties," says Valerie.

Padmini says, "I'll help cook."

Salif says, "That's super. I love Indian food."

Dahaba asks, "And who else?"

"Mr. and Mrs. Kariuki," says Bella.

Valerie says, "Who are they?"

Salif explains, "The principal of our school and his wife, who we stayed with. They were our hosts and they were very, very kind, especially the Mrs. She is large and generous and fun."

"Can we invite Qamar and Zubair?" says Dahaba.

"Yes, of course," says Bella.

"Can their mum and dad come too, please?" asks Salif.

"Sure," says Bella.

"And who else?" asks Salif.

"Your father's colleague Gunilla."

This time, Bella senses the presence of a ripple of tension from Valerie at the mention of Gunilla's name, which brings on a feeling of renewed apprehension.

"We know her," says Dahaba. "She's cool."

Bella asks, "By the way, when is Uncle Mahdi coming to pick you up for the movie? Maybe it is time you showered, no?"

Dahaba goes upstairs.

"What movie are you going to see?" asks Valerie.

Salif replies, "A film called *The First Grader*, based on the true tale of an eighty-four-year-old former freedom fighter during the struggle for Kenyan independence from British rule. Never having gone to school, he enrolls himself in primary school with six-year-olds. It's about the uneasiness his presence in the classroom creates among the educational and political authorities."

"Fascinating," says Bella.

"Mum, interested in coming?"

"Not my type of film," says Valerie.

———

A quarter of an hour later, Mahdi, Zubair, and Qamar arrive to pick up Dahaba and Salif. Dahaba immediately invites them to the dinner party tomorrow evening, and Mahdi immediately says that the family would be delighted to come. Bella introduces him to Valerie and Padmini, and she can see his flicker of recognition as he puts the names and faces together with all that he has heard.

Mahdi says to Valerie, "My children mentioned you were here visiting. I am so pleased to meet you."

Valerie says, "You have lovely children."

Mahdi welcomes Valerie and Padmini, and he smiles at both, a little too formally, thinks Bella. Nothing in his manner betrays that he knows anything about the legal rows and custody battles that have been raging in the family. He is impeccably polite, and he also treats Padmini with the respect due an honored guest.

Bella brings Mahdi tea and pours him and her some. Valerie and Padmini take their usual sundowners. But the conversation doesn't flow easily, and they are all relieved when the stairway echoes with the shouts of teenagers as the children and their friends roughhouse. Not that they lower their voices or make the slightest effort to calm down when they come into the room where the adults are. All four speak at the same time. Zubair and Qamar are impatient to get to the movie. "Dad," Zubair says, "we're going to be late."

Mahdi looks at his watch. He says, "You're not."

Bella says, "The impatience of youth!"

"Please let me finish my tea," Mahdi says.

"There is tea everywhere," says Zubair.

They troop out, still full of excitement, and the younger ones race each other to the car. Watching them, it's easy to forget that Dahaba and Salif have only recently lost their father.

Now that the three women are alone, the tension in the room is all the more heightened, and their conversation flows much less naturally. Bella points Valerie and Padmini to the liquor cabinet, saying, "Please do drink and be merry." She moves away on the pretext of warming up dinner after taking their order for leftovers from the afternoon's take-away.

Valerie makes herself a whiskey on the rocks and Padmini pours herself some red wine. Bella takes only water with a slice of lemon. They sip their drinks silently, evasively holding back what is on their minds despite the fact that a lot needs to be said. Yet not one of them is prepared to speak.

Finally Valerie slips out to the bathroom, and Padmini hurriedly says, "We owe you a big thanks, Bella, for settling the bills. I'll make sure we pay you back." When Valerie returns, looking much the worse for wear, Bella abruptly changes the conversation and talks about the Nairobi weather. How cold it can get at night up in the mountains and near the lakes! Bella is too wary to trust that nothing nefarious is afoot, and she is therefore extra solicitous, fearful of rousing Valerie's demons. What is more, Bella doesn't want the rapport between Valerie and Padmini to unravel now that they seem to be on course for departure back to Pondicherry. She is relieved when the conversation starts to flow again, with Valerie suggesting they eat at the big dining room table for a change. And they find a legion of discussion topics that Bella presses into service, such as the state of their restaurant and hotel business, the children's welfare, Bella's place in the children's lives—as well as Valerie and Padmini's future. For the first time since Valerie's arrival, Bella begins to feel the butterflies in her stomach settle.

Valerie says to Bella, "What occasion has prompted you to throw a party tomorrow evening? Of course, we are delighted that you've invited us too."

Bella is aware that it won't do for her to say that the party is their farewell party. "This is a welcome dinner for you, to which I've also invited friends of Aar's, most of whom you haven't met before. It is also a party I am throwing for myself now that my new life here in this new country is taking shape. In addition, I see this as a housewarming party."

Gracious for once, Valerie says, "Thanks for the invite."

After dinner, Bella drops them off at their hotel.

When she gets back home, Bella writes an e-mail to the Kariukis to give the house address and directions as she promised. Then she rings Marcella and leaves yet another message on her voice mail.

Finally, Bella takes the time to set up the darkroom. She puts all the equipment in place: an enlarger, an optical apparatus, a slide projector, sheets of photographic paper, a safelight, and the chemicals in which the paper will be immersed. To make sure everything is shipshape, she test prints a handful of photographs she took when she arrived here. The first images come out grainy and she isn't terribly pleased with them, but she works at the images until they are sharp and clean. And because she doesn't wish to sleep before Salif and Dahaba are back from the movies, she devotes half an hour to a long letter to Marcella, in which she brings the old dear of a woman up to speed on all that has transpired.

Salif and Dahaba get home close to midnight, full of beans and ready to chat about the film they saw. Bella, remembering that she has a dinner party to organize for tomorrow night, pleads exhaustion and retires to her bedroom, saying, "Good night. See you tomorrow, darlings."

20.

It is nine in the morning and Bella is in the kitchen drawing up her shopping list for tonight's dinner party when her mobile phone rings. It's Padmini, who offers to give a hand with the cooking. "And if you haven't done the shopping yet," she goes on, her voice low, almost whispering, "you can come and get me, and we can go to the Indian spice shop close to the Nakumatt."

"Would Valerie like to come too?" Bella asks.

"I doubt it."

"Is everything okay?"

"It was quite a fitful night."

Bella knows there is no point in questioning her further; it's clear there is a reason Padmini is not being more forthcoming. So she simply says, "Please expect me in an hour."

She showers, puts on a pair of slacks and a pair of sneakers, and knocks gently on Salif's door. "Wait," he says, and when he opens the door, he is dressed. "Morning, Auntie," he says. "What's up?" He is ready to roll.

She tells him what her plan is. He says, "I know the routine. You want me to stay put and look after my sister and the house, right?"

She hugs and kisses him and drives off to get Padmini, thinking about her plight, especially if she can't persuade Valerie to return to India with Padmini. She thinks to herself that one day, without warning, a door will open somewhere in Padmini's mind or, rather, a sense of despair will stroll in and take up residence. Then the poor woman will say enough is enough and she will leave Valerie. That is the damage that divided loyalty does, and the signs of an inevitable split are there. Bella can smell it the way you can smell an approaching storm. Maybe Padmini senses it is time she ups and flees, the way frightened people flee an oncoming hurricane. But Bella selfishly hopes that the women manage to leave together and that their parting of ways takes place after they are back in India.

Bella parks in front of the hotel and doesn't get out of the vehicle. She calls Padmini's mobile, but there is no answer, so Bella just waits; she does not want to risk running into Valerie. It occurs to her that they are behaving like a couple having a clandestine affair. But Valerie doesn't seem to care.

Bella's thoughts are interrupted by the arrival of Padmini, and she drives off in the direction of the Nakumatt shopping mall.

"So what is all this cloak-and-dagger stuff?"

"After you dropped us off last night, Ulrika, the lesbian who has a financial stake in that raided club, BIH, came to the door of our chalet, veiled."

"Veiled, as in looking like a devout Muslim?"

"Yes. And there was a man with her, a German. Ulrika was in need of a place to hide from the police. I didn't want to oblige them but Valerie insisted. So Ulrika slept on the couch, and her friend slept on the floor of our chalet. Early this morning, the man left, but Ulrika is still there."

It doesn't escape Bella that it is her own munificence that is now paying to keep Ulrika free. I might as well join the movement myself, she thinks. And of course, here in Africa, where gays are victimized, harassed, and harangued, they could do with all the help they can get.

"Any idea what effect the current situation will have on your plans for departure tomorrow?"

"No."

It's clear to Bella—and must be to Padmini too, Bella thinks—that Ulrika and Valerie have already had at least a fling. Will they continue their interrupted liaison now? Bella suspects that they might, which does not auger well for either Padmini's or Bella's plans.

Padmini says, "Valerie says that Ulrika is safe with us until tomorrow morning, when we are due to depart, thanks to your generosity in paying for the room until then. After that, she says, it's up to Ulrika to find another sanctuary."

"Is that arrangement okay with you?"

"No. What if the police find out where she is? We'll be considered accessories to the crime for offering shelter to a fugitive."

"What is Valerie's response to this?"

"She maintains that the likelihood of that happening is minimal and that we should give Ulrika shelter until an hour or so before we are scheduled to leave."

"Remind me when that is, your departure time."

"We are due to check in at Ugandan Air at five."

"Tight," comments Bella.

"I said it is too tight for my liking. But she insists that she wants to leave. She says she wants no repeat of what occurred in Kampala. She threw another stinker of a fit when she discovered you had paid the hotel bill up through tomorrow morning, by the way."

"Why?" says Bella. "Is the woman mad?"

"Anyhow, she was raving and ranting and calling you all sorts of terrible names until Ulrika and her friend showed up. Then she was singing a different tune."

"She still doesn't know how to show gratitude."

"Valerie doesn't know the meaning of the concept."

"So you are set to go?"

"Cross your fingers we are."

In the mall, Bella leaves Padmini in the spice shop and walks across to the Nakumatt. She gets arugula for the salad, and the olive oil, balsamic vinegar, lemon, pepper, and Dijon mustard she needs for her favorite salad dressing. She also gets pasta and peppers and tomatoes for the *penne all'arrabbiata* she is planning. For Padmini's dish, she gets basmati rice, chicken pieces, yogurt, fresh ginger, and fresh hot chilies, some green, some red. For dessert, she gets several types of cheese from the Nakumatt deli.

They meet at the checkout counter, and Bella pays. A youth elbows Padmini out of the way and takes hold of the cart Padmini is pushing. Not wanting to fight about it, they let him wheel it to the car, where Bella tips him.

They arrive home to a joyous brouhaha upstairs. Qamar and Zubair have arrived, and the four young people are up in Salif's room "having fun," as Qamar puts it, after a hug and a kiss from Auntie Bella when she looks in. Bella informs them that Auntie Padmini is with her downstairs, but that Valerie is delayed.

"But she is okay, though?" asks Dahaba.

"Of course she is."

"And she will be here in time for dinner?"

"Of course she will be."

Bella is surprised not to have received warning of their children's arrival from Fatima or Mahdi. Not that this upsets her, but it is unlike them. She checks her phone and discovers she has inadvertently turned it off. There are several messages from them explaining that they are attending a funeral service for a relative on the outskirts of town and so it made sense to drop the children at Aar's place first. Bella relaxes, happy that their relationship is already such that they don't have to stand on formality.

In the kitchen, Padmini chats with Bella as she goes about putting away groceries and rustling up some lunch—a dozen baked chicken drumsticks for the children, and, for Padmini and herself, some slices of mozzarella and tomato drizzled with olive oil and balsamic vinegar.

"Any news from Valerie?" asks Bella.

"Ulrika has been in contact with the German embassy in Nairobi to inform them of her situation."

"And?"

"The embassy will see what can be done."

"To my mind, this is the wrong approach."

"How so?"

"The diplomatic process is a lengthy one at best, and you don't want this to drag on longer than it has already. And the embassy may get in touch with the hotel management to find a discreet way of spiriting her out of harm's way. My only worry is that if any of this comes to light then matters may get much worse, at least in the short term. Lately this kind of interference by European and North American governments in local police matters in Africa and Asia has created diplomatic incidents."

"I had no idea."

Bella opens the oven and turns the drumsticks. Then she asks, "On what grounds are the police seeking Ulrika's arrest?"

"Valerie is under the impression that if they apprehend her they'll charge her with taking hefty fees to set up lesbians visiting from overseas with young African girls."

"Of course, we are all aware young African boys and girls are farmed out for such purposes to tourists all the time and there has never been any fuss about it." Bella sets out plates and tumblers filled with water and goes on. "In Mombasa, elderly white men openly frolic with young boys not even of shaving age. And in the seventies, Scandinavian women chased male teenagers in Gambia and Cape Town."

Padmini flinches at the mention of Cape Town but she agrees. "I saw it myself when I was there."

"There must be another reason why the police are now gunning for Ulrika. Why are they charging her with a crime they've chosen to ignore for so long?"

"Maybe she hasn't made the payoffs the authorities demand," ventures Padmini.

Bella calls up to the youngsters to come down and eat. They come to the table in high spirits, all of them yammering away at the same time and taking photos of each other and Padmini and Bella, even of the ingredients for tonight's dinner. Bella lets them serve themselves, wondering if they hear one another when they jabber like this. "Get your drinks yourselves and give us peace," she says, shooing them into the dining room.

After lunch, with the tables cleared and the dishes washed, Padmini prepares the tandoori chicken, mixing the spices she bought earlier with yogurt.

Padmini calls Valerie then reports on their conversation to Bella. It seems that things have taken a turn for the worse because the liaison in the German embassy is no longer picking up his phone and Ulrika and Valerie are stiff with worry. She tells Bella that Valerie is considering bringing Ulrika to the dinner tonight as her guest.

To this, Bella says, "That is decidedly not on."

"Knowing Ulrika, she may try to crash the party," Padmini says, sounding worried.

"Tell her she'll be turned away," Bella says, and she means it.

They have barely started to cook when Catherine Kariuki telephones to confirm that she will be coming but that James won't be able to; there's a security problem on the school grounds that he has to deal with.

Shortly after five, Mahdi and Fatima arrive. It's long before dinner, but Mahdi and Fatima are like family. Bella makes them tea and catches up with them at the kitchen table. Mahdi tells her that the Kenyan doctor they've consulted believes that Fatima's cancer is in remission, but Bella knows that Mahdi's optimism tends to run high.

Mrs. Kariuki's arrival alters the dynamics of the gathering. She cuts an authoritative figure, perhaps because she is used to being listened to by students. She is almost as tall as Padmini and broader, and she has a very strong handshake. She has known Fatima and Mahdi for a long time because Zubair and Qamar have been at the school since kindergarten. But this is the first time they are socializing.

Catherine Kariuki, when it pleases her, boasts a voice as booming as she is broad in the shoulders. Now she stands at the bottom of the stairs and hollers to the children to come and greet the adults. The four of them obediently come down the stairs single file, as if they were about to receive the blessings of Holy Communion. They extend their hands to her in turn, their heads bowed in deference, then step aside and wait to be dismissed. But within a few minutes, they have lost their shyness, and they go up to their rooms and bring down their cameras. Salif takes group photos in various combinations and Dahaba does single portraits. Bella can tell they are experiencing the special status that wielding a camera affords: stand here; smile and say "cheese"; put your hand here, chin up. The adults, even Catherine Kariuki, submit to them, following their instructions meticulously.

Fatima asks Padmini where Valerie is, and Padmini explains that she has been held up but is expected in time for dinner.

Then Gunilla arrives. Again, the dynamic alters. Bella introduces her around as Aar's colleague, and Gunilla goes around the room shaking hands with each of them until she reaches Catherine. The expression on Gunilla's face suggests she regrets not opting to say *"Namaste"* and keeping her distance the way Indians do. Fatima and Mahdi, who have heard so much about Gunilla from Aar, forego the handshake and give her a hug. Salif and Dahaba warm to her instantly, recounting their camping trip and taking pictures of her.

Bella encourages everyone to move from the kitchen to the living room. In an instant, they break up into smaller groups, some with their drinks on their laps, chatting, others on their feet, listening. Gunilla is tête-à-tête with Fatima; Padmini talks to Mahdi with animation, with Catherine chiming in. Bella, watching the groups merge and unmerge, wonders how much of Aar's relationship with Gunilla Mahdi and Fatima know about or suspect; or if Padmini, who knows about Gunilla's part in her and Valerie's release from detention in Uganda, will dare to raise the subject at all.

Having tired of taking pictures, Dahaba lends her camera to Qamar, who excitedly starts photographing everyone. Dahaba brings out the family albums, Gunilla's and her own. More photographs are taken of people congregating around the albums. Fatima begins to weep, looking at the photos of Aar, and Mahdi pats her back and comforts her.

Fatima vows to assemble the ones she has from their days together at school and university to make a gift of them to Salif and Dahaba.

Salif organizes a tour of the darkroom. Everyone is impressed, especially Catherine, who suggests that Bella teach a photography class at the school and that Salif and Dahaba become the school's designated photographers. When they return from the darkroom, they find that Bella and Padmini have set the table and are ready for people to be seated. There is still no sign of Valerie. Dahaba says she will call her mum and tell her to hurry up, but Padmini says she will do it and steps out of the room.

When Padmini gets back to the kitchen to help Bella with the food, she says that Valerie is on her way in a taxi but is caught in traffic. Padmini further whispers that she is worried that Valerie may be lying.

"Why would she lie to you? This makes no sense."

"That is the way Val is," says Padmini. "I have the bizarre feeling she is not telling the truth because she told me in the same breath that she had packed her suitcases and booked a cab to the airport for five tomorrow morning."

They bring out the food on large platters and put them on a side table in the dining table with plates, cutlery, and napkins. It's quite a spread: Bella's *arrabbiata* and arugula salad and Padmini's chicken tandoori, plus a fish curry and a rich array of vegetarian dishes, including lentils, chickpeas, and an assortment of Indian finger foods. Everyone is seated except for Zubair, who is taking pictures. Mahdi is presiding at the adults' table, Catherine having assigned him the duty "because you are the oldest man present." The children are at their own table.

The guests serve themselves, and the dinner seems to be a hit. Catherine, Mahdi, and all the children help themselves to seconds, and Padmini and Bella receive the guests' compliments gracefully. Fatima and Padmini are the only ones except for Bella who eat the arugula,

332 ➤ NURUDDIN FARAH

however; Padmini asks for the recipe for the dressing. Meanwhile, wine, water, and soft drinks flow like nobody's business, with Catherine emptying her glass as soon as it is topped up.

"How would you describe Kenyan cuisine, Mrs. Kariuki?" asks Mahdi. "No offense intended, but would you agree with the sentiments expressed by a Kenyan chef I once met who said that it is nothing more than bland peasant cooking?"

"The coastal cooking in Kenya is definitely not bland," says Catherine, "but then you may not consider the coastal cooking as representative of the indigenous food we used to eat before all these foreign influences came in. Kenyan coastal cooking is more like Yemeni food, with a touch of Indian cuisine. I love it."

"I would consider it Kenyan, but it is only a small area of the country," says Mahdi.

Catherine is mulling over what Mahdi has said. "Could you define what you mean by peasant cooking?"

"A cuisine lacking cosmopolitan influence, where the main purpose is to satiate hunger," says Mahdi. "I am thinking that in a place, a city, a country, or a region where there is a crosscurrent of cultures feeding off one another the kitchen becomes an amalgam of tastes. Like India." He turns to look at Padmini as if to seek her support.

Catherine appeals to her as well. "What do you think about this assertion?"

"India has suffered a great number of invasions," says Padmini. "It is a subcontinent with an ancient civilization, a huge population, and diverse cultures and faiths. I would say the cuisine reflects this multiculturalism. India boasts a cosmopolitanism far beyond that of many countries in Europe, including England."

"But both India and Kenya were British colonies," says Catherine.

"That's taking hold of the wrong end of the stick," Mahdi says. "In my visit to that island, I've found traditional British cooking rather bland and uninteresting, but more recently, Britain has benefited from the large influx of immigrants, especially from India and Italy, and British taste buds and cooking habits have benefited similarly."

"What is Somali cooking like?" Catherine asks Mahdi.

"The cultural crosscurrents passing through the Somali peninsula have altered the way we cook in the urban areas of the country, but they seem not to have penetrated beyond the cities and the towns," he replies. "I would say that we have borrowed freely from Arabia, India, and Italy, influences that set urban Somali cooking apart from peasant cooking. Our indigenous cooking rarely uses spices, and with its reliance on local grains, it sits heavy on the stomach. An ingredient like garlic is almost unknown. In cosmopolitan cooking, there is a variety of ways you can use the same ingredients to prepare a meal; peasants tend to eat the same food day in and day out. A Frenchman who taught at our school once complained that he had to come to Nairobi for his spices, even his garlic and lemon."

Catherine's mobile rings, and before answering it, she looks at her watch. Then she listens, nods her head, and get up from her chair with the suddenness of someone stung by an insect. Then she says, with equal abruptness, "It is my husband telling me that the chauffeur is ready to pick me up and that I must go." As if her abruptness has dawned on her only now, she adds, "I didn't realize it was so late, and I don't want my husband to worry."

She calls out to the children, who come round to perform what Bella refers to as their "salutations." They take one last photo with "Madame Principal," after which she pats them on either the head or the shoulders as if she were a pontiff delivering benedictions. Bella escorts her to the waiting car outside and thanks her for coming, sending her best regards to James. As the car moves toward the gate, which the guard opens, Bella notices that another car that is just arriving is blocking the exit.

This being Nairobi at night, the arrival of this unexpected car gives Bella a momentary worry. But then she recognizes the occupant of the vehicle, and in a moment, Valerie steps out, shielding her eyes against the headlights of Catherine's car. I'll be damned, thinks Bella to herself, the madwoman is here. But is she alone? Bella moves forward to greet Valerie, glad that Valerie's path and Catherine's have not crossed.

For the third time, the group dynamics change. It is like cards being reshuffled; there is no knowing how they will fall. It takes Bella less than a moment to determine that she won't ask Valerie about Ulrika because she is undoubtedly not supposed to be in the know, and in any event, this is a matter between Valerie and Padmini, no matter how much the outcome might affect her. With Valerie right on her heels, Bella walks into the living room, and a hush descends, broken by a squeal of joy from Dahaba, who runs toward her mother and hugs and kisses her. Salif stops taking pictures long enough to say, "Hi, Mum," from where he stands. Bella watches Padmini in nervous anticipation; she can tell that Padmini is as anxious as she is, neither of them knowing the outcome of the incident involving Ulrika. If Padmini, like Bella, has taken a gamble in coming to Africa, it appears that hers hasn't paid off.

Valerie acknowledges Dahaba's enthusiastic welcome then detours into a brief huddle with Padmini. Bella regrets that she doesn't have a clear sight line to both of them or the ability to read lips, but from Padmini's expression, she surmises that *l'affaire Ulrika* has been positively resolved.

Bella takes Valerie's elbow and steers her over to Fatima and Mahdi, and then, as soon as there is an opportune moment, brings her before Gunilla. She has to give Valerie credit: she remains composed and unflustered as she shakes Gunilla's hand. "Pleased to meet you," she says, smiling warmly. They chat a bit, only glancingly acknowledging that they have spoken before on the phone, and Valerie slips away before the conversation can turn to anything substantial. Bella is relieved that neither opens a can of worms in public, and she is in her own way grateful to them both, especially to the unpredictable and volatile Valerie.

Bella asks Valerie if she has eaten.

"I'm starving," she says.

"Come to the kitchen," says Padmini, "and see what Bella and I cooked. There is plenty left."

Bella keeps the children occupied with a spiel on photography so that Valerie and Padmini can have some time alone in the kitchen. She talks about what you need to produce photographs that can be sold to magazines and newspapers.

"I want to become a cameraman," says Salif, "and maybe a filmmaker. I'll be Somalia's best filmmaker, Auntie, thanks to you."

Bella asks what the others dream of becoming, and Qamar replies that she wants to become a literature professor while Zubair hopes to have a career in law. "What about you, honey?" she says to Dahaba.

"A medical doctor, to cure the sick, of whom there are far too many," Dahaba says. "I'll work for international charitable organizations, helping women and children, the poor and the homeless."

Qamar asks, "And you, Auntie Bella, what other accomplishments do you want to attain beyond all that you've already achieved?"

Bella thinks very hard to make certain that whatever she describes leaves room not only for Dahaba and Salif in her life but also for Zubair and Qamar, whose mother is in such precarious health. She reasons that perhaps it is just as easy to look after four children as two, especially children so wonderful. She hugs each of them and says, "For now, my plan is to start a photo studio here and look after Dahaba and Salif. And

I hope that you two," she says, looking at Qamar and Zubair, "will spend a great deal of time with us too. Because you are my family, you are all I have."

Dahaba, acting as spokesperson, says, "You are the world to us four and we love you, Auntie, love you to bits." And they go into a group hug.

Teary-eyed, Bella leaves them in haste and goes straight to the washroom to have a good cry. She looks at herself in the mirror and washes her face in cold water. She emerges, dry-eyed, to find Gunilla still chatting with Fatima and Mahdi about Aar. Fatima is admitting to the crush she had on him that he just shrugged off. She nods at Bella and concludes, "The boys in the class envied him, and the girls adored him. Aar was special," and then she lets her emotions take over, bringing her story to a tearful end.

Bella offers tea and coffee all around.

Mahdi and Fatima take the offer as a discreet signal that it is time they left. They exchange mobile numbers with Gunilla, making plans to meet at a time and place to be agreed later. Fatima says to Mahdi, "My sweet, let us round up our children and take them home, it is very late."

Bella says to Gunilla, "I predict that the children won't want to be separated and will resist going with their parents."

"They are winsome, all of them," says Gunilla.

"And they get on so well, the four of them," says Bella, looking in the direction of the kitchen and wondering where Valerie and Padmini have ended up. Bella feels like a shepherdess trying to gather her unruly flock and failing.

Gunilla says, "Time for me to go too, dear," and she is up on her feet. She stretches and says, "Must go to the gym tomorrow. I am out of shape."

"I haven't had a workout for days either," says Bella.

"I'll show you where my gym is, in Westlands," says Gunilla.

"We have a date," says Bella.

Fatima is back with Bella and Gunilla to report that Zubair and Qamar are, as Bella predicted, resisting leaving. Mahdi asks Bella if they can pick them up tomorrow. Bella says, "Of course."

Fatima says apologetically, "You see, with no school until next week, they get out of hand," although there is nothing to apologize for. They say their good-byes, and this prompts Valerie and Padmini to come out of the kitchen at last. They bid Gunilla, Fatima, and Mahdi good night, and Bella escorts her friends to their vehicles.

On her return, the children are taking pictures of Padmini and Valerie, and they want Bella to stand in the middle as Padmini and Valerie pose. Then there is a family portrait with Dahaba and Salif joining them and Zubair and Qamar taking photos in turn.

Before the children go to bed, Dahaba insists that she show Valerie the darkroom. Valerie is appropriately wowed and indulges her daughter's over-the-top enthusiasm. Then more good nights, the children yammering up the stairs until their voices fade behind the bedroom doors.

In the kitchen, the mood is ominous, but Bella bides her time, gathering the plates and piling them up in the sink. It feels good to push back the chaos she associates with Valerie and reaffirm this new life where there is no room for clutter. She brings in all the cups, glasses, and empty soft drink cans, and begins to wash up.

"Drinks, anyone?" asks Bella.

Valerie says, "Just water for me, please. I'll help myself." Bella hardly dares wonder if she is to regard this as a good omen.

"And you, Padmini?"

"More wine, please," replies Padmini. "And I'll do the same."

Valerie sips her water and says, "We are leaving at dawn, Padmini and I. I am packed and have booked a cab to the airport."

Bella cannot believe that matters are turning out this way, with Valerie drinking water and refraining from sowing rancor. She wonders if she can trust it.

Then, as if at Valerie's behest, Padmini says, "And we thank you for everything you've done. You've been the most generous host possible, especially considering your state of mourning."

And Valerie, if a touch begrudgingly, adds, "And we mourn with you. He was a wonderful man and proved himself to be a wonderful father to our children."

And what is there left for Bella to say but "Thanks"?

She is fond of silence, Bella reflects, in whose palatial space she can move around; she is seldom betrayed by the slip of her tongue, the way Valerie often is. But tonight Valerie seems to be a different self.

Bella asks, "Shall I call down Salif and Dahaba so that you can say a real good-bye?"

"Please, no," says Valerie.

"But why not?" says Bella in surprise.

"For one thing, I hate saying good-bye, and I can't stand the sight of Dahaba weeping and Salif making cutting remarks. I've never regretted doing what I did, leaving them. And I feel they are in superb hands with you—in fact, I trust that they will do better in your company and care than in mine." She pauses, and then goes on. "I love the darkroom, which I see as a wonderful illustration of your dedication to them, your interest in their well-being, and your intention to share the most important parts of yourself. If I speak with them again, I may muddle things. I don't want to leave them with conflict in their minds."

Valerie's mobile phone sounds. She looks at it, then nods to Padmini. "Our cab is here, darling."

Padmini again articulates their thanks, and they both rise to their feet. "We can see ourselves out," Valerie says, gesturing to Bella to stay put. Then she says, "Many things that ordinary people view as normal, including saying good-bye, are foreign to my nature. I have several selves, in fact: a private self that I am comfortable with and a public self that I find as demanding and exhausting as speaking a foreign tongue that I am barely familiar with. No doubt, you all think that I am rather unusual, uncouth in my outlook, ungrateful when I should be grateful. 'Good-bye' and 'thank you' do not figure in my vocabulary for reasons that have to do with my father and my upbringing. And so I would be lying to you if I use the very words I associate with a period of my young life that I viscerally hate to relive."

Bella thinks of the Somali wisdom that holds that what your parents don't teach, you will be compelled to learn the hard way from an unfeeling society. She is glad that Valerie is showing some signs of coming to her senses about her life and her priorities. But true to her word, Valerie neither thanks Bella nor apologizes, and she makes it clear that she does not wish to hug or to be kissed on the cheek. As she heads for the door, Bella takes Padmini in a tight embrace.

"Go gently, my friend," says Bella.

And then Padmini goes to join her partner in the waiting cab.

Acknowledgments

This is a work of fiction, whose germs developed in the soil of my imagination, even though the background of the events narrated here comes from other brains and other earths. However, I must make very clear that any resemblances to actual persons, living or dead, are purely coincidental.

A number of authors and their works, in ways both obvious and not so obvious, have played an essential role in the writing of this book, and I am grateful to them. Prominent among these are: Roland Barthes's *Camera Lucida* (translated by Richard Howard); Susan Sontag's *On Photography*; Barry Monk's *The Freelance Photography Handbook*; Sylvia Tamale's *African Sexualities: A Reader*; and *The Selected Poetry of Rainer Maria Rilke* (translated by Stephen Mitchell). The line *"La joie venait toujours après la peine,"* from Guillaume Apollinaire's poem "Le Pont Mirabeau," is translated by James Kirkup as "Joy always follows sorrow." The line "After the first death, there is no other" is from Dylan Thomas's "A Refusal to Mourn the Death, by Fire, of a Child in London."

A draft of this novel was, largely, written before the death of my favorite sister, Basra Farah Hassan, killed by Taliban terrorists in a Kabul restaurant bombing on January 17, 2014. Basra, in whose name friends of mine and I have founded the Basra Farah Funds for Women and Children, worked tirelessly for UNICEF and devoted much of her working life to improving the lives of those she met, wherever she was posted, in Ethiopia, in Darfur, in refugee camps in Pakistan, southern Africa, and Afghanistan. Everyone who knew her would agree that she strived hard to leave the world into which she was born a better place than how she found it. May her soul rest in peace.

Finally, I am grateful to many people who have hosted me, looked after me during my research travels: *Mahadsanidin!* My special thanks must also go to Faisal Roble, Fowsia Abdulkader, and Monique Lortie, who have volunteered to help set up the Basra Farah Funds for Women and Children: to all of you, I say *Mahadsanidin* too.

AVAILABLE FROM PENGUIN

Links

"This is the slightly abstract, slightly surreal territory where several Nobel laureates hang out, writers like Singer, Márquez, and Saramago, and it's no coincidence that Farah has been held up in their company . . . haunting."
—*The Christian Science Monitor*

Knots

"Audacious and irresistible . . . An intriguing, poetically intense, and deeply pleasurable read."
—*Los Angeles Times*

Crossbones

"Politically courageous and often gripping . . . a sophisticated introduction to present-day Somalia, and to the circle of poverty and violence that continues to blight the country."
—*The New York Times Book Review*

**PENGUIN
BOOKS**